THE FALL AND RISE OF PETER STOLLER

M PEPPER LANGLINAIS

ST. PETER IN CHAINS

ONE

1966

"GET him out or take him out." Peter's heart was in his knees, but he made sure it didn't sound in his voice.

Noise on the line as Jules Maier shifted. Peter pictured him tucked up in a dark, cramped flat with too-low ceilings and flimsy furniture. Someplace perpetually damp. Musty. And yet Jules would still somehow manage to look perfectly put together. Jules rolled out of bed perfectly put together. It was sinful.

"After all that work to get him in?" Jules asked.

Perfectly put together but, Peter was reminded, also a tad whiney.

Gordon had once told Peter he couldn't think of the men in the field as real people, not if he wanted to be able to do the job well. "Don't think of them as men you've met, had lunch with, drinks with," Gordon said. "Think of them as characters in a book or players in a game." Peter had wondered at the time whether Gordon thought of *him* that way, but he'd been too afraid of the answer to ask.

And now, with the file open in front of him and the face of Alexander Sepiol staring back from his desk, it was difficult advice to take.

Peter closed the folder.

"You know how this goes, Jules."

A heavy sigh. "I'll try to get him out, of course."

"Don't waste any time," Peter instructed. "And, Jules."

"Hmm?"

Peter pictured the arched eyebrow, the tiny smile. He was probably wearing one of those goddamned turtlenecks.

"Get yourself out as soon as you can. I don't want to have to send anyone in after you."

———

He hoped the drive to Oxshott would clear his head, but his mind continued to jump from Jules to Alexander and back again. Why wouldn't Alexander leave? How could they coerce him? Had Alexander had already given them away? If so, to whom? Was Jules really doing everything he could? Probably not. Jules was lazy. But if Alexander had leaked, Jules was also in trouble. Along with a half dozen more people in Brandenburg's Frankfurt.

Peter was surprised to find he'd arrived, his musings having stolen the time. The grass in front of the Lessenby's was dead with winter and flat with cars. Peter added his TR3 to the fleet.

He didn't bother to knock; he never did at the Lessenby's, and with the party, no one would have heard anyway. Gordon and Elinor held it every year at the holidays, this odd assemblage of people whose jobs were to be quiet and unseen, Gordon a gaunt anti-Fezziwig. Peter spotted him standing near the fireplace, Trevor Tillholm planted squarely in front of him, and he started in that direction, but Elinor Lessenby caught sight of Peter and moved in, arresting his progress. Her oversized hat forced him to rock back a bit on his heels; he then took a full step backward as her oversized body followed the brim. "Peter!" she shrilled as she held out a hand, "How did you sneak in without any of us noticing? Oh!" she laughed, not waiting for him to answer, "no, I know, it's what you do!"

Peter smiled and gave her clammy, bejeweled hand a quick squeeze.

"Don't you have a drink?" Elinor asked.

"I'm not…" Peter kept his face turned in her direction, though his eyes were everywhere and anywhere else. In one corner a group of secretaries, typists, archivists—"the girls" in other words—were giggling their way through whatever the old men in the top offices had done (or so they'd heard). Peter caught Miranda's eye, gave her a nod before solemnly returning to the end of Elinor's story.

"So I said to him, 'If you don't do it now, it will cost twice as much later, when it breaks for good!' If he runs the office the way he runs this house… Oh, but I don't expect you to say anything against him, of course," Elinor went on. "I've put you in a terrible position, haven't I? When of course you can't say a word. Not that Gordon would hold it against you. You know Gordon. Of course you do. Not at all the type to hold a grudge."

"No. He isn't," agreed Peter, glancing down as he realized he held a wine glass. Chardonnay. Where had it come from? Office work had dulled his edges.

For all her bluster, Elinor was astute; a man like Gordon Lessenby would not have been apt to tolerate her long otherwise. She gave Peter a sympathetic smile. "I'm keeping you from your friends."

Peter blinked surprise. "No," he said, "I see them all day anyway."

Elinor's smile lengthened. "You're a good boy, Peter. Now I think those girls over there are waiting for you."

Peter followed her gesture, and indeed Miranda's big, dark eyes were still on him, the other girls chattering but ducking their heads in his direction from time to time to check on his status. Throwing Elinor a knowing and apologetic smile, Peter disengaged himself from her, though as he walked away he was suddenly struck by the sad idea that Elinor Lessenby had no friends of her own in attendance. That was as it must be, but how lonely for her to have to talk to her husband's employees on such superficial terms because nothing deeper of their work could be discussed, and with no one else to engage her.

The twittering fluttered to a halt as Peter drew near. He lifted his eyebrows and made a point of looking at each girl in turn, favoring none of them, not even Miranda—*especially* not Miranda.

But Miranda was determined to make her relationship clear to the others, even if it was only professional. "You don't usually like chardonnay," she remarked.

"Not at the office," Peter admitted, then took a sip. As he tilted the glass, he let his eyes rove again, privately tallying the people he didn't know. There were five. No, six. He'd almost overlooked the man standing next to Ken Gamby, though now Peter saw him he couldn't imagine how he missed him. A trifle on the short side, sandy hair and hunched around the shoulders in a way that denoted discomfort. New fellow? Gamby was talking, too loudly as usual, and the unknown man was all but cringing. He looked over briefly, held Peter's gaze a second before turning away.

"Excuse me, ladies," said Peter. He held out his wine glass. "Miranda, would you?"

Miranda flashed Peter a look that suggested he probably shouldn't let her make any drinks for him any time in the near future, but she took the glass while the other girls pouted their displeasure at his parting from them so soon.

Peter decided against the direct approach, instead circling to join the men standing around Gordon. Gordon wasn't a talker, and he wasn't talking now; he listened as Trevor held forth on whatever headline in the day's paper had become his problem. It was the same patient expression on Gordon's face now that he wore in the weekly meetings, one of concern and compassion, one that never gave away how Gordon felt about the subject, assuming he cared at all.

Peter stood there but didn't pay any attention to Trevor's arguments (not that anyone was opposing him; Trevor argued with the world at large and did not require a concrete foe), his eyes traveling over the cluster. These were the older ones mostly, and a few young hopefuls, those who stood on the wire between in and out. Peter had no worries there. Gordon had a special fondness for Peter, something that went beyond the fact Gordon had been the one to recruit him—an affection that bordered on the avuncular.

After lingering long enough to catch Gordon's eye and receive a nod of acknowledgement, Peter turned his attention once again to where Gamby continued to tell rude jokes. The new fellow had drawn away, was at risk of becoming a wallflower. Who was he? Surely he knew *someone* at the party? Gordon wouldn't have invited just anyone.

Elinor had spotted the stranger, too, and was bearing down. "Charles," she said loudly, Peter supposed in order to be heard over Gamby, "you can't stand there all night. Come, come, meet some of the girls."

Peter risked a glance at the group of girls. By his reckoning, they'd eat this Charles alive. Peter stepped up to intercept.

"Who is this now, Elinor?"

"You again, Peter," Elinor replied, not unkindly. "I'm surprised the girls let you go so easily. But then, I guess that's part of what you're good at.

"This is Charles, by the way. Charles, Peter Stoller."

The eyes lifted to meet Peter's, a startling blue, then slid away again, embarrassed.

"No need to be shy, Charles, Peter doesn't bite. Charles is a cab driver."

Despite all his training, Peter was unable to completely hide his astonishment. "A cab driver?" He had enough sense, though, not to put voice to the logical follow-up: *Then what is he doing here?*

"He helped me this morning. You know I usually take the car, but it had to go into the shop, and I had so much to do for this party… Well, Charles here took me around all day, right through lunch, and after all that I certainly couldn't send him away without having tasted some of what he'd worked so hard for."

Reflexively, Peter glanced over at Gordon.

"Oh, Gordon knows, of course he does," Elinor told him. "He's fine with my having invited someone. It's not as if you're all going to talk state secrets here."

Peter looked at Charles once more. Charles, for his part, seemed very interested in his shoes, which were remarkably shiny. He was dressed more for church than for cab driving, and Peter wondered whether, when she'd called for a cab, Elinor had insisted on someone "dressed properly." It was exactly the kind of thing she was likely to do.

"Cabs must make for interesting stories," said Peter. "You see all types, I'm sure."

The head came up again, and those eyes. Charles wasn't a handsome man, Peter decided. A little too round from not enough exercise, maybe, and this made him appear soft. But the softness also bore a mark of kindness, not entirely unlike Gordon's patience. However, while Gordon could command a room without ever saying a word, Charles was liable to disappear in a crowd, become so much wallpaper.

"I wouldn't want to bore you," Charles said now, the voice as soft and kind as his figure. The eyes stayed on Peter this time, and Peter found himself absorbed in them, the way the light played in the brilliant irises.

No, no, thought Peter, and he made himself glance away, over at the girls again. Miranda's eyes were on him; she still held his chardonnay.

Back to Charles, whose own gaze had not wavered. Peter's lips stretched into an what felt to him like an unnatural smile. "Can't be any worse than whatever Gamby was going on about over there."

"Well, if you boys are all right," Elinor put in, "I just have to pop over and remind Gordon..." She was still talking as she sailed off in the direction of her husband.

"Party's a bit of a drag," Peter went on. "You don't know anyone here, and I spend all day with them." He wished then he still had the wine; it would have been a fine moment to take a sip, and his mouth was suddenly dry.

Charles turned away then to look toward the door, longingly Peter thought. "Elinor can be a bit of a bully," Peter continued, desperate now to hold some kind of conversation, "but she means well. Mrs. Lessenby," he clarified when Charles showed no immediate understanding but only blinked blankly at him. Charles nodded then, a short and decisive motion of the chin that Peter wasn't sure was agreement so much as acknowledgment. It was the kind of noncommittal gesture an old man might make, though Charles couldn't have been much older than Peter if at all.

"Look, if you want to leave..." said Peter, and those bright eyes found his face again. "You have your cab, don't you? No one is going to stop you, not even Elinor; she wouldn't raise that kind of a scene, though she might complain to the cab company later." He meant it as a joke of sorts, but it had just enough truth in it not to be very funny. So Peter took in a breath and laid the rest of it out: "I'll even go with you, if you like."

The blue eyes swept over him, down and up, before turning again toward the door. "You need a ride?" Charles asked.

"I have my own car. But we could meet... You're good with addresses, I assume."

"Your address, you mean." A statement, not a question.

Peter gave it to him. "You go on ahead while I make my excuses. Don't worry," Peter added, "I'll distract Elinor long enough for you to escape."

Taking care not to catch Miranda's eye, Peter first looked to where Gordon had been but found the group by the window had since disbanded. He stalked through the room, deftly avoiding being pulled into any of the various clutches of coworkers, and, having found no sign of Elinor or Gordon, moved on to the kitchen. There they were, the staff buzzing all around them, refilling glasses and replenishing serving platters, while Gordon leaned his back against the counter, head bent to listen as Elinor filled his ear with prattle. Sensing it might not be a good time— and moreover, it might be exactly the right time to go ahead and leave the party entirely—Peter began to back out of the room, but like a bloodhound, Elinor had caught his scent. Her talk came to an abrupt stop and Gordon's head rotated slowly in Peter's direction, pendulous, as if Gordon's thoughts were too heavy to hold up.

"Sorry," Peter said, "I'll just..."

"It's all right, Peter," said Gordon.

Peter stayed by the door. "I was just going to thank you."

"You're not leaving already!" Elinor cried.

Peter smiled ruefully, his attention focused on his boss. "You've seen my desk, it's covered." Alexander Sepiol's face flashed briefly through Peter's mind like a jagged bolt. How could he have forgotten so quickly? The response came just as immediately: a flash of intriguing blue eyes.

"You're going back to the office." It was a statement, not a question.

"Only to grab a couple things. I'll do the work at home. Reports," Peter added swiftly, "nothing sensitive of course."

"Of course," Gordon agreed. "Have a good night, Peter."

Peter nodded and fled. He crossed the living space in short order, very nearly made it to the door, then remembered he needed to grab his coat from the rack. Luckily, because he had arrived late, his hung near the top. He was just shrugging it on when Miranda materialized before him.

"Leaving?"

"Going to try and get some work done."

"Then I shouldn't be surprised to find a pile on my desk Monday morning?" She took a long sip of the wine in her hand, more chardonnay, though Peter's practiced eye detected the glass was too fresh to be his old one. Not enough fingerprints and smudges to have been handled by more than one person, and of the few prints he could see, none were his size. All Miranda. She was playing with him.

"I'm sure you're looking forward to it," he told her. "Enjoy the party." He went for the door without waiting for a response.

––––––––––

The drive back to London was eaten up by Peter's mounting curiosity—and unease. What on earth had possessed him? And yet there he was, off to meet someone he'd spent all of two minutes with at a party. But it was better than sitting at his desk waiting to hear Alexander Sepiol was dead. Or worse, Jules.

More so than usual, Peter was required to pay close attention while he drove. He was known to be careless in more than a few ways, but this stretched things even for him. Inviting this man to his flat? Peter switched the windscreen wipers on, then off, unable to settle on a setting as a light rain began to fall, the kind just enough to make it difficult to see clearly.

By the time Peter made it back to London, he half hoped Charles would stand him up. It was a big enough city; they might never cross paths again. How nice to be free of consequences born of a reckless moment. He found a parking spot up the block from his building and was surprised by the keen stab of disappointment that tainted his relief at no signs of a cab in the vicinity.

It was a nice part of town, though not the nicest; Peter had chosen the flat chiefly for the view. From his windows he could see two streets clearly and part of a third, would always know if and when he were surrounded, could see them coming. Now he walked up the thickly carpeted stairs, five floors in a building that topped out at six. Charles had left the party before him; if he were coming, he should already have arrived. Then again, Charles struck Peter as an intelligent man, so perhaps he'd allowed extra time. He wouldn't want to be found lingering outside the door.

Peter stopped just inside the door to his flat, his wet shoes squeaking on the tile of the entry. The same tile stretched into the kitchenette before being taken over by pale grey carpeting in the living space. Peter kicked off his shoes, went to hang his damp suit jacket over a chair at the kitchenette bar. Paused. Was that sloppy? But then he didn't want to appear too neat, either, too much a prig.

What was he thinking? He didn't want to appear anything. He was hoping *Charles* wouldn't appear at all. Wasn't he?

Peter moved through the flat with the restlessness of someone anticipating guests, unable to settle anywhere, yet having nothing to occupy himself with either. He picked up a book, set it back down, wondered if he should put it away entirely to keep from seeming too academic. But it was only one book. Without it, he might come across as unintelligent. He tossed the book onto the sofa. *Make him think I fall asleep reading at night.* If he even turned up.

A memory surfaced, Jules's dark, laughing eyes and teasing smile as he caught Peter reading ancient Greek poetry. Peter's throat constricted. He had no reason to worry about Jules; the man was lazy but good at his job when he could be bothered to do it.

Peter went to the rain-streaked window, peered into the vacant street. He went through the bedroom to the bath and washed his face, ran a comb through his hair. It was late. Was it too soon to give up and put on pyjamas? He was debating brushing his teeth when the knock came, so soft and hesitant Peter wasn't convinced he hadn't imagined it.

He opened the door to find Charles smiling sheepishly. He'd changed into different clothes, less church but far nicer despite being casual. He'd looked stiff and uncomfortable at the party, but now he seemed at ease, if still a little shy. "Hello," he said somewhat needlessly.

Peter pulled the door open wider to allow Charles to enter. "Should I take off my shoes?" he asked, noticing Peter's still in the entry.

"Whatever makes you comfortable," said Peter. It seemed like a diplomatic answer.

Charles slipped his wet loafers from his feet, but stayed parked in the entry as he surveyed the space. "It's very… white."

In addition to the light-colored carpet, the walls were white, the furniture equally colorless aside from a few accent pillows, and the table between the two sofas was glass. Even the brick surrounding the fireplace was white, the mantel bare of artifacts.

"It must be impossible to keep clean," Charles went on.

"Not so difficult. I'm not home enough to make a mess of anything."

Charles took a hesitant step onto the carpet, finally allowing Peter to release the door. He was suddenly very aware of his hammering heart and desperate for a task to keep him busy, so he went round to the kitchen proper. "Red or white?"

Charles seemed startled by the question, and Peter saw he had picked up the book from one of the sofas. "Hmm?"

"Wine."

"Red wine seems like an utter danger in here," said Charles, his expression a mixture of humor and what might have been honest horror at the idea.

"Only if you plan on splashing it around." Peter opened a low cabinet, out of which he selected a bottle. "Do you like cab?"

Charles had put the book on the table and moved on to studying the few pieces of artwork on the walls, Peter's concession to color in the décor. "The cab?" he asked, and Peter understood that Charles thought he had remarked on his guest's profession.

"Cabernet," said Peter. This was beginning to feel like a bit of a slog, what with him constantly having to clarify himself. All at once Peter was sorry Charles had come and wanted the night to be over.

But then, as Peter reached into the higher cupboards for glasses, Charles wandered into the kitchen. "Oh, yes," he said when Peter handed him the wine. "Let's live dangerously." And Peter's pulse rabbited.

Charles took his glass and went to settle himself on one of the sofas, Peter trailing behind him, though he stopped short of sitting right away. He wasn't entirely sure what Charles expected of him, and so, standing by the arm of the sofa, Peter stalled by taking a sip of his wine.

It wasn't natural for Peter to second-guess himself; he was, as a rule, a confident and competent man. And he'd had his share of flings—some were part of the job, others merely stress relief —but there was something different here. Peter thought he could really come to like Charles, if only they could get better acquainted. He just didn't know how to go about that bit. And he couldn't tell whether Charles wanted to go through all that effort.

The mirth that played around Charles's features didn't help matters. It gave Peter the disconcerting notion he was privately being made fun of, not something he was at all accustomed to.

He did not enjoy being taken for an amateur. And so Peter stood and sipped, watching Charles over the rim of the wine glass.

Charles appeared almost prim in the way he sat, not making full use of the cushions at his back but instead leaning a little forward, his stocking feet flat on the floor, the cabernet carefully held out over the glass table. His head was cocked, those bright blue eyes pinning Peter expectantly, and while Peter was certain there was amusement in the gaze, he detected something earnest, too, something like the shyness he'd seen at the party. It drew Peter in. He sat down.

There was room enough; when Peter had bought the two sofas he'd had the idea he wanted them to be long enough for him to be able to stretch out in full, either to read or nap. Not that he was ever home to do either of those things. But the furniture fit the space nicely, and at that moment it also gave Peter the ability to sit next to Charles without crowding him. Test the waters, so to speak.

Beside him, Charles relaxed a little, and finally drank some of the wine. This pleased Peter. It was a good vintage, and he didn't want to see it wasted. Charles seemed to realize just *how* good about halfway through, pausing to hold the glass in front of him as if for inspection before looking again to Peter.

"You like it?" Peter asked.

"It's very good."

"Only very good?"

"I don't know so much about wine," Charles admitted.

Peter let out a breath he hadn't realized he'd been holding. His eyes dropped to Charles's feet, where the toes wriggled in the brown argyle socks like a nervous tic. The rest of Charles was still, but those toes… It suddenly made Peter feel much better to think Charles might be a little nervous, that the humor he'd shown might be just so much false bravado. Peter felt the muscles in his back give as tension ran out of him like water out of a tap.

Charles was glancing around the room again. "It's a really nice flat," he said, and Peter began to comprehend that Charles was, in fact, a tad overwhelmed. Peter hadn't considered his flat could be *too* nice, but like the Lessenbys' house, perhaps it was just imposing enough to make a cab driver feel out of place and uncomfortable.

Or maybe, Peter thought now, the flat had given Charles the idea Peter thought he was superior in some way. That, like one might feed a stray animal, Peter was throwing Charles some kind of treat, a morsel that wouldn't last. So Peter finished the last of his wine, set the glass on the table, sat back and said, "Not very homey, though, is it?"

"Homey?" Charles echoed.

"A bit cold, in fact. I'd have done more with it—would do more with it—if I were home more, but..."

"Paperwork?" asked Charles.

Peter shrugged. "There are people at the office at least. Here it's just me, and I get bored in my own company before long."

Charles set his wine down, unfinished. "Maybe you should get a pet."

"No less dangerous than red wine," said Peter.

"A flatmate then?"

"Only the one bedroom."

Charles glanced over the back of the sofa to the door in the wall behind them, ajar and revealing just a corner of the over-sized bed. "Moving would be a hassle, I suppose."

Peter nodded gravely, as if the discussion were a deeply philo-sophical one. "Aside from the actual crating and lifting and what-not, there's having to let everyone know, changing your address all over the place, and your phone..."

"All the bloody utilities," Charles added.

"Exactly," said Peter. "And then you're expected to give a party besides."

"Hardly seems worth it," Charles agreed.

"It's a good location, and the neighbors are quiet," Peter acknowledged. "Would be difficult to find anything better."

"Nice amount of space, too," said Charles.

"All the white makes it appear bigger than it really is," Peter told him. "That and the windows. It's dark now, of course, but in daylight the place really opens up."

Together they spared a moment to stare at the long window that took up most of the wall behind the facing sofa, the drops of rain causing the lights of the city to blaze a fraction more brilliantly, if also unevenly.

"No shades?" Charles asked at length.

"They're an odd size. I need to have some made but haven't got around to it." In the back of his mind Peter was aware the discussion was bordering on absurd, but at least they were talking.

Laughter quirked at Charles's lips once more. "They'll be white, I suppose."

Peter felt a prick of annoyance but forced himself to answer evenly. "I hadn't really thought much about it. Like I said, I'm almost never home; I've lived here three years without drapes."

"In the bedroom, too?"

Like a marionette whose strings had been pulled taut, Peter felt his body come to attention, though he kept his posture relaxed. "Well, of course I did get curtains for the bedroom."

"Sun rises on that side," said Charles. "Would have you awake bright and early otherwise."

They were speaking in mazes, Peter thought, and wondered when they'd reach the clearing at the center. Or hit a wall. At that point he didn't care which, he just wanted to get somewhere, even a dead end.

"It was easier is all," Peter said. "Those windows are standard measure."

And there the labyrinth wall rose up, the artifact of a wrong turn taken somewhere in the cosmic scheme of things, opportunities neglected, a conversation gone amiss. The glasses sat on the table beside the book, they sat there in their socks and nice clothes, and the words dried up around them, leaving them no closer to anything than they had been at the Lessenbys' party. Peter felt another stab of disappointment similar to the one he'd had when he'd thought Charles wasn't coming, and he tried to imagine how he'd feel if Charles were to leave right then. Relieved? Or, like someone who'd found a good bargain but not snapped it up, would he regret letting Charles go?

Peter was used to knowing what he wanted; feeling ambivalent made him uneasy. A streak of decisiveness was key to his trade, and Peter liked to know his own mind. So he traced his feelings back, like Ariadne's thread. He knew he'd seen something interesting in Charles at the party; more than just sympathy for Charles's discomfort, there had been an attraction, despite some awkwardness. He wouldn't have made the move of inviting Charles over otherwise.

Peter looked at Charles, who met his gaze steadily and, seeming to understand Peter's conflict, once again eased the pressure by saying, "It's late. I should—"

Something in Peter's throat tightened. "I don't want you to go." It was a realization more than anything, a moment of self-discovery given voice. He was quick to add, "But if you want to, or need to…"

Keeping his eyes on Peter, Charles gave his head a little shake. "I'm just not entirely sure why I'm here."

A chill ran through Peter, the terrible harbinger of rejection. "You don't want to be?"

"That's not it at all," said Charles. "I wouldn't have come if I hadn't been… Hadn't thought you…"

Peter recognized the resurgence of the discomfiture Charles had shown at the party earlier in the evening. "Interested," Peter supplied. "You thought I was interested. And… Maybe you were also a little interested in me?"

Charles's cheekbones became highlighted in a pink flush. They were nice cheekbones, Peter decided, even with a slightly too much meat over them, and Charles was handsome after all, not in the spectacular way of someone like Jules Maier, but in the easily overlooked way of ordinary men.

"I like you," Peter said.

Those blue eyes again, bright and wide. "You hardly know me."

"My work requires me to be a swift and accurate judge of character."

"Paperwork…" Charles's voice trailed as Peter leaned in. As if taking a measure, their lips touched briefly once, twice, before making the third time count.

———

The ringing of the phone took on the phantasmic insistence that only occurs in the dead of night when the news is nothing but bad. Peter knew logically, as the sound drilled through his sleep, that the ring was the same as ever, but given the hour, he felt the trill was somehow grimmer. He glanced at Charles, dead in slumber, and slipped out of the bed as quietly as he could to take the call.

"Peter? I thought you'd never answer."

Jules's voice was tight, and Peter immediately discarded the rebuke that had first come to his lips, the reminder that Jules was not supposed to call him at home. "You're hurt. Did you get him?"

"You've got to come get me."

Peter's knees went watery. He leaned against the kitchen counter. "You know I can't do that. Where are you?" He was picturing Jules in the cramped flat again, now bleeding like a wounded animal. "How bad is it?"

"We trained together." His voice was shaking. A wounded animal, yes, frantic with fear. "A year ago, it would have been you out here instead of me. You have to come get me."

"I *can't*."

The line went dead.

TWO

1967

Peter halted his progress toward the door and turned, his coworkers slipping past him and making good their escapes. Trevor Tillholm was last, and Peter watched out of the corner of his eye as Trevor pulled the door closed in his wake, leaving Peter and Gordon alone in the large conference room.

The muffled sounds of post-meeting hall traffic and chatter subsided, and still Peter stood there. Gordon sat at the head of the table, his right hand absently fiddling with a pen that lay before him on the slickly polished wood. He wasn't looking at Peter, not directly; instead he stared into the distorted reflections on the table, at an imperfect Peter, rumpled, pulled apart in places by the natural grain.

Peter had no compunction about studying his boss openly, and not for the first time thought Gordon had aged quite a bit in the past months, his skin taking on a grey-blue tint, his cheeks sagging toward the increasing folds in his neck as if he'd begun to melt away.

"Not so many long hours at the office any more." Gordon finally looked up, eyebrows lifted; he even smiled.

"Not as much in the pipeline these days," Peter countered,

then softened it a bit by adding, "I hope I'm still doing satisfactory work?"

"Always." Gordon sighed, moved his head a fraction to stare out the window. "No word from Jules? Alexander?"

Peter had dutifully reported on the call from Jules, and after three days of no further communication, he had reluctantly sent MacAuley. But there had been nothing and no one to retrieve. Abandoned quarters. MacAuley had spent the better part of a month on the hunt, another ten days making sure of the existing network.

"But the network is fine," Peter offered. He knew it was weak. Without Jules and Alexander accounted for, they remained at risk.

The glance Gordon threw was sharp as a knifepoint. "For how long?"

"It's concerning," Peter allowed, knowing Gordon was watching, waiting for his answer. "For everything to go so quiet..."

"I'm surprised you're not champing at the bit," Gordon said with sudden vigor. "Usually you'd be begging to go have a look around."

"MacAuley's *had* a look around. There's nowhere else to look." And he didn't want to go. Of course he didn't. For once he was happy at home, had a personal life he enjoyed. An arrow of guilt pricked at Peter; he was comfortable while God only knew what had happened to Jules. Or Alexander. But most of his thoughts were for Jules.

"The way Trevor tells it—" Peter went on.

"Blast and damn Trevor to hell! You know he's the worst for building castles in empty fields. Let Trevor have his way and we'd have to quadruple the size of the Agency so we could half populate every other major power on the planet. Everyone's an enemy where Trevor is concerned.

"I want to know what *you* think," Gordon went on. "You've been behind that desk for over two months, swimming through the memos, all the minutia. Does it add up to anything?"

Gordon was rattled, Peter realized; he only ever got angry when he was rattled. Either Gordon had someone from the

Ministry breathing on him or he was honestly concerned about the potential hole in Frankfurt. Maybe both.

"I assure you," said Peter, "if I were receiving anything, even the smallest clue, I'd bring it to you directly."

Gordon's shoulders slumped and his back gave a little so that his spine fell against the leather of his chair, a man defeated. "We've been wounded, Peter. Someone has taken a pound of our flesh. Or maybe it was freely given." And he cocked an eye at Peter as if to invite a response. But Peter had no idea how to answer.

All at once Peter felt dull, almost bloated with ineptitude. It was as if being happy at home had left him full and sluggish. He resolved at that moment to do better. "I'll go through things with a fine comb, see if I can tease out anything."

"I want you there, Peter. If Jules will come to anyone, it's you."

And with that Peter's newfound resolve plummeted, doing a barrel roll for good measure before crashing. What would he tell Charles?

Charles knew Peter worked for a government office. He knew Peter sometimes traveled for work, although Peter hadn't since they'd met. And he knew Peter dealt in sensitive information, though *how* sensitive and *what kind* of information was something Peter had not elaborated on. Because he couldn't, of course. And Charles understood that, too, and never asked.

"How soon?" Peter heard himself ask, his own voice seeming to echo back from somewhere far away.

"We shouldn't lose any more time if it can be helped."

"Do you want me to check in with any allies? See what they're hearing, if anything?"

The hand fiddling with the pen grew more agitated. As a rule, Peter handled incendiary sites, not diplomacy; they had other men to handle the friendly side of things. Trevor Tillholm, for instance, who traveled to America and Canada and smiled and shook hands only to return growling and grumbling about how none of them could be trusted.

Gordon looked up, and Peter saw in his eyes the kind of

sadness usually attributed to basset hounds. "They'd tell Trevor, wouldn't they? If they were hearing anything?"

Peter shrugged. He had no clue what Trevor's relationship with his contacts was like, whether the Americans or Canadians would share their information with him. But knowledge was currency in the trade; with nothing to offer, Trevor was unable to purchase anyone's cooperation. They'd be relying on their allied countries' good graces. "Better angels," as one American president had put it.

"Or Michaelson," Gordon said, naming the agent who handled relations in India, and went on to name several other international liaisons. "Devon. Braithwaite. Jacobs. Leicester. Marshall." It was almost a code, or an incantation meant to conjure the help they needed.

And Peter had no ready answer. All he knew of these things came from the weekly meetings, like the one they'd just concluded, the one they'd held just to look at each other across the table and say, *We don't know, we haven't heard, no one's talking.*

The more Peter thought about it, the itchier it made him. Something really wasn't right.

Gordon read it in his face. "Ah, there's the Peter I know. It's starting to trouble you now, get under your skin." When Peter nodded, Gordon said, "Start with your men in Frankfurt. I'll let you know whether we need to have Trevor introduce you to his friends; I have to sound him out about it a bit first."

Peter nodded again and turned to go. He needed to map out an itinerary, have Miranda make his travel arrangements... But no. He'd do it himself, Peter decided; better not to let everyone know where he was going and when. There was no substitute for surprise, the moment when a man's very body gave him away: his posture, his expression, his eyes. On the outside chance anyone in the Frankfurt office was hiding something, Peter would be able to see it on him like a suit.

Miranda would be furious about it later, of course. She hated more than anything to be left out. The girls prided themselves on inside knowledge as much as the agents did, each basking in the reflected glow of her respective boss. Peter would be denying

Miranda a juicy tidbit of information by disappearing on her without explanation. But then again, she'd get miles out of being able to complain about him to her peers.

She was at her desk when Peter rounded the corner; his office held prime real estate down the hall from Gordon's own, and Miranda's desk was situated outside his door, a dinghy tied to his pier. Unfortunately for her, Peter didn't quite merit a corner office, and the nearest window was some meters off to the left at the end of the corridor, its watery light never able to reach Miranda's workspace. She used a desk lamp with a green shade that hung its sorrowful head over her work, the bulb a tired yellow that made Peter feel as if it were always winter and late in the day.

Miranda looked up as he approached; she always did, and Peter had come to suspect she knew the sound of his footsteps, the gait of his walk. "Headmaster have you stay late?"

"Something like that," Peter said, knowing she wanted more. Something in his stomach knotted, and he wasn't sure whether he felt slightly guilty for his evasion or a tiny bit gratified at having thwarted her. He went into his office without saying anything more and shut the door behind him. Then he waited.

A minute later his phone buzzed and Miranda asked, "Should I hold your calls?"

"Why would you hold my calls?"

"Well, the way you just swept in, and after having been in with Mr. Lessenby, I thought maybe…"

"I'll let you know if you need to hold my calls, Miranda. You'd be the first to know, in fact. The *only* to know, since you handle my phone line."

She didn't even reply, just rang off. Peter watched the light on his phone wink out. Waited.

A minute later: "Is it all right if I go to lunch then? If you don't need me to screen your calls?"

"It's fine, Miranda," Peter answered wearily.

"Do you want me to bring you back something?"

"No, I'll go out a little later." This time he was the one to disconnect. He waited a minute longer, just in case, but there finally came the sound of feet on the overpadded carpeting as a troop of women in dress shoes came clambering up the corridor. The Lunchtime Express. A burble of voices talking over one another, starting low but rising now and again until one or another hissed for quiet. And then it left the station, bound for the next desk to collect another girl before terminating at last in the canteen.

When they were well and truly gone, Peter began planning, first going through the meager reports stacked on his desk. Nothing useful there, no sign of activity at the Frankfurt flat, which of course was being watched. Peter looked again at the notes on the blood that had stained the chair and floor: "Unable to determine how much had been lost." No signs of struggle at the flat itself, though, so the wound—knife? gunshot?—had been sustained elsewhere. Had they followed Jules back? But no, MacAuley and others had visited the flat and gone unmolested. *So far*, Peter reminded himself.

He was thinking in circles. Setting the reports aside, he picked up the phone to make his travel arrangements instead. All the while he was aware of the lump forming in his throat. The grain of sand—the irritant—was the fact he was leaving, that he would have to leave Charles and be gone, possibly for a good, long while. And the more concrete the plans became, the bigger the pearl grew, until Peter was certain he would choke on his own misery.

By the time he came to the last of his reservations, Peter had ceased to attempt to hide his grief, and the woman in what they called the Stables finally asked, "I'm sorry, but are you all right?"

"What?" Peter asked. He had stopped processing anything but the simple logistics of travel. Name? Destination? Round trip? And then: *Are you all right?* It didn't play.

"You just sound…"

"I'm fine," said Peter. He tried to picture what the woman might look like. Short blonde hair maybe, and too much rouge; the kind of person to snap bubble gum. They'd been hiring younger and younger girls it seemed. Or the girls were just getting better at faking it.

He heard a deep intake of breath, and then she said, brightly and professionally, "So you'll be returning on which date?" Peter told her to leave it open, answered the remainder of her questions, and concluded the call.

Who knew how long he'd be gone? However long it took to mend the net and be sure it was sturdy. Half a year earlier he wouldn't have cared, might even have looked forward to the change in scenery, but oh, God, what would he tell Charles?

Nothing, of course. He couldn't tell Charles anything, not even where he was going or when to expect him home.

Adding to his agitation was that Peter had the nagging feeling he was taking the whole thing a bit too hard, was being too sentimental. Gordon had never wept for having to leave Elinor, so far as Peter knew. Then again, Peter could only imagine a break from Elinor would be something to welcome more than rue. Trevor wasn't married; Gamby had a wife Peter had only seen in photographs, a woman almost as large as Gamby himself. Gamby never mentioned her; Peter had no idea whether there were any children, much less whether Gamby missed his family when he went abroad.

As for Peter, he'd never before had anyone to miss. He'd dated, yes, even long-term (which Peter counted as anything lasting more than two weeks), but he had never lived with any of them.

Charles had moved in two weeks ago. Fast, certainly, but his flat had been taken out from under him when the landlord decided to move his ailing mother in. "Stay with me," Peter had said, surprising them both, but what was the use of having two spaces when they were almost always at Peter's anyway? He'd helped Charles pack his few things, and Charles in turn had bought bespoke drapes for the living room. Pale blue, "Just for some color," he'd said with that little smile, "but it won't make the room look too dark or too small." Charles had an eye for those kinds of things, Peter had discovered. He dressed well given his modest budget, knew where to find the best brands at bargain prices and how to match colors and whatnot. Unlike

Peter, who was only able to keep from clashing by following the strict advice of his tailor.

Peter had long been in the habit of ending relationships right before having to leave the country; it had saved him, and he liked to think the other party as well, a certain amount of anguish. But that was not an option with Charles. Living arrangements aside, Peter could not envision any circumstance in which he would be willing to let Charles go.

———

Peter pulled himself up the flights of stairs, his heavy heart having made him so much dead weight. He fumbled uncharacteristically as he thumbed through his keys, looking for the one that would unlock the treasure chest his flat had become—the place where precious things were kept. But today the keys as they shook in Peter's hands, the bolt as it obligingly released as commanded, sounded too loud in the hush of the hallway. As if giving away a secret.

Inside, Charles was stationed in front of the hob. Two pots squatted on the burners, and Peter could tell from the warmth in the flat that the oven was on as well. Not that it was unusual for Charles to cook; he did so at least twice a week, sometimes more often if he planned to be working. According to Charles this was his way of making sure Peter was taken care of. "I know you," Charles would say. "If I don't make it easy for you to eat, you won't eat at all." He wasn't wrong.

The door snapped shut like jaws and Charles turned to greet Peter with his usual smile, though it wilted at the sight of Peter's grim countenance. In turn, the evidence that Charles was unhappy—that *he* had made Charles unhappy—made Peter feel as if he'd swallowed a small, hard rock only to have it become lodged in his chest.

Charles's eyes fell on the briefcase still in Peter's hand, the worn leather thing that came home with Peter so rarely. "You have work tonight."

It was simply something to say, an opening gambit, a test of the mood in the room, and Peter knew this but still found himself snapping. "I don't usually."

"I didn't say you did." The tone was even, gentle, meant to be disarming. But the rock in Peter's chest was hard and jagged and hurt too much to attempt to extract. So Peter dropped his briefcase in the entry and went to the range instead, taking the spoon from Charles's limp hand.

"Your sauce is going to burn."

Charles stepped back as Peter began stirring with unwarranted ferocity, the tomato red paste threatening to wash over the sides of the pot and afflict the cooktop. "Anyway, I'm not bringing it home, I have to take it with me."

"Take it with you..." Charles echoed thoughtfully as if learning new words or a new language, his eyes never straying from the wooden spoon, even as Peter handed it back to him and went to shed his coat. When Charles only continued to stand there staring at the spoon, its bowl blooded by its work, Peter commanded, "Keep stirring."

Charles didn't. His eyes—those blue, blue eyes—shifted from the spoon to Peter in something like bewilderment. Peter felt cornered by them, accused, pressed into explanation. "They're sending me..." But of course he couldn't say where. "I don't know how long I'll be gone."

"For paperwork?" asked Charles. "Don't you have a courier or something for that kind of thing?"

"You should keep stirring."

"What kind of paperwork is so important...?"

"I work for the government, Charles. Some things are important, yes, *so* important that I have to fly all over the world to handle them. In person. You should stir the sauce before it burns."

Charles gave his head a tiny shake as if negating an unspoken thought. "But you're just..."

"No, *you're* just a cab driver. *I'm* a government official."

Of course the moment the words were out, Peter knew they were terribly and unforgivably wrong. He flailed internally for a moment, a man drowning in his own bitter bile, before seeking a physical escape. "I have to pack," he said, and all the courage he'd ever shown in his fieldwork—threat of guns, knives, torture —could not bear Peter up enough to look Charles in the face before stalking off in search of his suitcase.

The smoke alarm let out a piercing cry as Peter slammed the bedroom door.

———

Two days. He had gone two days without Charles's voice, or his smile, or the deliberate way he brushed past Peter, always making sure to touch even when there was plenty of space.

Peter wasn't supposed to call. One of the oldest rules in the book, if there were a book, though there wasn't. But Peter's leaving had been so stiff, so awkward, it preyed on him, making it impossible to focus on the work at hand. He could not be good at his job unless he made things right with Charles. So in a roundabout way, by Peter's figuring, he *had* to call.

But when he heard Charles's voice on the other end of the line, Peter's throat tightened against his words and he almost hung up.

"Hello?" Charles said a second time, and Peter jettisoned the one syllable that would come out.

"Charles."

A moment. "Peter?"

Charles didn't sound angry. Peter let out a breath, and with it his tension. He eased himself back against the pillow and head-board of the hotel bed. "Yes. It's me." There was a long silence. "I really shouldn't—" Peter began.

"Be calling," Charles finished.

Peter wished he could see Charles's face just then, to be able to tell if it was sullenness or sorrow that colored his words. They sounded remarkably alike a continent away and over an unreli-able telephone line.

"I just wanted to know you were all right," Peter told him. By which he meant he wanted to know *they* were all right, but he knew Charles would understand.

"Picked up some extra shifts," said Charles. "Been spending a lot of time at the library."

"You always were a fast reader."

"You sound tired," Charles said suddenly and with typical concern, and in that moment Peter knew all was well between them. "Is it late where you are?"

"You know I can't tell you."

"You'll get sick if you don't get enough rest."

"I'll be fine."

Silence again, but this time it was comforting in the same way simply having someone you love in the same room could be comforting, and Peter fell asleep listening to Charles's even breathing on the far end of the line.

THREE

"I TOLD YOU," Albine insisted in her halting English, "I put it all in the report."

Peter's German was fluent, and he had not asked her to speak English, but she seemed determined to do so all the same. There was something defiant in her tone, despite the averted gaze meant to show respect. That, or she was hiding something and couldn't look him in the eye.

"You're not in any trouble," Peter told her. He tilted his own head in an attempt to catch her eye. A pretty thing. Miranda would be jealous.

And suddenly Peter realized: Albine and Jules.

Typical Jules. Not completely out of the question for Peter under certain circumstances, either, though with Charles now in the picture, Peter hated to think what those circumstances would have to be.

He sighed. "I don't care what you and Jules did—"

Albine's head whipped up, her eyes wide.

"But are you hiding him?"

She was already pale, but Peter swore she went a shade whiter. Her rosebud mouth puckered as if his words were sour. She shifted in her seat, hands clinched in her lap.

It was a storeroom office, very different from the Castle in London. This place was small and stuffy, with no windows;

Peter felt he could hardly get enough air. Crowded shelves of cigarettes, perfumes—quick radio assembly and disassembly, if one knew which boxes to grab. Peter sat now in an uncomfortable folding chair, Albine facing him in another almost knee to knee, while out front Vasil worked the Intershop.

"He came," she confessed, and now for expediency she had lapsed into German, "he was hurt. He came to me."

"Here?" Peter asked, though he more wanted to know how badly Jules had been hurt. Peter's brain seized on the remembered sound of Jules's choking sobs, his plea that Peter fetch him home. *Well, I'm here. Where are you?*

Albine gave her head a tiny shake, her sleek blonde hair bright under the fluorescent light.

"Your flat," Peter deduced with an inward sigh.

A stiff nod.

Peter waited. When it became clear no further information was going to be volunteered, he asked, "And?"

She blinked rapidly at his sharp tone and ducked her head again. "I couldn't let him in."

The words were so low, Peter leaned forward and asked her to repeat them. "Couldn't? Why?"

"My boyfriend was there."

"Oh, for God's sake." That was in English, and Albine clearly understood the tone if not the idiom. She curled in on herself, shoulders hunching over her knees.

"So where did he go?" Peter asked.

"I don't know."

"Where did he go?" Sterner.

"I don't know!" She was sobbing outright now, shoulders jogging up and down. The storage room door opened and Vasil looked in; Peter waved him off.

"I told him he should go to hospital," Albine told him.

"Why would you tell him such a thing?" For the first time Peter was honestly angry rather than merely exasperated. "You know he can't do that."

"It's better to be in prison than be dead!"

Peter didn't agree. And he didn't think Jules would either. But he chose not to argue the point.

"Why didn't you say this sooner?" asked Peter. "Tell me this sooner? Why didn't you tell MacAuley?"

Albine lifted her beautiful, miserable face. "He promised to come back for me. To take me to England."

Peter was confused. "MacAuley?"

"Jules!" Now she was the angry one, a woman to whom promises had not been kept. A dangerous thing. "My boyfriend, he is Stasi. He protects me. I could not let Jules in my flat. But I would have gone with him at any time. Instead he—" She waved a hand.

The Stasi boyfriend didn't much worry Peter; it was in Albine's file. In fact, she had been encouraged to maintain the connection in case it became useful. Still, she was a stupid girl, he decided, for letting Jules stumble off on his own.

"Did he say anything about how he'd been hurt? Where was he hurt?"

Albine gestured to her left side. "It was under his jacket."

"Gun? Knife?"

She threw up her hands. Her tears were gone now; she was done with this, done with Jules. "I don't know."

"Why didn't you go with him then? That night?"

"I couldn't! I waited to see if he would send me a message, tell me where to meet so we could go. But I never heard anything."

And this, Peter saw, was all that mattered to her. Jules had gone away without her. He'd left her there in Frankfurt an der Oder with her Stasi boyfriend and a job that could get her arrested, tortured, executed, when all she wanted was to be away and safe somewhere. It was why she'd taken the job to begin with: the promise of a better life on the other end of it.

A package of digestive biscuits—the chocolate kind that Charles was especially fond of—caught Peter's eye. He reached over to the shelf and took them, opened the wrap, offered the open end to Albine. She shook her head.

Peter bit into a biscuit and considered. What would he have

done in Jules's place? Of course, MacAuley had already investigated every avenue. But then, MacAuley hadn't been at the Bastion with Jules, hadn't trained with him. And if Peter knew Jules, his old friend would be counting on Peter's intimate knowledge of him to find him. Jules had made it so Peter *had* to come.

Albine was frowning at him in undisguised distaste. "Do you want some tea with that?" she asked (English again), the words dripping with derision. *How very English of you to sit there and eat a biscuit.*

And yet you are so eager to get away to jolly old England, Peter countered mentally and took another bite.

1953

The Bastion was little more than a collection of cabins in the woods of Yorkshire, the dormitories sagging with age and often leaking, the main house in only marginally better repair as recruits were assigned to fix things, but in keeping with their training it was all done slapdash with whatever was on hand.

Peter had been there two weeks when Jules arrived and joined his dorm. Jules strolled in during break, set his bag on Peter's bed, and flashed that brilliant smile. "Is this one taken?"

"Yes." Peter was lying on it at the time.

Jules took a seat on the edge of the bed all the same. "Are you sure?"

From his bed across the room, Stephen Lyons peered over the book he was reading. Peter pushed himself up on his elbows and glared at Stephen until the glint of Stephen's wire rims disappeared again. Then Peter turned his attention to the man seated on his bed. "Pretty bloody sure." He pushed the bag with his foot and it clattered to the warped floorboards.

Jules sighed as if Peter had disappointed him. "It's Italian leather, you know. From Florence." But he made no move to retrieve it.

"Doesn't get you much here, mate," Peter told him.

Jules chuckled. "It's not prison. You're here of your own free will, aren't you?"

All at once Peter was very aware of this stranger's dark eyes on him; they seared, making Peter feel hot and uncomfortable. But he stopped himself from squirming, forced himself to meet the new recruit's gaze.

Still, it was Stephen who spoke up from behind his book. "They found Peter at uni. He's every kind of special."

Jules lifted an eyebrow. Then he stuck out his hand. "Peter, is it?"

Somewhat reluctantly, Peter shook, though it was awkward in his semi-reclined state. "And you are?"

"Jules Maier. They found me at the scene of a break-in." He reached down and scooped up the bag, bouncing up from the bed as he did so. "Which ones are free?"

The one to Peter's right was vacant, but for some reason Peter hesitated to volunteer it. Stephen said, "Closest to the door in this row. Or last one in that row. I'm Stephen, by the way. If anyone cares."

But Jules was eyeing his options. "Why is no one in that one?" he asked, indicating the bed beside Peter's. "Do you snore or something?"

"Wouldn't matter where you slept if he did," said Stephen. "That bed's only just available. Byrne joined ranks last week."

Jules stepped over to Byrne's abandoned bunk and set his bag on the faded chambray coverlet. Glossy leather, well worn—truly a handsome and expensive bag, Peter noted. "A break-in?" he asked.

That vivid grin again. Jules was swarthy looking, dark all over: hair, eyes, skin that suggested a Mediterranean heritage. And he carried himself like a prince. If he was a thief, he wasn't sorry for it.

"They gave me two choices," said Jules. "Either way, I'm at Her Majesty's pleasure."

The bell rang. Stephen slapped his book shut and said, "Best get your things into the trunk and come on." He gestured at the scarred wooden chest at the foot of the bed.

Jules lifted the lid and dropped his bag in without bothering to unpack.

"Not planning to stay?" Peter asked, and Jules looked briefly startled, though the smile was back quickly enough.

"Dunno yet. We'll see if there's anything worth staying for."

There must have been, because he stayed, and after the first week or so Peter quit expecting to find Jules's bunk empty in the morning. Still, they weren't friends. Friendships didn't form at the Bastion, more a grudging trust born from necessary reliance on one another. Each man had his strengths, and in exercises they worked together by dividing the mission into who was good at what. Peter was good at languages and codes; it was what he'd gone to uni for. And Jules could get in and out of just about anywhere... and lift any number of objects while he did it.

1967

The location of Albine's flat was a matter of record, and Peter was not keen to risk a meeting with her Stasi boyfriend, nor did he need to see the spot where Jules had stood and bled. It was more a matter of determining where Jules would have gone after.

MacAuley had scouted, of course. But MacAuley had not trained with Jules, and Peter was now betting Jules had orchestrated whatever getaway he'd made (please, God, that he made one) so as to require that little bit of insider understanding in order to find him.

"He might have made it over the Oder," MacAuley had reported. "And from there, who knows?" It was the fact Jules had not reported in that had everyone shrugging and throwing up their hands. Blown, injured, on the run, and not heard from all added up to one general sum: Dead.

But Gordon clearly didn't think so. Or, at the very least, he felt a need to be sure.

"It's a wild goose chase," Peter confided to Charles one night. Charles made appropriately sympathetic noises, and Peter added, "I'm sorry I can't tell you more."

"No idea when you might be home?" Charles asked.

"No," Peter sighed. It was the same whenever Peter snuck in a phone call; he couldn't tell Charles anything, and Charles had nothing much to tell. Charles tried to make light of some of the tourists in his cab, but every conversation was weighted with their ongoing separation. Not just physical distance, but their lack of shared experience was creating a mental and emotional rift as well.

"I hope you're able to find your lost paperwork soon," said Charles, and Peter tried not to laugh. Jules would have been amused to be coded as "paperwork." God knew he hated it enough. Anything that required reading or writing. Jules was too restless for that; he needed to always be moving and doing.

Peter rang off and looked again at the maps until his vision began blurring. He didn't need them; he knew his way around. But he kept hoping for inspiration to reach up and grab him, for the lines to somehow form a message. If Jules had wanted to get through to him...

Peter froze.

This wasn't about him knowing Jules. It was about Jules knowing him.

———

There had been little enough left in the dark, dank flat Jules had used as a hideaway. Vasil himself, along with one other agent, had gathered the remains and cleared the site. He'd passed all that along to MacAuley, and Peter now had it in the file.

"No photos?" Peter asked Vasil. Gertrauden Park was dead and empty as they walked, but at least there was no snow; it was a remarkably dry winter.

"No time," Vasil said. "We didn't know who might be watching the flat. They may even be watching us now."

Peter wasn't terribly worried on that score. If anyone had been watching Vasil and Bernd, the Intershop would have long since been hit. "It didn't look tossed, the flat?"

Vasil shrugged. "It was messy, sure, and a chair pushed over, but nothing crazy."

"And Alexander Sepiol?" Peter wondered aloud.

Vasil only shook his head. "Nothing."

Peter sighed. What he had was all he would get. *You're smart,* Jules had once told him, *but are you any good in the field?*

If he wanted to be found, was hoping to be rescued from wherever he was, Jules had better be playing to Peter's strengths.

———

"Progress?" Gordon asked when Peter called.

Peter was reluctant to voice his suspicions, so he said, "Not really. Found out the girl saw him after he was injured but wouldn't let him into her flat."

"The Stasi boyfriend," Gordon grunted.

"Yes."

Silence. Then Gordon asked, "Do you think he made it over the river?"

"Possibly. Likely, even. Though I don't know what good it would have done him."

"We have friends there."

"I'm not sure Jules knows any of them," said Peter. "Or would trust them if he did. We have friends enough *here,* and he took off anyway."

"You think something is wrong."

"Something *is* wrong. Jules is missing, and Alexander Sepiol—"

"Probably leaked," said Gordon.

"And yet if someone knew about Jules, knew enough to shoot or stab him, they haven't moved against the rest of the local network."

"So Alexander only gave them Jules," Gordon suggested. "One name only, minimize the damage."

"Yet Jules led them to the safe house, and to Albine…"

"He may have lost them first. I would hope he wouldn't risk going any of those places without being sure he wasn't followed."

Peter hoped so, too, but the memory of Jules's panicked voice invited doubt. "He wouldn't have gone very far," Peter mused, just thinking aloud now. "But why didn't he come out when MacAuley swung through?" *Or for me now, if I'm the one he wanted?*

"You're doing fine work, Peter," Gordon told him, his voice unaccountably sad. "Give it another week, and if you don't learn anything new, come home."

Peter's heart gave a little leap toward his throat. Charles. In a week he could go home to Charles. "Hopefully it won't even take the week," he said.

Gordon took it to mean Peter felt sure of the investigation. "Good man," he said and rang off, leaving Peter to the quiet roar of his own thoughts.

FOUR

1953

IT WAS their second exercise together. Peter, Jules, and Wyn Blevins, also from their dorm and in Peter's opinion too high strung for the work. Blevins was short, fair, and nervous, utterly useless in any situation that required quiet or confidence as this one did. Peter could only assume Blevins, acting as team leader this outing, had chosen him and Jules to make up for his own shortcomings. And Peter couldn't be very surprised when Blevins went missing.

"They've caught him, I bet," Jules muttered.

The goal was to retrieve the documents from the opposing team's cabin while simultaneously avoiding capture and defending their own intelligence. Jules would have been the proper one to send, of course. Peter was just there to decipher whatever they managed to get. In any case, Blevins had got it in his head to go after the documents and leave Jules and Peter to defend their own cabin.

"Serves him right," said Peter. "He knows you're much better at it. A good leader delegates according to one's strengths."

"We should go after him," Jules said.

"Be my guest." Peter glanced around the shack. "I can hold down the fort."

But Jules swept the file off the table and stuffed it into the inside of his coat. "You're smart. But are you any good in the field? Come on. We can't leave him out there on his own."

Peter started to protest, even as he followed Jules to the door with the idea of taking their papers back, but Jules turned with a smile and held a finger to his lips. With the choice to either stay in an empty shack and wait for an enemy agent to arrive or go with Jules, Peter opted to follow Jules into the woods.

1967

There were papers spread over the hotel bed, everything in the file. Now and then Peter would pick up a page and move it in hopes of discovering some hidden pattern, as if the pages themselves were bits of code that simply required the right arrangement to crack.

Meanwhile, his mind whirled. *You don't know if he's even alive,* he reminded himself. *He was wounded... but mobile... One can be badly wounded and still motivated to keep moving... Infection... He would have needed to get help, but from where?*

They'd been taught to sew themselves up if necessary; Jules would have had a kit for that. But depending on the severity of the injury, Jules might still have needed medical attention.

Peter pawed through papers until he found the list of local friendlies. Frankfurt an der Oder didn't have a large network. Vasil, Bernd, Albine, and until recently Alexander Sepiol, whose questionable loyalty Jules had been there to verify. It seemed they had their answer, but the extent of the damage remained unclear. MacAuley had deemed the network secure, and Peter had seen nothing counter to that, but Gordon wanted to be sure. Short of finding bodies, Peter didn't know if that was possible.

"It's not a key operation," Peter had told Gordon earlier that night over the phone. "It's not Berlin."

"One trickle can become a flood," said Gordon. "Vasil may not know much, and Alexander didn't, but Jules..."

Yes, Jules knew the names and faces of enough agents to be worrisome. Better to secure him, dead or alive.

Get him out or take him out. Isn't that what he'd told Jules about Alexander? And now here he was in the same position.

Not exactly, though. Peter spoke fluent German and, with the proper identification, passed as a native. He could stay unmolested in a hotel while Jules's foreign looks had forced him into hiding lest he attract too much attention.

We should have sent someone else. A memory of fair little Wyn Blevins passed through Peter's mind. He'd have looked the part, though he'd never have managed it. Last Peter had heard, Blevins was manning a radio in Denmark, where he could be as nervous as he liked without bothering—or endangering—anyone.

1953

Peter could hardly fathom how Jules managed to move so quickly and yet so silently through the undergrowth. It was early autumn, and leaves populated the ground, but Jules might as well have floated on air for all the noise he made. Peter stayed close, trying to step where Jules did and be just as quiet.

The opposing team's cabin came into view, and Jules stopped, so Peter did too. The cabins were old and little more than shacks, wooden with windows on three of the four walls and a door in the fourth. Inside were a chair, a bench, and a table. No working electricity, but they each carried torches anyway. It was about midday now, but it being autumn, they would lose the light soon enough. As it was, the day was overcast and somewhat dark.

Jules held up a finger as he studied the cabin, and Peter resisted the urge to slap it away. After a moment, Jules lowered his hand and turned to Peter, eyes glinting with excitement. "Go knock on their door."

"What?"

"Tell them we'll trade our intel for Blevins."

"He's not worth it. Besides, then they'll have me, too. Where are they? Not all in the cabin, surely?"

"We passed one coming over. That's why I went wide east to avoid him. He's probably on his way to stake our place."

Peter shivered, suddenly cold despite his wool coat. He jammed his hands into the pockets. This wasn't what he'd signed up for; he was strictly a linguist with a mind rapid and logical enough to crack codes and distill information. But they all had to train, get their feet wet in the field. "You won't like all of it," Gordon had told him when Peter had finally agreed to join, "but you need to have an understanding of what the men out there are going through, the decisions they face."

"Don't worry," said Jules. "I'll get you out." He nudged Peter with his elbow, and Peter reluctantly started toward the cabin.

1967

"I expect to be home by the end of the week."

Silence on the line. Peter hadn't exactly expected screaming—Charles wasn't that way—but he'd thought there would be *some* happy response. "Charles?" he asked, thinking maybe the connection had dropped.

"Sorry," said Charles. "I'm happy, of course. I was just thinking I need to go to the grocer's. What would you like for your first meal back?"

This was Charles's way; he showed his love practically and efficiently by making sure Peter's clothes were clean and he never went hungry. It sometimes made Peter feel like a pet. Or a plant, even. Less an individual and more something requiring care and feeding, an item on a to-do list.

"You're all I want," Peter said. And in that moment, it was true. Peter pictured Charles standing in the kitchen—next to the sink, he decided—crinkles around his brilliant blue eyes as he smiled, one had running through the thinning hair that was going from fair to white at the temples. There was something sturdy about Charles, and safe, and Peter had a piercing moment of wanting to be home and comfortable and, yes, cared for.

From the other end of the line came a heavy exhalation. "It happened very fast, didn't it? Us?" Charles asked.

Peter's mental wheels spun backward. "Are you...?" But he wasn't sure what to ask, or maybe just afraid of the answer.

"It surprised me is all," Charles admitted, and Peter imagined him leaning against the counter now for support. "I'm not saying I'm sorry because I'm not," Charles added, a streak of defiance in his tone, as if he dared Peter to make him apologize. "I'm only thinking I'm amazed how much I miss you, even after a few days, when we haven't even known each other that long."

Peter slowly let out the breath he'd been holding. "I miss you, too. I..." He wasn't quite ready to say it, but Charles seemed to understand.

"I know," said Charles. "I feel the same."

1953

"You've always loved me just a little."

Peter glanced up from his desk, caught a glimpse of dark hair and a flash of white teeth. "Bugger off."

"You'd like that, wouldn't you?"

Peter watched out of the corner of his eye as Jules dragged over the chair from a neighboring desk. What passed for a library was yet another dark and slightly damp room lined with shelves with desks crowded in the center. High windows let in what little light filtered in from the trees. In Peter's opinion, it wasn't a place fit for books. People were one thing, but books deserved better.

"You don't have to hide it from me," Jules said.

Keep writing. Don't look up. "Hide what?"

"You *do* love me, I think. And because you do..." He slapped a book onto the desk. "You're going to help me with this."

Peter drew back from the tome as if it were something distasteful, though really he was looking to introduce more space between himself and Jules. "It's a history text."

Jules leaned in. "I can't keep all these names and dates straight!" he hissed. "I don't know how you—how anyone—can do it!" He threw himself against the straight wooden back of the chair. "And I don't see why it matters, either."

"Of course it matters," said Peter. "These names and dates are key to successful relations the world over."

"You're such a diplomat." But it was said affectionately, almost wistfully. "That's not what I'm headed for, though. I'm going to be out there." Jules jerked his chin up at a window. "In the trenches. It's all I'm good for. Front lines, cannon fodder."

"It's not all you're good for," Peter said quietly. "But it's what you're best at. And we need men like you."

Jules burst into a grin. "See! I knew you loved me!"

Peter sighed, a strange mixture of relief and disappointment flooding his system. Jules hadn't meant anything by it, but for a terrible moment Peter had been worried the truth was out—and yet, in that same moment had come the freedom of not having to hide it any longer, and a willingness to take whatever consequences were involved. Now secrecy wrapped itself around him again like a heavy coat he never took off. A coat that couldn't keep him warm.

1967

There was nothing in the file, Peter was sure of it. He'd gone through the papers every which way he could think to, but there were no clues, no hidden messages from Jules. MacAuley hadn't missed anything.

Only one other place to look.

He could have gone to Vasil for the key, but he didn't. Later, Peter would only be able to say that "something felt wrong" and he'd wanted to investigate outside the network. It wasn't entirely true; though he'd told Gordon something was wrong, he didn't have any inkling just *how* wrong. He only wanted to cut out a step. It was late, the Intershop was closed, and Peter had no desire to go to Vasil's house, but he also didn't want to wait until morning. So he broke into the (no longer) safe flat instead. In truth, the building was so old and brittle he probably could have kicked the door in, and given the neighborhood it was unlikely anyone would intervene if he had. But not wanting to support even mild curiosity, Peter quickly, quietly, and efficiently picked the lock.

It was the third floor of a five-story walk-up, a slapdash kind of place that seemed to have been meant as temporary, but then no one made the effort to tear it down and now it was collapsing on its own. Peter's guess was it had been hastily built as shelter for those displaced by bombings during the war, but no one could be bothered to take responsibility for it. Perfect for people who wished to remain nameless.

One room with one window. Vasil and Bernd had stripped it of the few wares: the one plate, cup, knife, fork, and spoon; the single blanket (there had been no pillow); and of course the phone. Only the rusted metal frame of the bed and the heavy wooden table were left; Peter guessed the mattress and chair had been poached by locals who'd noticed the flat's vacancy.

At the sight of the nearly bare room, Peter deflated. It appeared doubtful Jules had left behind any clues, or if he had, very probable those clues had been obliterated when the flat was swept—by Vasil, then MacAuley, then the locals. But he'd come all this way, and at such an hour, so Peter was determined to make a thorough investigation.

The floor was greying, rough wood, and it was impossible to be entirely silent due to it bending and squeaking under Peter's weight. He slipped his shoes off to minimize the noise, and then also his socks when they kept getting snagged on splinters. His feet were none happier for it, and he foresaw an evening spent with tweezers in his near future.

The bed first. There was no light; the bulb, if there had ever been one, had gone the way of the mattress and chair. Peter pulled a small torch from his overcoat pocket and began examining the bed frame as if the rusty flakes harbored some secret. His reward was nothing but an aching back.

He sat back on his heels and considered. What might Vasil and MacAuley have overlooked? The very question made Peter's heart plummet; MacAuley was good at his job, which was why Peter had sent him to begin with. He would not have missed anything. All at once Peter was tired, and this exercise seemed futile, ridiculous even. What made him think Jules would have left something only he could find?

Peter switched off the torch and allowed his eyes to crawl over the room as they adjusted. Nothing carved in the floor or desk—too obvious, would have been found. And if it had been on the chair or in the mattress, well, tough luck there.

His eyes settled on a dark patch of floor near the desk, and for a moment his mind fell to static as he began to understand it was blood, old blood, soaked into the floorboards. Yes, there where the chair would have been, the place Jules would have been sitting when he called and begged Peter to come bring him home.

Peter forced himself to his feet, made himself walk over for a closer look. He took out his torch again but couldn't bring himself to fully illuminate the stain, Jules's life leaking away. He turned the light toward the desk instead, though he had no hopes for it; he only needed to focus on something else.

It was wood, lighter in color than the floor thanks to a coat of varnish. Scratches covered the surface, years of things thrown onto and slid across and, based on a few dimples, probably dropped on it. Peter moved for a closer look and found the expected swear words cut into the tabletop, a few women's names and crude drawings to accompany them. He ducked under the table, too, not because he expected to find anything but because he couldn't stand not to be thorough. There was a drawer, he discovered, shallow and without any handle; he had to slip his fingers under the lip of it and pull it open. The drawer was tightly fitted and, given its reluctance, largely unused. Of course there was nothing in it. MacAuley would have been equally thorough, after all, even if Vasil hadn't. Still, Peter shined his torch into the far corners of the drawer, skimming the little bit of graffiti that had worked its way off the desktop; some of their agents were evidently more enterprising than others. He was trying to shove the drawer back into place when a line of letters caught his eye.

They were nonsense, or seemed to be, scribbled faintly in pencil and easy to miss amidst the other scrawls. An alphabet

gone wrong or acronym run amok: ABPZPTCVTFQTTFLDIAL-
WOUVDVANEBD

Peter had to bend close to make it all out, the letters were so lightly written and crowded by other, darker inscriptions. Easy to miss. Proof that if one doesn't expect to find anything, one almost never will.

It had been years since he'd seen Jules's handwriting, but Peter was certain Jules had left this for him. A code, Playfair by the looks of it, which presented an entirely different problem: Peter had no idea what the key word was.

Time enough for that later. Peter drew a small notebook from his coat, and a pen, and took down the line of letters, checking several times over to be sure he'd got it right. He only hoped Jules had, too; codes were not counted among Jules's strengths.

Though he had what he'd come for, Peter didn't feel right leaving immediately, so he made a perfunctory examination of the rest of the little room, checking the window sill and collapsed shutters for any other messages, and going back to the desk drawer twice to be sure there wasn't anything more than the one line.

The horizon was going from dark to pearly grey by the time Peter slipped his socks and shoes back on. He was eager to get out before any other residents of the building could note his visit. A sense of triumph washed over Peter, the satisfied feeling of a job well done, but it was tempered by sadness—with this new evidence, it was unlikely he'd be going home at the end of the week as planned.

Charles would have to wait.

1953

They had him before he even reached the door; an arm snaked around his throat and his arms pinned behind his back, and Clarkson shouting, "I've got another one!"

Peter went limp, forcing Clarkson to bear his weight, little enough though that was. From inside the cabin, Gamby hissed, "Don't go shouting about it! Get him inside."

Clarkson shoved Peter through the door. "He was just walking right up like he was in for a visit."

Gamby frowned at Peter. "What's your game, eh?"

"We only have the one chair," Clarkson pointed out. And there was Blevins, tied to it, eyes wide. He was trembling hard enough to see, and Peter wondered the chair didn't shake apart beneath him.

"Let Blevins go, and you can have our intel," said Peter.

Gamby snorted. "And you, too, I suppose."

"I'll stay if you like. Decipher the papers."

Gamby stared hard at Peter for a long moment. They did not know one another well, were not cabin mates; Gamby was expansive in every sense of the word, and Peter was the opposite, thin as Gamby was thick, quiet as Gamby was loud. But they were both tall and both shrewd, and they sized one another now.

"Let him go," Gamby ordered, and Clarkson released Peter.

"You could have taken him!" Blevins complained, and Peter frowned at him.

"I'm here to save you, you nit."

"By failing us? Where's Maier?"

"Yes, where *is* Maier?" Gamby asked.

"Taking care of Tillholm, I expect," said Peter. "Why did you send him?"

"Same reason you sent Blevins," Gamby said. "No one wants to spend any time with him."

With a sympathetic glance at his team leader, Peter felt beholden to answer, "Blevins sent himself, actually," which sent Gamby into a roar of laughter.

"You're getting off mission," Blevins muttered.

"Wish we had a gag for him," said Gamby.

"Just use his sock," suggested Peter, earning a look of disbelief and betrayal from Blevins.

Clarkson dove for Blevins's feet, and Blevins kicked him away.

"Don't really," Gamby told Clarkson, then turned a wry face to Peter. "Not enough rope for his feet."

"This is *not* how this is supposed to go!" Blevins insisted. "Standing around chatting like you're at the club."

"Not a lot you can do about it, though, is there?" Gamby asked.

Blevins turned another accusing look on Peter, and Peter wished he knew what Jules was up to. He could only stall so long.

"What about the papers?" Clarkson asked, and Peter sighed. He was out of options.

"Sorry," he said to Gamby, and the big man had just enough time to look perplexed before Peter swung.

1967

After taking a run at the code and coming up empty, then sleeping off a bit of the night with the idea a fresh brain might help, then waking and showering and trying again with the same result, Peter called Gordon.

"What does it say?" Gordon asked, and Peter was forced to admit his failure.

"I've tried all our current key words," said Peter, and though he didn't want to sound as if he were making excuses, he added, "There's a chance Jules did it incorrectly."

"He left it for you to find," said Gordon. "He would have used a word that meant something to the both of you."

That had occurred to Peter, of course. Except he couldn't think of any one word that fit the need. "I'll think on it," he said.

"Good. It's fine work you're doing, Peter."

"Thank you, sir." The words warmed Peter; they always did.

FIVE

1951

HE'D FIRST MET Gordon Lessenby purely by accident—Gordon's accident, not Peter's own. Peter had been prompt as ever to a meeting with Dr. Davidson in that esteemed old man's cluttered office, where they were to suss out the finer points of some inscriptions on fragments from Tusculum. It had become generally accepted that Peter was Davidson's pet, and if the professor hadn't been almost as ancient as the artifacts, there would have certainly been further assumptions made about the relationship. There still were, but far fewer than if Dr. Davidson had been younger.

It was dusk, Peter recalled, the sky was purple with it, and he'd spied one fine star hanging over the buildings as he'd crossed the grounds at his usual brisk pace, forcing himself to slow once inside the permanent twilight of the college hall; it wouldn't do to arrive puffing and out of breath. He took the stairs up one flight, then two, drawing deeply of the stale air that circulated within but never escaped the heavy stone walls. The place was a nest for old dodos, all of them squawking and flapping at one another and taking no notice of the outside world or their own imminent extinction. Peter did not think to join them by going into academia and becoming fresh blood for the old system to pump; he knew himself well enough to realize he was too impatient to be an instructor, and that writing treatise after treatise over the same arguments would only bore him. At most Peter had the vague notion of doing some kind of translation work. At least then the texts would always be changing and some might even be interesting. He was cutting his teeth on this idea as he began more and more to assist Dr. Davidson, getting a taste for it.

"There will always be a need for turning one language into another," the professor often encouraged. And that evening Gordon Lessenby had come needing something foreign broken apart and put back together.

Peter knocked and, without waiting for an answer, opened the door—another signal of his impatient nature. Dr. Davidson sat behind his desk, the silver-white hair combed back, the watery eyes and toothsome grin turning Peter's way. And another, darker set of eyes also turned, and in the second of them raking over him, Peter felt he'd been finely combed by them, evidence picked off his person in a kind of optical assault. He scowled at the intrusion, and at the stranger who stood in front of Dr. Davidson's desk.

The man was a couple inches shorter than Peter, but so were many men. Broader, too, but so were many. The man's coat seemed to Peter too heavy for a fine spring evening, and it covered too much of the man's body for Peter to determine a shape. But the face was lined and slightly baggy, as if it had once been fuller and had lost weight. Peter guessed the man was of an age with his own father; the dark hair was showing streaks of grey at the temples. But the eyes were most certainly keen, and Peter felt no desire to walk any closer to allow the man any better a look at him.

But Dr. Davidson was waving one liver-spotted hand. "Peter! Yes, we had been planning... Oh, but this is Mr. Lessenby, just in need of a little help with an odd..."

Lessenby had not taken his eyes from Peter. "Close the door, if you would," he directed. Reluctantly, Peter stepped over the threshold into the office and did as bid.

"Mr. Stoller here is one of our best linguists," Dr. Davidson enthused, and the pride Peter would normally have felt failed to well; he rather wished the professor would not draw attention to him.

The dark eyes made another pass over Peter. "Stoller. Sounds German."

Peter was not sure whether it was an accusation, but he answered as if it were. "If so, it was long enough ago no one in our family can trace it."

"I'm sure they could," Lessenby said, "but my guess would be they wouldn't want to."

Dr. Davidson's head began to swivel between the two men standing in his office. "Well, now, whatever his family, Peter is a solid citizen, I believe," he said, and Lessenby pegged him with a sharp look. Davidson's frail hands flapped like a moth that had been pinned while still alive. "It's not as if I've researched him," the professor went on, "but..."

Irritation bubbled up in Peter's chest. "You can call my father if you like. I'm sure he'd be happy to discuss it."

Lessenby looked again at him. "Do you speak German?"

And for a moment Peter was confused. "At home?" he asked. "No."

But Davidson was quick to make things clear. "Peter speaks and reads just about everything. Except Sanskrit and Hindi, all those types. But if it's European, Asian, or Arabic, he has it covered."

"If I show you something, could you read it?" Lessenby asked Peter.

Curiosity warred with indignation that this man who had been so rude would now ask for a favor. "I won't know until I see it," Peter answered stiffly.

Lessenby turned to Davidson. "And you're sure you can't read it?"

"Well, but German isn't my language," the professor told him, "and even still, this doesn't look like any German I've ever seen." His pale hand tapped a paper on his desk. Lessenby slipped it from under Davidson's fingers and held it out for Peter's perusal.

Peter didn't take it; he merely stepped close enough to look. Then after a moment frowned and did take the paper, as if holding it and viewing it more closely would make it make sense. "It isn't..."

And then he saw. "Oh, Jesus. What is it? Like a test or something?"

"You understand it," Lessenby said.

"Well, no," said Peter, "it would take some time to... Whoever wrote this used at least fifteen different... They took bases from some languages, and—Look, the start of this word is Icelandic, but this bit here is Old Gutnish, and they've Frankensteined a whole letter by..."

Davidson beamed at Lessenby. "Told you he was bright, didn't I? He had that down in less than two minutes."

Peter offered the page back to Lessenby. "I feel sorry for whoever has to take this test," he said. "What kind of teacher does that to his students? What a headache."

"I think, Mr. Stoller," Lessenby said without taking back the paper, "you are going to be the one taking this particular test."

Automatically, Peter turned to Dr. Davidson. "Professor?"

"Mr. Lessenby works for... the government," Davidson said delicately. "And it seems none of their people saw what you did in this bit of paper."

Peter's eyes drifted back to Lessenby, who had shoved his hands in his coat pockets as if in mute refusal to take back the cryptic message. And all at once Peter understood. This man had come, had purposefully put Peter on the defensive in regards to his roots, tacitly questioning his national loyalty, because now there was no way to say "no" to this task without seeming unpatriotic.

For a second, Peter was tempted to crumple the paper in his hand.

But then he reminded himself this was exactly the kind of work he'd been planning to do after uni. And if he did well with this, might he be offered more? There might be no more interesting work than whatever messages the government needed translated.

Peter was aware of Lessenby's eyes on him, was sure the man read his thoughts even as they cascaded through his brain.

"How quickly do you need it?" Peter asked.

But instead of answering, Lessenby turned back to Dr. Davidson and said, "We'll have to put him someplace. Can't have him loose with it."

Davidson's rheumy eyes blinked in Peter's general direction, though it was always difficult to tell how much the old man could actually see. "I think we can spare him for a few days. If I know Peter, it won't take him long."

———

He was not even permitted to return to his room and gather any of his things. Instead, Lessenby assured him they would see to it he had everything he might need... Whoever "they" were. The government, Peter supposed, wondering at what large and lumbering agency of which this Mr. Lessenby might be a cog. An agency so inefficient none of its people could manage a linguistic task a university student could manage.

Or maybe no one else wanted the job.

Maybe it was something like a grocery list and no one could be bothered to translate it.

But then again, who would go to such lengths to disguise such a mundane bit of information?

Despite himself, as Peter was ushered into the back of the waiting car, Lessenby's hand hovering near his elbow so that Peter sensed it but never actually felt a touch, Peter found he was intrigued. He now wanted to translate the thing, just to prove he could, and just to reveal what was hidden so that maybe he could also figure out why.

Peter had shifted over in the seat with the expectation that Lessenby would sit beside him, so he was surprised when the man closed him in and made no move to get in the car. Instead, Lessenby opened the front passenger door and said to the driver,

"Take him to the estate and see him settled then come back 'round for me. I've got a couple other things to finish up with."

The driver—as it was nearly dark Peter could only catch the halo of the man's broad profile in the light of the lamps glaring through the windows—nodded and put the car into motion without a word. He did not speak to Peter and Peter thought it best to keep to himself. He concentrated on the turns, the scenery, trying to determine their direction and where they might be going. Wherever it was, there was nothing else nearby, no town with which Peter could orient himself. More than an hour later (but less than two, Peter noted) they rolled up to a tall iron gate fitted into a stone wall. With a wave Peter took to mean he should stay put, the driver got out and approached an intercom; Peter tried to listen but could hear nothing through the glass, nor was he brave enough to attempt to roll the window even a little. After a moment the driver returned. They sat. Waited. And some minutes later an older man in a heavy brown jumper came out and opened the gates.

The car eased through, slow and silent.

At first there was nothing but grass on either side, slightly overgrown from what Peter could tell in the dark, its unevenness suggesting it had not been mown recently though it was short enough to say it *had* been cut at some point. Then there came trees, though Peter couldn't have said what kind. They grew in what might have once been neat rows, but the trees were old enough now to stretch and lean out of line. Peter counted six to each side. Then the world opened again and ahead of them was a house—an estate, really, as Lessenby had called it, its wide brick wings unfurling on either side of a porticoed central hall. It looked not unlike a university building and so did not inspire much awe in Peter, who was all too familiar with similar structures.

The car turned in the circular drive and came to a stop. Peter automatically tried the door and discovered it could not be opened from inside. The driver climbed out but did not open Peter's door; as Peter ducked and peered, the driver went up the steps to the house and, as if timed, the door opened and a matronly silhouette appeared in the warm glow from within. The driver gesticulated at the car; the matron nodded as if it were all in due course. And then the driver returned and freed Peter.

———

The woman *was* matronly, Peter decided, her white hair pulled up in a grandmotherly bun, though she had fewer wrinkles than Dr. Davidson. She led Peter into the almost too warm hall and asked, "Have you eaten, dear?"

Peter had. He'd been expecting a long night with the professor and had equipped himself for it by having a large meal prior.

"I suppose you'll be wanting to get straight to work then," said the woman, who had not offered a name by which Peter could call her. She bustled farther into the house and it took a moment for Peter to understand he was meant to follow. Down a corridor, around a corner, into the back right of the central part of the building by Peter's calculations, and yes, there was a window into a large garden at the back, early spring flowers only just coming into bloom. Through the glass Peter glimpsed the wings of the house on either side.

The room was darkly paneled. It had a hodgepodge of book-cases and a table that looked more meant for a kitchen than a library. A single wooden chair, a stack of notepads and a cluster of pens. This was where he would spin straw into gold.

"Loo is out here to the left," the matron informed him. "Mr. Lessenby will be along with your things. Are you sure you wouldn't like some tea at least?"

Peter accepted the offer of tea and privately questioned whether he'd be given a bed. Or was he expected to push through until the work was done? If so, what of his things did Lessenby expect him to require?

Peter took a seat and stared moodily out at the dark garden. He didn't want to start the work until he had his tea and was reasonably sure he'd be left alone. Very little annoyed him more than interruption when he was trying to concentrate. A few minutes later there was the telltale rattle of ceramic being carried on a tray and the matron appeared with a cup, saucer, sugar bowl, a creamer of milk, and a plate of sliced lemon. "I can bring honey if you like," she told him as she laid each item out to his left, but Peter shook his head, and after she'd closed the door, he pulled the paper from his pocket and began to look it over.

The penmanship was sloppy—possibly it had been written rapidly—and based on the slant had been written by someone left-handed. But no, it couldn't have been written all that quickly, not if the person had been required to use all different bits of languages; no one could have memorized such jumble. Might as well make up a whole new language. It would be easier to learn than this.

Drawing over a notepad and selecting a pen, Peter began to work.

————

He was not sure how long he'd been at it, though it seemed to him the sky was getting lighter by the time Gordon Lessenby opened the door and said quietly, "You should sleep."

"I'm not tired," Peter said, though it was a bald lie; he was exhausted, but he did not want to give up his momentum.

"Let's see what you have," said Lessenby, and Peter bit down on his irritation and handed over his notes though not with much grace.

"In some cases it's just one letter that's from another alphabet," Peter explained as Lessenby's brow wrinkled. "It's all nonsense from what I can tell," he added. "Made-up words mostly. I've done as much as I can, but I'll need my books for a lot of it."

"Fine work." Lessenby handed back the notepad. "But I'm going to insist you get some rest. I've brought some things, fresh clothes and all that..." He went to the door, paused and waited for Peter to follow. As Peter unfolded his long limbs, they protested their treatment at having been hunched up for so long.

It must have showed; Lessenby nodded as if he'd proven something.

Peter followed Lessenby back through the same halls he'd come down. But instead of going back to the center of the house, they cut through and back and down into the east wing. At first Peter thought he'd be housed in the cellar, then suddenly there was a staircase and up they went to a corridor lined with doors; Lessenby stopped at the third on the left. "This is you. I'm right down there." He pointed to the last door on the right.

Peter didn't answer. He opened the door and went into the room, closing the door behind him without a word. It was spacious. The furniture looked old, antique even. On the brocade counterpane sat one of Peter's own overnight bags, and inside it he found some of his clothes neatly folded, and pyjamas, and his shaving kit.

He could not keep himself from frowning at the idea Lessenby had been in his room. Only Lessenby? Or had there been others? Had Lessenby sent someone else to gather his belongings?

But his brain was too exhausted from the work to think about it very long, and his body was sending up warning flares that it might also soon cease to operate properly. And so, extracting his pyjamas, Peter changed, dropped his bag and worn clothes onto the floor beside the bed, and then himself onto the bed, kicking and pulling like a child at the cover and sheets because he was too tired to get up and turn them back. Once he had fought his way in—which took more effort than getting up again would have—and was satisfactorily tucked under, Peter fell almost immediately into a black and dreamless sleep.

He was so sure Byron would be beside him that he woke groping for the warmth of a body that was not there. Sunlight slanted in from the window whose curtains he'd failed to close the night before, the brilliance illuminating his outstretched arm and the empty expanse of mattress. But despite the light, it wasn't warm.

Peter struggled to a sitting position and took in his surroundings with refreshed eyes. Of course Byron wasn't here, he—Peter's train of thought came to a screeching halt. Byron hadn't gone to his room last night, had he? No, he'd known Peter was planning to work with Dr. Davidson, had been a bit irked about it in fact. But it would be just like Byron to let himself in and lay in wait, putting on that hurt and languishing air as if he might waste away from neglect. And if he had, would Lessenby...?

But at that junction Peter's mind went blank; he couldn't not formulate in his imagination any interaction between Byron and Lessenby. The two did not correspond. The jarring juxtaposition made Peter's head hurt.

He threw back the covers and made to dress, finding a bathroom in what he'd thought was a closet. Maybe it had been; it was roughly the size of one. The water in the shower was only lukewarm, so Peter kept it short and was just finishing buttoning his shirt when the knock came.

"You'll want something to eat," Lessenby said without preamble when Peter opened the door. "And if you write down which books you need, I'll see you get them."

Peter followed Lessenby downstairs and to a dining room too large for just two people. But the sideboard was filled with covered salvers emitting delicious smells, and Peter was suddenly hungry. He trailed after Lessenby, whose own plate remained sparse as he opted for a couple sausages and some toast. Peter, on the other hand, heaped eggs, sausages, toast, beans, and ham... and then decided he would have to make another pass for the rest.

"Breakfast tea?" Lessenby inquired as Peter joined him at the table. A pot and cups Peter was sure hadn't been there a moment before now squatted at one end. "Or you might rather have juice," Lessenby went on as Peter tried to decide how close to sit. Across was better than beside, he thought. And Lessenby had not chosen to sit at the head of the table.

"I'm sure we have some, if you want any," Lessenby went on,

sounding like an uncle who was unused to having children visit. When Peter gave him a blank look, he added, "Juice, I mean."

"Tea is fine," said Peter. He set his plate down and waited, standing beside his chair.

"No need to wait on me," Lessenby told him as he poured tea. "Sit, eat." He leaned to set a cup in front of Peter then poured another for himself before settling into his own chair. "Table is too big to do it sitting," Lessenby explained. And it was —a wide expanse of polished mahogany separated them, the gleaming teapot a kind of island that neither could have reached without stretching or standing.

He was more than half done with his breakfast before Lessenby spoke again. "Is there anyone you should call? Anyone who might be worried were you not to be around for a couple days?"

Peter froze, just for a moment, then forced himself to continue eating as if the words had not startled him. But he knew what they meant: Lessenby knew about Byron. Either Byron *had* been there, or... Peter tried to remember whether he had anything in his room that pointed to Byron. Notes, maybe. Byron often left him little notes, and though he threw most away, there might have been a stray or two. Or perhaps Byron had left a new one.

"We don't want a hue and cry, you understand," Lessenby went on. "And if anyone were to ask Dr. Davidson, well, he'd know to tell them you are on a research trip of sorts. But maybe not everyone would ask Dr. Davidson."

Oh, Byron *would* ask the professor, but would not be easily satisfied by a vague response. Byron would demand to know where and why and for how long.

"If a student were to suddenly be declared missing..."

"I don't think they'd go that far," said Peter, and he was surprised at how even his voice remained. "Students go off for a few days now and then. Maybe they get called home, maybe they just need a break. We're adults, not children."

"Yes, well, we'd like to avoid a fuss all the same. Of any kind."

Peter nodded. His plate was empty. But since Lessenby wasn't going for seconds, he wasn't sure he should.

"You haven't answered my question," Lessenby said. And when Peter blinked at him, "Is there anyone you should call?"

Suddenly tired of the tiptoeing, Peter sighed and asked, "Why are you pretending not to know?"

For what seemed like a long time, Lessenby stared at him from the far side of the table. Then, having seemingly come to some conclusion, he nodded and asked, "How long have you known Byron Milton?"

"Not long. A few months."

"How many is a few?" Lessenby pressed. "I'm sorry, but in my line of work it pays to be as specific as possible. Are you still hungry? There's plenty more."

Peter realized Lessenby understood his need not so much to eat, though that was a side benefit, as his need to get up and move rather than face him down across the dining table. It should be a conversation rather than an interrogation. He gratefully stood to fetch more breakfast.

"Four months," Peter said. "We met right before the winter break."

"But didn't spend break together."

"No." More ham, more eggs, and when he returned to the table a fresh cup of tea was waiting.

"You went home for the holiday?"

Peter shook his head but had the feeling that, once again, Lessenby already knew the answer. "I was invited to stay with a friend and his family in Switzerland."

"A close friend? Someone who might notice you're gone?"

Another head shake. "No, I just helped him in history so he felt he owed me. We don't even share any courses this term, so I haven't heard from him."

"And Mr. Milton…"

"I should probably give him a call to keep him from worrying."

"I get the sense he is as romantic as his name," said Lessenby.

So there *had* been a note. Peter was unable to suppress a grimace at the thought of Lessenby reading it. "Byron is..." Peter searched for a word. *Ardent* came to mind, but that was not the picture he wanted to paint. He settled on, "Devoted."

"And he will be upset if you are gone very long?" Lessenby asked.

"Yes," said Peter. "But if I talk to him, I might be able to keep him from making a scene about it."

"Would he? Even if he knew you were all right and just away doing research?"

Peter could not think of a way to explain that Byron would make a scene if Peter asked to study alone for a few hours, much less if he went away unexpectedly. Truly, Peter knew he needed to end the relationship, but he hadn't the emotional energy to deal with the fallout. And so it dragged on in cycles of Byron's melodramatic antics: First his avowals of love, then his furious protestations of Peter's perceived lack of caring, followed by silence, then weeping, and then they returned to the start of the wheel. The tide came in, the tide went out.

"What kind of scene would he make?" Lessenby pressed, and Peter realized the man was sincerely concerned.

"I don't know," Peter said. "So long as he hears from me, I don't think he'll get frantic. But if he doesn't... He'd probably start with my professors..." But even as he said it, Peter realized it wasn't true.

Lessenby saw something in Peter that informed him of this fact as well. "You're thinking of something else."

"Doyle. Another friend. Byron would actually probably go to him first."

"The one you went to Switzerland with?"

"No. I've known Alec longer; we attended public school together."

"Alec Doyle is the name?"

Peter nodded numbly. Was Byron even now shouting at Doyle, accusing him of hiding Peter's whereabouts?

"Byron is... jealous?" Lessenby ventured.

Peter nodded again.

"Does he have reason to be?"

Peter could not squelch the flare of irritation that the question ignited in him. Eyes flashing, he challenged, "Does it matter?"

Lessenby sighed. "Imogen, show Peter to the phone, would you?" And as Peter turned to find the matron from the previous night hovering in the dining room doorway, Lessenby continued, "Peter, do write down the titles of those books you need. The sooner we can get them, the sooner you can be back with your friends."

———

The books were delivered that afternoon, which gave Peter time to get over the disaster that had been his conversation with Byron. Peter had tried to explain, even as Imogen hovered under the guise of managing the breakfast dishes (it was the kitchen phone), he was off on some research for Dr. Davidson, and yes, Byron could go and ask Dr. Davidson himself if he liked. Sorry and sorry and sorry again that it had come up so unexpectedly and he hadn't been able to let Byron know ahead of time. And no, he didn't know when he'd be finished, but of course Byron would be the first to know when he was back. And still the call had ended with Byron ringing off in a huff.

After that, Peter had walked the garden in attempt to shake the overspill of Byron's emotion, until Imogen hailed him for lunch, which he took alone in the oversized dining room. As the last of his ploughman's and piccalilli disappeared, Imogen had informed him his books were waiting for him, and he'd followed her down again to the room where his notes still lay and fresh tea had been waiting, his textbooks and dictionaries standing in a neat line under the window. Embracing the opportunity to put all else from his mind, Peter had gone right to work. Now and then fresh tea and baked goods materialized at his elbow; he ate and drank some without tasting and more often let things sit untouched. He was interrupted at one point and asked if he wanted to stop for dinner. He did not. More muffins appeared.

And then, finally, he was finished.

———

Peter sat back against the unforgiving wood of the chair and rubbed his eyes. It made little sense, but he'd checked and rechecked, and it was as close as he was going to come to a translation.

He rolled his neck and let his eyes travel out the darkened window. It was late. Or early. Would they bundle him into the car and take him straight back or wait until a more reasonable hour? Maybe they were all asleep themselves.

"They." Though he had only seen Lessenby and Imogen (and only Imogen since breakfast), Peter thought of them in terms of a collective, as if there were more people in the house, haunting the shadows and taking care not to be seen. He had no real reason to believe this other than intuition, or maybe mere fancy. But whether there were two or twelve, he was at the mercy of their hospitality... And had no idea how to get back to his room.

He stood and stretched, his limbs admonishing him sharply for spending so much time hunched up over his work, and was eyeing the latest offerings that remained on the table when the door swung silently open and Imogen slipped in bearing a fresh tea tray. "Oh!" she exclaimed when she saw Peter had moved from his seat. "Finally decided to take a break, did you?"

"I'm finished," he told her as she placed the new teapot on the table and took up the old one. He glanced at his watch, which had been his brother's and was due for a new strap before long. It *was* early, after two. "I hope I didn't keep you up."

"You get used to all hours in this job," Imogen said.

"And a lot of baking," Peter deduced. It won him a twist of the lips as Imogen tried not to smile.

"Don't get cheeky just because you swooped in and saved the day," she told him with mock severity.

"Did I?"

But she was already at the door. "Wait here," she instructed.

"I'll fetch Mr. Lessenby." She disappeared, tray rattling with cold tea and stale biscuits.

Peter turned circles in the tiny room, his eyes falling periodically on the notepad filled with his work. Had he really saved the day? The translation itself made no sense; he'd broken and rearranged it in every way he could think to, but nothing he tried made it coherent. At least not to him. Maybe it would make sense to Lessenby.

He'd paused to skim his efforts one last time when Lessenby slouched in. "Imogen says you've finished."

"I've done as much as I can," Peter said, handing over the notepad.

Lessenby took his time, flipping page by page, many of which were filled with nothing but scribblings and marginal notes. And yet Lessenby seemed to be reading it all, as a calculus instructor might do in order to follow a student's work. Every now and then Lessenby's eyebrows would rise then fall as his forehead would crease then clear.

"And this is the sum total, is it?" Lessenby asked as he came to the final pages of the pad.

"That's it directly, bit by bit and piece by piece," said Peter. "I've marked where languages change and which part belongs to which language..."

Lessenby lifted his dark eyes from the notes. "It's good work. And quick. But you must be exhausted. Would you like to go back now or stay another night?"

Peter hadn't expected to be given a choice and therefore did not immediately know how to answer. But then Byron swiftly crossed his mind, like something flying past a window that one senses but does not fully see, leaving only an impression: "bird" or "leaf" or "bit of litter." And so with only the vaguest sense of why, Peter said, "I'll stay here, I think. No use making anyone drive at this hour."

Lessenby nodded his approval. "Don't forget your books."

———

He brought his packed overnighter down with him to breakfast next morning. He'd managed to squeeze in all but two of his books; those two he carried tucked under his arm.

They went through a similar ritual as the previous day, with Peter following after Lessenby and sitting across from him as they ate. It was only after Lessenby had finished his toast that he spoke. "We could do with a few more like you in the Agency."

Peter took a couple more bites of egg before saying, "I'm not sure I follow."

"You did something none of our core translators were able to do."

"Is that remarkable?" Peter asked. It was an honest question. Languages came easily to him, always had, which was his prime reason for studying them. Why do anything difficult? But he had no idea whether translators were common or not; he hadn't done that much forward thinking.

Lessenby countered with a question of his own. "Did you understand any of what you translated?"

Peter shrugged. "I understood the words, when there were whole ones. They didn't make much sense. I tried rearranging..." He stopped there. Maybe it was a bad idea to show he'd been curious enough, ambitious enough, to go beyond merely working out the jumbled letters and made-up words.

"But didn't come up with anything," Lessenby finished for him. When Peter shrugged again, Lessenby continued, "Perhaps you'd be interested to know that some of our people *did* make sense of it. Thanks to your help, there is a good chance we'll be able to stop something very bad from happening to some very good people."

Peter waited for the feeling of pride to fill him, but it didn't. In fact, he felt strangely hollow. He had come to the end of this odd detour, and in a couple hours he would be dropped back into his everyday life. Classes, and much more mundane translations, and Byron to deal with.

"You have another year before you graduate?" Lessenby asked. This time Peter nodded around a mouthful of sausage. "And what will you do after?"

"Translation work, I suppose," said Peter. It was the first time he'd ever said as much aloud and worried it showed a lack of foresight and planning on his part. "I don't want to teach," he added, just to prove he *had* thought about it.

Lessenby looked interested. "You would take more jobs like this one?"

"Food is better here than at uni," Peter reasoned.

"So long as we keep feeding you then," Lessenby concluded with an avuncular smile. "Well, and Imogen likes having young ones back in the house. Don't you, Imogen?"

Once again Peter turned to find her standing in the doorway. The woman was dead silent when she walked. "I like anyone who can appreciate a good meal," she said. "And the young ones always do."

"We'd pay you a consultancy, of course," Lessenby added. "And then maybe after you graduate, if you decide you'd like to come full on..."

Come full on into what, exactly, wasn't clear. But Peter didn't have any other solid prospects either. He had no intention of closeting himself in a dusty, overstuffed office like Davidson's, much as he liked and respected the man. He nodded and, not wanting to cheapen himself by appearing too eager, said, "Yes, well, maybe."

"You've got time," Lessenby told him. "Just an option to keep in mind. And for now..." Lessenby stood, and Peter took that as his cue to do the same. He reached down for his bag and orphaned books and followed Lessenby out to the front hall then down to the waiting car while behind them Imogen erased the traces of their passing.

SIX

1967

"I'M SORRY," Peter said again. He felt he couldn't say it enough in the face of Charles's obvious dejection.

"Found a paper trail, did you?" But the levity came out strangled.

"Something like that. If it weren't important... If it weren't something only I could do..."

"Well, they've sent the best, so it must be important."

"I'm wrapping it up as quickly as I can. But you know how these things go." *Except no, you have no idea.*

"Dotting i's and crossing t's."

"Yes."

They fell into their comfortable silence, each content to know the other was there, even if they were only tethered by phone cords. Charles's breathing became so steady Peter began to wonder if he'd nodded off, but then Charles said, "I've got a shift, so..."

"Right. Don't pick up any bilkers."

"You either."

Peter did not go to Vasil, but Vasil came to Peter.

"Something happened at the safe flat."

"You really shouldn't have come to my hotel," said Peter, though of course the damage was done.

"Another walk in the park would have raised more suspicions. And you can't do all your shopping at the Intershop." Vasil took a seat in the chair in the corner, leaving Peter to either sit on the bed or remain standing. He opted to stand.

"What happened that's so important?" Peter asked.

"We have residents watching, listening. Someone went to the flat, stayed a long time."

It was a split-second decision whether to admit it or not. Nothing in Vasil's posture suggested he knew or even suspected Peter was the one to visit the flat. But Peter had seen Vasil lie straight-faced to Stasi, too.

"Did anyone see him? Or her?" Peter asked.

Vasil shook his head. "Only heard him walking around. Or her," he added with a twist of his lips that suggested he found the idea of a woman there amusing. Perhaps he was thinking of all Jules's conquests.

"And did you check on the flat?"

Vasil shrugged. "There's nothing there worth being concerned about."

"Then why come to me to report it?" Peter asked. "And did you consider the person might have left something behind?" Vasil only shrugged again, so Peter continued, "Are you suggesting I take a look?" In daylight, it might be possible to see more.

Vasil pushed himself up from the chair. "You can if you like. I only thought you should know."

Peter frowned at Vasil's lack of interest. "In your mind this case is closed."

"Alexander Sepiol is gone. Jules Maier is gone. What they did to one another, who knows? I was worried when it happened, that it might spread to the rest of us, but..." Another shrug. "It seems to have stayed between them."

"And a strange visit to Jules's flat in the middle of the night does not alarm you," Peter surmised.

Vasil's lips twisted again as if he were trying not to smile. "Bernd will check. But it was probably nothing more than a vagrant." He cut his eyes at Peter, and Peter knew he knew.

"Let me know if he finds anything," said Peter.

Vasil nodded. "You will be going back soon?"

"Yes. I don't think there's much more I can do here."

Vasil extended his hand, and Peter shook it. "The big fish almost never come," Vasil said. "Mr. Maier must be very important."

"I only needed to be sure..." Sure of what? Gordon had been worried about potential leaks in the network, that whoever made Jules—or whoever Jules had made—had more names on his (or her) list, but Peter could not pretend that was his real reason for traveling to hostile parts. Much as he'd hated leaving Charles, he'd needed to be sure of Jules, as sure as he could be under the circumstances. And now he *was* sure. Not that Jules was alive—he still didn't know—but that Jules had thought of *him* in his moment of need.

Vasil still stood there, waiting, and Peter shook off his wandering thoughts. "But it seems the network is fine," he concluded.

"It's always a shame to lose good men," said Vasil as he stepped toward the door.

"Let's try not to lose any more, then, eh?" Peter asked.

Vasil turned, hand on the knob and a hard look in his eye. "We always try. But we cannot promise. That is the nature of the job."

It was Peter's turn to nod. Vasil left without another word.

1953

Peter had speed and the element of surprise on his side, but with Blevins unable to help, he was outnumbered. As Gamby reeled and lumbered, Clarkson jumped onto Peter's back, or tried to— Peter shrugged him off without too much effort; Clarkson's hold was not strong. But then Gamby was advancing, and Peter had no doubt of *his* hold being strong enough.

Blevins, meanwhile, was hopping up and down in his chair, making a racket but otherwise being typically useless.

"Hold him!" Gamby roared, and Clarkson snatched at Peter's arms, but Peter leapt aside so that as Gamby swung he very nearly hit his own man. Peter was aiming to make an end run for the door and never mind Blevins when Blevins startled them all by springing out of the chair and knocking Clarkson flat.

"And you're rubbish at knots!" Blevins said.

"How—?" Peter began.

"Stop talking!" ordered Blevins. He grabbed Peter by the arm and steered him toward the door like an angry headmaster, which was ridiculous considering Peter had a good six inches on him.

Gamby came to his senses then and started after them but too slowly; as Blevins and Peter stepped out into the rapidly darkening woods, the wooden door of the cabin swung shut, revealing a grinning Jules. "It won't hold him," said Peter, and sure enough a thudding followed, the flimsy wood rattling.

Jules pulled something from his pocket and snicked it onto the rusty hasp that served to secure the cabins when not in use. A padlock, just as corroded as the hardware.

"Where'd you get that?" Blevins asked.

"They leave them in the desks when they open the cabins."

Gamby was banging and shouting. "He'll splinter the door before long," Peter said.

"He'll wear himself out first," said Jules.

"We still didn't get the papers," Blevins mourned.

"Who said we didn't?" Jules reached into his coat and pulled out a file folder.

"Those are ours," Peter said.

"No..." Another folder emerged. "These are ours."

Blevins's mouth fell open.

"Come on, then," Jules said as he tucked both folders away. "Back to camp." He started walking, Blevins alongside and staring up at Jules as if he were some kind of savior.

Peter didn't move. "And where is Tillholm?" he asked.

Jules half turned and shrugged. "Probably lost. And you will be, too, if you don't keep up."

1967

They keep them in the desks.

The memory struck Peter's brain like lightning. It could, of course, be a coincidence. Jules had no reason to remember or reference that particular training mission; they'd completed plenty others. He'd probably simply thought the desk drawer in the flat was the safest place to leave a message, the likeliest place for it to be found, assuming anyone—preferably Peter—looked closely enough.

And yet Peter found himself murmuring aloud, "What else?" Was the key word to the cipher related to that mission as well?

Peter tried "padlock" but came up with gibberish. He flipped again through all the papers in the file, but nothing stood out as a possible key. He tried "Albine." Didn't work. He wracked his brain for the names of other girlfriends, but there had been so many, none of them especially important; Jules went through women like colds through Kleenex.

"Don't Blevins on me." Peter could all but hear the words whispered in his ear, a phrase Jules had coined... after that mission.

Blevins.

NETWORKCOMPROMISEDSLUBICECABIN.

Peter stared at it for a minute. Two. Then said to the empty room, "But we don't have a cabin in Slubice."

———

"Compromised how?" Gordon asked.

Peter strove to keep his voice even, patient. "I only know as much as the message."

"What cabin in Slubice?" Gordon went on. "Why wouldn't he go to one of our friends there, one of the safe—?"

"He's probably not sure how far the rot goes," Peter put in. Damn Jules and his suspicious streak; he could turn one bad agent into hundreds. Yet something warm rose through Peter at the same time. Jules trusted *him*. Wanted *him*.

"We haven't got a cabin," Gordon complained.

"No," Peter agreed and was on the verge of explaining about their training mission, about Blevins being the key, yet something reined in his tongue, and for a moment he was confused by his own resistance. He never kept things from Gordon. Gordon, who knew Peter's secret and protected him, using his silent power to keep anyone who would move against Peter (Trevor Tillholm sprang immediately to mind) at bay.

Peter comforted himself by thinking it would all come out in his report anyway, so he wasn't really holding anything back.

"You'll have to go have a look," sighed Gordon. "I'm sorry, Peter. I know you're eager to get home."

Was he? The thought of Charles swimming about the flat like a lone fish in a too-big bowl put a dent in Peter's heart. But there was something else in Peter that was jubilant at the prospect of seeing Jules again.

It might only be a body you find. Peter pushed the thought away. Jules was a survivor. And Peter would be his savior.

———

"I've picked up a trail," Peter explained.

"A paper trail?" Peter could hear Charles's voice pushing the words up at an attempt at levity, but there was something tired and sad weighing them down, making them unable to fully fly.

"Yes. I do hope it won't be much longer."

Silence. And Peter couldn't blame him, really; what could one say?

"You're not even supposed to be calling me," acknowledged Charles. "So I'm grateful for what I can get."

"My work doesn't usually..." Peter's voice trailed. He made token visits to various satellite offices, but most of his work stayed in London. But he was tired of explaining; it was beginning to feel like defending.

Charles seemed to understand. "I know." Sad again. "Rotten timing, really."

It *was* rotten timing, the worst possible moment in a relationship for an extended absence. They'd only just got their bearings and hit their stride, and now it was all off kilter again. *And it has nothing to do with Jules*, Peter told himself. *It would have been rotten no matter the reason.*

But there was a tiny part of his brain, buried deep, which thought otherwise.

———

Peter steered clear of the network. He left Frankfurt an der Oder without any further message for Vasil, and he entered Slubice without announcing himself to their friends there, either. If Jules was even partially correct, it was better to play things close.

He checked into a quiet hotel on the north side of town, the kind of place tourists didn't know existed, and was grateful his Polish was as good as his German; no one looked twice at him. Not wanting to garner attention, Peter wandered the city, always keeping a pace that made him appear to have purpose. Finally, he found what he was looking for. He was going on a camping trip, he explained to the shopkeeper. Well, it was *almost* spring, wasn't it? And it had been a remarkably dry winter. No, he had a tent, but his clothes... Soon Peter was kitted out for walks through the woods despite the shopkeeper's conviction they would have more snow before winter was over. He bought a map as well, remarking his was old.

So began days of tromping through the wooded areas around Slubice, of which there were plenty. The people at the hotel came to know Peter as a nature lover, someone who went out and took down notes about the various animals that crossed his path on his hikes. It became necessary to avoid an old woman named Berta who was an avid bird watcher and would corner Peter whenever she could so as to discuss her hobby at length.

She seemed to live in the hotel and spend her days in the parks. No family left after the war, only birds, and she was convinced some of them were her dead sons come to visit her.

To maintain appearances, Peter took pictures on his walks and had them developed at the chemist down the road. He wasn't much of a photographer, but the other guests oohed and aahed gratifyingly enough when he showed them.

It was late on the sixth day when Peter saw the mark on the tree. Lovers' initials, easily overlooked: JM + PS inside a heart. And Peter's own heart beat a little faster.

He took a picture and walked on. *I went wide east...* Peter checked the sun, nearly gone, and turned away from it.

It was all but dark by the time Peter came upon the cabin. On any other day he would already be back at the hotel; he didn't even have a torch with him, so he didn't see the cabin until he was almost upon it, an old hunting box that leaned distinctly to the right as if tilting its head in a perpetual question. It was as warped as anything at the Bastion, weathered to colorlessness, brittle and splintering like a fighter spitting teeth in defiance of his opponent—in this case, time.

Peter drew a deep breath. Jules had made it this far, but was he still alive? Peter tried to steel himself against the possibility that the ending would not be a happy one, but at the same time his traitorous brain insisted, *There's no smell of decay. He's alive, he has to be.*

He stepped toward the door, which no longer fit neatly to its frame. The gaps showed no sign of light or life, however. Everything was quiet and still.

What if he's gone already? Moved on? Didn't think you were coming? Lost faith in you?

The tumble of thoughts was like a fist pressed to Peter's abdomen.

Then came a noise like a boot sliding across a hard floor, followed by the clear sound of a gun cocking. "Don't move."

Peter's heart leapt into his throat at the sound of Jules's voice —rough and raw but so very alive—but he forced himself to remain still; he hadn't come this far to let Jules shoot him. He kept his eyes on the door, though it was getting increasingly difficult to see anything in the growing dark. "Jules, it's me."

Screeching as the door protested being thrown open. "About damn time!" And suddenly there were arms around Peter, a face pressed to his neck as Jules heaved sobs into his coat.

"You usually smell better," said Peter.

Jules pulled back. "Shut the bloody hell up."

Peter noticed the stiff way Jules moved, as if to minimize contact on his left side. "Your injury?"

Grunting, Jules gestured at the shack. "I'd offer you refreshment, but…"

"You can't spend another night out here," Peter told him. "I'm not sure how you've managed it this long."

In the dark Peter sensed rather than saw Jules's lips twist up in that familiar smile. "You never could have. But that's why you have the desk job."

"I've done my share," said Peter, putting on the tone of one with superior rank, a tone that concluded the discussion before it could begin in earnest. "Now get your things and let's go."

————

He could not take Jules back to his own hotel; the patrons had come to know him too well for that. Too many questions. So instead Peter checked into an even smaller, more out of the way place of the sort people averted their gazes and never asked anything. Then he handed the key off to Jules, who was waiting outside. "You get cleaned up," Peter said. "I'm off to call Gordon, and then I'll be back to check on you."

Jules's mouth went white at the corners. "Call him from here."

Peter fleetingly wondered whether the people at his hotel would look for him if he stayed gone very long, or if they would just go through his belongings.

"You'll want to debrief me," Jules added, a smile playing at the edges of his lips.

Every fiber in Peter's body twanged with tension. Jules had

always known how to bait him. "Why the woods?" he asked. "Why didn't you…?" He gestured at the hole in the wall that passed for a hotel.

Jules's features fell into more serious lines. "Come up and I'll tell you."

Peter's tension gave way to a flood of resignation, and Jules smiled again, knowing he'd won.

Jules always won.

SEVEN

1953

SOMETHING LANDED on the bed beside Peter, and he reluctantly opened his eyes then jerked backward so abruptly he would have fallen off the mattress if Jules hadn't thrown an arm over him to hold him in place.

"What are you doing?" Peter demanded. He pulled the covers tighter around himself.

Jules was laughing. "Don't bother. Those blankets aren't thick enough to hide anything."

It was Sunday, the one day of the week they were allowed to sleep late, though that had never stopped Jules; *every* morning was one in which the rest of the cabin was forced to all but prop him up for inspection. "What are you doing up?" Peter asked.

"Well, *I* didn't have an all-night chess game."

"It was best of seven," muttered Peter. "And I won."

"Of course you did."

Peter was suddenly very aware of the heat of Jules's hand on his back and the quiet in the cabin.

"No one else here," said Jules, and Peter silently cursed him for being able to read him so well. A need to put more air between them prompted Peter to throw off the blankets and

Jules's arm, sit up, and swing his legs off the bed, effectively turning his back on Jules.

"And why are you waking me then?" Peter asked. And waited. But there was no answer.

He turned and looked over his shoulder. Jules had rolled onto his back, was staring up at the beams of the ceiling. "Sometimes I think I should have just taken the prison time."

"You don't like it here?"

The dark eyes found him. "Do you?"

No. But Peter couldn't bring himself to say it; doing so felt ungrateful. "I don't think we're meant to enjoy it."

"Like school," said Jules.

"That's what it is, really. Occupational training."

"But you liked school, didn't you?" Jules asked. "You're good at it."

"Being good at something isn't the same as liking it."

Jules sat up abruptly. "Yes! That's it exactly!"

Peter didn't understand, nor was he particularly interested. He went to his trunk to find fresh clothes. "Wear that navy blue jumper," Jules told him. Peter frowned but pulled out the recommended jumper without comment.

"And the tennis shirt underneath," Jules went on. "You know, that sort of dusky lavender one."

Peter stopped and stared at the man on his bed. "Miss playing with dolls much?"

Jules grinned. "That's you. A doll." He bounced off the bed. "I'll leave you to it. See you at tea."

"Where are you—?" But Jules was already gone.

Peter looked into his trunk at his neat stacks of clothes, his books and notebooks. Almost against his will, he bent and teased free the tennis shirt.

Well, Jules *did* have an eye for fashion.

1967

"You carry a razor in that thing, I hope?" Peter asked as Jules tossed his beaten bag—the same leather bag as that first day—onto the dented mattress.

"Yes, but I'm left-handed," answered Jules, and Peter watched him slip his filthy coat off, allowing it to slide from his left arm onto the floor.

"How bad is it?" Peter asked with a nod at Jules's left side.

"Well, I'm not dead. Help a fellow out."

Peter frowned, not understanding.

"I can't pull it off on my own," Jules said, plucking at the discolored jumper. "My left arm..." He lifted it roughly halfway and winced.

"You're funning me," said Peter.

"You know me," countered Jules. "I wouldn't have gone this long in these clothes if I'd had a choice."

Peter still did not move. "Cut it off then. Not like it's worth saving."

"Your knife or mine?" Jules asked.

Peter sighed and fished a folding knife from his coat pocket, held it out for Jules. But Jules wiggled the fingers of his left hand and smiled apologetically.

"Oh, come on," said Peter. "You're not completely helpless."

Jules took the knife and cut a rip into the ribbing at the bottom of his jumper, then began to pull the material apart. It gave way easily enough at first, stopping mid-chest. Jules grimaced. "I can slip my arms out now, but you'll have to get it over my head for me."

Peter closed his eyes and sent up a silent prayer for patience. "You'll want me to shave you next."

"I wouldn't say no."

When Peter opened his eyes, Jules was grinning. Irritation percolated through Peter. "Call the maid."

"You're prettier."

Peter sighed and scanned the room. "There's no phone."

"Places like this..." said Jules. He had worked his arms free of the jumper's sleeves but was struggling to pull it over his head with only his right hand.

"I need to call Gordon," Peter said, "arrange to get you home, *that* looked at," he nodded at the angry-looking laceration the jumper had revealed and wondered what it had cost Jules to have to sew it up on his own, possibly repeatedly as threads wore out. It looked itchy and painful, and a spike of guilt pierced Peter. "I'm sorry it took us—took me—so long."

"Then help me get this bloody jumper off!" Jules flapped the two hanging sides of fabric, making him look like an exotic but ridiculous bird.

Peter was taller by a couple inches, and Jules needlessly ducked his head—the curls dark and beautiful for all they were unwashed—to allow Peter to pull the ruined garment over. "You've got something clean?"

"Cleaner, anyway. In my bag." Jules was already shedding his trousers, adding them to the pile of discards.

Peter stepped away and turned his back, searching again for the nonexistent phone. "I'll have to go back to my hotel. You'll be all right—?"

The sound of water running caused Peter to turn. From the tiny, tiled cave came a low moan, though whether it was pain or pleasure Peter couldn't distinguish. He wasn't sure Jules differentiated between the two. In fact...

A thought propelled Peter to the bathroom doorway. There was no door. There wasn't even a shower curtain; the entire room was tiled with a drain in the floor. "Who stabbed you?" Peter asked.

Jules turned. "Care to join me?" When it became clear Peter wasn't of a mind to play, Jules sighed and turned off the water. "Was going cold anyway. Throw me a towel?"

Peter leaned over and took the thin, worn bit of fabric that passed as a towel from the rack; it was damp from shower spray. "It was Albine," Peter guessed.

"You have a deviant mind; I like that." Peter backed out of the doorway as Jules cinched the towel and made for the bed, the skin around his cut a bright red.

"It's not a professional job," said Peter. "Jagged, and without enough force to kill you. A woman, then, or someone who didn't have it in him to kill you. Or both."

Jules nodded as he fished fresh clothes from his bag. "But it's not what you think," he said.

"What do I think?"

"That she was jealous, caught me with someone else."

Peter didn't deny it.

"She did it because I found out," said Jules. "About the network, and about Alexander Sepiol."

"What about him?"

"They killed him."

"Who?"

Jules had trousers on, at least, but now he held up another jumper and frowned. "I'm going to need more help."

"Not a single button-up?" Peter asked.

"At this time of year?"

"Sit," instructed Peter, and Jules perched himself on the edge of the bed. Peter shoved the neck of the jumper over Jules's head. "It's like having an overgrown toddler. You're on your own for the arms."

Jules groaned and complained but managed to get his arms through the sleeves. "And now, Daddy, you absolutely must feed this toddler."

"Who killed Alexander Sepiol?" asked Peter.

"I'll tell you all about it over dinner."

Peter eyed Jules. The man had lost weight, of course, over the weeks of living in the middle of a nature preserve, but he wasn't painfully thin. "What *have* you been eating?"

"Whatever I could catch or steal." Which meant he hadn't fared too badly. "But I'd kill for an honest meal."

"I'm going to have to find a telephone anyway," said Peter. "Go shave. I can't take you anywhere looking like that."

Jules had a taste for luxury but had, Peter had learned over the years, an indifferent palate, which meant he wasn't picky about his food. So Peter installed them in a relatively dark, semi-empty restaurant—the kind where it was dim enough that you didn't see your plate clearly, but then again, no one would ever be able to swear they saw you there, either. As it was, Peter had the urge to squint to see Jules sitting just across from him. Jules, on the other hand, was entirely devoted to his dinner.

"Does it hurt?" Peter asked, picking at his rolada.

"Does what hurt?" Asked around a mouthful of bigos.

"The wound."

Jules stopped eating long enough to breathe and sat back against the banquette. "Yes. But you get used to it." He huffed a laugh. "Well, those of us out here in the trenches, anyway."

"Why me?"

"I trust you."

"You could have trusted MacAuley," said Peter.

Jules sniffed and went back to devouring his stew. "He didn't even see the message."

"And wouldn't have been able to read it if he had," Peter pointed out.

"But you did," Jules grinned. "Good old Peter."

"What happened to Alexander Sepiol?"

Jules's chewing slowed to thoughtful. "I was trying to find him, talk him into coming out."

"I thought you'd already spoken to him."

"Once, yeah. And he said no, he couldn't leave. Had a girl. They always have a girl."

"So do you," said Peter.

Jules dismissed this with a wave. "Not the same. This was a girl he wanted to marry. Wouldn't go unless we could take her too."

Peter frowned; it was the first he'd heard of this.

"I was going to ask you for papers for her," Jules said. "But then I couldn't find Alexander." The bigos was gone. "This is like old times, eh?"

Peter pushed his plate across the table.

"*Really* like old times," Jules went on as he accepted the offering. "Don't you ever eat?"

An image of Charles standing at the stove flashed through Peter's mind. "Only under the right circumstances."

"Moon has to be full or something?"

"What makes you think they killed him?"

"I was at Albine's, saw a note from Vasil."

"To Albine?"

Jules shook his head. "Dunno. But it was Vasil's writing. Said to cut A. S. because he wouldn't play for the team."

"And Albine found you snooping," Peter deduced. "Not like you to get caught."

Jules grimaced but didn't reply, instead putting all his energy toward finishing Peter's chicken.

"It's enough to be getting on with," said Peter. "I'll call Gordon from my hotel, arrange for us to get back so you can file an official report."

Jules nodded, and he cocked an eyebrow. "Will Miranda be around to help me with that?"

Peter refused the bait. "You'll have whatever help you need." He pulled out his wallet and handed more than enough money over to Jules to cover the cheque. "You know the way back to your hotel?"

It was an unnecessary question, and Jules's expression said as much. "You're not leaving?" he asked as Peter slid free of his seat.

Peter paused at the strangled note in Jules's voice; Jules never panicked.

"It goes deep, I think." Jules was all earnestness now, not a shade of jest in his face. "And they know I know."

"But they don't know you're here. They don't know *I'm* here; they think I went back to London." It wasn't exactly true; Peter had no idea what Vasil or the others thought. But he kept his tone confident.

Peter watched as Jules's shoulders released their tension. "You didn't tell Vasil? About the message?"

Peter shook his head. "Didn't feel like something he needed to know."

"Points for keen intuition. Knew I could count on you. Still, the sooner we're gone, the better I'll feel."

"You think the Slubice network is affected?" Peter asked.

"No idea. Not a risk I was willing to take, though."

Understanding flooded Peter. "So you went tribal."

"In case they were circulating my picture, yeah." The rolada was gone. Jules

tossed money on the table and stood. "Walk with me?"

"If *you* want to get back to London, *I* need to get back and call Gordon."

Jules muttered something that sounded suspiciously like "pet."

"Well, and it's a good thing for you I am his pet," said Peter, striving to keep his voice down as heads began to swing their way. "You'd be out in the cold until you died otherwise."

Jules hung his head in a suitable display of repentance, though Peter knew it was all for show. Indeed, not a second later Jules was peeking up at him and smiling again like a child checking that Daddy wasn't really angry. "You're his pet and I'm yours."

Another thought of Charles skidded across Peter's brain: the absent way Charles stroked Peter's hair when he laid his head in Charles's lap while they watched the evening news.

Jules's eyes glittered, birdlike, as he watched Peter's face. "Ah, you have a new pet."

Peter shook his head. "No, I'm just... Tired. And you must be ready for a real bed."

"Whatever passes for one in that place," Jules agreed. "Though maybe I should come with you. In case Gordon wants to talk to me directly."

Peter snaked his way between the tables, aiming for the fresh night air. The space was narrow, and Jules was forced to follow behind, which Peter supposed was just as well; he wasn't quite ready to look Jules in the eye and send him away. So he did it while looking at his shoes.

"The people at my hotel know me too well," he said, consciously weighting his words with apology. "If I bring you back with me, it *will* be noticed. And if you're even a little bit right about the network..."

"I'm right. About Frankfurt, anyway. And my guess is they know our friends in Slubice, too."

They stopped on the sidewalk, just outside the restaurant door. The night air bit at them; though it had been a dry winter, it was still a bitterly cold one. Peter dipped into his coat pocket for gloves then, with an eye toward Jules's bare hands, held them out to him.

"First your dinner, now your gloves," said Jules. "You certainly know how to court a man."

Heat spread through Peter in spite of the chilly air, pricking his cheeks and the back of his neck. "Go back to your hotel and stay there until I come for you."

Jules lifted his eyebrows and held up his freshly gloved hands. "Sounds promising."

Peter turned away then and started walking, using all his willpower to keep from looking back.

———

He called Charles first.

He knew Gordon should be the priority, but something drove him to Charles instead—a need to transfer the tingling feeling Jules gave him to a safer receptacle. But he couldn't explain that to Charles, couldn't even mention Jules, and only found himself more frustrated than before.

"Something's wrong," Charles said.

"No," Peter insisted. "I found the missing paperwork."

"But you don't sound happy about it," said Charles.

"Well, you know..." Though of course Charles didn't. "It means more work in the long run."

Silence, and Peter pictured Charles's furrowed brow as he tried to figure out what Peter meant. It was so damned difficult, having to talk in circles all the time. "You would rather it had stayed lost?" Charles ventured.

"I only wish I didn't have to be the one to take care of it," Peter told him. "But it does mean I'll be able to come home soon. In fact, I'm going to call Gordon now and arrange it."

"Now you sound happy." Peter could hear Charles's smile, not the teasing kind Jules always offered, but something genuine and warm. His frustration ebbed. Of course he'd phoned Charles first; Charles *was* the priority, his priority. Putting Charles first was the same as putting himself first, for somehow, at some point in time, Peter had, without realizing, come to rely on Charles as his conduit to the sane and mundane. Charles was a piece of normalcy in a skewed and unbalanced existence, a shaft of sunlight forcing its way through drawn curtains. It was easy enough to overlook such things when one worked in an office every day, even if the office was piled with government secrets. But being out in the cold and dark forced Peter to appreciate the light and warmth Charles embodied.

"I am happy," Peter said, the warmth filling him up—not the prickling heat Jules gave off, but a comfortable and contented feeling. "I'll be happier still to see you."

"Call Gordon then," said Charles. "And come home to me."

____

EIGHT

____

"CHARLES?"

Peter dropped his scuffed and battered suitcase in the entry. It had taken longer than expected to get home; Jules had insisted on all new papers with names Vasil wouldn't know, and he'd refused to leave out of Germany, so they'd worked their way deeper into Poland and flown out of Warsaw. Every new obstacle had chafed at Peter to the point he'd become very short with Jules, dropping him at an Agency flat with nary a word before heading home.

But as he stood in the open doorway of the flat, the warm welcome he'd been hoping for failed to transpire. It was late, true, but Peter was certain he'd told Charles what day he'd be home, had reemphasized it on the phone calls he'd braved making from overseas. He recalled his words to Charles clearly: "My flight is coming in pretty late. You don't have to wait up, of course."

And with the typical hint of laughter in his voice (the one Peter had learned not to take personally), Charles had said, "Of course I'll wait up. I can hardly sleep without you here to begin with."

Suddenly aware of the door pushing against his back and leg, Peter stepped the rest of the way into the flat and allowed it to close. Looked to his left at the kitchenette, spotless and empty.

Let his eyes sweep the living area, also spotless and empty. It was just like when he'd lived alone.

A cold, crawling fear blossomed in Peter's stomach. *He wouldn't have*, he assured himself. *He might be out, but he's not gone forever.*

Still holding his briefcase and dragging his bag along behind him like a sad, stray dog, Peter moved forward, his trained eyes darting in search of data: a finger smudge on the glass tabletop, a deserted library book, any sign of inhabitance. Simultaneously he stretched his ears in an effort to pick up any possible sound: movement in the bedroom or attached bath, steps nearing the door that might mean Charles was coming home.

But there was nothing.

All at once Peter felt as if a lead weight had been tied to the threads of his heart, dragging it down out of his chest and into his gut. He dropped the suitcase handle and stood there beside the sofa, unable to move. If a bullet had been coming at him at that moment, Peter supposed he would have stood there and taken it, never bothering to duck or dodge.

"Charles?" he asked again, but this time it was nothing more than a weak whisper. Peter hated that he sounded needy, hated that his heart was breaking; surely he should be made of stronger stuff. He should at least check the bedroom, the closet, verify that what he suspected was, in fact, the truth. But a numb sort of heaviness had settled over him like a mantel, a tiredness in his limbs that kept him rooted there, made him want to crumple except that he was too drained even to move that much.

He wasn't sure, later, how long he remained there. At some point he could no longer hold himself up, and he half stumbled the two steps to the sofa and fell onto it and into sleep. The next morning consciousness returned slowly, reluctantly, in seeming correlation to the growing light filtering through the drapes, *those* drapes; unsticking his eyelids and seeing them and remembering, Peter thought he would probably have to get rid of them. He would never have peace of mind otherwise.

Is it true? Peter asked himself this as he tasted his own bitter tongue, as he forced himself upright to sitting and ran his hands absently through his mussed hair. He thought back to that last phone call three nights before, picked at it like a scab. But Charles had sounded the same as always, no hint of disaffection. Peter had faith in his talents and training, and moreover in his bond with Charles; he was sure he would have heard it in Charles's voice if there had been a problem.

"A note." He said it aloud, thickly because his mouth was dry and sticky, and began to scan the flat, what he could see of it from where he sat, which wasn't much. He needed to get up, unpack, shower. *Clean yourself up*, he thought, *then worry about him.*

It, he argued mentally. *No. Him.*

Peter pushed himself to his feet, only to be momentarily nonplussed by motion at the corner of his eye. It took him a minute to realize he was still wearing his overcoat. The flapping of the hem had drawn his attention. He shed the camel-colored wool and let it slip onto the couch.

Lurching past the suitcase and briefcase, Peter made for the bedroom. If he'd had any lingering hope that Charles had been there all along, it was swiftly dashed. The bed was neatly made, unslept in. Both night tables were clear, too, excepting the phone on one side and a framed photograph of Peter and Charles on the other. Charles's side. He'd left the picture behind.

Peter brought his hands to his face, rubbed at it vigorously in an attempt to get blood flowing. His eyes stung, hot, surprising him with tears; he couldn't remember the last time he'd cried. He felt childish for it now but also powerless to stop it. So he stood there shaking and letting the sorrow out until he was at last able to draw in a deep breath and keep moving.

He went into the bathroom, thinking to splash water on his face, or better, shower. Yes, that was what he'd been planning to do. He pushed the door closed behind him and avoided looking in the mirror, only catching blurs of his own actions, never allowing himself to see what he, Peter Stoller, looked like as a man abandoned. He had unbuttoned his shirt, was pulling his arms free of the sleeves and thinking absently of Jules and his knife wound, when a smudge of color drew his attention. Peter looked at the closed door, which held two hooks, and on each hook was a bathrobe. His was indigo, Charles's crimson.

And they were both there.

Peter's heart gave a little leap. *The closet,* Peter told himself. He dropped his shirt onto the bathroom floor—Charles would have scolded him—and flung open the door, almost running. He pushed the sliding door aside and discovered, yes, all their clothes, his and Charles's, neatly arranged.

"Where are you?" Peter wondered aloud. He found himself glancing left and right as if expecting Charles to crawl out from under the furniture or otherwise materialize. But of course he didn't.

Peter looked again at the clothes hanging in the closet, the neat stacks of sweaters on the shelves. Were they all there? Could Charles have left most of his things, taking only a few? But Charles did not even own a suitcase, no, not even a duffel, had never needed one; Peter had taken the only luggage.

What do you know? The facts, Peter demanded of himself as he began to prowl the flat in earnest, searching for a telltale note. *You spoke to Charles three nights ago. You've come home to an empty flat. Charles is gone, but clearly intends to return. But why no note?*

The answer was obvious. Charles hadn't left a note because he had seen no need for one. He'd expected to be back sooner.

"So where are you?" Peter asked again as he opened drawers and rifled the contents, flipped through the pages of books. He was only doing it out of habit now; he knew he would not find anything. He considered he might have to begin checking with the cab service, local hospitals... This last thought left Peter cold. If Charles was in hospital, his family might be in attendance, and Peter had not met them, was not even clear on whether Charles had told them...

A shiver ran through him, and all at once Peter became very aware of his lack of shirt. He decided he would shower, yes, just as he'd planned, and maybe Charles would come home in the meantime with a story about having to cover the overnight shift. They would laugh at the drunken antics of tourists and hardened locals alike and all would be well. Peter was so convinced of this that by the end of his shower he was acutely disappointed to find himself still alone in the flat.

Like a good mother, Charles kept the contact information for his cab company tacked to the side of the refrigerator. Peter stared at Charles's neatly printed writing for a long time and tried to devise something to say when he called. He was usually good at thinking on his feet, smoothing paths for himself, but that was when he only had himself to think about. Peter didn't want to say or do anything that might jeopardize Charles—his personal comfort, his work environment—and so began to prepare himself accordingly. When he felt ready, he slipped the paper from its magnet and went to the phone.

"Yes, I'm looking for one of your drivers, Charles... I never got his last name," Peter said when the line was answered. He used the same breathless rush of words of any harried person, leaving no space for the other party to speak. "I think I left a library book in his cab last night, and I rather need it back. It's overdue as it is."

There came a gruff bark of a laugh. "You've seen him more recently than we have then. Charles hasn't been in for two days."

Peter ignored the small seizure in his chest and pushed through with his playacting. "Well, does he have a number? Or is there a lost and found or something?"

"I can't give you his personal number," the man said, "but we have a lost and found all right. You're welcome to come down and look. Though if I know Charles, he probably took the book back to the library for you." Another laugh. "If you see him, tell him to get back to work, would you?" He hung up without waiting for Peter's response.

Peter felt a sort of fog rolling in, clouding his thinking. He glanced down at himself, still in his bathrobe. *Should get dressed,* he told himself. Small steps, one thing at a time; that was the only way he would be able to get through it.

He was on his way back to the bedroom when the knock came. Not loud. But then it came again, more insistent than before. He glanced down at himself again wearing nothing but his dressing gown. Another knock. Peter ensured the robe was secure and went to the door.

Jules was there, grimacing, dark eyes wide. Dark smudges emphasized the bags under Jules's eyes, which were themselves red-rimmed and bloodshot, the eyes of a man who'd not slept well.

"What are you doing here?" Peter asked. "You should be—"

Jules put both hands on Peter's chest and thrust him back into his flat, entered after and kicking the door closed behind him. "I know where I should be. But I couldn't..." His eyes were everywhere. "You're alone?"

"I'm somewhat in the middle of something, Jules," Peter said tightly. How dare Jules demand even another minute of his time? He'd neglected Charles more than enough already.

"Yes, you are," Jules agreed. His gaze found Peter's luggage, still standing beside the sofa. "Good, no need to pack. But you do have to get dressed. Now. Quickly."

"Has the medic seen you yet?" Peter asked, wondering whether Jules needed a psychiatric evaluation.

"You don't live alone, though, do you?" Jules asked. "Where is he?"

Cold washed over Peter so thoroughly he began to tremble. Jules nodded. "I thought so. Get dressed, grab whatever passports you have on hand."

"You know what's happened to Charles?" Peter asked.

Jules gave Peter another firm shove, this time in the direction of the bedroom. "No time. Get dressed.

"How well do you know him?" Jules called the question from the living area as Peter searched out fresh trousers.

Peter didn't bother to answer; it was none of Jules's business, and anyway, Jules knew everything he needed to know to answer the question himself: Peter didn't live alone.

Peter exited the bedroom and found Jules stationed in front of the windows. "They'll be coming. Do you have what you need?"

"They who, Jules? What's going on?" Peter kept his voice patient and even, unwilling to allow Jules's anxiety permeate him. It was, perhaps, understandable that after everything they'd gone through Jules would be jumping at shadows. But Peter's chief concern now was finding Charles. His duty to Jules was done.

"Charles Toulson, that's his name, isn't it?" Jules asked as his eyes roved the streets and pavements around the building. The cold Peter had felt before returned, icier than before.

"What of him?" Peter asked, his lips almost refusing to move, so frozen did he feel.

"They're here," said Jules, and Peter looked down to where a car snaked its way up the block, stopping to park some way down. It could have been anyone. But then a big, bulky body leveraged itself from the driver's seat. Gamby. He went to the back door of the car and opened it, and someone smaller with steel-colored hair and a growing bald spot emerged.

"Gordon," Peter said dumbly.

"There's a back exit." It wasn't a question, and Peter wasn't surprised; leave it to Jules to case the building.

"He's probably just here to get a full report on..." Peter gestured with an open hand, indicating all that had happened in Frankfurt, Slubice, and with Jules in particular.

Jules's near-black eyes met Peter's hazel ones. "It goes deep, Peter. And high."

Like with Vasil at the hotel, it was another of those split-second decisions. Stay and face Gordon, try to determine if Jules was correct? Or take Jules on faith? Peter was used to being able to trust his own judgement, had been successful in going with his gut, but at that moment he found himself unable to get his bearings. He had no reason to believe Gordon meant him any harm. Why should he, when Peter had done nothing wrong? But Jules's near panic was beginning to seep through the tiny holes in Peter's surety.

"If you're not home, there's nothing to worry about," Jules said. "You haven't burned any bridges by being out."

"Where is Charles?" Peter asked, as if dipping a toe into a pool to check the temperature.

"I'll show you. But we must go *now*."

Peter glanced at his suitcase. "You have a car?"

The grin Peter knew so well flashed across Jules's face like lightning in a dark sky. "No, but you do."

———

His car was around the corner, not because he'd wanted to hide the fact he was home but because it had been late and there was no parking on his block at the time.Jules tossed Peter's bag in the boot while Peter wedged his briefcase between the seats. "Where are we going?" he asked as Jules jumped in beside him.

"C and I."

Peter's hand dropped from the ignition, and he turned to stare at Jules, sure now that Jules really had gone mad. But Jules merely blinked back at him. "I told you I'd show you, didn't I? He's down at C and I."

Confinement and Interrogation.

Peter started the car. He didn't even see where he was going, navigating through a haze of acute fear. If Jules was correct... If Charles was being held... "But why?" he croaked.

Jules did not answer.

"How do you know?" Peter asked as they pulled up in front of the orange-red brick building, square, bars over the windows. An old warehouse, or maybe even an asylum, who could know? A place meant to keep things in or out, or both. Yes, that was it, of course; a place to keep things apart.

"It's amazing what open ears and closed eyes can win you," said Jules. Then, as Peter opened the car door, "What are you doing?"

"You said you would show me."

"They'll have noticed I'm gone by now, and they're discovering you're not home either," Jules said.

Peter stared at him, one foot already on the pavement.

"You go in there, you might not come back out," Jules insisted.

"Is that all?" Peter asked. He climbed the rest of the way out of the car and slammed the door shut behind him.

Jules scrambled out after him. Peter stopped and waited by the door, its red-brown paint the color of dried blood. Panic was crawling up Peter's throat, but he swallowed it. He had to be brave, for Charles's sake if not his own.

"I've nothing to hide," Peter said, as much to himself as Jules. "They have no reason to hold me. Or Charles."

"Are you sure of him?" Jules asked.

The question stopped Peter's breath.

"Is he worth it?" Jules pressed.

And somehow that one question broke Peter's fear into shards, like ice left to melt on hot asphalt. "Absolutely." He pulled open the door.

———

He was all too aware of Jules's presence close behind, pressing him as they moved down the pool-colored corridor. It smelled of sweat and antiseptic; their shoes squeaked on the uneven linoleum. Above them, the fluorescent lights jittered, giving everything a flash-bulb feeling, as if a series of photographs were being taken. *Time of my life*, thought Peter. *Wish you were here.*

Peter stopped at a reception window protected by sliding glass, the top half doubly defended by a metal grate. A frizzy-haired blonde sat at the desk, absorbed in a paperback, her glossy fingernails wrapped tight around the edges in a way that made Peter think she must have come to the good part, the climax of the story. He tapped at the glass below the grate, and the girl held up one manicured finger in an indication that they should wait. A few seconds later, having finished the paragraph she'd been reading, she inserted a finger in the book and finally gave Peter her attention.

"Mr. Stoller," she said with some surprise.

"Beverly. I'm here to see Charles Toulson."

Beverly's brow furrowed, and for a moment hope spiked through Peter. She didn't know who he meant, Charles wasn't here. But then she said, "I thought only Mr. Lessenby was allowed to see him."

Peter smiled at her the way he smiled at the girls in the Castle. "Sandra was supposed to call ahead and clear it, but you know how these things fall through the cracks." And when Beverly still hesitated, he nodded his head in the direction of the reinforced door to his right. "It's not as if we're going anywhere."

Beverly's overly pink mouth worked for a moment as if literally chewing over his words. Finally she reached under her desk and a low hum sounded; the door clicked free of its locks. Wooden, with a large glass pane interlaced with wire mesh, it looked newer than the building around it. As Peter pulled back the brushed chrome handle, Beverly said, "I'll have him brought to room three."

Beyond the door, the corridor was narrow; two men could not walk abreast. Peter knew it had been designed to prevent detainees from being able to bolt. He imagined Charles being herded through with agents before and behind, with no opportunity for escape. The tall walls and high ceiling gave the whole of the place a canyon-like feel, tight and claustrophobic. Peter wondered what would happen if there were ever a fire.

Behind him Jules was all but stepping on the backs of Peter's shoes; Peter could feel the anxiety coming off him like heat as they came to the end of the hallway and turned a corner. While the corridor remained narrow, now there were doors and long windows to the left that showed big, empty rooms that also had long windows in them. The observation rooms. Agents would stand there to watch interrogations that went on in the rooms beyond, boxes inside boxes. But better to be cross-examined in one of those rooms than taken downstairs to the rooms without windows, the rooms where no one saw what was done to you. Those rooms were commonly referred to by agents as "The Tombs."

Peter's heart gave a tiny flutter of fear. Was Charles downstairs? But as they came to the third door, Peter saw an agent already stationed outside the door. He was a square man with a military haircut possibly meant to minimize just how grey his hair had become. He stared straight ahead, as unmoved as the

Queen's guard, as Peter pulled open the door to the observation room and entered, Jules so close behind Peter thought he would start pushing again any moment.

"The farther in we get, the harder it will be to get out," Jules hissed in Peter's ear.

But all Peter's attention was for the man on the far side of the glass. Charles slumped brokenly over the table, head down, though Peter could see the two-day growth of hair climbing the cheeks, a mixture of fair and grey that suggested a turning, the onset of age. *He must hate that*, Peter thought. Charles prided himself on his grooming; the wrinkled clothes, his own unwashed body would be a torment for him. Peter's heart clinched; his hands formed fists involuntarily. Jules noticed and took a step back.

"What reason do they have for treating him this way?" Peter demanded. He turned on Jules. "What else did you hear?"

Jules darted a look at Charles and grimaced. "They seem to think he was siphoning information off you..." At Peter's outraged expression, Jules put up his hands. "Look, I don't know! But the question was whether you knew about it, or..."

Peter was shaking, utterly furious, though more on Charles's behalf than his own. Let them do what they liked to *him*, Peter, he was qualified to take it, but Charles was innocent until they had a solid reason to believe otherwise. "Evidence?" he asked.

Jules only shook his head; he didn't know. "How did you meet?" he asked. "When? Do you bring any work home, anything sensitive? You're the smart one, Peter; you tell me what evidence they might have."

"Then why did you warn me?" Peter asked, his eyes fixed on Charles.

"I owe you that much, don't I?"

"Can you get us out?"

When Jules didn't answer right away, Peter dragged his eyes from the interrogation room. "You're not documents, Peter," said Jules.

"Neither was Alexander Sepiol."

"And look what happened to him. Where would you go?"

"Let me worry about that. You just get us out." He turned a thoughtful frown to the window. "Elinor was the one to invite him, you know," Peter said. "To the party. She thought she was being nice, asking the man who'd driven her around all day..." Acidic suspicion began to drip through Peter, pooling at his core, and he yanked open the door to the observation room and stepped inside.

———

Charles didn't bother to look up at the sound of someone entering the room; if anything he curled farther in on himself. Peter leaned against the door and waited. It took everything inside him not to go to Charles and gather him in his arms, but there was something cold now at Peter's center as doubt began to spread. His heart was no longer pumping blood but ice water.

"Charles," Peter said.

The head came up, the haggard face revealed. Charles's cheekbones were accentuated by lack of the robust foods he was used to, his skin sallow for want of sun. His lips were dry and cracked, and dark circles puffed under his eyes, the prominent red veins of which made the irises all the more blue. And yet to Peter's shame Charles was the one to ask: "Are you all right?"

Peter choked.

"I told them," Charles went on earnestly, and he looked at the mirror knowingly, "I told them you hadn't done anything."

Peter moved forward, bypassed the empty chair, knelt on the floor beside Charles's seat. He put his hands on Charles's knees and looked up into the worn face. "Tell *me*, then."

"What's to tell? They asked me where we met, how long we've been together, whether you ever brought work home with you..."

Peter nodded, playing the patient solicitor with a child in the witness box. "And what did you say?"

"I told them the truth. About the party, and when I moved in, and..."

"And?"

"And that you have a briefcase that you sometimes bring home. You know, the brown leather one. I always know whenever you bring it home that you'll be up late, working."

"Are *you* all right, Charles?" Peter asked. "Did they hurt you?"

Charles didn't answer. Peter sat back, slid his hands off Charles's knees, rose and sat down across the table.

"This is more than paperwork," Charles mused.

"You've always known I do more than just paperwork, haven't you?"

Charles gave a tiny shrug, sullen, like a teenager's.

"Were you ever tempted to look in my briefcase, Charles?"

The blue eyes flashed, and Peter recognized the red flush of anger that rode Charles's cheekbones. They didn't fight often, Charles was too easy going for that, but when they did Charles grew vivid and bright in his ire.

"Why should I be?" Charles demanded. "I don't care about your work, only worry..." Charles was staring at the mirror. He was no fool; Peter was sure he knew someone was out there, wondered whether Charles pictured nameless, faceless men in dark suits... Or someone in particular. Gamby? Gordon?

"Worried?" Peter asked suddenly.

Charles started out of whatever reverie he'd been indulging.

"Why worried?" Peter pressed. He was a hound who smelled blood and was on the trail. "I only just traveled for the first time since we met. Other than that I've been home. I work regular hours, haven't been out late. What reason would you have to be worried?"

Charles's mouth opened but no answer came. It was an expression Peter knew well, not on Charles, but from work; it was the look of a man who had said something that gave everything away. It was *not*, however, the cagey visage of a man trying to salvage the situation or save his skin. Charles was caught and he knew it, but he wasn't deft enough—*trained* enough—to talk himself free.

"For whom are you working?" Peter asked. His heart was thundering, the adrenaline racing through him as a light sweat broke out over his body. He didn't have time to examine the emotions, figure out whether he was sad or angry or resigned or all of these; he would do that later, in private.

Charles appeared stricken. He was visibly terrified, a sure sign he was no professional.

"We can protect you, Charles," Peter said, and to his own ears his voice was dull and flat. He'd plateaued, was on automatic pilot. "But you need to cooperate."

"Protect me how?" asked Charles.

Peter's heart plummeted. He was surprised by the free fall. "Are you working for another country? We could arrange to send you back in exchange—"

"Really, Peter?" Charles scoffed. "I don't even own luggage."

Peter felt the sharp stab of a sudden headache; he propped an elbow on the table and rubbed at his forehead with his hand. "That doesn't mean..."

"Have you ever seen a mouse thrown into a river?" Charles asked abruptly. "Mice can swim. But a river... It's too big for them, the water moves too fast. The mouse will try, of course, it'll fight the way all creatures do when it's life or death, but eventually it gets swept away. It drowns."

For an inane moment Peter wanted only to ask Charles why and when he'd ever thrown a mouse into a river. It wasn't like Charles to be cruel. But then, Peter had to assume he might not know what Charles was really like, that all he knew of Charles was so much playacting. Peter, who had prided himself on his sound judgment. He felt something inside him start to crumple.

"You're saying you're the mouse?" Peter asked.

"No. You are," said Charles.

Peter stared. He turned the pieces of their conversation this way and that in his mind and tried to piece together the puzzle, but nothing fit. There was no big picture that he could see. And Charles looked back at him, his drawn face sad and in earnest. *He really is worried*, Peter thought. *Worried about me, but why?*

"Someone threatened..." Peter began, his brain working furiously to fill in the blanks. He folded his hands together and rested his chin on them, watching Charles for a reaction. Charles obliged by darting another look at the mirror.

The hairs on the back of Peter's neck rose. His chest was suddenly paralyzed and air ceased to pass in or out of his lungs. He fought the urge to turn and follow Charles's glance, again wondering who Charles thought was on the other side of the glass, and instead focused his gaze on Charles and silently asked the question, hoping despite his doubts and their seemingly long separation they knew each other well enough for Charles to understand.

Charles stared back, and for a minute Peter despaired. Then Charles closed his eyes and pinched the bridge of his nose. Blinked. Paused to wipe at his closed eyes once more. Blinked.

Peter pushed his chair back from the table. "Is there anything else you'd like to say? Besides calling me a drowned rat?"

"Mouse," Charles corrected somberly.

The door to the observation room flew open, and Jules was there, eyes bright as a magpie that has spotted something shiny. For the first time since arriving, he appeared not simply at ease but chipper. "We should go."

Peter looked to Charles, who was staring, stunned, at Jules. "He's a friend," Peter assured. "In fact, Jules here was my lost paperwork."

"You can explain that to me later," said Jules. "But we should go now if we're going to go at all."

"Go where?" Charles asked hoarsely.

"One thing at a time," said Peter. To Jules, he said, "What about the guard?"

"I'm going to send him for water. But you need to be ready." With that, Jules was gone again, the door swinging shut in his wake.

"I don't even have a passport," said Charles.

"We'll get you what you need," Peter promised. He rounded the table and took Charles's hand. "You trust me?"

The vivid blue eyes met Peter's briefly, then darted toward the door. "And him?"

"I've known him a long time. And he owes me more than a little favor." Peter drew Charles to his feet as Jules burst back into the room.

"For God's sake, Peter, the camera!"

Air whistled through Peter's gritted teeth, the release valve for his exasperation. "Charles, go with Jules. I'm right behind you." He was already dragging the chair over to where the video camera hung on the wall.

"No point in it now, is there?" Jules asked. "Just come on!"

And this is why he's in the field and I'm not, Peter thought. But he'd done his fair share of hotfooted missions, usually was brilliant at thinking on his feet. It was the weight of emotions sinking him now. Charles was right; he was the mouse, fighting the current.

Jules led them back out to the main corridor, Charles between them like a prisoner and Peter bringing up the rear. They walked swiftly, with every sign of having a purpose, but they did not run. Down past rooms four, five, six… Around a corner and there were the lifts at the far end of the hall. Jules hit the down arrow.

Peter balked. "Down?" he asked, his throat swollen with sudden, irrational fear. The Tombs were down.

But then Jules went to the stairwell door to the right and pulled it open. "Up. Quickly." He pulled the door shut again after them, making sure it wasn't seen as having been used.

Charles found himself in front now. "How far?"

"All the way," said Jules. "I hope you don't mind heights."

In truth, it wasn't a very tall building, only four stories. They came to the roof and Jules said, "And now we go back down again."

Charles looked at him as if he were mad. "You're joking."

Jules pointed to a fire escape. "They're so sure of being able to keep everyone in, they don't bother with all the ways out."

The oversight seemed impossible to Peter, but he didn't have time to dwell on it. Charles turned to him, his face white. "Can't we just tell them the truth?"

"Too late for that, mate," Jules put in, and Peter thought he was unnecessarily cheerful about it. "You're officially a fugitive now. Better fly before they close the cage door."

"I'll go first," said Peter as Charles paled further. Peter made for the fire escape, the cold metal biting into the fine skin of his palms; he could hear Jules giving Charles instructions as he climbed down: "Wait until he gets to the first landing and then start. No sense taxing that old thing with too much weight."

Peter made the first landing and immediately felt the shake of another body coming down the ladder. A dizzying number of climbs later, he reached the pavement, Charles and Jules coming after.

"My car..." Peter began. It was in front of the building and only had two seats.

"Give me the keys," said Jules. Peter did, and Jules ran to the mouth of the alley and peered out. Evidently he found what he was looking for; he began waving someone over. Peter squinted, tried to make out the person—a woman, that much he could see, which was hardly surprising. Jules spoke to her, handed her the car keys, and came back to where Peter and Charles stood.

"She'll bring it to Paddington for us. You cold, mate?" Jules asked Charles, who had begun to shiver.

Immediately Peter felt terrible for his neglect. He shed his camel-colored coat and put it over Charles's shoulders.

"Best lose ourselves," said Jules. He glanced at Charles again. "We can get him cleaned up at the station."

After one more check by Jules, the three of them exited the alley and joined the throngs of London.

NINE

PETER HAD a handful of passports and enough training to doctor one on the fly so that Charles officially became Arnold Hanley, at least long enough for them to leave the country. Jules had opted to take his chances, so after unloading Peter's luggage from the car at Paddington, he kept the car—and the girl who'd delivered it. Peter had his misgivings, but at the same time knew Jules to be able to talk himself out of and through almost anything, the mess in Frankfurt an der Oder notwithstanding. "I'll give them a good story," Jules promised. Peter wondered whether he'd ever get to hear it.

2 MONTHS LATER

It was hot out, and Peter would have much preferred to be sitting under the umbrella of a café table, stretching his lunch over a couple of hours. But there was no stopping Charles. His taste of freedom had sent the two of them rabbiting across Europe in the general direction of Turkey and Greece, though with so many detours Peter wouldn't attest they'd ever get that far. At least not any time soon.

Charles had yet another of his guides open in his hands, and Peter wondered if Charles ever *saw* anything of the places they visited, what with having his nose in a book all the time. Not that it made any difference to Peter. He'd seen it all before and continued to see—and to think—unable to turn off his eyes or brain.

"There," Charles said, stopping on the pavement and pointing. "That church was built in 1022. Did you know?"

Peter's eyes raked the Gothic tower, the stone so old it would always look dirty and wet. Or maybe it genuinely was dirty and wet. Peter had to remind himself that sometimes things really were as they appeared. "I do now."

The finger moved left. "And that bridge—"

"Charles."

Charles dropped his arm, and those bright blue eyes traveled to Peter's face, wide and expectant.

"I have to wonder," Peter said, carefully measuring his words, "how or when did you learn Morse code?"

Peter saw everything in Charles's body tighten, as if a screw had been turned somewhere inside. But the face remained open and remarkably blank.

"That day in the interrogation room," Peter went on, "you blinked the signal for 'affirmative.' Do cabbies learn Morse as a matter of course?"

Charles shrugged, but to Peter's expert eye it was more of a jerk than a fluid movement. "Doesn't hurt to know it," Charles said, his tone offhanded. "Not a crime."

"No," Peter agreed. "It's not a crime." He waited to see if there would be more, if Charles would weave a garland of excuses or lies, tie ribbons around to make the crown of thorns more beautiful if not more comfortable. But Charles only stood there with that half smile Peter was beginning to think of as more of a smirk, the smug expression of a man who has just checkmated his opponent.

Or maybe it meant nothing.

Peter didn't know any more, for the first time in his life could not trust his instincts. His internal compass had been damaged by the magnet that was Charles.

"Tell me about the bridge then," said Peter, and Charles visibly relaxed, brightened, a happy tourist once more. And as

Charles rattled on about ancient Romans and citywide fires, Peter told himself none of it mattered. Not only the city's history but theirs. He'd followed Charles across the Channel, and he'd follow Charles over this bridge—reconstructed most recently in 1736—and whatever other waters and bridges presented themselves. Whether they were moving toward or away from the truth or were merely turning in circles, Charles would navigate with his guides and maps and Peter would allow himself to be led. He was surprised to find he didn't mind.

"Wouldn't now, of course," said Charles, stopping halfway across the bridge to look into the deep green river that sauntered smoothly beneath them.

"What?" Peter asked, drawn from his thoughts.

"Burn. The old one was wood. This one is stone."

"Something to be said for building bridges that can't be burned," said Peter, but Charles was reading through the guidebook again, and if he heard Peter he chose not to answer.

ST. PETER AT THE GATE

ONE

PETER FELL BACKWARD INTO WATER, shattering the placid blue surface and sinking beneath, and the liquid closed over him as if he had never touched it, never existed, turning a newly undisturbed face to the sky. He flailed for a moment, all instinct, before a calm settled over him and he spent precious seconds marveling at the way the light sparked and played above, a mirage of Heaven. Peter was a good swimmer; he knew he could, he *should* push himself to the surface. All at once he realized he had no idea how he'd ended up in the water to begin with. Was this an ocean? It was warm, this water, and clear.

But then the water began to cloud, red-brown, and Peter realized he was bleeding, bleeding into the pristine water and ruining it. He looked upward again through the stillness, and through the mists of his own blood could see Gordon standing above him, lord-like, a gun in his hand.

Peter opened his eyes and was met with Charles's blue gaze, an ocean of another kind resting on the pillow next to his. "You're awake," said Peter.

"So are you." Charles's breath held the faint scent of the pastilles he habitually chewed, fruity and sweet, and Peter idly thought they should probably find a dentist if Charles was going to keep eating candy.

"You're gone again," said Charles softly.

"No." Peter forced himself to focus on the face across from his. The room was only just starting to lighten, so that the air around them seemed to be grey, almost foggy, as if night were created from tiny particles now dissipating as the sun rose.

"You need a hobby," Charles insisted. "Something to keep that mind of yours occupied. You're going to keep having these dreams until you find something else to fill your brain."

"What should I do? Scrapbook?"

Charles winced, and Peter's heart was drawn down into his stomach by some invisible thread that, had Peter been required to name it, would probably have been guilt. The albums that held all their travel photos were Charles's particular pride; he'd spent what to Peter seemed an inordinate amount of time putting them together, then had walked Peter through them all like someone reading a storybook to a child, as if Peter had never been to any of the places, had not, in fact, been beside Charles each and every step of the way.

Peter understood, of course, Charles's desire to relive what had been on the whole a lovely four months. But in Peter's (now ex) profession, reliving things was more a hazard than a joy. He had no knack for nostalgia. Forward was the only direction Peter knew how to move. It was either that or stand still, and standing still got you shot.

Charles rolled away from Peter, sat up and plucked the coverlet off his legs in a strangely mincing gesture, as if not to disturb the bedclothes more than necessary. "It's Saturday," he said as he climbed from the bed.

"Is it?" Peter had long since lost track of days, though Saturdays were a good point of reference. Charles always worked Saturdays. Peter sat up slowly, and for a moment he experienced the weight of the water from his dream, could sense it trying to force him back down to the mattress. He felt lightheaded, but he fought it and remained upright. "Big group?"

"A good size." Charles took a sweater from his bureau. "We're headed into the season, so they keep getting bigger."

It was a ridiculous dialogue, one they had some variation of every week. At some point that afternoon or evening, Charles would come home—possibly bringing dinner if he didn't feel like cooking—full of stories about the tourists he'd guided through the streets of Salzburg that day, and Peter would nod as he chewed and have absolutely nothing to offer to what would inevitably become an entirely one-sided conversation.

"Peter."

He snapped to, found Charles frowning at him, clothes stacked neatly in hand as he readied to dress. "I asked if you had any plans for the day." The tone was gentle as opposed to accusatory, which only made Peter's lapse seem worse.

Peter ran his hands over his face, massaging to encourage the blood to flow. "I'm sorry, I..." He made himself move, get out of bed, though he didn't want to. "The shopping maybe."

"Oh, good," said Charles with almost too much enthusiasm. "I started a list. It's on the kitchen counter."

Peter went to the closet, pulled out some trousers and a shirt. "English or German?"

"The list?"

"The tourists."

"Oh. German today, I think. I should look at my notes before I go." He glanced at the shirt Peter had selected. "You'll want a jacket with that. It's a little cool out these days."

Peter nodded to show he'd heard. Charles tucked his clothes under his arm and shuffled into the bath while Peter slowly and deliberately buttoned his shirt, armoring himself to face the day.

———

It wasn't so *fast*, Peter thought as he meandered through the grocery, dutifully consulting the list Charles had left for him, the neat block letters staring up at him with a kind of determination and insistence. *And he still pronounces a few things wrong.*

But then, Peter argued inside his head, *we've only been here seven weeks. And he's nearly fluent.*

Could just be the type who is good with languages. You know for a fact he's good with his tongue.

A warm crawl made its way up Peter's back as his mind took

a turn he hadn't expected. He stopped walking, forced himself to focus on the paper in his hand. Asparagus. Charles didn't even like asparagus, but he cooked it because he knew Peter enjoyed it.

It's a long game, Peter thought. *He's playing you.*

But there was nothing to play for. Not any more. Peter no longer worked for British intelligence, had no access to any useful information.

He knows Morse code and picked up German faster than is typical. Did he already know it? Charles had once said he'd taken some German in school but that it hadn't stuck, but maybe it had come back with use. Still the questions harangued Peter. *What other languages does he speak? Why would someone who had never been out of England prior to six months ago need to know these things?*

Peter closed his eyes briefly. He was making himself dizzy, chasing the same questions around his head day after day. Charles was right. He needed a hobby, something to occupy his time and mental space.

He opened his eyes to find himself standing in front of the asparagus, the banded phalanxes marching through the marshes of water intended to keep them moist. How long had he been there? Peter squeezed his eyes shut again in the hopes of fending off an impending headache.

Peter selected a bunch of asparagus, dropped it into his handbasket, looked again at the list and turned in search of tomatoes, only to be confronted with a body taller and wider than his own. *"Entschuldigen Sie mich—"*

"Peter."

Peter's gaze rose from the shirt that took up most of his field of vision and came to rest on a familiar face, though it took him longer than it should have to understand what he was seeing.

"Gamby?" His heart froze in his chest. *They found us.* But of course he'd always expected they would eventually. Gordon was good at his job, and—though it pained Peter a bit to admit it—so was Ken Gamby.

"You've gone domestic. Do you get your hair done once a week, too?"

Peter stepped around the man he'd once worked with, thinking motion would mask his trembling; he was rattled in the literal sense, but better if Gamby didn't see. "You've come all this way to insult me. I'm flattered." Yes, good, the words came out steady.

"You know better than that," Gamby told him as he followed Peter to the pyramid of tomatoes. He picked one up and handed it to Peter. "This is a good one."

"Now look who's domestic." But Peter put it in the basket.

"Wife grows them."

Peter had no answer for that. He'd known Gamby was married but had never heard the agent talk about his family. Peter went back to his list, the neat letters now signifying the safety of order and good sense. Mushrooms. But Charles hadn't specified what kind.

"It's Gordon," said Gamby as Peter craned in search of where the mushrooms might be.

Momentary confusion, but Peter did not allow it to show. "What of him?"

"They're throwing a net around him."

Peter spotted the mushrooms in the far corner and turned his steps in that direction.

"If Gordon goes, they'll give Tillholm his seat," Gamby went on.

"Should we be having this conversation in a public grocery?" Peter asked. "Or at all, really, under the circumstances?" He frowned hard at the collection of fungi, trying to remember when he and Charles had last eaten mushrooms and what they'd looked like. Not white, he was sure. Brown. Big? Portabella? Had Charles chopped them up?

"He loved you," Gamby said.

An image of Gordon holding a gun flashed through Peter's mind. "Past tense."

"What are you planning to cook?" Gamby asked, and Peter turned, startled by the exasperation in Gamby's tone.

"What?"

"The kind of mushroom will depend on what you're planning to make."

"You cook." It was a flat kind of statement, something to be filed away like hundreds of other pieces of useless information, Peter's brain starving for sustenance.

Gamby shrugged. "Wife's no good at it. And neither are you from the look of it."

In defiance, Peter grabbed a carton of mushrooms and tossed it into the basket. Only later would he realize they were white after all.

———

"You still living with your friend?" Gamby asked as he trailed Peter up the pavement.

"You're following me home now?" Peter countered. Though no one bothered to step aside for the tall, thin man carrying the grocery sack, Gamby's larger-than-life figure cut quite a swath on the streets of Salzburg.

"I don't have to follow you. We know where you live."

Confirmation. "Then you already know the answer to your question." Peter rounded a corner, moving from a bustling main thoroughfare to a slightly less congested side street, and Gamby kept on his heels, an unwanted bodyguard. They walked through the artificial canyon of buildings that curved around and away and turned two more corners before Gamby reached over and took the groceries from Peter's hand.

Peter stopped walking.

"So you can get your keys," Gamby explained.

Allowing Gamby to isolate him did not seem like a top-of-one's-class move. When Peter failed to reach for his keychain, Gamby asked, "Why Salzburg?"

The sudden question threw Peter, and it took him a moment to answer. "You'd have to ask Charles. I let him pick."

Gamby snorted. Impatient, he started walking again, taking Peter's groceries with him. "Come on, then," he said as he trudged two doors down to Peter and Charles's building, "let's see if we can't turn this into something edible."

———

Partly because it was too early for wine, and partly because Peter felt it wouldn't do to be even slightly impaired with Gamby around, Peter set a kettle on for tea while Gamby made himself strangely at home by going through the cupboards and icebox. Though Peter had never cared much about the kitchen, he now found himself privately thankful Charles had insisted on a flat with one large enough for two people; Gamby's bulk counted as at least one and a half, his bull-like form corralled by the L-shaped countertop and the small dining table at which Peter went to sit in an effort to stay out of the larger man's way. He watched Gamby collect odds and ends and set them on the counter, very like what Charles did most evenings. But when the kettle whistled, Peter was up again and squeezing past Gamby to get at the tea mugs. He took his prizes to the far end of the counter to pour the hot water and steep the tea, all the while watching Gamby from the corners of his eyes.

"If you were hungry, we could have just gone to a café," Peter finally allowed after watching Gamby laboriously dice an onion. He took his tea back to the table, abandoning Gamby's on the counter to either be drunk or grow cold.

Gamby threw the bits of onion into a pot he'd set heating on the stove. "Garlic," he muttered, turning in a circle. *Like a dog*, Peter thought, observing from over the rim of his cup. Then Gamby said more loudly, "Better to do it here."

A tiny stab of fear drove its way through Peter, all the more potent for its needle-thin blade, but he strove to sound nonchalant. "Do what exactly?" For the first time he wondered whether the flat might be wired; was someone listening? Peter only just prevented himself from checking under the table, though he knew they'd never be so obvious as to put one there.

But Gamby had found the garlic and was devoted to chopping it, his hands too big to do so gracefully. It occurred to Peter that

Charles would have had it done in a tenth of the time. This was followed by the belated idea that Peter shouldn't be too comfortable with Gamby wielding a knife in close proximity. Too late to do anything about it however.

"It would have been you," Gamby said once he'd tossed the garlic in with the onion. Peter almost hated to admit it smelled good, whatever it was.

"I'm afraid I don't follow," Peter told him.

Gamby paused long enough to sip some tea then went to work on a box of capellini, which he poured into a second pot to boil. "You were heir to Gordon's throne."

"But not any more," said Peter.

"You don't want it?"

Peter was momentarily stunned by the question, but Gamby's expression prompted him to state the obvious. "I can't have it."

Satisfied with his culinary efforts, Gamby rested against the counter and took up his tea once more. "Why did you run?"

Peter felt suddenly overwhelmed by the incongruity of having this man in his kitchen, cooking a meal, drinking tea, and talking old office gossip. If it was meant to make him feel at ease, it wasn't working. Peter's nerves were taut, and the faux friendly sheen only overset him, driving him to the point. "Why are you here, Ken?"

Gamby's brow cleared, going from furrowed to smooth, and Peter instantly realized this was hard work for his ex co-worker. He was used to being muscle, the intimidator, and inclined to be direct in his dealings. Having to visit Peter and make nice was not Gamby's strong suit. Peter mentally kicked himself for not catching on sooner. Chalk it up to rusty skills, but it was still shameful.

He'd given Gamby a straight shot now, however, and Peter saw the whole of the agent's form relax as they got down to business. "If Tillholm takes over, it will be a disaster. Can you imagine? The way he jumps at every shadow? He'd have us spread too thin, be picking fights with every ally."

Peter pictured Trevor Tillholm—short, nervous, as agitated as a terrier—hunched into Gordon Lessenby's chair at the head of the conference table. It was a bad fit. "That still doesn't explain why you're here."

"Doesn't it?" Gamby asked. When Peter didn't respond, Gamby swallowed visibly, and it pleased Peter to imagine the man's pride was stuck in his throat. The words, when they finally came, were pushed out in a rush of breath, a painful birth. "We need you back."

The confession fell like a sledgehammer to Peter's chest, causing a brief arrest of his heart. It was like an earthquake, this sudden shift from fearing that Gamby had come to drag him back in chains to realizing he was being asked to return in triumph. And as with any earthquake, Peter would need to wait for the shaking to stop before assessing the damage.

Gamby returned to his pots, and Peter stared at the broad back as Gamby drained the pasta, added it to the onion and garlic and then went in search of Parmesan. Peter didn't bother to guide him, not to the cheese, nor to the plates or utensils. Gamby hunted and gathered and eventually brought heaping plates to the table, which Peter took as a cue to make more tea. He was filling the kettle when Gamby finally grunted, "Well?"

"Well what?" Peter asked. He had the same uneasy feeling he got when Charles was angry and Peter wasn't sure why. Like they'd had an argument without Peter realizing it.

Gamby heaved a sigh. "Will you come back?"

"If Tillholm's the problem, get someone else. Why not you, for that matter?"

"They won't have me," said Gamby. "I'm too..." He paused in his eating. "How did Gordon put it? Divisive."

"Well, and everyone hates me equally, so there's that in my favor," said Peter as he set a mug beside Gamby's plate. "But how does Gordon have any say, if they're dragging him out in a noose?"

The front door of the flat opened before Gamby could answer, and Charles's voice traveled from the tiled square meter that served as an entry. "Did you cook, Peter? It smells love—"

Peter knew the risks of freezing when cornered; his job had

primed him to stay quick on his feet. But as he listened to Charles's voice come closer, his steps grow louder as they progressed off the entry tile and onto the hardwood, all Peter could do was stand there while Gamby continued to eat, placid as a cow.

". . . ly," Charles finished as he stepped into view from where the wall cornered to form the kitchen.

Peter suddenly realized the mug of tea he was clutching was burning his hands. But he couldn't make himself move.

Charles stopped short of the kitchen Lino, a lopsided half smile on his face as he took in the scene, though Peter knew from experience the amusement was simply a shield for Charles's discomfort. "I see you found something to occupy yourself," Charles went on.

Gamby had the grace to stop eating then. "Do you want some? There's plenty."

Peter saw the upturned corner of Charles's mouth twitch. "I'm not sure there's room at the table."

Indeed, it was a small table, as the size of the flat necessitated, and Gamby took up a good portion of it. But Gamby rose and went to the pot on the stove. "There's space enough. Sit."

Charles threw a look at him that Peter could not decipher. With a jerky motion, Peter pulled out a chair for Charles, who entered the kitchen with the air of man going to execution. As well he might, Peter reasoned. It was the same feeling Peter had upon first seeing Gamby, but there would be time enough to soothe Charles later.

Gamby returned to the table, set the fresh plate and fork in front of Charles with more grace than Peter would have guessed was possible for such a large man, leaving Charles to murmur his thanks. Gamby didn't answer, instead asking, "What are you standing there for, Peter?"

Peter set his tea in front of Charles, a weak peace offering, and took a seat. He pushed the pasta around with his fork and watched Gamby shovel his in, not daring to look at Charles, though he was aware of movement on that side of him; by the sound and feel of things, Charles was eating. This was confirmed a minute or so later when Charles remarked, "It's good."

"My grandmother used to make it," said Gamby, adding as if it somehow mattered, "She was Dutch."

For lack of other options, Peter took a bite. The noodles had gone lukewarm, and they snaked down Peter's throat, the oil slippery on the roof of his mouth. He made himself swallow nonetheless. He couldn't have said whether he chewed. He kept his eyes on his plate, and on the area of table immediately surrounding his plate; if he stuck it out long enough, the meal would eventually end and Gamby would leave.

And then what?

Peter's eyes darted in Charles's direction. Salzburg had been good for him—all the traveling had been, had suited Charles so that he'd begun to appear younger and more fit than when he and Peter had first met. Happier, too, until that afternoon. Now Charles had fallen in on himself, shoulders rounded and head ducked as if to form a protective shell. And all it had taken to transform him, to make him look like he'd caught a cannon ball in his gut, was the sight of Gamby.

And yet Charles was too polite to demand Gamby's departure. Christ, he was too polite to turn down Gamby's proffered dinner. Peter felt a rise like mercury inside him, though he wasn't sure with whom he was angry. Charles for being too nice? Gamby for being such a thug? Or himself for doing nothing more than watch it happen?

Peter pushed his plate away, and Gamby looked up, his own dish nearly empty. "You don't like it?"

"I'm not hungry," said Peter.

"Never did eat much, you skinny bastard," Gamby remarked. He pushed back from the table and took his plate and mug to the sink. "You think about what I said."

"I don't know what you want," Peter told him.

"I told you."

"You said..." Peter glanced uncertainly at Charles, who was no longer eating so much as quietly fiddling, twirling the pasta on his fork as if to create art or perhaps read his future in the whorls. *To hell with it,* Peter thought. *He'll find out one way or another, whether he's supposed to know or not.* "You said you need me back. But I still don't understand why or what for."

"Come back and I'll show you."

And then Gamby was gone, the door of the flat slamming with finality, the echo of his leaving hanging in the air between Peter and Charles like the knolling of a funeral bell.

____

TWO

____

CHARLES immediately and silently went to work on the kitchen, and Peter knew better than to intrude. Charles was neat by nature, but his methodical sanitizing of the sink, the counters, the pots and plates spoke to something deeper than a simple desire for cleanliness. Peter stayed at the table and watched Charles's hands turn red from the heat of the water. After a few minutes, he rose and took up a dishtowel and began to dry the dishes and put them away.

The room seemed suddenly too big without Gamby there to take up most of the space. Peter envisaged himself and Charles as two planets separated by a vast expanse of airlessness; in Peter's mental picture they rotated slowly, each moving in its orbit, with not enough gravity between them to pull them together. But what did they orbit? What was their sun?

"You can't go back."

Peter tightened his grip on the plate he'd been drying, not out of anger but because the sudden sound of Charles's voice had startled him. But Peter saw how Charles's keen blue eyes found the white knuckles, watched the conclusion being arrived at in Charles's mind.

To Peter's surprise, the resolve in Charles's face hardened. "You can't," he said again, flatly, like a teacher telling a student one could not add two and two and make it five.

Something contrary in Peter reared its head, and instead of doing the easy thing, possibly the right thing, and telling Charles he had no intention of going, he said instead, "Well, you did say I should find something to do."

"Not this."

"It's what I'm good at, Charles. You're good at tours, and decorating, and German apparently, and I'm good at..."

"Paperwork?"

Peter pressed his lips together. The old joke was no longer funny.

"It's a trick, a trap," said Charles. "They lure you back and lock you up."

It was, of course, Peter's secret fear, but it irritated him to hear it aloud. He wanted to believe Gamby was in earnest. He wanted to believe the Agency needed him.

"That plate is plenty dry, by the way," Charles remarked. "Try this mug."

Peter turned and shoved the plate into the cupboard with more force than was strictly necessary before making to snatch the mug from Charles's hand, only to have it slip, chipping as it bounced against the lip of the counter on its way to the floor. They each stared down at it for a long moment before Charles said softly, "Hope you weren't too fond of it."

Peter slapped down the dishtowel and went for a walk.

———

The minute the door banged shut behind him, Peter realized he'd made a mistake. They lived in a densely populated area of the city near the old part of town, the part the tourists frequented; this made Charles's job easier but Peter didn't much feel like fighting his way through the crowded streets, even to get to the park or walk along the river. He could not bring himself to go back inside, however, so after standing on the stoop for a good two minutes—long enough for him to notice the flicking of lace window coverings in the ground floor flat as a curious lodger surveyed him—he made himself take a few steps, moving deeper into the neighborhood and away from the concentration of foot traffic.

It was a sunny day, though from the manmade ravine in which he walked Peter could only admire the way the sun slanted against the topmost portions of the buildings. He was left in their shade, abandoned to the chill of the shadows and the cut of the wind as it coursed between the structures. Warmth hovered above him like angels in Heaven, taunting Peter with the notion that he could never hope to reach it. Nor would it deign to descend and bless him. And so he slid from street to street, a snake going ever deeper into tall grass. If he could not reach Heaven he might at least hide from its strike.

For a while Peter only walked, his steps automatic. He was unable to focus on any one thought, to devote himself to any particular line of reasoning. *Charles* flashed through his mind, and *Gamby*, and *home*, but he was incapable of chasing any of these things through to a finished or fully formed concept. The words bounced as balls might in an empty room, first high and far, then gradually lower and slower until they rolled to a stop.

Peter stopped too, and saw the sun had gone behind the buildings; it was getting dark. He turned around and headed for home.

Except Salzburg wasn't home.

The thought was so arresting and felt so full after his previous amorphous snatches of ideas, that Peter almost stopped walking again, in fact paused mid-step and had to make a conscious effort to keep moving. He had been so sure when he and Charles had left London that it wouldn't matter where they lived, that home would always be wherever Charles was. But it wasn't true. If home was where the heart resided, as the old adage said, then certainly Charles owned a large portion of that real estate, but England, Peter saw with sudden clarity, being the country he'd not only spent his childhood in but also to which he'd given his adult livelihood to secure and protect, held a large claim as well.

Of course, due to his work, Peter had spent his fair share of time away from home. Some operations required months of entrenching in a foreign city...

Another idea came unbidden, and this one was unwelcome as well: *Why had Charles chosen Salzburg?*

. . . Entrenched.

Peter stopped walking again, and an old woman shot him a glare from behind thick spectacles as she dodged round him on the pavement. It took an additional minute for Peter to gather himself enough to take another step. As he did so, he realized he was trembling, and it had nothing to do with the cold.

———

The kitchen was empty when Peter entered, cleared of all signs of the afternoon's activity, and upon first consideration the flat was roaringly silent, but as Peter grew still in the middle of the lounge he came to realize there was a faint hiss coming from the bedroom—the sound of the shower.

Relief poured through Peter, even as the noise of the water brought back to him sharply, if briefly, his dream of earlier that morning. For an instant Peter could feel the waves closing over his face, could almost believe he was drowning where he stood, but the sensation receded almost as quickly as it had come. The relief, however, remained, and it took Peter a moment to understand he had been afraid in those first few seconds after entering the flat, afraid that Gamby had returned and taken Charles away. He remembered all too well another time he'd come home to an empty and abandoned space.

The shower cut off abruptly and silence thudded into the vacant air. Peter waited, listened to the bedroom door swing open then softly shut again as Charles closed it behind him— Charles couldn't stand to leave it open even a crack, it was a privacy issue for him, and Peter found himself wondering once again what Charles might have to hide—and the soft pad of Charles's slippered feet as he came down the hall.

It was a tiny flat, with small windows that made it always seem dark despite the plain white walls and a number of lamps.

Charles had used his good taste to decorate it, had tried to balance the cavernous feel by sticking to lighter wood and fabrics, though he hadn't been able to resist peacock blue accents. Peter would have chosen something already furnished (and airier, more modern), but that wouldn't have suited Charles, who had never been entirely comfortable in Peter's old place in London, even after moving in and hanging drapes.

And so Peter stood between a television console constructed to look older than it was and a traditional-looking loveseat (the room was too small for a full-size sofa) flanked by two tables that might have been hatchlings of the console, each with a lamp that Charles had thoughtfully left switched on for Peter's return. This was the room in which Peter often spent his days reading the papers and following the international news, living vicariously; he hadn't the taste for novels or history except as it pertained to the present. It was a room Peter often felt the urge to duck into, though the ceiling was no lower here than anywhere else in the flat. But the yellowish light of the lamps created the kinds of shadows that suggested a low-ceilinged cave, and Peter was taller than average. And at that moment, as he listened to Charles scuffling in his direction, Peter felt too tall and too obvious, a badly positioned piece of the furniture.

Charles arrived clad in his favorite green pyjamas, a tome from the English bookseller tucked up under his arm. He stopped short at the sight of Peter, and Peter detected in Charles an impulse, only just squelched, to glance toward the door. Peter fleetingly pondered what Charles might be looking for, but Charles's eyes—with noticeable effort—remained on Peter.

"You came back."

It was said with incredulity, and Peter sensed something loosen within him as the tremble he'd felt the beginnings of earlier while on the street went rushing through him at full speed. Charles set his book down and pulled the throw off the loveseat, moved to drape it over Peter's shoulders. "I told you you'd need a jacket."

Peter allowed Charles to fuss around him, obediently settling down onto the loveseat as prodded, and enduring swathing and re-swathing in the blanket until enough of him was covered. "Did you think I wouldn't?" Peter finally asked. "Come back, I mean."

Apparently satisfied with his handiwork, Charles stepped back. "Yesterday I wouldn't have doubted it. But then, yesterday you wouldn't have stalked out like that, either. I'm going to make you some tea."

Watching Charles walk away, increasing what was beginning to seem like a yawning vastness between them, gave Peter more of a chill than his evening stroll had done. Despite the fringed border that tickled and annoyed his neck and hands, Peter pulled the throw a little tighter around himself, all the while watching Charles move through his meticulous ritual for making tea. Peter tried to imagine him as a spy. For whom? To what end? It wasn't the first time Peter had asked himself these questions, but his revelatory flash during his walk had given him a new avenue to explore. It was like seeing something entirely new and different in a painting one looked at every day. Now Peter felt the need to step back, look both more closely and yet keep a greater distance so as to view the big picture. Did this new information alter the image as a whole? Did it change the way he felt about it? Was there anything else he'd missed?

Or maybe he was simply seeing things. Maybe his brain was that bored, his training that ingrained, he had no choice but to pick apart everything and everyone around him.

But the Morse code. The German. "Why Salzburg?" Peter asked abruptly as Charles stirred the tea in the cup, the spoon chiming against the ceramic. Charles set the spoon aside and carried the cup—it was a proper teacup; Charles preferred them to mugs—to where Peter sat.

"Hmm?"

Peter made no move to take the steaming drink. He kept his eyes on Charles's face. "Why Salzburg? Why did you choose here over any other place we could have lived?"

Charles's face seemed to fold down the center, the frown collapsing his features from brow to chin. "I thought you liked it. But if you don't, we could—"

"This isn't about me. Why did *you* choose it?" At the back of his brain, Peter saw a red light go on, a warning. He was aware he had adopted an interrogatory tone, that he was setting up a verbal divider and was very near the edge of something, though he wasn't sure what, or where he might land were he to lose his balance and fall.

Charles set the rapidly cooling tea on one of the side tables then sat beside Peter on the loveseat—there being nowhere else to sit aside from the floor—and stared into the kitchen, where the light was still on over the sink, weak and yellow, doing more to deepen shadows than shed light. "I'm not enough for you any more," Charles said, and Peter thought the words sounded as if they were being dragged out unwillingly like small, vicious creatures from their den. "Maybe I never was. And now your friend—"

"Gamby's not a friend," said Peter.

But Charles only stated it again. "Your friend has turned up and what? Said something to make you think I...?"

Charles finally turned to look at Peter, the brilliant eyes searching for something, and Peter found himself holding his breath, afraid to move.

"I don't think anything," Peter said after a long moment. "I only asked why you chose Salzburg."

"You thought I had a reason," said Charles.

"I wondered if you did is all. And you're plenty enough for me, Charles. I wouldn't go anywhere without you." Peter held up an edge of the blanket draped over his shoulders. Exhibit A. "Who else would take such good care of me?"

Charles cracked a smile but it only partially warmed his icy eyes, which continued to hold visible reservation. "I do sometimes question how you ever got on before."

"I didn't. Much." It wasn't entirely a lie. Life before Charles had been markedly different, filled with take away meals and long hours at the office—or long stints of business travel—if only to avoid going home to a cold and empty (and airy, and modern) flat. But then, he'd always been able to go home.

Charles sighed and reached for the teacup. "It's gone cold. I'll make you a fresh one." He rose and started for the kitchen, and for a second Peter found himself hating the sound of Charles's slippers as they hissed along the floor.

"Don't," said Peter, standing as well and shedding the throw. "I'll take a hot shower instead."

"Peter."

Peter stopped, but Charles wasn't looking at him, was pouring the tea down the sink.

"If there's somewhere else you'd rather be..." And now Charles did look up, and even across the dimness of their flat the eyes were vivid sparks of color. "It's a big enough world."

Something showed in his face, Peter knew, his homesickness written in bold strokes, because almost immediately Charles's expression became grim as he said to Peter, "Anywhere but there."

"They need me," Peter told him. "Gordon—"

"Can take care of himself," Charles interjected with a harshness that surprised Peter. "My concern is you."

The drowning mouse. After all that had happened, being confined and interrogated and forced to flee the country, Charles still somehow felt the need to worry for him.

Peter took in Charles's rigid posture. On most issues, Charles was amenable, and all at once Peter realized he was used to having his way, had grown accustomed to Charles's acquiescent nature. Now Peter felt like a spoiled child, right down to the desire to stomp his foot; it was not a pleasant feeling.

Charles's gaze darted to Peter's tightened fists, and Peter saw him slump slightly. "You're going to go."

"I need to..." But Peter wasn't sure what he needed. To prove himself? To find out the truth? They were asking him back, throwing open the gates that Peter had thought were locked forever.

Charles had rinsed the teacup and was now drying it as gently as if it were a baby. "If you go, you'll stay."

Peter hesitated, unsure whether Charles meant the Agency would confine him or that Peter would stay of his own will. Either way, he'd made it a personal rule never to lie to Charles if he could help it, sins of omission notwithstanding, and he did not want to promise now that, should they attempt to return his cog to the machinery of the Agency, he would resist. So all he said was, "That cup must be more than dry by now."

"Maybe I was hoping for a genie," said Charles, but he put the dishtowel down and returned to cup to the cupboard. Then, with a sigh, "Give me a week to settle my tours."

Peter's heart hiccoughed in his chest. "What do you mean?" And when the blue eyes turned toward him, so vivid they were clear even from across the dimness of the flat, Peter shook his head. "No. You can't."

Charles's expression went stony. "You can but I can't?"

"*You're* the one they don't trust. They might not lock me up, but you... " Peter inhaled deeply and willed his heart back to a normal pace. "I'll talk to Gamby, suss things out. Maybe you'll be able to join me once I've cleared the way." *Once I've learned the truth,* he didn't say.

Charles's expression morphed back into concern, and in that moment Peter wanted to believe Charles was innocent of whatever shadowy doubts had crowded his mind. So far his love and need for Charles had outweighed any other concerns he might have. But now Peter was worried the scales might be tipping. Willful ignorance was one thing for an ex-agent, something else for an active one.

Yet a surge of love for Charles, and a sense of fairness to him, prompted Peter to add, "And if you don't hear from me—if they hold me—run."

THREE

"WHAT ABOUT *HIM?*" Gamby asked almost immediately after Peter had agreed to return to London. Although Charles was out giving a tour, Peter had decided against staying in, well aware that doing so would encourage Gamby to make another visit. So he'd gone out to walk amidst the throngs strolling along the Salzach, the people availing themselves of the unseasonably fine weather. He'd known Gamby would be watching, waiting, impatient for an answer.

"He has a name," Peter replied mildly. When Gamby only sniffed, Peter added, "And he's staying here."

"Do I hear a heart breaking?"

The tone was so flat, so mild, Peter was tempted to look at Gamby to see how serious he was, whether he was enjoying Peter's discomfort, but stopped himself from giving Gamby the satisfaction. "He has a good thing here," said Peter, his manner equally level as Gamby's had been, "and I'll be back before long."

Peter sensed the quickening tension in his companion, though Gamby kept his voice disinterested. "You're not planning to stay in London?"

"No. I'll see things sorted and then come home." The last word nearly stuck in Peter's throat; he was almost positive

Gamby would hear the way it was dislodged and thrown out to follow the others. Salzburg wasn't, could never be, home.

They strolled along in silence for some little while, Peter overly aware of the hulking man beside him and wishing Gamby would go away. He had his answer. What more could he want?

"I can arrange for him to come with you," Gamby finally said, his words long and low and reluctant.

"No." Peter hoped he hadn't answered too quickly; from the corner of his eye, he perceived the quick turn of Gamby's head and could feel the appraising gaze, but Peter forced himself to continue looking only ahead. He tried to take comfort in the notion Gamby wasn't pushing to have Charles return with him. Could that mean the Agency no longer had any interest in holding Charles? Did it mean Gamby was on the level when he said the Agency needed him?

After a moment, there came a shift, and Gamby's broad shoulders relaxed slightly. "You're beginning to doubt him."

Peter felt something hard drop through him like swallowing a cold bullet, but he kept his face still, his eyes forward.

"How soon can you be ready?" Gamby asked.

"Three days."

"Two."

Peter shrugged, was startled when one of Gamby's too-large hands clapped him on the back. Peter wondered if Gamby had done it to make him react; the slap between his shoulder blades, followed by the squeeze of his shoulder compelled Peter to finally look at the man next to him. Peter wanted to pull away but didn't, and Gamby's hand remained on Peter's shoulder for a minute or two. It was as if Gamby had snared something and was unwilling to release it. When Gamby stopped walking, Peter was obliged to stop as well.

"I'll see you back at the Castle then," said Gamby.

Peter blinked at him, one rapid movement of his eyelids. "In two days."

Gamby gave a decisive nod and the hand came free of Peter's jacket and hung in the air for a second as Peter processed that his companion was waiting for a handshake.

Slowly, Peter placed his hand in Gamby's.

He stole it back as quickly as he could.

————

Peter opened the envelope and tried not to think about the worry on Charles's face, still there after Peter had assured him Gamby would not be visiting again. Their parting had been perfunctory, always Peter's preferred way of doing such things though he'd had other reasons for it as well this time.

"They'll still be watching me," Charles had said.

"Yes."

"And what about you?" Charles persisted.

"Don't worry, I'll handle it." But the concern never left Charles's expression, could not be masked by his smile, had seasoned their swift farewell kiss, Peter sensing Charles's inclination to cling.

Peter shoved the memory aside and pulled the plain card from the envelope the woman at the train station's ticket window had handed him. The only thing written on it was an address. It was Gamby's writing. The address was a familiar one, a flat off Bayswater owned by the Agency, a place to stash people.

Peter checked the envelope again but found no key.

They would be waiting for him.

He sat back in his seat, closed his eyes, and listened to the regular sound of the wheels racing along the tracks. The noise didn't quite drown out the thud of his heart.

————

A third-floor walk-up, really a converted attic, but it had been well renovated and nicely maintained, one of the better properties the agency held, and Peter was surprised Gamby had counted him worthy of it. There was no one outside the door, of course, but when Peter turned the knob, it did not resist. He pushed the door only a crack, was taking in the weak sliver of grey light coming through the windows (the flat faced south-west) when the knob was ripped from his hand as someone opened the door the remainder of the way.

"Lurking are we?"

"Miranda." At least it wasn't a couple of Gamby's thugs waiting to cart him in, though Peter wasn't certain that would have been any worse.

She wore a too-tight sweater and a too-short skirt and was holding a glass of red wine. "They sent me to make sure you have everything you need. Not chardonnay," she added, offering the goblet.

But Peter merely stepped past her, suitcase in hand, and went to stand at the windows. Besides it being a cloudy day, the sun was nearly gone. "Turn on a light, would you?"

He could hear her frustration in the way she released the door, allowing it to slam shut under its own weight. *Reinforced*, Peter noted. *And no spyhole.* A second later a lamp switched on. "They thought you might like a friendly face is all."

"Then why did they send you?"

It was cruel and he knew it, but Peter also knew he needed to set his boundaries and make them clear, as much for himself as everyone else. So he drove the wedge in and began to hammer, did it before he could think too much about it, before he could possibly change his mind. But he was too much of a coward to turn around and look at the resulting cracks.

He heard the glass being set down and the sound of arms sliding into a coat. "If you need anything, call the office. Number's the same. I assume you remember it."

Peter almost turned around then, almost apologized. He later wondered whether it would have made any difference. But something between fear and stubbornness paralyzed him at that moment, and he found himself seeking his reflection in the window glass, then looking for the mirrored twin of the lamp which made one corner of the space bright and inviting while the rest—including where Peter stood—remained dim and cold and grey. Was reflected light still light? Yes, Peter decided, though it held no warmth.

Behind him the door snicked open once again before closing more softly than before.

Peter discovered he was still holding his suitcase. Several more minutes passed before he felt sure enough to put it down. Because for just a moment he thought he might not stay.

———

It was not a large space; a Japanese screen divided the bed and a bureau from the rest, and what passed as a kitchen had been crammed in under the eaves so that Peter was required to nod his head forward if he wanted to use the sink or the two-burner hob. An actual wall separated the bathroom (shower, no tub). But everything was clean and fairly new, had been made as homey and cozy as could be managed, and someone—Miranda, Peter supposed—had stocked the small refrigerator with all the makings for sandwiches. Leave it to Miranda to assume he was incapable of cooking anything more sophisticated.

Peter didn't unpack; it felt better to live impermanently. He turned once, twice around the place, too restless to sit. He was bored already, should have come on the morning train and gone straight to the Castle to get things started. He briefly rebuked himself for having scared off Miranda then concluded he'd rather be alone than in her company. Though he wished he'd thought to ask after Gordon before sending her away.

He stopped again at the windows. It was dark now and over a couple rooftops Peter could see a mostly black slice of world that he thought must be Hyde Park and, beyond that, more distant lights of the city. He considered going out, but after thinking of everything that would entail—putting his coat and shoes back on, locking up, walking—decided he was too tired and abruptly collapsed onto the scratchy, too-new sofa. It was brown and tweedy and cheap, and Peter wondered what had happened to the old one, which had been soft and worn and probably taken from someone's castoffs.

He was never sure how long he sat there. Later he would remember seeing the rejected glass of wine on the table beside the door; there was an ornamental bowl there, too, that Peter suspected held the key to the flat, though he didn't bother to get up and check, only let his gaze travel lazily over the room until it was arrested by the phone squatting on the table beside the sofa. He began to reach for it then stopped himself. Everyone expected him to make that call, which was exactly why he couldn't, not right away. A cold lonely fell over Peter. It was an old, familiar feeling, one that told him more than seeing Gamby or Miranda that he was back on the job.

And waiting was a large part of the work. Peter sat there, his mind drifting to past long stretches of sleepless nights—he refused to think of Charles, did not want to picture his anxious anticipation of the phone ringing—until a sound outside the door brought him back to attention. The door was too close to the floor to see anything moving under it, but Peter was sure he'd heard movement. He waited for the knock, or perhaps for the door to simply open, Miranda not having locked it, but nothing happened.

A minute passed. Two. Peter finally rose and went to the door. Put his hand on the knob and held his breath. Outside there came the sound of something—someone—coming to a stop just on the other side of the door.

Peter thought of the gun folded into the clothes of his suitcase. Let his breath out slowly and silently. Pulled open the door.

———

The sight of Gordon Lessenby had an unexpected effect on Peter. A tremor ran through him, his throat tightened, the corners of his eyes began to sting. He had the sudden, disconcerting urge to sob on the shoulder of this man who, for most of Peter's adult life, had been his mentor, all but his father, and then had turned his life inside out and sent him into exile. At the same time, something hot and sharp entered Peter through the soles of his feet, a spike of fear and anger. Had this all been a trick to get Peter back to London? And was Gordon here to take him in after all?

Before Peter could act or speak, Gordon held up a finger and, obedient and well-trained child, Peter pulled himself in line. Gordon tapped two fingers against an ear and Peter nodded his understanding. "Could have sworn I heard something," said Peter, taking care to keep his voice pitched low, the tone of someone talking to himself. He left Gordon standing on the threshold, closed the door on him, and went to work.

It took twenty minutes to be thorough, but once he was sure he'd found all the listening devices, he let Gordon in. Gordon swept the room, double-checking, but Peter hadn't missed any.

"Why are you here, Peter?" Gordon asked.

The words fell on Peter like a blow so that he almost rocked back on his heels, but he made himself remain still. He took in Gordon's straight posture and trim figure; clearly life was not all bad, for Gordon looked far healthier now than he had when Peter had last seen him. No longer melting into a baggy suit, Gordon wore a smart jumper and trousers that fit him properly, and his skin color was warm rather than pale.

And how must I look to him? Peter asked himself, feeling at once travel-worn and hollow, like an underfed orphan. Peter wondered who had replaced him in Gordon's pantheon, tried to imagine who might have taken his place as Gordon's right hand, and a stab of sorrow twisted in his heart. Whoever it was, they were clearly taking better care of Gordon than Peter ever had.

"What did you hope to be able to do?" Gordon asked, not unkindly, and Peter was pulled back into the moment.

"Whatever was needed. Gamby said..." But what *had* Gamby said? Not much.

"Do you know what happened after you left?" asked Gordon, and again Peter's world tottered slightly. "Did Gamby tell you? We hung a curtain over it, had to. But it's too late to get you out tonight, and by tomorrow it will be too late to get you out at all."

Frustration mingled with hurt and Peter's head suddenly felt tight, the room too hot.

Gordon stepped over to the window. The low-hanging clouds

had begun to spit rain, leaving blurry comets of water on the glass. "They're going to figure out you've found the bugs soon."

"All these places are wired," Peter snapped. "It won't surprise anyone that I might think to look for them and switch them off." When Gordon only nodded, never taking his eyes from the street below, Peter asked, "Why did you come then? Why did Gamby bring me back, if there's nothing I can do except..." He splayed his fingers as if Gordon might throw him something, or perhaps hoping to catch whatever he was missing.

Gordon did Peter the honor of turning, surprise written on his features. "To see you, of course." He paused. "You didn't bring Charles." It was not a question, and Peter felt no need to answer the remark.

Gordon went back to looking out the window. "Your office is just as you left it," he said. "Though Miranda has been reassigned..." It seemed he might have more to say on that but thought better of it.

"Miranda was here when I arrived," said Peter, suddenly desperate to keep Gordon there, to dig in and unearth something, extract some treasure from the past. Whatever was buried between them, Peter had the urge to bring it to light. *Keep him talking*, he thought. It was an old trick, and Peter had always been good at it when in the field.

But Gordon had been doing this longer, had taught Peter all the trade secrets, and knew a pitfall when he saw one, even when camouflaged. "I know," was all he said, but he said it with a gentle smile, one Peter had not seen in years, and Peter was immediately reassured.

"Get some rest," Gordon instructed as he moved toward the door. As he took hold of the knob, he looked over his shoulder. "Why didn't you bring him?"

A bolt shot through Peter at the seemingly innocuous question; he felt the very molecules within him burn with a warning. It was as much a trick as Peter had tried to play: the parting question, embedded in kindnesses and sympathies.

But this was Gordon. If he asked, there was a reason he wanted or needed to know.

Peter opted for hedging. "I think the reasons for that are pretty obvious. And not terribly relevant." The last bit sounded sanctimonious, even to Peter's own ears, but Gordon's expression never changed. He only gave a short, quick nod of understanding.

"Good night, Peter."

He was gone before Peter could reply.

FOUR

THE GATEKEEPER GLANCED up with a lack of attentiveness Peter found a tad alarming. Surely such a role required more than a passing interest in those coming and going. But all Peter saw was the dark flash of the man's gaze before being greeted by a crown of untidy brown hair as the gatekeeper took up a pen and his log, and when the question came, it sounded more bored than official. "Name?"

Peter didn't answer.

"Name?" the gatekeeper asked again without looking up.

Peter continued to wait, and after a moment there came a huff and the head lifted. *Just a boy,* Peter thought when he saw the smooth visage that, even in irritation, showed no wrinkle of the brow, no signs of age. All the boy's sentiments were pooled in those dark eyes.

"Peter Stoller," said Peter before the boy could raise a fuss. "And I suggest you pay closer attention to your work."

Peter watched the flow of emotions cross the young man's face. From the initial irritation, to resentment at having this older stranger reprimand him, and finally recognition of the name, which seemed to engender a mixture of surprise and fear. Only the skin around his eyes and along his jaw moved, but it was more than enough to read him; the boy had not yet learned the crucial skill of remaining still, and Peter felt something like pity and possibly concern pass through him. How would such a one fare in the field? The young man's lips parted slightly, as though he should say something, though nothing came out.

Peter saved him the trouble. "How is it they put you out here? You can't have been in the service long."

"No, sir." The boy stood in belated acknowledgment of being in the presence of a superior, his chair clattering behind him. "But there's no one else in."

"No one?" Peter asked sharply.

"Well, not many. Not enough. There's been a bit of, er, reorganization going on. I'm Martin, by the way." For a moment Peter was not sure whether the boy meant his first or last name, but then Martin added, "Simeon Martin. Simeon with an 'e' in the middle. Even though it's pronounced like Simeon without an 'e.' My parents..." But either Simeon wasn't sure what to say about his parents, or Peter's expression at bearing witness to this unnecessary flood of information prevented the junior agent from continuing.

"Tell me, Mr. Martin," Peter said gravely, "when you open your mouth, does everything you know fall out?"

The young man blinked for a few seconds before answering with equal seriousness. "I don't know, sir."

"Work on it," Peter told him. "Keeping it in, I mean. And find me Gordon Lessenby."

"He's not in," Simeon said, and Peter saw the boy's hand spasm as if wanting to clap itself over his mouth, though it stopped somewhere near the sternum and hovered there, splayed, as if he might place it over his heart and recite a pledge instead. "And anyway, Mr. Gamby said I should take you directly to him." He started around the desk, stopped short, went back and opened a drawer, from which he extracted a bright yellow visitor's badge. He handed it to Peter with an air of apology.

Peter clipped the badge to his suit jacket. "I might should sign the log, too," he suggested.

"Oh! Right." Simeon dutifully checked his watch and entered

the information then turned the ledger toward Peter for his signature. Peter noticed the young man's hands were shaking, that his notation in the log had been made jerky with the gratuitous motion.

"You seem nervous," Peter remarked.

"No. Well…" Simeon appeared to consider, and Peter pinpointed with ease the moment the young man came to a decision. "No. Sir." He moved around the desk again and waited for Peter to join him, then led his senior up the familiar staircase to the bank of lifts. "Sorry," Simeon murmured, and when Peter looked a question at him, "they said you weren't allowed to be unescorted in the building."

"I would expect nothing less," said Peter, taking care to hide the wound the words had inflicted. He'd known, of course, in the rational sense that he would not simply be permitted free run, but to hear it said so plainly made it suddenly clear to him his heart had not been privy to the same communiqué. It was always jarring for an agent, Peter reflected, when heart and mind had a difference of opinion. Or was that true for everyone, regardless of their work? He realized he didn't know, had never had the luxury of knowing anything different from his job. Even his relationship with Charles was predicated on his work experience. It was such a stark and terrible insight that, when the lift doors opened, Peter half expected them to reveal a pit into which he must either step or be thrown.

But Peter stepped into the lift without incident, and as Simeon looked to join him, asked, "And who will act gatekeeper while you're nannying me?"

Simeon stopped uncertainly on the threshold of the lift, the back of his left hand positioned to keep the door from sliding closed as he looked over his shoulder and through the wrought iron railings to his abandoned post below.

"Didn't they give you a procedure?" Peter snapped impatiently when the dark eyes returned to him wide and full of indecision. "Should you call for someone?" *Jesus, don't they teach them to think any more?*

Simeon was looking over his shoulder again. "There is no one."

Something in Peter quickened, prompting him into motion. He exited the lift. "There's always someone." He went to the railing and looked down on the lobby, the gatekeeper's empty table, the logbook still open. Anyone could walk in off the street. Had Simeon even locked the desk?

Peter realized as his heart thudded in his ears that he was afraid.

He turned to Simeon. "Where are they? This place should be busy this time of the morning."

Once again Peter could see Simeon's mind working as he assessed how much he should say. And then came that moment of decision, and with a deep breath, "There's been a bit of a purge."

"When?"

"After you..." His voice trailed and Peter wondered what sort of "curtain" Gordon had hung—what the official word was versus the rumors, and which was closer to true. "Sort of broke into factions," Simeon continued. "Lot of people just waiting for Mr. Lessenby to step aside, a few others trying to walk him to the door."

"And you?" Peter asked.

"I haven't been here long enough to pick a side," said Simeon.

"And where does the purge come in?"

"Well, what with Mr. Lessenby's wife..."

"Elinor?"

"So they cut away everyone around him, just in case. I mean, you were gone, and then those smart enough put some distance."

"You mean Gamby and Tillholm."

Simeon shrugged. "Some even went so far as to move to a new building. Which is why no one is in this one."

"Then what are you being punished for?" asked Peter.

The dark eyes flashed at him and the shoulders stiffened. "Sir?"

"You must have made someone unhappy to be stuck with gatekeeper duty in a nearly abandoned building."

Peter could tell from the rueful twist of Simeon's lips he was right. "Insubordination, sir."

"Toward whom?"

"Mr. Tillholm. Sir. But he was—"

Peter held up a staying hand. "I don't need to know. And you need to find someone to escort me upstairs or else man the desk."

He watched as Simeon considered his options and once again thought how green the boy was, giving everything away on his face. Not thinking near fast enough, either. Had it been a field situation, it would have been nothing short of disaster. As it was, it stretched Peter's patience to near breaking.

Then Simeon took a set of keys from his pocket, held up a finger indicating Peter should wait a moment, and turned to hurry back down the stairs. Peter watched long enough to figure out Simeon meant to lock the front doors, preventing anyone else entering while he was away from his desk. Not an eloquent solution by any means, but it did the job. Would he hang a sign too? One of those clocks with the moveable hands, *Will Return...?*

Peter didn't wait to find out.

Turning back to the lifts, Peter slapped the button and the patient and waiting car slid open. Peter stepped inside and pressed '6.' He had one glimpse of Simeon's surprised and outraged expression through the bars of the railing before the doors divided them. Now Peter only had to hope the lift would be faster than Simeon's ability to hit the emergency stop. Or would he simply call Gamby?

But no, if Peter had read the boy right—and he was pretty certain he had—Simeon would try to work around those in authority. Not so much out of fear of further reprisals as out of a sense of superiority and a need to prove he could handle the situation on his own.

The lift slowed, stopped, opened to allow Peter to exit. It was his old floor, the top floor, where his office had stood at Gordon's shoulder, making Peter readily available to the throne at any given moment. Trevor Tillholm had occupied the sixth floor as well; Gamby had been stuck on five, though Peter wondered whether he'd moved up since then. But Gordon had said that Peter's own office, at least, was as he'd left it. Small comfort, the idea of not having been immediately replaced and all memory of him scrubbed.

But it wasn't his office he'd come to see; it would be locked anyway and Peter no longer had a key. So Peter turned his steps in the other direction, toward Gordon's office.

Simeon had said Gordon wasn't in, but Peter was willing to wager Sandra would be, and as expected, when he turned the corner he was greeted with the familiar bounce of her blonde waves. Sandra was possibly younger than Gordon but she was certainly older than Peter, and her dedication to her brilliant golden hair made for a stark contrast from her lined face; one would almost have thought it was a wig except investigation by curious parties had proven Sandra's twice-monthly visits to her salon were, in fact, very real.

Now those blonde masses swayed in Peter's direction as he approached, and Sandra's hazel eyes lit with undisguised fondness as she recognized whom it was. "Peter!" He thought she started to get up but apparently thought better of it before completing the motion, so that she only hopped in her seat before forcing her hands to stay flat on her thighs. By the time he reached her desk, she had composed herself thoroughly, peeking up at him through over-mascaraed lashes with something like a coy reprimand. "Gordon isn't in. And you shouldn't be wandering loose."

"So I've been told." Peter awarded Sandra a swift kiss on the cheek and perched himself on the corner of her immaculate desk. "But I know you can fill me in on everything I haven't been told yet."

"Peter," Sandra said again, and this time it was a low warning as to an errant schoolboy. But Peter knew by the way she glanced left, right over her shoulders that she was prepared to let a few tidbits of gossip slide. More than facts, of which Peter usually had a full share, Sandra had always been good for the temperature of things.

"They tossed your office right after," Sandra admitted. "Didn't find anything useful, good for you. And now Gordon's locked it and won't let anyone touch it."

"Why not?" Peter asked, even as he mentally attempted to catalogue his old office's contents. Remaining stubborn on such a point would surely never help Gordon's cause; what reason could Gordon have to resist so strongly?

And now Sandra gave Peter the look at told him he shouldn't have to ask such a question. "He's waiting for you to change your mind and come back."

Peter opened his mouth to tell her Gordon had just the night before been not terribly happy that Peter *had* come back, or maybe to say he hadn't realized that was an option, but something inside him cautioned against letting this bit of information fly. Sandra was a gossip, after all. "I don't think I'm very welcome here," Peter said instead.

The breathless arrival of Simeon seemed almost direct evidence of Peter's testimony. The young man turned the corner almost at a run, but slowed when he spotted his quarry. Protocol disallowed Simeon to take Peter to task for having bolted, but the dark eyes were hot enough to convey the unspoken message.

"Young Mr. Martin," said Peter, and Sandra straightened in her chair, all business now as she shooed Peter off her desk.

"I don't know when Mr. Lessenby will be in," she said, too loudly. "He's in and out at all hours these days."

Peter ignored her, though he obediently abandoned her workspace and approached Simeon. "I assumed Gamby had been moved up."

"Into Mr. Lessenby's office?" Simeon asked.

Peter gave a nonchalant shrug.

"We'll walk down to five," Simeon decided, angling for the stairwell.

"I hope you learned a lesson at least," Peter told him.

"That you can't be trusted?"

"That no one can be trusted."

"As I hear it, you learned that one the hard way," said Simeon. The stairwell door whined open and Simeon stood back to allow Peter through ahead of him.

"Then consider yourself lucky I gave you the short and easy tutorial."

Behind them the stairwell door swung shut with a resounding clang.

———————————————

FIVE

———————————————

WHEN THEY CAME to the assistant's desk outside Gamby's office, Peter nearly balked. But years of training had given him the ability to keep moving despite any shocks or sudden upsets. And was he upset to see Miranda sitting there? Was he really all that surprised? No, Peter decided. He was not.

Miranda rose at their approach. She hardly spared a glance for Simeon, choosing instead to focus her defiant stare on Peter. But Peter opted to pretend he was nothing more than a guest, perhaps one unfamiliar with these people and this place. He looked around with all the offhand curiosity of a man on a mere interview. And it was Simeon who spoke.

"Peter Stoller here to see Mr. Gamby."

Miranda finally turned her eyes in Simeon's direction. She gave him a short nod of dismissal, and Simeon made a sharp, smart one-eighty and stalked off the way they'd come, never bothering to take any kind of leave of Peter.

"Still winning everyone over, I see," said Miranda. Peter only stared blandly. With a sigh, Miranda turned and gave a quick tap on the office door then pushed it open before Gamby could even respond. "Mr. Stoller is here."

From over Miranda's shoulder, Peter watched Gamby's expression, but if his assistant's lack of formality bothered or surprised him, Gamby didn't show it. He looked as much like an oversized boulder as ever, even as he stood and motioned Peter in, his eyes still trained on whatever lay in the folder spread open on his desk. But as Peter moved nearer and the door clicked shut behind him, Gamby flipped the file closed and finally looked up to greet his visitor.

Peter sat without being asked, wondering at the singularly uncomfortable wood-and-leather chairs Gamby had selected for his office. With their straight backs and overwrought carving they appeared practically medieval, and felt it too. Still, Peter was slim enough to fit between the unforgiving arms without feeling pinched; he couldn't imagine what some others in the office might do under the circumstances. Not sit, he supposed. And maybe that was the point. Maybe Gamby was not keen to invite company to stay long.

Gamby appeared one step behind when he realized Peter had already settled himself. Peter watched the larger man smooth one meaty hand down his front as he resumed his own seat. Gamby opened his mouth to speak, but Peter held up a finger to stop him then pointed it at the intercom on Gamby's desk. Gamby furrowed his brow at Peter, started again to say something, but then the intercom beeped and Miranda asked, "Do you want anything, Mr. Gamby? Tea?"

Gamby looked the question at Peter and Peter shook his head.

Gamby's massive finger flattened the intercom button. "No thank you, Miranda."

"Send her on an errand," Peter intoned quietly once the Gamby had lifted his finger. Gamby frowned but must have seen something in Peter's expression that prompted him to press the button once more.

"Miranda, I need some pens."

"Sir?"

"Pens. And not these useless things from whatever cabinet or closet you ladies keep. Go down to the stationer and find something that works for God's sake."

There was a long silence of the kind that might make one

wonder whether he's been heard before Miranda answered, "Yes, sir."

"And bring back lunch," Gamby added. "You know what I like and," with a glance at Peter, "I guess you probably know what Mr. Stoller likes as well."

"Yes, sir."

From outside the office door came the sound of a desk drawer opening then closing, the wheels of a chair over carpet. Finally, the tread of feet getting ever farther away.

"Satisfied?" Gamby asked his guest.

"Where is everyone?" Peter countered.

"Rats leaving a ship," said Gamby.

"And Gordon is the captain," Peter deduced.

"He doesn't have to go down," Gamby told him.

Peter was suddenly very aware of the hard and unyielding chair that surrounded him as neatly as any trap. "This is why you need me."

"You're already out…"

"And I suppose there's nothing left of my reputation to lose."

"Not like you're on pension," said Gamby. "Living off your mum's money, aren't you?"

It took effort for Peter to keep his expression neutral.

"You know we know," said Gamby. "Everything. But does *she* know? About…" He spread his meaty fingers wide.

Peter sidestepped the question. "I'm never sure how much you know, Ken. More than I ever did about you, it seems."

Gamby smiled but it failed to light his eyes. He took hold of a picture frame near the edge of his desk and turned it, held it up for Peter to see. A red-haired woman almost as sturdy looking as Gamby had her arms around two boys; Peter guessed them to be anywhere between eight and eleven years old. "My wife and two boys," Gamby said. "Not in town," he added, setting the picture down. "I try to get home on weekends. Except when I have to go haring off after you."

"You could have waited until Monday. Or sent someone else."

"There's no one to trust."

"But you trust me?"

"I trust your loyalty to Gordon, if nothing else," said Gamby.

Again Peter became all too aware of the hardness of the seat beneath him; the leather padding provided no relief. The back of the chair was too high, too straight. There was no way to get comfortable.

"What of Elinor?" Peter asked, though he opted to refrain from adding it was young Mr. Martin who had brought her up.

Gamby shifted in his overstuffed leather chair, though in Peter's mind Gamby himself was plenty enough stuffing. "I'm not cleared to tell you anything about that."

"And yet you're hoping what? That I'll take the blame for whatever it is you won't tell me so Gordon can be let off the gallows?"

Another shift, so that now Gamby was all but squirming.

"I'll see..." Peter began and Gamby leaned forward with anticipation. Peter stopped speaking to eye him, the way a mouse might stop and hold still when it senses a cat ready to pounce. When Gamby made no further moves, Peter started again. "I'll see if I can clear him, *and*," he pronounced loudly and emphatically as Gamby pulled in breath to protest, "if not, we can revisit whether *my* falling on *your* sword would do anyone any good."

Gamby resettled in his seat. "I don't know what you hope to do to help him, if not take the heat," he said. "We've tried everything else. Trevor is leading a band of witch hunters, all of them foaming at the mouth."

"One thing at a time," said Peter. He extracted himself from the chair. "I'll need my office."

Gamby rose as well. "You'll have to ask Gordon for it."

But Peter had turned in anticipation toward the office door, and moments later it opened without so much as a knock, revealing Miranda with three bags in hand: one from the stationer's and two from a deli up the street. "Didn't have enough hands for drinks," she told them.

Peter took a step toward her, thinking to relieve her of some of her burden, but she took a half step away and went around him, setting all the bags on Gamby's desk. "Those are the best pens they have. One blue, one black. I doubt accounting will let you expense them."

Gamby only grunted, then said to Peter, "Will you be needing an assistant while you're here?"

Miranda stopped short.

Peter didn't look at her, was careful to keep his eyes on Gamby. "Give me Simeon Martin."

Gamby's eyebrows went up and he grinned. "Should've guessed you'd want a boy."

Peter ignored the implication, instead peeking with interest into the deli bags on the desk. "This one smells familiar." He picked up the bag and brushed past Miranda. "Thanks for lunch."

His back burned from the daggers Miranda drove into it with her eyes as he left.

———

Peter chose to take the lift this time, even though it was only one floor; there was an element of escape involved, the juvenile feeling of having slipped under the headmaster's awareness. It seemed unlikely Gamby would insist Peter continue to be escorted everywhere—even if he wanted Peter under constant supervision, it was clear the staff requirements would not bear it out—but the moment was a kind of limbo, indeed his entire situation was a purgatory, he was being allowed out of Hell but not into Heaven, not without a good deal of penance first.

Back on six, Peter paused and swung his head toward Gordon's corner but almost immediately dismissed the idea of returning to Sandra. She wouldn't have his key, and her big mouth went both ways; it wouldn't be long before anyone who came into the building would know he was there. Peter's window of opportunity was therefore limited.

He turned instead in the opposite direction and went to his old office, which was locked as expected. The desk outside the door that had once been Miranda's was now clear of all traces of having ever been inhabited, though the old phone still sat on the corner and the wood remained polished because the cleaning crew took pride in its work. Peter set his lunch on the desk and opened first the right drawer then the left, but aside from those strange crumbs of occupancy that all drawers gather, they were empty.

Tilting his head for a look underneath, Peter saw there was a shallow middle drawer of the kind that hangs right above the desk's knee space. He opened it, and there lay the last vestiges of Miranda's service: five plastic pushpins of varying colors, a blue Biro with no cap, a wooden pencil with broken lead, two bent staples, and four paperclips that had surely been left behind because they were no longer shiny.

Well, he didn't need them to be shiny. Selecting a large one, Peter worked quickly, bending it to his requirement. He was at the keyhole of his office door when someone behind him asked, "What are you doing?"

Peter didn't bother to stop, much less turn around. "What does it look like, Mr. Martin? Though maybe I should have you do it, just to check you learned something before they hatched you."

Before Simeon could formulate an answer, the lock offered a tiny click of submission. Peter rose and pushed the door open just a crack, angling himself to prevent Simeon's curiosity getting the better of him. "Get your desk sorted," Peter told him, "and then find out who has the job of keeping track of Charles Toulson."

At these orders, Simeon glanced at the desk and noticed the lunch bag. "Do you want...?"

But Peter had already closed his office door firmly, if quietly, behind him.

Truthfully, it was shameful the office locks were so easy to pick. But then, no one in the building should have had anything to hide. And the Castle itself had always been secure, though Simeon Martin's assignment as gatekeeper suggested things had fallen off significantly. Peter wondered briefly whether Simeon had been sure to find someone to cover the gatekeeper's desk—or worse, whether he'd even thought to unlock the lobby doors—before giving it up as none of his concern.

Peter leaned against the door and surveyed the room. Not having been in his office since before his final business trip some nine months before, he could not immediately pick out all the tiny signs of intrusion, though it came back fast: the bronze lion statue that he normally kept on the second shelf had been moved up one tier, and Peter was sure if he bothered to check the books themselves they would show signs of riffling; dirt had been spilled and leaves shed around the two potted plants on the windowsill, the plants themselves now brown and shriveled, Gordon's moratorium on the office seemingly having extended to the cleaning crew (the thin layer of dust bore this out); pictures hung slightly askew on the walls, and a framed antique map of London remained leaning against the filing cabinet (Peter discovered upon inspection that the hanging wire had come free on one side and no one had bothered to fix it, much less had they bothered to replace the paper backing where it had been ripped away in search of anything that might be hidden); the neatness of the stack of files and papers at the right corner of the desktop, balanced by the matching leather-bound date and address books on the opposite side—Peter was never so tidy.

Leveraging himself away from the door, Peter had not gone two steps into the room before the intercom on the olive green desk phone beeped. "Is this, um...?"

With a sigh, Peter crossed the room and pressed the answering button. "What is it, Mr. Martin?"

But the office door was already opening, with Gerald Kerr filling the doorframe while Simeon made a helpless gesture behind him.

"Gerry," Peter acknowledged warily. Not quite so big as Gamby, and possessing far less hair, Gerry Kerr was probably the best in the nation at his job, which was building security.

"Mr. Lessenby say you could be in here?" Gerry asked.

"Unfortunately he's not in," said Peter. "I wasn't able to ask."

"Then how did you get in?"

Peter could tell from his tone Gerry already knew, and even if he didn't Peter felt the steward should be smart enough to make an educated guess, so Peter didn't bother to answer. If he were in real trouble, Gerry would have turned up with several squires ready to throw him out. Because he was alone, Peter concluded Gerry only meant to make a show.

Indeed, Gerry's lips twisted in a way that suggested he was trying not to smile. "Always were a cool one," he said. "Didn't believe them when they said you'd gone. Then didn't believe them when they said you were back."

Peter wondered who'd said, though he supposed Sandra was a fair place to start. "Gamby asked me in to help with something. I don't expect to be long. Just a few weeks."

Gerry got serious again. "I'll have to clear this with Mr. Lessenby."

"Of course."

"Can't have even emeritus agents wandering loose."

"I understand." Though Peter didn't. His mind was racing. Emeritus? Was that the story Gordon had put out? Explained why Sandra had the idea Peter might come back.

"If you're going to be here, get yourself a badge. A real one," Gerry said, gesturing at the bright yellow Visitor still clipped to Peter's lapel.

"Naturally."

Gerry remained in the doorway, reluctant to leave, and Peter supposed that was his right; the steward's role was to see things in distinct contrast of black against white and to act accordingly, so that being faced with such a grey area left him uncertain and with no right answer to the question Peter's presence posed. Nor could Peter answer the question for him, though the way Gerry looked at him, Peter was sure he was longing for just that. But Peter no longer had the power to give an order, could not tell Gerry to go, no matter how much they both might wish it to be so easy.

And so Peter waited it out, until Gerry nodded as if something sage had been said and took a couple steps back, Simeon only just darting out of the way. "I'll just go see if Mr. Lessenby might be in yet."

"Good idea," Peter told him, then offered a compromise. "I'll make sure Mr. Martin stays with me in the building until we're squared away."

Simeon shot Peter a dark look that clearly conveyed his mistrust, but Gerry appeared much eased by this pronouncement, and his relief made him generous. "It's a formality is all. You always were the best of them; see how they couldn't do without you? Mr. Lessenby must be that pleased to have you back in the Castle."

Peter tried to smile, was surprised to discover it hurt. In the end he succeeded only in lifting one corner of his mouth, the corresponding eye crinkling in simulated gratification, so that the one side of his face became a theatrical mask of comedy. But by then Gerry was already gone.

Simeon stepped into the vacated air of the office doorway. "Alistair Wingfield," he said.

Peter's brow wrinkled, and irritation at not immediately understanding made him sharp. "What?"

"He's the one tasked with coordinating all the information about, you know, your friend."

It took Peter a second longer still to understand what Simeon was trying to tell him, and he wondered at Simeon's seeming desire to be delicate about the matter. "Fast work," he acknowledged, even as he mentally called up all he knew about Alistair.

"I already knew," Simeon said baldly. "But you went into your office and shut the door before I could say anything. Do you want your lunch, by the way?"

Peter frowned slightly at Simeon's off-handed manner, which bordered on insolence. But the dark eyes met his with an openness that belied the suspicion that Simeon had meant anything more than what he'd said; it was the boy's lack of filter, Peter realized, that caused him to come across as disrespectful. One more thing to work on. Christ, where was the Agency finding them these days? And what was it teaching them?

Simeon held up the deli bag as if Peter might require a visual aid to answer the hanging question, and Peter's frown deepened as he shook his head. Time to start the lad's on-the-job education.

"Alistair's an odd choice," mused Peter. "He's an archivist with a background in ciphers." The same job Peter would have had if Gordon had not selected him as heir apparent.

"Didn't he serve in the military?" Simeon asked.

Peter nodded. "And you're to address him as Major Wingfield."

Simeon's eyebrows rose in surprise. "Am I going to talk to him?"

Instead of answering, Peter asked, "Is your desk settled?"

Simeon glanced over his shoulder. "Well, I have that thing," he said, pointing to the telephone and intercom. "All the other assistants seem to have typewriters. Do I need one?"

"Probably. In the off chance I need you to type anything."

Peter's dry tone was lost on Simeon. "Maybe I'll wait and see then," he said.

"If you think you're well enough established," Peter began and was gratified by the alert response in his assistant, the way Simeon drew himself up, squaring his shoulders as his eyes widened slightly in anticipation, "we'll go and see the Major now."

SIX

MAJOR ALISTAIR WINGFIELD WAS A NEAT, sharp-looking man with a tidy steel-colored mustache riding his upper lip, though it did little to compensate for his steady loss of hair. He wore his suit as he would his uniform: smartly and with purpose. Within the paneled walls of his office, the Major ever appeared to be a shining sovereign among pennies, surrounded as he was by papers and dust. The small window behind him added to the feeling; in the mornings it remained grey and lifeless, falling in the shadow of the building across the way, and in the afternoons its brief moment of utility wherein it accessed any kind of outdoor light only emphasized the motes that floated and swirled in the room, making the space feel small and thick with polluted atmosphere.

If the Major minded any of this, he bore it with the stalwart resolve of his rank, just as he tolerated Peter's and Simeon's visit. He answered Peter's knock with a "come in" that sounded as much like an order as an invitation and didn't immediately look up from the work spread across his desk.

"Peter," the Major intoned, though how he knew without lifting his head was a mystery, "I'd heard you were coming back. And who is your friend?"

"My assistant, Mr. Martin."

Simeon shot Peter a look that suggested Peter had just

thrown him to a lion, but Peter ignored it; he was lacing together his remaining patience as he waited for Major Wingfield to continue the interview. After another minute, the Major set his pen aside and graced them with the full force of his clear, grey eyes. They skidded over Peter to Simeon. "Don't make them like they used to, do they?" he said, and Simeon's cheeks blazed red. Peter said nothing.

"Sit down then," said the Major. "I can guess why you're here."

The chairs in the Major's office were decidedly less cramped than Gamby's but not much more comfortable. Peter surmised they did not see much use. The Major had so few visitors, and his work was so solitary, he didn't even require an assistant. Still, the Agency probably would have given him one if he'd asked. But the Major eschewed such signs of status; he knew his own worth and needed nothing and no one to buoy his esteem. Having an assistant would have only given him something else to trouble himself with, cutting into his ability to focus solely on his work.

"I have some concerns about Charles's... integrity," Peter began. Beside him, Simeon gave a little start, but Peter remained still as the Major's grey eyes scoured his face; if Wingfield were looking for the symptom of a falsehood, he would fail to find it. Peter's words had not been a lie.

Satisfied, the Major selected a notepad from the scatterings of his desktop and picked up his pen. "And what causes these concerns?"

But Peter's lips pressed thin, his mouth set in a recalcitrant line.

"You've come here to tell me this but won't give me more?" the Major asked.

"I only want to know if, from your perspective, I have just cause for my suspicions."

There came another long moment of the Major's scrutiny, while in the next chair Simeon began to fidget.

"With me away..." Peter went on.

"Yes, he'll have the opportunity to be more open about his

work. Assuming there is any," said the Major. "But he's no fool, Peter. He'll know we're still watching. In fact, if he has any training he'll know we're looking that much harder now."

Peter's nod conveyed disappointment as much as understanding, his eyes dropping to the carpet.

"I'll keep you apprised should anything significant occur," the Major offered in gruff consolation.

Coy as any girl, Peter looked from under his eyelashes at the severe figure seated before him, and only just prevented himself from smiling. The visit couldn't have gone better if he'd scripted it.

Adopting a tone once reserved for his father, Peter said, "I appreciate it, sir." He rose and Simeon scrambled to follow suit. "We won't take up any more of your valuable time."

Behind the desk, the Major shook off his momentary sentimentality and bent himself back to his papers. "Always were a good man, Peter."

"Thank you, sir." Peter had his hand on the doorknob, Simeon crowded close behind in an unseemly eagerness to depart, when the Major spoke once more.

"It was the German, wasn't it?"

Startled, Peter turned to look at him, but the Major only had eyes for his work. Peter had to clear his throat against a sudden tightness in order to answer. "That was part of it. Yes."

The Major nodded but offered no other commentary, and Peter and Simeon made good their escape.

———

"What just happened?" Simeon asked, working to keep up with Peter's long strides through the corridor. Now and then a head would turn their way from the desks they passed and there would follow a stillness like that of a stunned animal at the sight of Peter Stoller, the rumors made real.

"You shouldn't have to ask," Peter told Simeon. "You should be able to work it out for yourself."

Silence. It lasted long enough that Peter glanced at his

companion, took in the slightly furrowed brow, and had some pity. "I'll give you a hint."

The dark eyes looked up hopefully, hungrily.

"Did you see what was on the Major's desk?"

"Papers?"

"*Think* about it. *Picture* it. Don't just say the first thing that comes into your head."

"But there were papers," Simeon said in defiance. "And a pen. That notepad. His phone. A couple books."

They had arrived at Simeon's desk, Peter's office. Peter waited. Simeon watched him, searching his face for a clue, but Peter's expression remained maddeningly neutral. "The books?" Simeon finally asked.

"You're only guessing."

"But it's the right answer," Simeon concluded, triumph sparking his eyes.

"Guessing will work some of the time, though making an *educated* guess will increase your odds. What made you guess it was the books?"

The light in Simeon dimmed a little. "Because there wasn't anything else."

Peter sighed. "For one thing, the books weren't dusty. Nor were they on the shelves with his others. The top one had been much read, if the condition were anything to go by."

"Maybe he bought it second hand," Simeon suggested.

Peter nodded his approval. "Very good, Mr. Martin. Now you're beginning to think."

"But what was it?" Simeon asked.

"You didn't notice? You should have," Peter said when Simeon gave his head a tiny shake. "Not the kind of thing you might expect to find on the desk of a man busy with ciphers and reports on the movements of potential adversaries. To a good agent, it would stick out like a sore thumb."

Simeon's eyes flashed again, and he flushed; Peter could see he was working to keep his tongue in check. "You'll learn," Peter soothed. "It takes practice, which is what this apprenticeship is meant to give you."

Simeon's anger was instantly replaced with speculation. "Apprenticeship?"

"The book," Peter insisted. "Can you picture it?"

"It was blue..."

Peter once again waited, but nothing more was forthcoming. "And?" he finally prompted.

"It was blue," said Simeon. "That's all I saw of it."

Peter gave up. "It was a copy of Jane Austen's *Persuasion*," he said.

Astonishment crossed Simeon's features. "Really?"

"And beneath it was an equally battered anthology of poems by Byron."

Peter watched as this information resolved itself within Simeon's brain. "The old man's a romantic!"

"So it would appear," said Peter.

"And you used it against him by giving him a sob story about your... friend," Simeon went on.

Even as unpracticed an eye as Simeon's could detect the shuttering of Peter's expression, the eyes growing cold and the body still, a living model of reproof. When Peter spoke, the tone brought to mind water at the bottom of a deep, dark well.

"Mr. Martin," said Peter, "where is my lunch?"

———

The abused deli bag was fragrant enough to declare its contents without Peter having to open it, and he immediately set it aside. He wasn't hungry, he decided, not even for his favorite sandwich from a place he never thought to patronize again. Funny, Peter thought, how the moment something you want becomes readily available it loses its value.

He was debating whether to simply throw the bag away, arguing with himself over the need to take it outside to keep the office from smelling, when the intercom beeped. "Is this...?"

Peter pressed and answered. "Yes, Mr. Martin?"

"Mr. Lessenby is—" Simeon cut short as a low voice interrupted, followed by a light knock at Peter's door. As Gordon entered, Peter dropped the lunch bag into the wastebasket beside his desk and rose to greet his visitor.

And here was Gordon as he'd always known him, so very different from the night before: the suit slightly too big and just wrinkled enough to draw attention, the tie a tad too loose and askew. Peter wondered whether Gordon had given up buying work clothes, being so close to retirement. Perhaps he was making the best of what he already had, unflattering as that wardrobe might be.

"Sorry to interrupt your..." Gordon gestured at the crumpled bag, sole occupant of the trash bin.

"No need to be," Peter assured. He was suddenly, inexplicably nervous, had to swallow against an unbidden knot that had formed in his throat.

"Sit," Gordon told him, taking up one of the two chairs across the desk from Peter. "Oh," he added, and his fingers dipped into his trouser pocket to produce two keys on a thin metal ring. "For your office and your desk." He leaned forward and set them on the edge of the dusty mahogany.

Peter did not reach to take them. Instead, he kept his palms flat on the wood in front of him, not trusting his hands not to tremble should he lift them. "Thank you. I trust Gerry spoke to you?"

Gordon made a noise that Peter took as affirmation. "Your old badge should be locked in your drawer there."

Peter nodded, wondering why Gordon had bothered to come to his office when he could just as easily have called Peter to his. Why had he come to the flat the night before, for that matter? To see Peter, he'd said, but why? What was he looking for?

"Of course, you could just go home," Gordon said, and Peter's wall of curiosities shattered like a stone through a window. "Leave them to it."

"Leave them..." Peter repeated faintly, urging his mind to keep up.

"A deer in the wood," said Gordon. "And if the hunter notices a second deer?"

"He goes for the easier target," said Peter.

"You're an easy target, Peter."

"I know. It's why I'm here. Give you the chance to run."

"Run where?" Gordon asked. "These woods are my home. And they'll always be full of hunters, poachers. They may spare me today, but they'll be back for me tomorrow."

Peter scowled. He couldn't like Gordon's resignation, and he certainly couldn't like Gordon's dismissal of the help Peter was trying to give. "Are you throwing me out?"

Gordon's brows rose as he made his point. "I'm trying to save you, Peter. So you can be a hunter instead of hunted. So you can walk in the open instead of having to hide." Gordon rose to his feet, and Peter saw in the movement that Gordon schooled his body carefully, making each muscle wait its turn so that the overall effect was that of an aged man, slow, struggling. But underneath was all the energy and ability of someone far younger, faster. Smarter.

Gordon caught Peter looking and smiled. "If they think you're already injured, they get sloppy." He turned to go. "You should call Charles, you know," Gordon added without looking back. "It will only look the more suspicious the longer you put it off."

He was gone before Peter could stammer a reply.

————

He stared at the phone a long while before reaching instead for the keys Gordon had left on his desk. Peter's hands were cold, but the keys were colder still, and the metallic clank they made seemed remarkably loud in the otherwise quiet. Using his thumb to separate them in his palm, Peter selected the smaller of the two and unlocked his desk to retrieve his badge, avoiding making eye contact with the photo, his face, and yet also that of another person—someone younger and more assured of his moral high ground, ready to defend it against all comers, to swing first and negotiate later.

The Visitor badge went sliding across the desk, vehemence backing the toss, and coming perilously close to spilling over the edge. But it was with more care that Peter picked up the phone.

What day was it? Peter wondered as he listened to the rings. His eyes fell on the old agenda at the corner of his desk, outdated now by nigh on a year. *Tuesday*, he thought suddenly. Not too many tours on Tuesdays.

"Hello?" Charles sounded breathless, as if having rushed for the telephone. Peter hadn't noticed how many rings there had been. Many, he suspected.

"Hello?" Charles said again, and now he was beginning to sound angry. Peter could picture his frown, the way the skin around Charles's eyes tightened when he was upset.

"Charles," Peter finally said, if only to alleviate his own imagination, but his voice rasped unexpectedly, forcing Peter to clear his throat.

"Peter? Where are you?"

"At work. The office. But I wanted you to know I—"

The office door opened, arresting Peter's train of thought and revealing Simeon looking confused. "Does the light on the phone... Oh."

"Who's that?" Charles asked.

"My assistant," said Peter.

Simeon remained in the doorway, his nose wrinkled. "Smells in here."

"They gave you an assistant?" Charles asked.

"Why don't you make yourself useful, Mr. Martin, and empty this wastebasket," Peter suggested, and Simeon's eyes darkened with mutiny, though he moved to do as told.

"You must not be in much trouble then, if they gave you an assistant," Charles went on.

"This one is every kind of trouble," Peter said as he watched Simeon pick up the offending trash bin. Simeon eyed Peter in return, his expression an odd mix of sullenness and curiosity. Peter made a shooing motion with his hand in attempt to move him along. "But I guess I asked for it," he added with a sigh as the office door finally closed.

"Asked for it?" Charles echoed.

"Well, I chose him. Boy's in want of... something," said Peter.

On the other end the line was ominously silent, and slowly Peter realized he'd said something wrong, though a rapid mental review failed to produce the culprit. "Look," Peter said, "I have a lot to catch up on, I just—"

"I'm sure you do."

"I just wanted you to know I made it in all right. Would have called last night, but..." But nothing, of course. It hadn't been so very late. Peter had spent the evening turning circles in the flat, unable to settle, only working to exhaust himself enough to get any kind of sleep.

"You're very busy," said Charles. "I understand."

But Peter rang off worried that Charles understood something he didn't and afraid of what that might mean.

SEVEN

PETER SLOUCHED BACK to the Agency flat that night and wondered, upon entering, whether he would be expected to find his own lodgings before long. It had become difficult to guess how lengthy his tenure might be—that it would be temporary remained absolute in Peter's mind, but what he'd first assumed would be a matter of weeks now looked like it might be months depending on the turns of events. Not knowing made Peter feel itchy. In fact, the whole setup pricked at him; the longer he stayed, the more worried he became they *would* lock him up after all, haul him down to C&I for show, just to let Gordon off the hook.

And Gordon... Jules had said the breaches went high, had intimated Gordon was part of that. But Gordon showed no sign of wanting Peter in chains. If anything, he seemed to want Peter gone again. Or was Gordon afraid Peter would ferret out the truth? But no, Peter was good, but never as good as Gordon.

Christ, what a mess.

Peter dropped his briefcase on the sofa. It felt good to carry it again, to have something solid in his hand, something that cast him as a man of real work and purpose. Even if it was all show and no substance, Peter could pretend, maybe even make himself believe.

But alone in the flat, the masquerade was suspended. The

empty space was painful; Peter felt his lungs tighten the way they might in exceedingly cold air and knew the ache was caused by the vacuum the flat posed, its silent implication of a long and lonely night. And the likelihood of many more ahead.

He tried to think what he used to do in the time before Charles—*B.C.*, thought Peter abstractedly—and took faltering steps toward the refrigerator with the not entirely fully formed idea of at least having something to eat. Yes, and some wine would be good; if he drank enough of it, he would cease to care about being alone.

Of course, the contents of the icebox had not magically changed in the course of the day, and the only things in it were the components of a sandwich, some canned lemonade, and the stoppered remainder of whatever wine Miranda had tried to give him the night before. Poisoned, for all Peter knew. Might there be an unopened bottle in one of the cupboards? He was checking when the knock came.

It was the kind of staccato rapping in which each knock was sharp and distinct—one, two, three—all knuckle. Peter paused, frowning around the edge of the cabinet door, his pique at being alone evaporating at the arrival of unsolicited company. Not because he was relieved but because, in the contrary way of mankind, having someone suddenly turn up only made Peter want them to go away. And so he stayed still, his eyes watching as the doorknob was tried. But Peter had locked it.

"Peter?" The voice was muffled through the reinforced door but still easy to identify. There came the jangle of keys; Gamby must have given her one, Peter realized, and tasked her with keeping an eye on him.

Peter slammed the cupboard shut and stalked to the door, yanking it open just as Miranda was about to fit the key into the lock.

"Oh," she said, "you *are* here."

"And so are you," said Peter. "Why?" He stayed in the doorway; if she wanted in, she would have to push past him.

Miranda leaned to her right in an unveiled attempt to see around him into the flat. "I... wondered..."

Peter wondered, too, what she might be looking for.

"Have you eaten?" Miranda asked abruptly.

"You came here because you wondered if I've eaten."

She finally looked at him. "I came to ask why you didn't want me back as your assistant."

"Gamby not treating you well?" Peter asked.

Miranda huffed. "This would be easier if there were food involved."

"I didn't realize it was difficult," said Peter, but he stood back finally, holding the door open in unspoken invitation. After a moment's hesitation that Peter was sure was only for show, Miranda stepped inside.

"Settling in?" she asked, and Peter watched her sweep the room with her eyes.

"Want a sandwich?" was his only response. "Seems to be all I have."

"There's a really good Indian place around the corner," Miranda told him, then squinted at him thoughtfully the way one does at something in an aquarium tank at the zoo, as if Peter might be a novel, as-yet-unencountered kind of species. "Do you like Indian food?"

The question felt insulting, though Peter supposed it was more the way she looked at him that bothered him. As if he should have a placard giving his scientific name, his natural habitat, and the details of his existence. Miranda had been his assistant for four years, and Peter had the notion she should know whether he liked Indian, just as she knew he didn't like chardonnay. But aside from occasionally bringing him back a salad or a sandwich for his lunch, or making a reservation for him for dinner at his club, Peter realized he and Miranda had never had cause to discourse on likes or dislikes of the mundane variety. Still, he'd always assumed Miranda's interest in him— and it was an interest he had been very aware of—extended to her knowing all about him. Or that she was at least intelligent enough to pick up all the clues (just as he knew she liked reading biographies and had a weakness for shoes and handbags, though she almost never spent a penny on new clothes).

Well, but what hints had he given her? Peter reasoned that it was unlikely he'd ever come into the office reeking of curry. "Yes," he said. "I like Indian."

Miranda surprised him by dropping her purse and settling onto the sofa. "There's a phone book…"

But Peter gave his head a small shake. The way Miranda's eyes roved the room tweaked something in him; he felt it as acutely as a pinched nerve. "Let's go out," he said.

And no, he was sure he hadn't imagined the fleeting consternation that crossed her features. But she stood and picked up her bag once more, flashed Peter a smile, and preceded him over the threshold, down the stairs, and onto the rapidly darkening streets of London.

———

It was one of those middling restaurants that was too pricey for students but not really nice, either. The tables had white clothes draped over them, but the chairs were plastic with puffy vinyl seats. They served beer but not wine. Peter opted for water.

They were silent as they reviewed the laminated menus, Peter surreptitiously watching the top of Miranda's dark head, split neatly by the vivid white line of her parted hair. All at once he missed Charles with a great, knotting, aching heartsickness that Peter thought—had he had anything in his stomach—might have made him violently, physically ill. As it was, this feeling sat in him like a stone, and he wasn't hungry any more, at least not for anything he could eat.

Miranda finally lifted her head and smiled when she saw he was looking at her. Miranda's smiles usually passed as sincere, even when they weren't, but now Peter detected the strain at the far corners of her lips. Or was it that he'd been away long enough to see her with fresh eyes: the too-thick face powder and layers of lipstick? She fiddled self-consciously with the roll of silverware and he noticed the polish on one of her French-mani-cured nails was chipped.

"So," Miranda said, and Peter watched her eyes dart in his

direction then back to the silverware, "how are things with Charles?"

Hearing his name pushed the stone further up Peter's gullet, and he was forced to take a deep breath before answering, if only to ensure he could speak. "Is that really what you want to talk about?"

He'd surprised her, he could tell from the jerk of her chin, though she was quick to hide it. "I was only trying to be polite."

"And how is... What was his name? Denis?"

Miranda laughed, a bright but not beautiful sound, more like shattering glass than the poetic tinkling of crystal. "I can't believe you remember that!"

"My job is to remember," said Peter.

"You always were so serious," she said.

"Was I? Am I?" Did he know this about himself? Peter wasn't sure. He'd always thought of Charles as the serious one.

"Are you happy?" Miranda asked.

Peter looked at her long and hard enough to be considered rude, trying to read whether she meant the question, and whether his answer would matter to her one way or the other.

"I'm not happy without Charles," he replied. "But I miss the work."

"And you can't have both," Miranda supplied.

Peter didn't answer, and the waiter came to the table to take their orders and whisk away the menus. As Peter sipped at his water and wondered why the restaurant had wine goblets but no wine, Miranda asked the question she'd put to him earlier at the flat, "Why didn't you ask to have me back as your assistant?"

"Easier to take someone unassigned than to poach," Peter told her, and then asked his question again too, "Do you not like Gamby?"

Miranda shrugged with only one shoulder. "He'll never be you."

Peter understood immediately. Miranda wasn't being flirtatious; her ambition was showing. "You mean he'll never be king of the Castle."

"You could have had it, Peter," she told him. "If you'd stayed instead of running off... When you left, it was as good as a confession."

"I didn't confess anything. There was nothing to confess."

"It looked like guilt." Peter watched the shadow pass over her face, doubt becoming resolution as she took a final step. "And then Gamby, too."

"What about Gamby?" Peter asked.

Miranda made a display of reluctance, though Peter knew she was dying to say more, that she would say more without his needing to prod. "After..." She waved a hand that Peter supposed was meant to encompass his and Charles's escape. "Gordon sent Gamby to bring in his wife," she said.

A dart shot through Peter, setting all his nerves on alert. "Gordon thought Elinor had something to do with...?" But with what? Whatever was going on, whatever Jules had hinted at. Whatever had landed Charles in C&I. But was Charles a willing participant? For that matter, what had happened to Jules in all this?

"She ran, just like you." Miranda went on, her tone thick with accusation.

"As good as a confession," murmured Peter, drawing the lines between the dots. "Someone tipped her off." Could Jules have gotten out there that fast? Was Elinor as innocent as he was, or had Peter thrown his lot in with the enemy?

"And do you really think it was Gordon?" Miranda pressed. "That Trevor is right about him, that Gordon circumvented justice in favor of love?"

"The heart leads people to do all manner of strange things," said Peter.

But if Miranda perceived the self-implication in his words, she ignored it. "Gamby went to get Elinor. He was supposed to wait for Milligan to join him but, according to the statement he filed, he had the feeling something was off and decided not to wait any longer. Went in on his own. But Elinor was already gone."

"You're saying he let her go."

Miranda's eyes flashed signals across the table at Peter as the waiter returned with their food and took his time arranging the bowl of rice, the lamb, and yellow curry. When the waiter had made his final bow and left, Peter asked, "And so why isn't he gone then?"

"Because why go after a little fish like Gamby when you can catch Gordon instead?"

Peter waited for Miranda to serve herself, but she only continued to stare at him until he was finally forced to ask, "Aren't you going to eat?" He wondered whether, during gossipy lunches, entire tables of food went untouched by the assistants as they focused on the juicy verbal tidbits instead.

But now Miranda dropped her eyes as if chastised and began to spoon rice onto her plate. "I've never..."

Peter took the rice from her but Miranda did not immediately relinquish her hold on the bowl.

"Should I do it?" she asked.

"Do what?"

She made a gesture at his plate, and Peter surmised she was asking if she should serve him. "It's not tea, Miranda," he told her, gently tugging the rice bowl free.

"Well I've never had a meal with one of my..." She gestured again, this time at him. "So I don't know what I'm supposed to do."

"I'm not your anything now," said Peter.

"Still my superior."

"I'm not so sure," he said. "It's not clear where I rank now; I'm something of a ghost."

"Does it bother you?"

Peter took a bite of lamb to keep from having to answer. He chewed slowly, savoring the flavor; though he and Charles had spent time in India during their travels, there was nothing quite like having it back home in London. *Home...* An image of Charles in the flat in Salzburg flashed through Peter's mind—Charles, seated alone at their little table. Well, but Charles didn't actually much care for Indian food, in India, London, or anywhere else.

Swallowing the bitterness along with the spice, Peter asked,

"So you're saying Trevor is overlooking Gamby's seemingly obvious transgression in order to go after Gordon?"

"Certainly looks that way."

"And Gamby must know this," Peter went on. "He must know what people think about him." Peter was surprised to discover he felt sorry for Gamby. "But if there are two deer in the wood…" Peter murmured.

"What?" Miranda asked.

"What use is it bringing me in, then? If Trevor won't go after so easy a target as Gamby, if he's so set on Gordon, why would he bother with me?" Peter asked.

"Maybe he supposes he'll sweep Gamby up later," said Miranda. "After all, Ken hardly stands between him and the throne."

"I don't either. Not any more."

"I doubt Trevor sees it that way. Haven't you heard what everyone is saying?"

In an industry where one was required to treat rumors as potential fact until proven otherwise, sometimes even having to err on the side of caution by acting on them, gossip could be both a savior and a sin. Peter knew his reappearance would have started the horses out of the gate, but he had no idea what direction they might run.

Miranda snorted at Peter's blank expression. "They're saying Gordon is prepping to install you so he can abdicate before Trevor cuts his throat."

Peter understood then. The game was to redirect the hunter's attention. Peter was wounded, perhaps, but he could still give Trevor a fair chase, giving Gordon enough time to set things right and get away. How long would Gordon need? How long would he, Peter, have to act as decoy? And could he run faster than Trevor could shoot?

"That's easily scuttled," said Peter as he reached for more curry. "Gamby was the one to call me back, not Gordon."

Though Peter was intent on his food, he could feel the concentrated intent of Miranda's gaze. "So it's not true?"

Peter raked her with a disapproving look. "You came looking

for me at my flat because you wanted the upper hand in office gossip?"

Miranda's lips twisted. "I wanted to know you were okay. I'm used to being the one looking after you." The line of her mouth struggled into the semblance of a smile.

"You haven't had to look after me in a long time, Miranda," said Peter. He set his fork down and glanced behind him, and the waiter appeared almost immediately, nodding so hard he bent nearly double when Peter murmured his request for the bill.

"But you're alone now," she said.

Suddenly Peter's body felt heavy. He'd eaten too much. He wanted to crawl back to the flat and sleep.

Something in his face gave him away, he realized, as Miranda began to sputter. "Not forever! I only thought you must miss him and..." Followed by her attempt at sympathy. "Gamby wouldn't let you bring him?"

But Peter wasn't willing to let her build that bridge. "He's not a pet," he spat, and at his shoulder the waiter took three hasty steps backward, staying only close enough to hand Peter the statement at full arm's length. Peter didn't bother to look, simply pulled his card from his wallet and handed it over. "It's not a matter of signing a release and getting permission to keep him," he continued.

"I know. I'm sorry," Miranda said.

"And Gamby did offer," Peter went on, his words gaining speed; it was as if his insides had been ripped open and he was compelled now to spill them, the strength of his accumulated irritation at the way everyone tiptoed around Charles, would hardly speak his name—as if Charles had died, or worse, the relationship had—pushing the words out. "But I'm sure you can understand why Charles might be reluctant to accept Ken's generosity."

Peter realized he was breathing hard, nearly panting, and made himself inhale long and slow; he felt as if he'd just tossed his still-beating heart onto the table, and from Miranda's wide eyes he guessed she thought the same. He wondered how unsightly she found it.

But she surprised him by leaning forward and laying her hand over where his rested on the table. "I'm sorry," she said again, giving each word a careful kind of clarity that Peter supposed was designed to prove she meant them. He slid his hand out from under hers and the waiter returned, edging cautiously toward the table with the slip for Peter to sign.

Peter slid his card back into his wallet and stood, nimbly sidestepping the waiter's new spate of nods and bows, suddenly craving the outdoor air. He stopped just outside the restaurant's doors and drew in deeply as Miranda caught up to him. She threw him a look that was equal parts irritation and concern before lifting her own chin to the sky. It was dark now and they simply stood there on Queensway, staring at the strip of starless blue than ran between the buildings like an overhead river and letting people slip and duck past them on the pavement until Miranda finally asked, "Would you ever go back to girls?"

Peter started walking.

EIGHT

SHE DIDN'T FOLLOW HIM, for which he was grateful. Once safely restored to the flat, he began a thorough examination of everything in it. The wiretaps were back, he discovered; they had probably done that while he was at the office. It was no less than he would have done were he in Gamby's place. The devices would be back tomorrow, then gone for a couple days, then back again once Gamby thought Peter would be too complacent to check.

But were they the reason Miranda had wanted to eat in the flat? So their conversation could be recorded for her boss? But no, why would she want Gamby to hear her confide all the suspicions about Gamby's role in Elinor Lessenby's escape? Or had she gone off script?

Peter turned these questions over in his mind, patiently collecting and disabling the bugs, and all the while trying to discern what in the flat might have been Miranda's goal. The way her eyes had flown all over the room... She'd been looking for something, he was sure of it. The wires? If Gamby had been the one to have them installed, she'd have already known they were there.

Maybe it wasn't a question of what so much as whom. Miranda would know Charles wasn't there. Had she anticipated Gordon might visit the flat?

But no, of course not. Peter sat up from where he'd just pulled a tap free from the underside of his mattress base, and for a moment his train of thought veered slightly off track as he wondered what anyone listening at the agency might hope to hear going on in his bed. It was a terrible place for a bug should anything actually happen on the bed; the mattress itself would muffle anything anyone said and movement would result in loud squeaks, cracks, and groans from the bed frame. Not at all useful. Who on earth were running things these days?

Which brought Peter back to his initial epiphany.

Miranda had been looking for signs of Simeon.

Peter got to his feet and glanced at the bed, unmade from that morning, which would have irritated Charles. Maybe whatever serf Gamby had sent had bugged it because he knew nothing *would* happen obstruct the sound or disturb the microphone, that the bed would be untouched aside from sleep and the mic would work just fine for picking up sounds from anywhere else in the flat. Was this the manifestation of his watchers' assumption of Peter's loyalty to Charles? And if so, should he feel gratified or slighted?

Would you ever go back to girls? Peter shook his head, though whether he was answering the question or dismissing it even he didn't know. He hadn't ever gone for girls in the first place, not outside of the job. But perhaps Miranda was hoping to be an *inside* job.

Exhaustion blotted the growing list of questions from Peter's brain as he redoubled his focus on sweeping the flat. He went so far as to check his suitcase, shaking out the clothes until the neat stacks became a tumbled pile, making sure his gun was there and had not been tampered with, then feeling along the lining for any telltale lumps. He flipped through the pages of the book Charles had given him "for the trip" and checked under the dust jacket to be certain. It was an old library book rescued from the discard bin, a German novel that Peter hadn't bothered to open much less read. Something about the offering annoyed him; Charles should have known he didn't read novels. Especially not ones that ran so long as this one... Maybe Charles had hoped Peter could use it in self-defense if the need arose. Peter tossed it back into his suitcase where it landed on the clothes, teetered, and made a slow descent down the soft mountain.

———

It ended up in Peter's briefcase the next morning—*Ein Kampf um Rom*, so maybe Charles really had meant to be funny—if only to give the bag some weight. The gatekeeper glanced at it, but he'd seen all manner of things going in and out of the building and only asked, "Is this from our library?" Peter pointed out the stamp that ran along the top edge of the book, and the gatekeeper said, "Didn't think so," and dropped the tome back into the briefcase with a thud.

Simeon was at his desk, astoundingly alert and almost vibrating with anticipation. He stood up the moment Peter rounded the corner, was talking before Peter could fish his office key from his pocket.

"The Major, he brought this," Simeon was saying in a rush of breath. Peter paused on the threshold, looked down at the sealed A4 envelope in Simeon's hand. "Told me not to open it. As if I didn't know better."

For a dread moment Peter wasn't sure he wanted it, wasn't sure he wanted to know, but Simeon was all but thrusting it at him as if it might be filled with poison. Which it very well might, though not of the kind Simeon was worried about. With some reluctance, Peter took the envelope between two fingers and his thumb. "Thank you."

A last glance at Simeon's face, the concern in it, before he closed the door told Peter that his young protégé did understand the nature of the Major's toxin after all.

The envelope lay on Peter's desk while he tried to find other, more important things to do, but of course there was nothing else. He was there as a target; no other work would be entrusted to him. Peter thought briefly of Simeon and wondered whether the boy's association with him would taint him; should he let young Mr. Martin go? Back to whatever he'd been doing before?

Like Major Wingfield, Peter did not have any real use for an assistant. But he was hesitant to set Simeon free. In Peter's view, Simeon was a kind of orphaned animal unlikely to survive the wilds of the Agency without shelter, no matter how feeble Peter's protection might be.

With no other prospects—should he stop by and see Gamby? But he really didn't want to—Peter finally slid his finger along the pasted seal of the A4 and slid free the sheets of paper (there were several), a quick scan bringing illumination to what appeared to be terms of an unspoken agreement being brokered by the Major.

The first five pages were details of Charles's activities the day before. A tour, a trip to the market, and apparently a very long conversation with the English bookseller, with a side note that the conversation was in English, though the bookseller spoke it only brokenly; it seemed the man embraced the opportunity to practice whenever Charles stopped by. Much of the dialogue simply consisted of the bookseller, whose name was Diederich Aachen, asking how to pronounce certain authors' names. Herr Aachen evidently found English names equal parts troublesome and amusing, and Peter could picture Charles's patient smile as the man quizzed him over this and that, holding up books and pointing to the covers, asking over and over again, "And this? How do you say this?"

A scan of the remaining log entries released a valve in Peter's heart of which he had not been aware; nothing out of the ordinary for Charles, who had taken his books and groceries home and stayed in. Aside from one phone call—the one from Peter— there had been no others, and Peter was able to continue cherishing his mental image of Charles at home alone, spending his evening curled up with a book.

While you went out with Miranda, Peter reminded himself but quickly pushed the traitorous thought aside. It wasn't so much Miranda, of course. Peter had no interest in her outside his need for information from whichever sources he could draw it. But thinking about Charles being so alone and so isolated, while he'd been out with someone... *anyone...* Peter briskly reminded himself that he'd spent the night alone in his flat just as Charles had done, and without (with a glance at his briefcase) even a good book to read.

The bulk of the pages from the envelope were log entries from previous dates, and each had some query or another written in the margins. Some were as simple as, "Why?" Others were longer: "Who did he mail this to?" next to a note about a letter Charles had dropped in a box and, "Could not trace this call. Do you know?" beside an entry wherein Charles had stepped into a phone booth during their travels to Brazil.

Peter understood then that the Major was offering an exchange, a way of cobbling together a more thorough picture of Charles, his habits and activities. It was exactly what Peter had hoped for, but also the thing he most feared. A tightness crept into this chest and stomach as he considered what it meant to be spying on the man he loved… Did it say more about Charles or about Peter, this lack of trust? Could Peter plead training and instinct? He didn't think so. But he also knew he could not rest easy until he was sure of Charles. And in the meantime, Peter's participation in the surveillance would prove that he had not left out of guilt, though if he was supposed to take the fall for Gordon, perhaps that worked against plan.

At the very least, answering all the Major's queries gave Peter something to do. He had only just begun to wade through them, pausing to try and recall various dates, times and trips, when his intercom beeped. "Um…"

"Yes, Mr. Martin?"

"Mr. Tillholm? Here to see you?"

Peter didn't much like the squeak in Simeon's voice. "Send him—"

The office door opened before Peter could finish, and there stood Trevor Tillholm, natty in a suit almost as dark as his slicked hair. The eyes behind his black-framed glasses were so pale as to be almost clear. But though Trevor usually showed a certain amount of nervous energy, he seemed quite steady as he stood in Peter's doorway.

Peter slid the pages back into the envelope and stood.

"Trevor." He gestured to a chair and noticed how Trevor balked, the way his head jerked back slightly and he rocked just a little on his heels, physical resistance to the implication that Peter maintained the authority to command him to sit. And all at once that steadiness was gone, though Trevor tried to hide its loss behind something meant to pass for a smile.

"Peter," Trevor said, easing into the office and closing the door behind him. "I'd heard you were back. Didn't quite believe it."

"I don't quite believe it myself, though I don't expect to stay long."

Trevor was eyeing the envelope Peter still held, his curiosity evident. "This is what you're working on?"

Peter only smiled. "Won't you sit?"

"I only stopped in to see for myself," said Trevor. "Gordon called you in?"

"Gamby actually." No sense in lying about anything so easily verified.

Trevor's eyebrows went up a tick. "Gamby? What on earth for?"

"I'm sure it will be covered in the next meeting. Are they still on Thursdays? My calendar is sadly out of date."

"It would be, wouldn't it? I should tell you," and here Trevor did sit down, just on the very edge of the chair Gordon had settled into the day before, and hooked one knee over the other, "in case you hadn't noticed, though I'm sure you have, that we're not all in the same building any more. Some of us have been moved closer to, ah, the higher powers."

Peter sat down as well. "Did seem like the building was a tad deserted," he confided with a small frown, "and I get the feeling I'm not being told quite everything... But I'm sure they'll catch me up as we go along."

He could see the thoughts flowing behind Trevor's eyes, and for a moment, the way Trevor started to lean forward, it appeared he might tell Peter something, invite him into a confidence. But then Trevor drew back again. He squared his shoulders and gave a neat nod, then stood, and Peter stood again too, thinking how it was like being in church, the up and down, and maybe he should send up a prayer just to cover all his exits.

"I'm sure you're right. They will," Trevor was saying. He paused at the door, hand on the knob. "And watch it with that boy Gamby's fobbed off on you. Bit of a troublemaker. You'll want to keep him on a tight rein."

"I'd noticed," Peter agreed, schooling his lips to keep from smiling. "Can't even type."

"Should have stolen Miranda back," Trevor said with a sniff. "At least then you'd know what you're working with."

Peter gave an oh-well shrug as Trevor let himself out of the office without bothering to shut the door behind him, watched as he gave Simeon a disapproving frown as he passed. Not to be outdone, Simeon frowned right back until Tillholm was gone from sight. Then Simeon rose and came to lean his head in around the doorjamb. "Must have been important for him to come back here. He doesn't enter this building unless he absolutely has to."

"I'm sure he had other business and simply decided to take the opportunity," said Peter. And when Simeon didn't show any signs of moving, "Bring me some tea, would you? Sugar, no milk. And close the door."

————

Peter exited his office some time after the lunch hour, annotated notes in hand and ready to return to Major Wingfield. It had taken no little time to think back and recall all the incidents the Major had queried (Peter almost wished he'd had one of Charles's scrapbooks for reference), and some Peter had no knowledge of and therefore no answers for. These were few, but the fact they existed at all planted a dark seed in the pit of Peter's abdomen.

He'd been so focused, he'd worked through lunch (and Simeon hadn't thought to remind him, much less ask whether Peter wanted him to bring him anything), and so was planning for a late meal or possibly an early departure altogether. But as he swung open his office door, Peter was greeted with the sight of Miranda perched on the edge of Simeon's desk. She was smiling and chattering at him, her pale legs appearing long in contrast to the decided shortness of her black pencil skirt, her high-heeled feet crossed at the ankles.

Peter's eyes went swiftly to Simeon. How was the boy taking this onslaught of female attention? But Simeon's expression was remarkably blank, almost to the point of stony, his dark eyes hot with what Peter could only classify as dislike.

Miranda was either blind to or ignoring Simeon's lack of enthusiasm as a steady of stream of what Peter supposed was office gossip flowed from her too-red lips, though when Peter emerged she stopped and turned her smile on him. *It's like a lamp,* Peter thought, squinting despite knowing better. And not the warm kind. More like the ones they used in interrogation.

"Did you need something, Miranda?" Peter asked. "Or does Gamby not keep you busy enough?"

She shrugged. "Just trying to be friendly with the new gir... er, boy." And she flashed her teeth again at Simeon, who only continued to stare.

"He's too young for you, Miranda, go away," said Peter.

She slid off the desk. "If he's too young for me, he's definitely too young for you."

Having become the subject of the conversation appeared to jolt Simeon out of whatever loathsome stupor Miranda's lecture had induced in him. "I'm twenty-six!"

But Miranda was already walking away, and she did not slow her stride, merely tossed a look over her shoulder, and whether it was meant for Simeon or Peter to catch neither of them knew.

Peter waited until he heard the lift chime and the doors slide closed before holding out the envelope for Simeon to take. "Hand this off to Major Wingfield. Then you're free to go for the day."

"What are you going to do?"

The alarm in Simeon's voice surprised Peter, and he took a moment to scrutinize his assistant, observing his tense shoulders and worried mouth, so like when Charles said the exact same thing.

"I'm going to lock up and go home as well," Peter finally said, relieving Simeon's suspense. "Unless you know of a reason I should stay?"

Simeon gave a shake of his head. "No. Sir."

Peter glanced in the direction Miranda had gone. "Did she say something to set you off?"

"She said a lot of things," Simeon said, sounding bitter. He stood. "None of it worth anyone's time."

Peter nodded and turned back to his office to collect his briefcase and be done. He had an evening of debugging the flat ahead of him. And maybe he would stop somewhere for take away. How strange to be back within reach of all the places he'd missed only to have their names and locations flee his mind. He was now required to begin building a new list, so that by the time he returned to Salzburg he would have twice as many places to regret leaving.

AFTER NIMBLY MANAGING chopsticks to pick noodles straight from the rapidly warping container, and then scouting out and neutralizing the reinstalled wiretaps, Peter phoned Charles. It felt wrong that the call was merely another on a list of to-dos, and not even the priority; Peter knew he should *want* to talk to Charles, but now that their contact was a part of Peter's overall plan, a cog in the machinery, it took on the metallic taste of a chore.

Peter wondered as they exchanged bland pleasantries whether there was any way to get answers to the Major's questions, which had become Peter's own. *Who did you call in Brazil?* Peter imagined asking, and more importantly, *Why didn't you tell me?*

But instead he found himself only half listening to Charles recount a tour group of school children he'd herded through the Altstadt that morning. "Just happy to get out of regular classes, I imagine," Charles said.

"Mm."

"And you?"

For a moment Peter was confused, his brain still fogged with inattention. "I don't have classes," he said, grasping onto the last thing he could remember hearing.

Charles gave an odd hiccough of laughter. "No, I didn't

suppose you did."

"It's pretty boring, really," Peter told him. "I don't see that my being here has much use."

"So you'll be coming home?"

The hope in Charles's voice squeezed Peter's heart. "As soon as I can. That's always been the plan." A little lie for the record; Peter had no doubt they were being listened to.

"Don't stay any longer than the book I gave you allows for," said Charles.

Peter thought he'd have to be pretty desperate to even *start* reading that tome, much less get all the way through, but he didn't tell that to Charles. He was about to make some innocuous comment about whatever books Charles might be reading when he was startled by a sharp knock on his door.

"What's that?" Charles asked.

"I don't know," Peter admitted. "Hang on." He set the receiver on the table and crossed to the door.

"Mr. Martin," said Peter when faced with a somewhat worse-for-wear Simeon. It had begun raining at some point in the evening by the look of him. "Why are you here?"

"He made me stay," Simeon complained, pulling another A4 envelope—or perhaps it was the same one as before—from the safety of his jacket and thrusting it at Peter's chest. "And then I didn't even know where you lived, so..."

"It couldn't wait?" Peter asked.

"If it could wait, he wouldn't have made me sit there, would he?"

Peter swallowed the immediate consternation that arose at Simeon's tone and strove to remain temperate. "Well, does he need a reply?" When Simeon only offered a blank stare, Peter sighed. "Come in and sit down."

As Simeon sagged onto the sofa, Peter returned to the phone. "I'm sorry, something seems to have come up."

"So I gathered. Your assistant?" The question held the tang of something sour, as if it had been asked through pursed lips.

"Yes..." Peter was distracted by the envelope he held. He

recognized a stray pen mark near the flap; the Major was nothing if not frugal with his resources.

"Do you think...?" Charles began, dragging Peter's thoughts back to the pseudo-conversation they were having. Whatever Charles was about to ask, Peter realized from the way he spoke that it was costing Charles something to voice it.

"What is it, Charles?" Peter asked quietly, gently, all at once sorry for any and every pain he'd ever visited upon this soft, sweet man, for being negligent over the phone, for ever thinking ill of him, suspecting him of wrongdoing.

From the sofa, Simeon watched intently.

Charles cleared his throat and with the tone of someone rallying asked, "How soon can I come over?"

"What, here?" Peter asked, glancing at Simeon. How much of the conversation was the boy able to follow? "I'm not sure it's safe yet—"

"I don't like being apart from you," said Charles. "I don't like not knowing whether you're eating properly, getting enough sleep..."

"I'm fine, Charles. I—"

"Have an assistant for all that, I know. But I'd rather be the one taking care of you."

You and Miranda both, Peter thought. "I can ask Gamby tomorrow." He had the notion there was a puzzle in all this, that if he could just pull together all the pieces he'd have the complete picture.

"Ask Gordon," Charles said.

Peter glanced at the envelope in his hand and wondered how much his answer depended on its contents. Took a deep breath. "Fine. I will."

The line fell silent, Peter itching to end the call but not wanting to be unkind, and Charles obviously reluctant to be finished; Peter felt his hold as keenly as if Charles were standing there, grasping onto him. "You'll call tomorrow?" Charles finally asked.

"Of course," Peter said with relief as the conversation bumped against conclusion. "Goodnight, Charles."

"Goodnight."

Peter set the receiver in the cradle before anything more could be said. He glanced at Simeon, who was unabashedly staring at him. "Have you eaten, Mr. Martin?"

"No."

"You can help yourself to whatever is in the flat if you're hungry," Peter told him as he opened the envelope and skimmed through the contents. At first he wasn't able to understand what he was seeing. There were some grainy photographs he was required to squint at to make sense of, and these were followed by one-sheets describing each person in the photos, their names and known facts. The only person in the photos who did not have a corresponding profile was Charles. And he was in every picture.

———

"I hope it was worth it," said Simeon, and Peter started; he had forgotten the boy was there, and now he was standing at Peter's shoulder and grasping a thick sandwich in his right hand. At a glance Peter guessed Simeon had utilized the last of whatever provisions Miranda had stocked.

"I don't know yet," Peter told him repressively. "Sit down with that before you make a mess."

Simeon shrugged and stepped over to the small table where Peter had eaten earlier that evening while Peter began a closer inspection of the pages. "Tell me about your family, Mr. Martin," he instructed.

"But you're reading."

"I won't have anything for the Major tonight, and even if I did I don't know where he—How did you find me?"

Simeon took a gulping swallow of a large bite of sandwich. "Asked Miranda."

Peter gave a small sigh.

"Don't like her much, do you?" Simeon asked.

"Our personalities conflict," said Peter. He frowned at a grainy black-and-white of Charles standing on a street corner in

Greece. The man he appeared to be talking to had greasy black hair and held a cigarette. The profile said the man was a jeweler but ...

"I don't have any family," said Simeon and Peter stopped to look at him. The boy's eyes burned defiantly, as if challenging Peter to taunt him for this revelation. But Peter merely asked, "None?"

Simeon shrugged as if trying to reduce the fact in consequence. "Both my parents died when I was at uni."

Peter only nodded. Orphans and outcasts were favorite targets of the Agency, people who had nowhere else to go and no one else to turn to. They were so grateful to be given a purpose and makeshift family their loyalty lasted longer.

"No siblings?" Peter queried, his eyes drifting back to the page.

"No. I have an aunt, but..."

Peter nodded again.

"I don't like her much, either," said Simeon.

"Your aunt?"

"Miranda."

Peter looked up again. He wasn't surprised, of course, not after having seen the interaction between Simeon and Miranda earlier that day. But he *was* curious.

"There's something about her... It's not right," Simeon said, a deep and thoughtful frown bisecting his features.

Maybe the boy had some instincts after all.

"It's late, Mr. Martin, and I have a lot of work here," said Peter. "I'll see you in the morning."

———

One, maybe two, and Peter would have been able to believe it was coincidence. He wanted very much to be able to believe that.

But six... Charles had had contact with no fewer than six known operatives during their worldly travels, including one he continued to meet semi-regularly in Salzburg. Not the bookseller, no, but the man who ran the *Laden an der Ecke* where Charles bought his steady supply of pastilles.

There were no notes from Major Wingfield, no written queries; Peter supposed the information spoke for itself. The unasked question was, of course, why? To what purpose? Whose side was Charles—and by extension Peter—on? Though if the Major was sharing such information, it meant he trusted Peter enough, that Peter had passed some kind of test, which had been Peter's goal all along.

Or perhaps it was an implicit threat.

Peter went through the pages again and again and tried to create a reason, aside from the obvious. But nothing held. There was no logic to any of his fabrications, only the deep desire to wash Charles clean of conspiracy, of treason.

The sky was going from dark to light. Peter went to the bed though he was sure he would not be able to sleep, then woke with a jolt some time later as the sun broke through the windows and lit the flat, the caught rays warming the small space like a greenhouse.

What grows here? Peter wondered as he lay within the wreck of sheets. It was beautiful, yes, but it had been born of the dankest decay, its roots nurtured in something foul.

———

"Everyone's been calling." The moment Peter turned the corner, Simeon was out of his chair and talking. "The Major, of course, and then also Mr. Gamby, and Mr. Tillholm, and Mr. Lessenby..."

Peter stopped short of his office door, fingers going still in his pocket where they had been searching for the key. "All of them?"

Simeon nodded. "What was in that envelope?"

Peter thought as he extracted the key, fit it into the lock. The Major... Had he shared this intelligence with anyone? He would have had it a long time, but why sit on it? Someone else knew, but whom? Or really, the question was this: to whom did the Major adhere? Where did his loyalties lie?

The answer seemed obvious in Peter's mind as the office door swung shut behind him. The Major was an old-school man given to romantic fantasies of years gone by. He'd be Gordon's man, through and through. And because Peter was also one of Gordon's men, there was the chance of a kinship, an alliance.

The Major and Gordon first then. Once Peter knew their thoughts, he could better deal with Gamby and Tillholm.

Pulling the envelope from his briefcase, Peter marched for the Major's office, was disconcerted when he got to the door and found Simeon at his elbow. "You should be handling my desk," Peter told him.

"Why? Everyone who's likely to come by has already been."

Peter attempted his sternest expression. "This isn't—"

"Is that you, Stoller?" a voice from inside the office called. "Don't hang around outside the door. Get in here. Oh, and you've brought the other one," the Major said as Simeon followed Peter, adding grudgingly, "Guess it's the only way he'll ever learn.

"What do you make of it, then?" the Major asked as Peter sat down clasping the A4 so mercilessly his thumb created wrinkles like fissures spreading from the point of impact.

"I'm wondering why you sent it. That is, there were no notes that I could find, so..."

"Didn't seem fair for you not to know." The Major eyed Peter carefully. "But maybe you already did."

Peter kept his face blank, his body still, while beside him Simeon stared at him with wide, dark eyes.

"Take note," the Major said, and Simeon swung his gaze in the direction of the man behind the desk. "A good agent knows how to play Mr. Wolf's Dinnertime.

"Gordon assured me you didn't know," Wingfield went on, turning his attention back to Peter. "I suppose you read it all. Every one of them a Soviet contact of some kind, from East Germany and the Republic proper. And that one from Cuba."

"You've forgotten China," said Peter.

"Yes, China. Heard a rumor the boys in Hong Kong had gifted you with a gun when you stopped over, and now you know why."

"They knew?" But even as Peter asked, he realized of course they had to have known. His men would have been recceing the man in question, would have seen Charles with him. The Major's answering expression only confirmed that Peter shouldn't have needed to ask.

"Guess you can appreciate Salzburg, too, now," the Major added.

Peter bit his tongue against the rising tide of irritation within him. He understood the Major felt he was doing him a kindness —if in his brusque and efficient military manner. But the pill was no easier to swallow for having it shoved down his throat.

"I need to speak with Gordon," Peter said suddenly, rising, and a bewildered Simeon did the same, darting looks of concern at his mentor and darker looks at Major Wingfield who sat nodding.

"I've briefed him, of course," said the Major.

"I'd expected as much. Who else, if I may ask?"

The Major reared up like a proud horse. "I only report to one man."

Peter nodded. "Thank you, Major."

"You're a good man, Peter. Would have had them bring you back sooner. Better yet, never let you leave in the first place. Might've saved some trouble all around."

———

Sandra greeted Peter's approach with a smile, though it quickly turned faulty when she noticed Peter's grim expression. "He's been waiting for you, dear," she said as Peter brushed by, Simeon on his heels. But Sandra put out a hand and took Simeon by the arm. At his questioning look she gave her head a shake.

The office door closed with a definitive click as it latched.

———

Peter tossed the envelope onto Gordon's desk. "You told him to give these to me?"

Gordon's basset hound eyes regarded the increasingly worn A4. "No. But I knew he probably would."

"And why didn't you tell me? Months ago, instead of letting me know now how..." Peter ran out of words, turned a tight circle on the industrial rug in front of Gordon's desk.

"Sit down, Peter," Gordon coaxed gently.

Peter stopped and looked at him, this man he'd loved and trusted more than his own father; now everything felt like a deception of some kind. Even the offer to have a seat smacked of trickery.

When it became clear Peter would not sit, at least for the moment, Gordon said, "What would you have had me do? I couldn't have relied on you to run him, not with your personal involvement."

"You thought my ignorance would be my bliss."

"It surprised me when you left," Gordon admitted. "Something I never would have thought you'd do. I knew then that whatever the two of you..." Gordon sighed. "You chose him over us, Peter, plain and simple."

Peter sat then. "Clearly I didn't have all the facts when I made that decision."

"You didn't give us a chance to give you any facts." Gordon used his thumb to pick at a hangnail, all the while eyeing Peter speculatively. After a long moment, he said, "Wingfield said you suspected something might be going on."

"Not until after we'd already... And even then, nothing specific," said Peter. "Nothing I could have brought to you that you could have acted on."

"But you asked the Major whether he had anything more solid."

In the space between his tongue and the roof of his mouth, Peter felt something bitter beginning to form. A sour taste slid down his throat and made his stomach start to turn.

"He's asked..." Peter began, and Gordon's eyebrows went up expectantly. But Peter felt he might suddenly be sick, could feel sweat forming across his brow.

Gordon sat up suddenly and patted the envelope. "These are only the ones we know about. There may yet be more."

Peter fought an overwhelming dizziness, drew a deep breath, and forced himself to speak clearly and evenly, maybe even with purpose and conviction, though to his own ears the words sounded hollow.

"Charles has asked to be allowed to come over and stay with me while I'm here."

Gordon fell back against the padding of his leather chair as if struck by a physical blow. "Seems odd. To come back to the lion's den, as it were."

Peter did not feel enough loyalty to go so far as to explain the plan to slip Charles into the country once Peter had taken over the surveillance duties or at least had the surveillance team on his side in the matter. It was clear now that the lines lay differently than Peter had at first assumed, but he knew better than to admit in this moment that kind of collusion with a suspected enemy. Given that, Gordon would have no choice but to suppose Peter's allegiance was at best divided, and at worst...

"We hadn't been getting along," Peter said. "I couldn't shake the feeling..."

Gordon nodded sympathetically.

"And now I know there was good reason for it," Peter went on, and the acrimony in his voice was no act, though try as he might he could not rid himself of the impression he was wronging Charles more than Charles had wronged him.

"It is difficult to live with someone you can't entirely trust," said Gordon, and Peter's eyes flew to his face, lined and drawn and sad. Of course Gordon understood only too well; his wife Elinor was the reason Gordon was now frowned upon by so many, her treasonous activities having cast a long, cold shadow.

"What motive do you think he might have for wanting to come back?" Gordon's question was a gentle probing, like a doctor testing a sprain.

But no matter which way he turned it in his brain, Peter could not guess at Charles's goal. "He said he wants to be the one taking care of me. He's... frightened for me maybe, or..."

Peter came to a blockade in his thoughts. And all at once Jules's voice was whispering, *It goes high.*

"You believe him?"

"Yes."

"Doesn't trust Gamby?"

Peter shrugged. "Does Gamby know?"

"About this?" Gordon asked, his fingertips brushing the envelope on his desk. "No."

"Trevor?" queried Peter, but Gordon shook his head. "You've played it close," Peter said wonderingly, but Gordon did not offer any explanation.

It goes high.

"We can arrange for Charles to come to London," was all Gordon said. He was watching Peter closely now, and Peter supposed Gordon was looking for some sign of reluctance, if not an outright balk. Despite his deep desire to do just that, Peter could not find any useful excuse to deny Gordon his prize catch, who appeared all too willing to swim right back into the Agency's net.

Peter's mind tossed out the image of Charles in the interrogation room at C&I, unshaven and anxious, and Peter's breath stopped in his throat. His turning stomach stalled and tightened, and he forced himself to swallow for fear if he didn't make whatever was crawling through him go down, it might come up. "You'll meet him at the station," he croaked.

"We don't want to scare him. If he senses danger, he'll run. We'll wait until he's somewhere more isolated..."

"The flat," Peter said as his sickness became more acute.

"It would be the easiest thing," Gordon acknowledged. "You don't have to be there."

"I'm not a child," Peter snapped, his ire rising past his growing horror and beginning to balloon. "You don't have to tell me my beloved pet is being sent to live at a farm."

Gordon's face sagged, and his body followed, the whole of him slumping, dwarfed by his chair. "I realize this is difficult."

"Do you?" Peter challenged. "Tell me, did Gamby let Elinor go, or did you? Could you not stand the thought of her stepping into a trap? Was it *difficult*, Gordon?"

Gordon blinked, the lids moving slowly, and for a moment Peter thought Gordon might not know what he was talking about, even entertained the concern that Gordon might be showing early signs of senility. But then Gordon said, the words drawn out, "There is no evidence Gamby let Elinor go..."

"But there's also no evidence he didn't," Peter finished.

"The only difference between your case and Gamby's was that he chose to stay. *Was*," Gordon reiterated, "until we had this evidence that Charles Toulson..." His fingertips fell on the envelope once more, sliding it slightly back and forth across the slick polish of his desk. "And maybe he'll tell us Gamby was with them all along. We don't know. Hopefully he'll be able to answer any number of our questions."

"And I'm the bait," said Peter numbly.

"You said he asked to come. How do you know you're not merely an excuse? That he doesn't want to come to London to meet yet another contact?"

But Peter did know. Somehow, he did. And yet he had nothing to support such an argument and an envelope filled with evidence to the contrary. "*Ein Kampf um Rom*," he breathed, the words barely a sigh as he rose.

"What?" Gordon asked sharply, and Peter guessed his use of German had startled him. The war was near enough in memory that the language was yet considered unfriendly, even when on the correct side of the Wall.

Now Peter shook his head to show it was nothing, meant nothing. "What should I tell Charles?" he asked.

"Give us two days to get him cleared. Then tell him you'll meet whatever train he comes in on. And Peter," he added as Peter nodded and went for the door, "steer clear of the German. No need to make anyone any more suspicious than they already are."

Peter smiled wanly. "But it's the perfect thing, you see? My speaking German will draw their fire, give you time to run." And he slipped out before Gordon could answer.

____

TEN

____

"WELL?" Simeon asked the moment Peter turned the corner, thus arresting Peter's spiraling misery. Still, it took Peter longer than it should have to focus on his protégé; the young man stood behind his desk chair, obviously too worked up to stay seated.

"What's going on?" Simeon pressed, and his hands tightened reflexively on the chair's padded back.

Peter shook his head, made for his office door. "Nothing." He stopped short on the threshold. "You don't happen to speak German?"

Simeon grimaced. "Not very well. I mean," Simeon went on hastily as Peter's expression sharpened, "we had this neighbor woman when I was... Anyway, she was German, always shouting at me and my friends in German. Mum said she'd been displaced by the war or something. Told me to be nice. And this woman, she liked to bake pies and pasties, so..." Simeon offered a shrug as if this explained something, but in Peter's mind it did not.

"So?" Peter prompted.

Simeon gave him a look that suggested Peter should have been able to form a reasonable conclusion without having to ask. "So I started going to her house."

"To eat pie," Peter said.

"Yeah."

"And you learned German this way?"

Simeon shrugged again. "A little. Her English wasn't very good, and all her books were in German, too."

Peter opened his mouth, even went so far as to draw in a breath to pursue the line of questioning, then expelled the air in one quick huff and gave up, reaching instead for his doorknob.

"Where's your envelope?" Simeon asked as Peter pushed open his door.

Peter realized he'd left it on Gordon's desk. "I don't need it," he decided. It wouldn't do to have it lying around the flat in any case, since Charles would be coming. Though how long Charles would be staying and how much opportunity he would have to poke around was an as-yet unanswered question.

Gordon would give them one night at least, surely? The Major was a romantic, but from experience Peter knew Gordon lacked that sentiment, the way he'd handled the defection of his wife being a primary example. And if he was at all worried that Peter might tip Charles off, let him go... That they would run again...

For a fleeting moment Peter considered going right then to the train station; he could be back across the Channel before anyone knew what was happening, back with Charles, never mind any lingering questions.

"Sir?" Simeon asked. "Are you all right?"

Peter tightened his grip on the doorknob to stop his trembling. "I'm fine, Mr. Martin. And now I need to make a phone call." No sense putting it off. He stepped the rest of the way into his office and allowed the door to swing closed behind him.

Charles's tone over the line mirrored Peter's own solemnity as Peter informed him he would have leave to come to London in two days' time.

"Well, that's good news then..." Charles said, his relief evident in his tone, though Peter still detected apprehension.

Is it? Peter wanted to ask, but he knew if he did it would not only make Charles anxious—and therefore all the more eager to come—but would be thought of by the service (because of course they were listening) as Peter attempting to warn Charles off. They didn't know of Charles's treacherous activities yet, but it would all spill out soon, and every call would be carefully re-examined for signs of Peter's involvement. And yet even as Peter worked to shield himself, his mind spun hopelessly in search of ways to bring Charles under his protection.

But out of his mouth came, dull and resigned, "I'll meet you at the train, once you tell me which one you're on."

"Gordon was the one who said it was okay?" Charles asked.

"Yes." The thought of absconding returned: *Maybe I should go. Pack up in the night and...*

"Is there anything you'd like me to bring you?" Charles asked. "More books?"

And here is where Peter's fragile mechanism broke. "Jesus, Charles, do you really think I have time to read?" His eyes fell on where his briefcase leaned against his desk like something tired, and Peter wondered at how he'd been carrying a book, a German book, in and out of the building day in and day out. But the gatekeeper had hardly raised an eyebrow. Perhaps he'd assumed it was for work.

The phone line had gone silent, the way a room goes silent when someone enters and announces bad news. It was a mournful nothingness.

"I'm sorry," Peter finally managed. "I've..."

"It's all right," said Charles.

But the words did nothing to fill the empty hollow that stretched between them, and as Peter wondered how best to extract himself and ring off, Simeon opened the door and said, "It's Mr. Gamby, sir."

"Takes good care of you, does he?" Charles asked.

Peter shifted in his chair in a vain attempt to make himself comfortable. "Gamby?"

"The assistant."

"He's a bit of a disaster, really," said Peter, and in the doorway Simeon frowned. Peter paused to ask him, "Is he here?" and when Simeon shook his head, "Tell him I'll be right down."

Simeon slinked away but left the office door open.

"I should go," Peter sighed into the receiver, and whether it was resignation or relief even he couldn't tell.

"Two days," said Charles. "Is your number the same?"

"The office number is, yes."

"Will I get to talk to this assistant of yours? Does he answer your line?"

"Unfortunately," answered Peter. "Though almost anything would be better than having to deal with Miranda. Why are you so interested?" Peter asked suddenly. "You've asked about him... Oh, God. You're jealous."

Peter marveled that it has escaped him in previous conversations, was prepared to berate himself on the sagging of his observational skills, but then contented himself with the notion that the prospect of any kind of romantic relationship with Simeon had been so far from his own mind he hadn't come close to guessing it would be anywhere near Charles's.

"Maybe you'd fall in love and find a reason to stay in London," said Charles.

"This is your big worry?" Peter asked, then called, "Mr. Martin!"

Simeon appeared in the doorway once more.

"Am I attractive?"

The young man went instantly pink and his dark eyes looked anywhere but at Peter. "I don't... I mean, for, you know, I'm sure... I have a girlfriend!"

"See there?" Peter said into the receiver, "He finds me revolting. You may go, Mr. Martin."

This time Simeon pulled the door closed behind him.

"He'll have me done for harassment now," said Peter.

But on the other end of the line Charles was making an odd noise; it took Peter several seconds to understand he was laughing. Peter couldn't recall the last time he'd heard Charles laugh. Not since their travels, and even by the end of those Charles had become serious, his lighthearted moments fewer and more forced. "Poor thing," Charles finally managed, and Peter pictured him wiping at his eyes; Charles always cried when he laughed too hard.

"You can apologize to him on my behalf when you call with your train schedule," Peter told him.

"Two days," Charles said again. Then, "Good luck with Gamby. You won't tell him I'm coming?"

"Should I?" But Peter already knew the answer.

"No," said Charles.

"Don't trust him?" Peter asked, thinking of Gordon's earlier question.

"Do you?" Charles countered.

"I won't volunteer any information he doesn't need," said Peter without really answering the question. "But the longer I keep Gamby waiting the more curious he's going to get."

"All right then." Charles's tone was laced with reluctance, and a spike of irritation drove itself through Peter; why did Charles have to be so clingy? It would all be so much easier if he'd loosen his grip.

Yes, Peter told himself grimly, *so much easier to toss him to the wolves if he didn't have such a hold on you.*

Still, he must have said something suitable to end the call because next thing Peter knew, he was setting the receiver back in its cradle. He took a moment to massage his forehead with his fingertips and clear his mind then went for the door. "Call Gamby and tell him I'm on my way," Peter told Simeon as he passed his desk but was halted by Simeon's almost sullen tone.

"Her name is Katy. Katy Shaw. She's a fashion designer. Or wants to be."

Not tracing this new spurt of information to its origin, Peter frowned. "What?"

"My girlfriend."

Peter considered for a moment. "Mr. Martin, you have an almost unnatural need to be free with your personal data."

Simeon flushed. "You're the one who—who..."

Peter raised a hand. "And I apologize." A pause. "And have you known her long?"

The dark eyes sifted Peter's features, trying to discern the trick, the joke, but Peter's face was as blank as ever. "Three months. Almost four."

"Be sure you vet her," Peter told him, turning again for the bank of lifts. "You never know who they may have tossed in your way."

ELEVEN

"TOOK YOU LONG ENOUGH," grumbled Gamby as Peter entered his office. Peter glanced questioningly back at Miranda's vacant desk, and Gamby said, "You always seem to want her gone. You didn't get along?"

"Not as much as she wanted," said Peter as he eased the door closed behind him.

"Girls were always after you," Gamby sniffed, "for all the good it did them. And how's that boy of yours?"

"Learning."

"I'll bet he is," said Gamby, but Peter ignored it. He walked slowly along the wall of the office, taking in the various framed photographs and asked, "What's so important?"

"I didn't say it was important. But I'd heard you're carrying around a big German book?"

Ah, there it was. The gatekeeper had noticed after all, and now Peter at least knew to whom the man answered. "Not as if I have any real work to do," Peter told Gamby, pausing to regard a picture of Gamby and Gordon taken, based on the large red bow over the door behind them, at some holiday party. The photo was grainy and ill lit, and Peter wondered when and where it had been taken.

"Sit down, Stoller, you're making me nervous."

Peter shrugged and crossed swiftly to one of the torturous chairs, folded himself origami-like into its clutches.

"Have you seen Trevor yet?" Gamby asked.

"He came to see me. Doesn't seem to have his sights trained on me yet. Though my assistant mentioned he'd asked for me this morning, so I'll need to find out what that's about."

"Did he call or come by personally?"

"I don't know," Peter admitted. "It's Thursday isn't it? Are meetings still on Thursdays?"

"We don't have them, not like before," said Gamby. "It's a divided court, Gordon holding his own here and Trevor over there. No one knows what anyone is doing any more. I often get the sense we're not doing much of anything."

Peter frowned. "But who took over my field offices? You?"

"I don't run agents, you know that. I'm all watchdog and muscle."

It was a minor distinction considering Gamby did walk the dogs, meaning he decided if and when an agent needed to be watched and set the agents who watched him (hence his surveillance of Peter), but the ultimate answer was Gamby hadn't inherited Peter's position, so Peter let it pass. "Trevor?" he asked.

"He's the diplomatic side, for all his lack of diplomacy. Just last week he was shouting down the Americans over something he felt they'd bungled. We won't keep any friends that way.

"Gordon's doing it himself," Gamby continued. "You saw he didn't replace you. Well, he didn't shift your workload either. He's been cradling it like a baby, waiting for you to come back and pick up where you left off."

"He can't have believed I would," said Peter. Unless Gordon had assumed—maybe even known—that Peter would discover Charles's true allegiance? And had also known Peter would side with the Agency once all was revealed?

For a split second Peter wondered whether Gordon would go so far as to fabricate the evidence against Charles, but no, the photos had seemed real enough. Charles *had* met with all those Red agents.

"What are you thinking?" Gamby asked.

But Peter shook his head and stood, glad to be released from the confines of the carved wood and unforgiving leather. He only just stopped short of stretching and yawning. He would need to be sure he had time to quiz Charles before Gordon or his men came to collect him. No guessing or talking around it; Peter would need to be direct, however uncomfortable it made Charles. Or him.

"You going to see Trevor?" Gamby pressed.

"I'll ring him," said Peter, glancing at his watch. He'd missed lunch again. "I don't fancy going over there if I can avoid it."

"Don't blame you," said Gamby. "I'll just warn you, I'm going to let him know about the book. Get him curious enough to start following you. Pull him off Gordon a bit until we can get Gordon into fighting shape."

Peter thought again of how fit Gordon had appeared that first night in his flat, and the show of age Gordon seemed to put on for the office. Had Gamby noticed the difference? Or did he, like so many others, assume Gordon was wearing himself down?

"Thanks for the warning," Peter said. "But I don't know how you're planning to help Gordon. So far he seems uninterested in doing anything to save himself. If you could convince him to retire..."

"He won't until he's sure the Castle is secure."

"The Castle is falling down around his ears. There's nothing left to secure. If Trevor is the new direction of things, we won't be autonomous for much longer. They're going to absorb us into some other office, maybe break us apart and hand us out like candy to whomever's been behaving."

Gamby scowled. "That's what we have to stop from happening."

"Do you think you can?" Peter asked, his eyes drifting back to the wall of old photographs.

"If we prove our worth..."

"They'll only work harder to claim us for their own," Peter finished. "If we were quiet and didn't cost them anything, they'd gladly forget we exist."

"Not with Trevor whispering in their ears," said Gamby, and Peter turned to him, his gaze so piercing Gamby shifted uncomfortably in his chair, moving slightly to his right as if to evade it.

"There's your answer then," said Peter simply. "You'll have to shut him up."

———

Simeon was conspicuously absent when Peter returned to his office, but Peter's annoyance dissolved when he discovered a sandwich and still-hot tea waiting for him on his desk. Perhaps Miranda had given Simeon some advice on the care and feeding of his boss.

Peter took his time with his lunch, in no hurry to deal with Trevor. He even took an extra minute to stick his head out after eating to check whether Simeon had returned. He hadn't.

Time to draw their fire. Resigned to the task at hand, Peter returned to his desk and dialed Trevor. "Oh! Mr. Stoller!" yelped the girl who answered the line. She sounded shrill and oddly nasal over the line, and Peter wondered whether it was the connection or if she really spoke that way.

"He's gone out to a meeting," she said. "Shall I have him call you?"

"Only if he wants to."

Peter had only just rung off when there came a tapping on his door. It opened before he could answer. Peter had expected Simeon, froze when he saw it was Miranda instead. He watched narrowly as she grinned and slipped into the room, acting for all the world like someone getting away with something.

"I wasn't sure you were in," she said as she eased the door closed behind her in a deliberate way that proved a desire to be discreet. "What with..." She jerked her head back toward the door, and Peter gathered she was referring to his absentee assistant.

"And you weren't at your desk earlier, either," he replied, his tone dismissing any possible condemnation of Simeon Miranda might have been hinting at, even as he eyed the glossy black handbag that hung from her shoulder. Had she only just come back from wherever Gamby had sent her? "Why are you here now?"

"I heard you have a book."

It was a business built on keeping secrets, but Peter had long ago learned that, internally at least, information circulated quickly and widely when passing through unofficial channels. It took somewhat longer for it to wend its way through the approved irrigation system.

"What of it?" he asked now.

"It's German?" Miranda asked.

"An old library book. Charles thought I'd enjoy having something to read during my trip."

"And have you? Enjoyed it?"

Peter frowned at her strangely mincing progress across the carpet; she walked not in her usual, purposeful way, but as if on a tightrope: slowly and carefully, one hand on her purse as if to keep her from swinging off balance.

"I haven't even looked at it," Peter told her, and was surprised when Miranda stopped and nipped at her lip, the picture of indecision.

"But you've been bringing it in and out of the building," she said.

Of course, if Gamby knew, Miranda would know too. "Yes," Peter said. "Keeps my briefcase from feeling too light. What's this about, Miranda? I've already chatted with Gamby about it."

He observed her eyes drift down to where his briefcase leaned against his desk, the faded and overworn spine of the book only visible as a sliver nested in the leather. "Can you read German?" he asked.

Miranda gave her head a tiny shake, but Peter read it not so much as an answer to his question as her seeming to negate some unspoken thought. She was talking to herself in her head, perhaps arguing with herself over something. And then, as she came to a conclusion, her eyes trailed back to him.

Peter watched one of her hands—the one with the chipped polish—clench and unclench over her handbag and knew. He was up and coming around the desk before she had the gun entirely free of the fabric.

"Take it," he told her. "I don't know what you think it will tell you, but..."

It was a Browning, Peter noted as he took her hand and the weapon in both of his. He had expected she might release her hold on the gun, relinquish it to him, but instead she gripped it more firmly, a small, sad smile on her face. "I signed it out from upstairs," she said of the gun.

"Miranda..."

He tried to at least turn her aim away, gentle her arm downward, but she stiffened her muscles and made her hold rigid. "I always did like you, Peter."

"You can have the book," he told her. Something inside him knotted as his mind made an unwanted connection. "You were working with him all along."

"It wasn't personal," said Miranda. "You were just a job. When it became clear you weren't... That is, when we figured out I wasn't your type..."

"You threw Charles in my path instead." Peter gave a sharp laugh, though it was far from delighted. "And now you say it wasn't personal." His fingers tightened over her hand and the gun, and in response her finger tightened on the trigger.

But Brownings, Peter knew, had heavy pulls. And Miranda didn't seem to have much experience. As she was forced to adjust her grip in order to get enough leverage, Peter released his hold, stepped back and turned away, bending toward his briefcase in search of the book and whatever message Miranda seemed to believe it contained.

Loud, Peter thought when the shot pushed him forward, as if to help him reach his goal. *Stupid girl didn't bother to sign out a suppressor.*

And it was the last thought he had for some time.

———

Later, when they asked him why he hadn't disarmed her, Peter would be forced to admit he was sure Miranda hadn't wanted to shoot him; he'd trusted if he handed over the book, she would leave. In the end he was simply lucky he'd moved and she wasn't a better shot.

It was Simeon, naturally, who turned up and pulled Peter out of his grey stupor by jostling him, all the while saying, "Oh no," and, "I'm going to be in so much trouble."

Peter did not much like being moved and started to say so, but realizing he had a limited amount of time and energy concluded it was more important to convey what he knew. "Miranda," he said, the name coming out as a sigh. "Book."

"Just... wait," Simeon said, half clambering over where Peter lay to reach the telephone on the desk.

Peter tried to say it louder, more clearly. "Miranda. Book."

Receiver to his ear, Simeon turned to Peter and nodded to show he'd heard, but Peter was not convinced the boy understood. And then Simeon turned away and was babbling into the phone.

Peter stared at the ceiling and wondered how long he'd been lying there, bleeding into the low pile of the rug. The blankness above him began to swim, and Peter's eyelids grew heavy.

"I'm sorry, Mr. Stoller," Simeon said, reappearing at Peter's side, and his voice seemed too loud somehow. Peter wished the boy would go away and leave him alone. Let someone who knew how to handle things...

And then Simeon was pushing him over onto his right side. "I have to put you like this to slow your bleeding out. Can you hear me?"

This last was said close to Peter's ear, and if Peter had had the strength and proper angle, he would gladly have swatted the boy.

"You said it was Miranda?" Simeon went on, filling the silence with his breathless chatter, as if the faster he talked the faster help would arrive. Clammy hands pulled at the bracelet of Peter's wristwatch, catching some of the hairs on Peter's arm as Simeon hunted for a pulse. "Something about a book?"

But Peter couldn't answer. The dam of numbness had been

broken and pain was beginning to trickle free, originating at the wound in his side. Every intake of breath now came with an increase of radiating ache, fingers of burning agony poking through and reaching out to the rest of his body. Peter decided he would gladly give up all his blood if that meant the hurting would stop.

The world in front of his eyes—the corner of his desk, his crumpled briefcase upon which he'd evidently landed—gave way to tendrils of creeping fog. Peter's throat burned, and his chest seemed to vibrate with each hammer of his heart, though the beats seemed to be slowing, like a wound clock unspooling to stopping. Oh, but it was doing its best, his heart. It was giving all its strength to each pound, despite being utterly broken.

And beside him Simeon continued to talk, the words faltering then becoming rapid and insistent, though Peter could no longer make any sense of them. He felt as if cotton had been crammed into his ears, all the sound around him muffled by his heartbeat.

Peter hadn't realized he was cold until the warmth at his back moved. Hands were on him, rough and gentle at the same time, working his suit jacket off of him, prodding at the place where the bullet had struck. Peter thought he saw Gordon in the doorway, hands stuffed in his pockets and the usual sad and sober expression on his face, Simeon hunched beside him as the response team did its work. But then blankets were on him, and he was lifted, and the world tilted and went black once more.

TWELVE

HE AWOKE with all the urgency engendered by the knowledge of impending danger, jerking into consciousness as though sleep had been a struggle, an enemy to be thwarted. There was something important that needed to be said or done, someone who needed to be caught.

But before Peter could make sense of his surroundings, a face leaned over his, peering with eyes made puffy by lack of sleep. He was unshaven, looked even more sloppy and disheveled than was typical, and Peter twitched at the sight of him. "Gordon." His voice nothing but husk.

Gordon nodded as though satisfied. A nurse swished into the room, the sweetness of her angelic features belied by a flinty nature. With an aristocratic wave of one hand, Gordon was forced back from Peter's bedside so the nurse could perform her duties. "Awake are you?" she asked, though Peter had to wonder how she knew; she hardly looked at him. Her eyes went from the chart she'd taken off his bed to the numbers on the various pieces of equipment that surrounded him and back again. "Try not to move around too much or you'll pull your sutures. Are you in any pain?" And now, finally, her gaze lifted to regard him just long enough to see Peter shake his head. "No need to be brave about it," she said. "If you start to hurt, let me know." And she hung the chart on the bed and stalked out.

"Best possible care," said Gordon, and Peter turned his head to see Gordon perched in a frayed armchair, the kind of castoff found in the lesser flats held by the Agency. Gordon leaned forward, his elbows resting on his knees and fingers interlocked; only his fidgeting thumbs gave any indication of the energy or agitation held in his frame. When he caught Peter's eye, however, he lifted a brow and gave a half smile.

"Did you catch her?" Peter asked. Gordon responded by turning to the small table that stood between his chair and a clump of equipment, taking up a pitcher and cup that rested there, and pouring out some water.

"Can you sit up enough to drink?"

Gordon was slow to remove his hand from the cup, and for a moment Peter thought he meant to hold it for him like one does with a small child. But then Peter felt the full weight of the water shift into his hand and suddenly he had to work to keep from dropping it as Gordon let go. Peter's hand trembled, making it difficult to swallow as the water splashed around the edges of his lips, until at last Gordon reached over to steady the cup once more.

"We have not found her. Yet," Gordon said when Peter had his fill. He returned the cup to the table and resumed his seat. "But we know she hasn't left the country."

"The book," Peter said. "Charles was using it to get a message to her."

Gordon sighed heavily. "Peter..."

"They put her right under my nose," Peter rushed on. "And when she didn't take, they threw Charles at me..." Peter's throat tightened, threatening to close on him. "You have him at least," he finished and became aware he was shaking again. "Has he...?" But Peter wasn't sure what he wanted to ask or whether he wanted to know more than he already did.

"Peter," Gordon said again, "I'm sorry."

The shaking became so pronounced Peter wasn't sure whether he might be convulsing; he could only manage to stare at the faded blanket that covered him, watching as the shocks shot through his legs. He gritted his teeth against them and a second later they subsided.

"I should have paid better attention," Peter said. "It was a classic trap."

"You're a good agent, Peter," said Gordon. "And you did exactly what you were supposed to do, right up until the moment you dropped us for him."

Peter's neck felt oddly weighted; he couldn't seem to lift his head, felt forced to stare into a middle distance, the scarred Lino blurring before his eyes.

"You'd be proud of young Mr. Martin," Gordon continued. "He did a fine job of collecting Charles from the station this morning."

Peter spared a brief moment to wonder how that meeting must have gone before asking, "And what has Charles told you? About the book, the message?" He almost couldn't hear his own voice over the thrumming that had begun in his ears. It was as though he were standing beside an ocean with the tide rolling in, and everything sounded dull and distant by comparison.

"The book was meant for me."

Peter wasn't sure he'd heard correctly. He tried to lift his head to look at Gordon squarely but his head would only jerk as if caught by some invisible rein until finally Peter gave up and his chin swung to his chest, his head bobbing like a flower too heavy for its stalk. He pressed his palms to his eyes and let his fingers find purchase in his hair. "Jules was right," he breathed. "It goes right to the top." But somehow this new betrayal felt blunt; Peter could not absorb any more shock.

"Jules?" Gordon asked, his tone sharp with surprise. "What's he got to do with anything?

"I couldn't trust Gamby," Gordon continued. "I wasn't sure he hadn't let Elinor go. So when Gamby came to you, I began to worry. I shouldn't have doubted you, of course. But when you took off like that..."

And now Peter was shaking his head; this new information made no sense to him. "I don't... I can't..."

The warmth and weight of Gordon's hand on his shoulder startled him and he flinched.

"It's too much," Gordon said. "I'm sorry. You should rest and we can debrief you later."

Peter's gaze found Gordon's wrinkled suit sleeve and tracked its way up to the long, lined face. His eyes met Gordon's, the latter's red-rimmed and clouded with moisture. "No," said Peter. "Do it now."

"It can wait."

"Explain it, Gordon!" The quaking was embedded in anger now, enough that Peter felt he might shake into pieces even as Gordon's hand pressed down as if to still him.

"This isn't the place," Gordon told him. "And you have other visitors waiting."

Peter's eyes immediately darted to where the door stood open for visiting hours, but the threshold remained vacant.

"Mr. Martin has been very worried," Gordon said, moving now for the door. He leaned out into the hallway and motioned with his hand, and like a genie Simeon materialized shortly thereafter looking sheepish and uncomfortable.

"I don't like hospitals," Simeon said with an apologetic grimace as he slinked toward the bed, hands jammed into his pockets as if trying to avoid any contact with his surroundings. "But you're awake now at least."

"I'm sure you've been keeping vigil over my lifeless form," Peter remarked dryly.

"Well, if you were lifeless you'd be—" Simeon began but broke off when Gordon frowned in his direction. One of Simeon's hands escaped its pocket to rub uncertainly at the back of his neck. "Office is full of flowers."

"Where were you?" asked Peter.

"You told me to be sure about Katy."

It took Peter a moment to recall. "Your girlfriend."

"I was trying to figure out if she was..." Simeon glanced at Gordon. "Legit."

"And how were you planning to determine that?" Peter asked.

The outer edges of Simeon's ears began to redden. "I went to her flat." He looked from Peter to Gordon and back again.

"And?" Peter prompted.

Simeon's gaze dropped to his shoes. "She broke up with me."

Peter supposed there was more to the story but decided to let it lie. For someone who often readily volunteered information, Simeon was being decidedly guarded about this particular incident, and Peter guessed the hurt might be a bit too fresh to explore. Nor was it relevant. "I'm sorry to hear that," Peter remarked, if only to have something to say and bring an end to the subject.

But Simeon's head whipped up. "You ought to be! Just because you don't trust your own—"

"Mr. Martin," Gordon said, his voice low and warning.

"I never would have, if not for him! It's no way to go about having any kind of relationship, is it? Always worried about whether or not this or that person is lying, or hiding something, or..."

"It's part of the job," Peter said stonily. "You see what happens when you let someone or something slip through." He gestured at his hospital gown, in the vague direction of the wound in his side.

Simeon snorted and looked away, over his shoulder at the open door. "You can't live your life that way is all. You'll end up alone."

Gordon nodded solemnly. "It is a lonely lifestyle in many ways. Not right for everyone."

Simeon's face went white, his expression stricken. "I don't... I'm not saying ..."

"I know you're not," Gordon soothed. "It's an adjustment. Peter will see you through it."

The pronouncement startled Peter out of a grey study. The full force of his situation swam forward into his consciousness. Charles was in custody, extracted from Peter's life like a parasite. And Gordon? Peter darted a look askance at his boss. Despite all Simeon's protests, Peter no longer knew who to trust, could not help but question the allegiances of everyone around him. What was true?

"What did happen to Jules?" Peter asked.

Gordon regarded Peter for a moment, then looked to Simeon. "Visiting hours are ending, and you're so antsy it's starting to make even me nervous. Go on outside and wait by the car. We'll let you rest," he added to Peter as Simeon swiftly disappeared. "The doctors want to hold you for at least two weeks, but we'll see if we can't convince them to release you a little sooner. If you rest enough now," Gordon went on, holding up a hand to halt the visible protest surfacing in Peter, "we'll have a better case for your discharge."

Peter's eyes scanned the bare room. It was clear he wasn't going to get an answer to his question, not just yet.

Gordon grunted with some kind of understanding. "Place was like a greenhouse. Hospital made us take them all out. Which is why your office is now a jungle. You have a lot of friends, Peter." He puffed out a short breath. "Should I bring you something to read?"

"*Ein Kampf um Rom?*" Peter asked, unable to keep the bitterness from his tone.

"Charles is here now and able to answer for himself," said Gordon. "We no longer need the book. Gamby is clear and so are you."

Peter tried to wrap his mind around the fact that Charles's downfall was his salvation but was at a loss as to how to feel about it. Grateful? Relieved? He felt neither. Like Simeon's, his wound was too fresh and painful to probe, and Peter shied mentally just as he might have recoiled from someone poking at an open injury.

Gordon read Peter's lack of response as exhaustion. "You're in no condition for this just now, and I shouldn't leave Mr. Martin too long. I'll have the nurse bring a magazine if you like."

But Peter shook his head and lay back down. Suddenly all he wanted was sleep, the only way to turn off his brain and escape the weight that seemed to have been thrown over him like a blanket. He closed his eyes and sensed rather than heard

Gordon's hesitation. A minute or two passed before Gordon's steps sounded, slow and growing ever fainter as they departed Peter's bedside and left the room.

Peter waited a few minutes longer, but sleep refused his invitation. With his eyes closed Peter's thoughts were only that much louder and denser, as if packed into the darkness behind his lids. In the hopes of releasing the cerebral clamor and relieving the pressure, he opened his eyes and looked for something—anything—on which to focus. But the room was bare and uninteresting; there was not even a television.

Best possible care, Peter thought, *for someone serving Her Majesty's Government and living off the taxpayers*. He closed his eyes again. And fell into water, warm and relaxing as a bath. It closed over him like an acceptance, and he drifted lazily through the broken light, sinking slowly until commotion sounded from around him, dragging him back toward the surface.

"He's spiking a fever," someone was saying, and Peter was shocked with cold as his blankets were torn away.

"Infection?"

"I dunno. But his heart rate's high and his respiration is down."

The waters of Peter's peace became roughened as hands clawed at him, attempting to pull him from the comfort of the waves. He tried to shake them off, tell them to leave him alone, but the creatures (he could not see them, was too dazzled by the brilliance of the light) were viciously insistent.

"He's fighting it," one of them said.

Peter broke loose and dove down, eluding capture, and every time he sensed the nets he moved again, deeper and farther out to sea, until they finally gave up the chase.

———

The ocean was peaceful. Peter floated just beneath the surface, where the light could still find him. He let the water push-pull him and did not resist. It was a game it played with itself, this tug of war, and Peter was the rope. But the currents were gentle and temperate, and he did not mind being their plaything.

He went on that way for some time until a burning began deep in this chest and throat. Even still he strove to remain as he was, until another burst of noise and activity exploded around him, and Peter found himself swamped by the turbulence, which threatened to plunge him to the depths even as he was becoming increasingly aware of his need for air. Once more he fought, this time to rise, and when he finally struggled through to the surface he discovered there was no sign of land, no shore to swim toward.

Peter battled panic. He turned a circle and saw nothing but sea on every side, and now something in the water seemed to be wrapping itself around his feet, his ankles, ready to pull him back under. Peter kicked at it, thinking he should swim, but which way?

And then he heard someone speaking. Whether the words were for him he wasn't sure, couldn't hear them distinctly, but they meant someone was nearby. Peter turned another circle, looking for a boat, a raft, even someone just treading water, but what he spied was the end of a long pier. Kicking off the last attempts of the water to hold him, Peter swam in the direction of the splintered and weathered platform, using all his strength to cut through the increasingly tumultuous swells.

There was no ladder, and it was a fair distance from water to wood. Peter could make out the shadows of people on the pier, could hear their murmurings. And then one voice came clear: "Nurse! Nurse, he's..."

"Charles," Peter realized.

Charles's face appeared over the edge of the pier, followed by his hand, which he extended down into the open air, inviting Peter to take hold.

Peter reached up, stretched to close the gap. All at once he was so tired he didn't think he could hold himself up over the waves much longer. His fingertips brushed Charles's. Once, twice, and Peter was ready to collapse, to give up, but Charles leaned farther out and grasped him, hand then forearm, hauling him up out of the clutches of the rising surf.

―――――

Words spoken low and rapid like prayer filled Peter's left ear; he turned his head toward the sound but was not ready yet to open his eyes. He lay there, trying to assimilate the world around him: the soft hiss of machinery, the pillow lumped behind his head, the nostril-searing smell of antiseptic. And a hand over his, large, and too warm, and familiar.

"Not like you to be religious, Charles." But Peter's tongue was stuck in the bed of his mouth, dry and sticky, and his words tripped forward as nothing more than inarticulate mumbles.

Beside the bed an intake of breath, and the hand over Peter's tightened. "I'm here," then, "Nurse! He just tried to speak!"

Peter lifted his lids a fraction and a nurse entered his line of sight, forcing Charles to shift backward in the chair he'd pulled to the bedside, though the hand remained clamped to Peter's own. "You kept everyone on their toes, did you, Mr. Stoller?" the nurse piped, her voice cheerful and squeaky like new rubber soles on waxed flooring. She bent to peer at him and filled Peter's vision. Not as pretty as the last nurse but kinder; Peter supposed beautiful people were more able to be unkind than plain ones. "There you are," she said with a satisfied smile.

"Went for a swim," Peter told her, or thought he did, but he wasn't sure whether the words were working.

"Mm-hm," the nurse replied as if he'd made perfect sense, but Peter could tell by her tone that he hadn't. It was the same tone adults used with children talking nonsense. "I'm going to bring the doctor in for a look at you. Sit tight."

She moved off and Charles appeared in the space she'd vacated, eyes wide and blue and warmer than the sea Peter had just escaped. "Peter?" Charles was frowning, and Peter understood Charles wasn't sure how aware Peter was just yet. Peter moved the hand under Charles's to show his comprehension and attempted to work his tongue free for clear speech.

Charles saw the way Peter's mouth moved and asked, "Thirsty? Can you drink?" He turned right then left in search of water, all the while remaining tethered to Peter with his one hand. The standard pitcher and cup stood on a side table, and it was with obvious reluctance that Charles released Peter's hand so as to pour the water and insert a straw.

"Ah! That's progress," came a voice outside Peter's field of sight; Charles, the cup and straw were the limits of his world at that moment and all he really wanted or needed. The water felt good in his mouth and throat though schooling his lips around the straw took more effort than he would have liked.

The doctor and nurse approached and Charles withdrew with the water, and Peter lay back once more as a penlight filled first one eye then the other. "Very good," said the doctor. "Do you know who and where you are?"

Peter scowled. "Peter Stoller. In hospital for a gunshot wound."

The doctor nodded approvingly, light glaring from the lenses of his square spectacles each time he drew his chin up. "A little slurred," he said over his shoulder to the nurse, "but that's normal. Better than average, really. He doesn't appear to be confused at all, which is a good sign."

Peter caught a glimpse of Charles's dogged, hopeful expression, of the large hands with its squared nails now gripping the cup of water like an altar boy ready to present it at the appropriate moment. "When can I go home?" Peter asked, though as he voiced the question an arrow struck through him, a reminder that he had no real home now. He looked at Charles again and wondered how it was they'd let him come to keep vigil. Gordon was kind, but was he *that* kind? Had Charles made some kind of deal?

"It will be a while yet, I'm afraid," the doctor said. "We need to be sure you don't relapse." He turned away and began giving instructions to the nurse on what to put in various drip bags, how much of this and that Peter should be given. He left without any additional word to Peter, and the nurse went about her work while Peter and Charles stared at one another, the nurse crossing their shared gaze now and again to accomplish her tasks. When she finished, she smilingly eased Peter's bed into a semi-recline, told him to press the call button if he needed anything. Then she was gone.

Long, terrible silence. Finally, Charles held out the cup of water, a kind of offering, but when Peter tried to lift his arms to accept it, they trembled with the exertion. Charles pulled his chair closer and held the cup, even going so far as to turn the straw to the proper angle, and Peter drank until there was almost nothing left.

"More?" Charles asked. Peter shook his head.

Charles drew back to return the cup to the table, and Peter felt a terrible mixture of loss and relief at not having him so close. "They let you..." Peter began.

"I'm not being held, Peter," Charles told him.

"You made a deal."

"Not... Not like you think. Oh, Peter," and now one of Charles's hands moved to cover his eyes, a gesture Peter recognized as something Charles did when he was about to cry. "Would it make any difference if I swore I love you?"

Of course you love me, Peter wanted to say but checked himself with the realization that, despite his concerns about Charles's loyalties to queen and country, he'd never questioned that Charles loved him.

"You surprised us when you broke me out," Charles went on, the hand dropping to hang limp over the arm of the chair. And yet still Charles would not meet Peter's eyes. "Ah, God, this is for Gordon to explain. In debriefing."

"I want you to explain it. Now."

Charles continued to stare off into a corner of the room for some moments. "Gordon," he began hesitantly, the words drawn out as if being extracted from a mental fog, "getting close to retirement, and of course he'd been setting you up to move into his place."

"Common knowledge," said Peter.

"But Gordon had also become aware of a hole, and he had to be sure..." Charles shifted in the chair and at last brought his blue eyes to Peter's. "He didn't doubt you, Peter, not really. But he had to be sure it wasn't you, and he also had to protect you if they—whoever they were—were moving on you. You're a valuable asset," Charles offered with a small smile that lifted only one side of his mouth.

"He didn't know it was Elinor," Peter concluded.

"No. But he'd locked himself up, and he wasn't going to be in the loop after he retired anyway, so you were the best option, an obvious target."

"Lucky me."

"Lucky me, I should say," said Charles. "Gordon inserted me to test your strengths, so to speak."

"But it was Elinor who invited you to the party," said Peter.

"And Gordon who made sure she needed a cab for the day."

For a moment Peter thought he might be having a seizure, then realized he wasn't shaking; it was his world that seemed to quake around him, his very understanding of the people around him and his relationships with them. A chasm had broken open at his feet, separating Peter from his worldview and leaving the truth as a gaping hole to be negotiated.

"But then..." said Peter, but his train of thought braked stubbornly and refused to go further.

The nurse returned bearing a tray of something muddy that she said was stew. "Eat slowly," she told Peter as she trundled the table over and poured fresh water. "Small bites. And chew thoroughly." She looked to Charles. "Staying the night again, Mr. Toulson?"

But Charles ambled to his feet in the slow, stiff manner of someone who had not much moved in many hours, or perhaps days. "No, I should go tell it on the mountain..." He paused long enough to stab Peter with a beseeching look; Peter turned his attention to his bowl.

"Been here for days," the nurse told Peter once the shuffling sound of Charles's steps had fallen away. She leaned to arrange Peter's pillow as an aid in his sitting up to eat. "Must be a good friend."

"Drew the short straw more like," said Peter. He tried to lift his hand for the spoon but his arm was too weak from lack of use. He glowered at it as if doing so might frighten it into behaving.

"Need some help with that?" She drew over the chair Charles had evacuated and began to feed him like a mothering bird, tiny spoonsful of the beefy broth. "Got to get your strength up."

She chattered on in that vein, and Peter ignored her, his mind twisting with questions and new input. Had they found Miranda? What had been in the book? And why hadn't Charles just *told* him instead of hiding information for Gordon?

Oh, but they hadn't been sure he wasn't working with Gamby, and hadn't been sure Gamby wasn't working with Elinor... The pieces were creating a picture, blurry but starting to come into focus now. Peter found himself irritated that Gordon —and Charles?—had ever considered he might be a turncoat. But then was forced to grudgingly admit he'd have done the same in Gordon's position. Well, hadn't Gordon mentored him after all? And as for Charles...

Peter's head came up so abruptly the stew-laden spoon the nurse was holding was knocked aside and she gave a chirp of surprise. "He's clear," said Peter, "and I'm clear. So that's all right then, isn't it?"

The nurse was daubing at the spots on the blanket where stew had spattered. "I guess so. Are you done eating?" The kindness she'd thus far shown was beginning to sound strained.

Peter wasn't listening. He had the nagging notion that the fact both he and Charles were on the right side of things should be the only thing that mattered, but he could not shake the bitter taste of the apple that had fallen from his personal tree of knowledge—that, at the beginning at least, he'd been nothing so much as a job for Charles.

And of course it meant Gordon had known all along how best to engage Peter's interest and affection, a fact that rankled more than Peter would have expected. Never mind the hurt of having been doubted, or needing to have been tested.

"I'll resign," he decided aloud.

"That's a funny way to put it," the nurse told him as she

began gathering up the remains of his meal. "I'll leave the water here for you." She maneuvered the table so that it rested beside the bed, the straw of the cup as near to the right height as could be managed so that all Peter would have to do to drink would be to lean forward. He nodded his thanks and she swished away.

"Wait," Peter said as she neared the door, and the nurse turned. "I don't want any more visitors."

"Sir?" And from the way she frowned and her brow furrowed, Peter knew she thought she must misunderstand. So he spelled it out.

"No one. Except hospital staff. In my room. Until I'm discharged."

"That could be days, even a week or more!"

"I'll get better faster if I'm not bothered," Peter told her. He even almost believed it, though he knew that he *would* be bothered, if only in his own mind. When still she hesitated, he added impatiently, "There's no rule that says I *must* allow people to see me."

"No..." Her eyes drifted toward the chair where Charles had sat for who knew how many hours or days.

Peter resolutely refused to follow her gaze.

"If that's what you want..." She was leaving it open for him to change his mind, possibly willing him to change it.

He didn't.

———

For the following six days, Peter he mulled his options. Resigning, upon reflection, seemed hasty, but an extended leave did not.

He would go home.

Or, rather, he would go back to where he'd come from, the house he'd lived in as a child before being bundled off to school, and where his mother still reigned. His father had passed the previous summer, and Peter's exile had precluded his attending the funeral, though he felt it unlikely he would have gone even if he'd been able. Indeed, Peter had not been "home" in almost four years, and only twice since his brother's death, stays that had been perfunctory and mostly chilled by the silence extended by all parties involved.

But Peter needed an escape. And after years of escaping his childhood, he now found it a refuge from his present confusion.

The hospital could keep Gordon, Charles, and the others out of Peter's room but could not stop them from being there once Peter was released. But it was Gamby Peter found waiting at the kerb, standing outside his illegally parked Jaguar, idly tossing and catching the keys with one hand. Peter wasn't sure whether he was relieved or disappointed.

"Where to?" Gamby asked. "Not the Castle, I'm guessing. Where'd you get the togs?"

It occurred to Peter he had no idea where the clothes had come from, though he recognized them as his. But certainly not the ones he'd come in with. "Someone must have left them with the staff," said Peter as he went around to the passenger side and climbed in.

"Why the embargo?" asked Gamby once they were moving. "You didn't say where we were going."

"Are my things still at the flat in Bayswater?"

"Far as I know." Gamby directed the car into traffic, muscling his way through in the same way Peter had seen him push his way through people. Gamby had turned intimidation and bullying into an art on every canvas.

"I'm taking a leave," said Peter.

"Nothing like a gunshot wound to make you want to put your affairs in order," Gamby acknowledged.

"Just need time to think."

"Six days alone in a hospital room not do it for you?" A pause. "Why *did* you shut them all out?"

Peter wondered at Gamby's excluding himself but didn't query it aloud. "Why did they send you to fetch me?" Peter countered.

"Toulson wanted to come, of course. Cabbie and all that," Gamby sniffed. "Gordon thought it might be better if he didn't."

Peter was aware Gamby was watching him from the corner of

his eye, looking for a reaction, a tell, but Peter was determined not to give him any. But somewhere inside him, Peter was conscious of a tiny warmth—pleasure in this testimony that Charles had wanted to be there.

"You know he's an agent?" Gamby pressed.

Peter kept his eyes on the windscreen. "I do now."

"You're angry they lied to you."

Angry? Was he? After six days of stirring the information in the pot of his mind, Peter still wasn't sure how he felt. He had moments of anger, and more of disappointment, and a few of depression; taken collectively, the jumble of emotions summed a kind of grey void, as if Peter's heart were now a wasteland.

"You should at least give them the chance to explain it all," said Gamby.

"They can debrief me after my leave," Peter told him.

Gamby was pulling the car to the kerb in front of the building that housed the Agency flat. "Doesn't make much sense if you ask me," he said. "Letting it hang over you while you're off wherever."

Peter threw wide the car door and got out without answering. Gamby, he noted, stayed put.

———

He had no key, but suspected he might not need one if they'd known he was being discharged, and indeed the knob turned when Peter tested it.

He eased open the door prepared for a full ambush but all he found was Charles on the sofa with a book open on his lap and a bag of crisps at his side. Charles lifted his head when Peter entered, his brilliant eyes wide and searching, and whatever he saw in Peter's expression caused his cheeks to redden as he dropped his gaze back to whatever he was reading.

Peter gave the sofa a wide berth and went for the area where the bed stood behind the divider. He found his suitcase standing sentry in the corner, placed it on the bed, and opened it. He was momentarily stymied by its emptiness but did not want to ask

Charles where his things were. So instead he took a moment to consider what Charles was most likely to have done, and then went to the small bureau and began opening drawers until, yes, he found his clothes neatly folded and waiting for him.

"What are you doing?"

Charles's voice came from so close Peter gave a start, socks avalanching from his fingertips. "Packing," Peter answered, pleased with how flat and solid his own voice sounded compared to the wavering note in Charles's words.

"Gordon says we can stay until we find somewhere else," said Charles.

Peter made the mistake of looking at him then, meeting Charles's slightly panicked visage. Peter was suddenly reminded of the horse his brother Phillip had been riding the day he died, the way it had rolled its eyes and flared its nostrils, had pawed the air in vain as it crushed Phillip beneath its bulk. The school's groundskeeper had been sent for a gun to put the beast out of its misery, but for Phillip it had already been too late.

And now, here on Charles's face Peter witnessed a terror similar to that horse's. What bullet would work to end his suffering?

Peter was surprised at the way his chest constricted and recalled the way the groundskeeper had cried after shooting the horse. At the time Peter had thought the man was wasting his grief, since Phillip was certainly the greater loss. But looking at Charles, Peter understood the sorrow the groundskeeper had felt. Peter had ended his share of lives in his line of work, but to end someone's happiness and leave them breathing was something else entirely.

Drawing in a deep, slow breath, Peter forced his voice to remain steady when he spoke, guiding each word with his tongue the way he would aid a shaky person in walking. "I'm taking a leave from the Agency."

The blue eyes crawled over his features. "A leave. For how long?"

"Open-ended."

"You've spoken to Gordon already?" Charles asked.

"No. But I don't think he'll deny me." Peter detected a thread of defiance in his own tone.

"And where are you... Or shouldn't I ask?"

Peter's dropped the pile of clothing he'd been clutching into the yawning suitcase. "Derbyshire, to see my mother."

Silence, of the kind that comes to people when in mourning, stretched between them, and again Peter thought of the horse and the groundskeeper, of Phillip and the ringing quiet that had followed the gunshot. He peered at Charles through his lashes, saw that Charles's gaze was on the floor, was surprised when a drop fell from Charles's chin to the rug. A tear.

"Are you so angry," Charles asked quietly, "that you'd rather be someplace you hate than here with me?"

A hot hand squeezed Peter's heart. "When?" he asked, because in a flash of comprehension it became clear to him what the real question was, what he most needed to know. "When did it stop being work and start being love?"

Charles blinked up at him, not bothering to hide or wipe the flow from his eyes. "That night. That first night. I almost didn't go to your flat. Do you remember? I almost told Gordon I wouldn't, *couldn't* do it... Oh, Peter, I fell in love with you the moment I saw you."

Peter's eyebrows lowered and he looked hard at Charles, trying to discern if his words were true.

"And then you were kind," Charles went on, his words surging now; Peter saw the quick in and out of his chest as he took fast, shallow breaths to fuel his speech. "It would have been easy if you'd been an arsehole, but you did everything perfectly— "

"Fell for your trick, you mean," said Peter.

"The *operation* went *smoothly*," Charles said. "You'd have wanted the same if the job had been yours."

Peter couldn't refute it.

"And then you went on that trip, and I began dreading your return, much as I wanted it, knowing you would come back and we'd spring you, close the trap on Elinor, and I would be extracted from the whole business. From you." Charles sucked in a shuddering breath.

Conception cascaded through Peter's brain. A hole in the Agency's information flow, so of course Gordon started at the top to be sure it wasn't his right hand. "I passed," he said.

"We'd usually spend at least half a year, but after two months we were sure enough of you," said Charles.

"You've done this before," Peter realized.

"It's what I do," Charles told him. "Help vet the knights."

Peter rubbed his eyes, turned back to the bureau to finish collecting his things. "I have to go."

"Peter..."

What had been a neatly stacked pile of shirts went sailing into the gaping mouth of the suitcase. "I gave it all up, Charles! For you, for a lie!"

"Love isn't a lie," Charles said quietly. "And I gave up something, too."

"Oh? What? Your next assignment?"

Charles shook his head. "When it was learned Elinor had flown... We still didn't know who the hole was. Looked like Gamby, but..."

"They didn't find Elinor, either," said Peter.

"It was one of the things I was working on," Charles said. "The network, following the strands of information..."

"Why didn't you tell me?" Peter asked.

Charles grimaced, and for a moment Peter thought he was physically in pain. And maybe he was. "I would have, even against orders, but I knew... I thought, at least..."

"I'd take it badly," Peter finished for him.

Charles gave one short bob of his chin, a decisive nod. "You'd be angry, regret having chosen me, having ever been with me." Charles's gaze drifted to the open suitcase spilling with clothes, and the implication was clear—Charles's fears were being actively realized.

"I didn't know I was so predictable," said Peter sourly.

"Stable," Charles corrected. "Sturdy."

"Loyal," Peter added, and there was a sharpness in his tone that pushed his point home. "Trustworthy."

"The longer we went on, the guiltier I felt, and the worse it would have been to tell you," Charles said. "And if the orders had been yours…" He let the unspoken conclusion hang between them, that if Peter had been ordered to keep something from Charles, he would have done so. Yet knowing he'd have done the same only made Peter feel shoddier somehow.

"And then Gamby turned up and I really didn't know what to think!" Charles continued. "Because he was the best guess at having let Elinor go. So why was he tapping you?"

"And yet you hid a message for Gordon in my book," said Peter. "I might've found it, you know, and figured it out."

Charles's lips twisted into a half smile, though the shimmering in his eyes suggested there were yet more tears in the wings. "I half hoped you would, actually. But I had a strong suspicion you wouldn't even open the book, much less find the message in it."

"Predictable again," Peter muttered, but he suddenly understood Gordon's visit that first night. Gordon had come to try and ascertain whether Peter was a traitor after all, and possibly in search of anything Charles might have sent… Miranda, too, had come looking for what she believed Peter had in his possession —a clue, if she didn't know exactly what to look for—but Peter had been carrying it around with him, none the wiser. "You could have just phoned him," said Peter.

But Charles shook his head. "Not with the way they've been watching him, and not with the way the other side has been watching me. Coming back here has blown me, of course, but I already found out what I needed to know."

"That Miranda was the leak."

"That, and where Elinor is," said Charles.

This declaration surprised Peter enough that he rocked back on his heels a bit and felt the hard wood of the bureau at his back. "Where?" he demanded.

"You asked why I chose Salzburg."

Peter stared hard at Charles and inside him something began to break apart the way assaulted soil crumbles into the ocean when it can no longer resist the elements beating at it. The impact of realizing he didn't really know Charles, might never really have known Charles... He'd been so secure once, in their relationship; in Peter's mind Charles had been as steady and unchanging and predictable as he now accused Peter of being. Peter had thought himself the clever one, but Charles had flipped the mirror.

Turning back to the bureau, Peter grabbed the last of his clothes and hurled them into his luggage. He found his gun in the bottom of the drawer and tossed it in as well. "I don't suppose you have my briefcase somewhere?"

Charles blinked at him, then turned jerkily left then right. "I... It's..."

Something else occurred to Peter. "Oh, for God's sake, are we wired?"

Charles had ducked more fully behind the dividing screen to extract the battered leather bag from where it had been tucked beside the bed. He held it out to Peter with obvious reluctance, and Peter snatched it from his fingers. The briefcase was light. Empty. Peter tossed it in with his clothes.

"We're not wired," Charles said, his voice low and heavy.

"Shall I check?" His vicious tone alarmed even him, and Charles flinched visibly, but Peter felt powerless to stop the sudden flow of renewed anger that now flooded his veins. He expended the rush of adrenaline by cutting his way through the flat, turning over the dining table, the chairs, while Charles watched wide-eyed and paralyzed. When Peter started to take apart the telephone, Charles finally moved. He crossed to where Peter was fumbling with the receiver and placed his hand over one of Peter's.

"Peter. Stop."

Peter dropped the phone and stepped back, shaking the hand Charles had touched the way he might had he been burned. The receiver dangled from the table and swung like a man at the gallows.

"I don't know you," Peter said, his voice vibrating with the excess energy pulsing through him; the entirety of his tall, thin frame was shaking.

A shade of bewilderment passed over Charles's features. "Of course you—"

"I thought I did but I don't. It's all been... And maybe I never..." The enormity of it was crowding Peter's ability to think. He needed to move, took the long way around the sofa to avoid having to pass Charles as he went for his suitcase.

Charles turned where he stood but did not attempt to stop him. Only watched as Peter tidied the clothes enough to make sure they didn't get caught in the closure before snapping the luggage shut.

"I'd call Gordon, but the phone appears to be broken," Peter said as he made for the door. "Do me a favor and send him a book."

———

Peter wasn't sure whether to be surprised that Gamby was still there, but he was glad of it. When Peter emerged from the building with his suitcase, Gamby climbed out of the car and went to open the boot. "Guess that's settled," Gamby remarked as Peter dropped in the luggage.

Was it? Peter wondered, suddenly terrified it was, that something had just ended—that *he* had ended it—without his realizing. He looked up at the windows of the flat. The glare of daylight made it impossible to see whether anyone was there. *Anyone,* Peter scoffed at his own thought. There was only one person who mattered.

"Forget something?" Gamby asked, hand on the boot cover and poised to shut it.

Drawn from his musings, Peter shook his head. "No, I..." Then changed his mind. "I might have."

"Take your time," sighed Gamby as he slammed shut the boot and leaned against the car to wait.

Peter sucked in deep, steadying breaths as he climbed the stairs a second time; his side was beginning to twinge from the movement after having been bedridden so long. He half expected Charles to have locked the door behind him, but the knob was loose when Peter tried it. Peter opened the door a crack and saw Charles had righted the furniture and was now kneeling on the carpet screwing the telephone receiver back together. He looked up and froze when he saw Peter. Peter could see all the muscles in Charles's back and neck knit themselves together more tightly; in his hands, the phone trembled slightly as the blue eyes, their wetness and red rims making them all the more vibrant, settled on Peter with some apprehension... And maybe, Peter thought, a tiny bit of hope?

Peter stepped more fully into the flat but remained on the threshold, hand on the knob, ready for a quick exit should this not go the way he hoped.

"Come with me," he said.

That same look of bewilderment, perhaps disbelief, came to Charles's features. "What?"

"To Derbyshire. I don't want to go alone. Come with me."

Charles released the phone and slowly stood. "But you..." Charles began to look around the flat as if he'd never seen it before. "You were so... I thought you'd gone. For good."

This confused Peter. "Do you want me to go?" he asked. It was an honest question. Had he misread something? But no, Charles's tear-streaked visage said otherwise.

"No!"

Charles advanced on him so quickly, Peter's instinct was to shrink back, but then Charles had his arms around him, was kissing him, though it took a moment for Peter to regroup enough to return the affection.

"Ah, God, Peter," Charles said with a happy sigh. And when he only continued to stand there with his arms around Peter, his head tucked up under Peter's chin, Peter answered rather stupidly, "You can meet my mum."

"I'd like that." Peter felt Charles's arms slide free and was instantly sorry; it was like losing a life preserver while floating in a vast ocean. "Just give me a minute to pack."

———

"More baggage," Gamby said when Peter returned, this time with Charles and his luggage in tow. Gamby dropped his half-smoked cigarette, crushed it under his toe, and went to open the boot once more. "Where to then?"

"St Pancras," Peter told him. He opened the back door of the car and held it for Charles then slid in behind.

Gamby took up his spot behind the wheel. "How long will you be gone?"

"Tell Gordon we'll be back in a month," said Peter. He glanced at Charles who was watching out the window as the streets passed and tried to imagine what his mother was likely to say or do when confronted with such indisputable evidence. The specter of those silent meals rose up like mist before Peter's eyes. "At most," he added.

"Best get back before Trevor moves into your office," Gamby warned.

Charles turned his head from the view and stared at the back of Gamby's thick neck. "Then drive faster."

ST. PETER ASCENDS

YEARS LATER TREVOR TILLHOLM would tell people he was the one to affect the succession, but Ken Gamby had been there and his story was somewhat different. Gamby's account stated Tillholm was on the brink of putting his own name forward when Gamby himself cut in with, "Peter Stoller is the natural choice, I would think," earning him a furious glare from Tillholm down the table.

But even before Tillholm could begin to break apart this new wall—and it was clear enough from his agitation he intended to —a Ministry man named Tarlington said, "Peter Stoller? I went to school with..." and Tillholm shut up as the wind began to change direction.

———

"What are you doing here?"

"I could ask the same of you. In fact, I'm certain I have more rights to the question." Peter stood, hand wrapped around the sturdy wood of the front door, too stunned to ask in his visitor.

Jules glanced over his shoulder like a man hunted. Well, and it was a feeling he knew well, Peter supposed. Was it habit, then, or was Jules honestly concerned about something? Still, the gesture brought Peter back to himself, and he stepped back to allow Jules inside.

"Nice place," said Jules, glancing at the impressively high ceilings. The house was an old stone behemoth Peter's mother referred to as a "cottage" and she'd redone the interior to suit her love of luxury. The heavy fabrics, dark wood, and slate flooring made the entry hall cave-like and stuffy, in Peter's opinion, and after a little more than two weeks he was almost ready to return to the Agency flat under the eaves, tiny though it was.

"This is where you come from?" Jules asked.

Peter led him to a lounge at the right of the entry. "How did you find me? Did Gordon send you?"

Jules flashed a smile that crumbled into a grimace as he threw himself into an overstuffed armchair upholstered in red and gold brocade. He looked well enough at home, Peter thought, what with his turtleneck and pressed trousers. Mum would love having him as a decoration.

"Gordon is actually the reason I'm here," said Jules.

Peter remained standing, too agitated at this unexpected visit to sit. He thought fleetingly of Charles out in the garden with a book and, boring as that was, had a sudden wish to join him. "Gordon *did* send you," Peter said, wishing to move the conversation along.

"I'm sure he would have, if anyone knew where he was," said Jules, his smile now thin and bitter.

Something spidery and frantic began to crawl in Peter's stomach, aiming up his throat. He swallowed it back and attempted to keep his voice level. "What do you mean?" And when Jules only stared at him, "Well then, who's looking for him? What's being done?"

The dark eyes sparked defiance. "I told you it went high. Yet you came back anyway, right into their fold."

Peter shook his head. "It wasn't... Maybe Frankfurt, I don't know what happened there, but not... It wasn't like you thought, Jules, they—" But Peter had not been fully debriefed, had left before that could be done, nor was he sure what Jules was cleared to know.

"Your friend is here, isn't he?" Jules asked.

Peter continued to shake his head, not to deny it, but to show it didn't matter, that whatever Jules was intimating, it wasn't true.

"And he's one of Gordon's," Jules went on. He leaned forward in the chair. "They *knew* you'd break him out. You were the perfect scapegoat, and running made you look guilty as hell."

"No," said Peter. "In fact, Gordon put the word out that I'd left of my own accord. That way the door was open for me to return."

"When he needed you to take his place at the guillotine."

Peter ran one hand across his forehead as if attempting to streamline his thoughts. "He didn't want that. Gamby did, but..."

Jules rose. "I should go. With Gordon gone they'll be asking you to serve as interim."

"Interim..." Peter echoed, his hand rubbing more frantically, urging his thoughts into sense. By the time he gave it up as fruitless, Jules was a ghost.

———

The air in the car was stuffy, despite the fact Peter had partially opened his window, and smelled of warm vinyl. Peter suppressed a cough, and Charles shot him an indecipherable look before going back to concentrating on the road with a fierceness Peter was unused to seeing in him. Charles had insisted on driving, of course, despite never having actually been a cabbie. Time and again Peter shifted his shoulders, resettled in his seat, sighing occasionally at the passing countryside.

"Tell me again what he said," said Charles, and Peter wondered whether Charles was looking for something specific in the story or just trying to keep up conversation.

"That no one knows where Gordon is. And that they'll want me to act as interim." Peter kept the rest of Jules's suspicions to himself. At best, he was preventing Jules from looking like a mental case. At worst... Well, but Peter didn't really believe it. Jules simply didn't have access to all the facts.

"Did Gamby send him then?" Charles asked.

"I don't know. He didn't say."

"Seems like the kind of thing Gamby would have come on his own for, is all," murmured Charles. Peter couldn't disagree, but he wasn't much interested in pursuing this circular dialogue either; nothing useful would come of it until they were back in London.

A new thought occurred to Peter. "Did you vet him? Jules, I mean."

Charles pursed his lips. "No. He wasn't one of mine."

Something stone-like settled in Peter's stomach, daring him to ask which of the knights *were* Charles's. But Peter was wise enough to realize he didn't really want to know.

"He came in rather backwards," Charles went on. "Or so I understand."

"They caught him stealing," said Peter. "That's all I know about it."

"Must've been some job to get the Agency's attention."

"He's good, no question."

Charles's hands tightened on the steering wheel. "He went out of his way to help you."

"To help *us*," Peter corrected. It would have been the time to relate Jules's fears, but Peter's tongue refused to loosen on the subject. All he said was, "Apparently Jules was operating under the same set of facts as me."

"But you know better now," said Charles quietly.

Peter didn't answer.

They dropped their luggage at the flat, and Peter left Charles there to unpack and restock the refrigerator while he returned the hire (Peter's mother having refused to let them use one of her cars, as if they were rambunctious teens liable to wreck it). Then he went straight on to the Castle.

"Good, you're here. Saves me the trouble of fetching you," said Gamby without preamble when Peter knocked at his office door. The desk outside remained vacant.

"No new assistant?" Peter inquired.

Gamby sniffed. "Everything's frozen up. With Gordon gone—I assume that's why you're here? Who told you?" He gestured to a chair, indicating Peter should sit.

"Jules Maier. And I'd rather not," Peter added. "They're terrible chairs, Gamby. Anyone ever tell you that?"

Gamby chuckled. "So they are. You have a dinner jacket, I hope? Man at the Ministry is champing to meet with you. Said he went to school with you? Just a formality; the job is all but yours. You should have seen the look on Tillholm's face—"

"What man?" asked Peter, then waved his own question aside and replaced it with the more important one. "Where's Gordon?"

"Don't know. No one does."

"Well, and so what are you doing to find him?"

"That's the crux," said Gamby. "With no one in charge, no one can do much of anything. Now here," Gamby bent to his desk and scribbled a note on a piece of paper. "That's the restaurant and the time. Be sure to get yourself something proper to wear."

As Peter reluctantly accepted the page, Gamby added, "The sooner you're installed, the sooner you can go looking for him."

———

"It's nice," Charles announced some two hours later as Peter stood in the middle of the flat, dressed in the hastily assembled finery and hardly able to breathe for fear of popping a button. How on earth would he be able to eat?

"You would know," said Peter. "Too bad you don't have the cab now, you could drive me over."

Charles appeared surprised. "What makes you think I don't —?" But he pulled his own question up short with realization.

Too late. The bitterness flooded Peter's mouth and he said with false lightness, "Oh, I'd forgotten. You weren't actually required to give up everything, were you?"

Charles blanched, all but for two ruddy spots high on his

cheekbones and a flush at the back of his neck. But he answered with an equal attempt at levity, "Yes, well, but lucky for you it means you have a chauffeur for the evening."

"Is the car nearby?" Peter asked.

"I can have it 'round in twenty minutes," said Charles.

"Making me fashionably late." For a moment they only stared at one another, and Peter saw the apprehension in Charles's clinched jaw. Finally, he relented by adding, "But better to go in knowing who is there than waiting to see who turns up."

Charles's jaw loosened but the smile was strained. "Then I'll be back in twenty."

Peter watched the door swing closed and wondered whether Charles was as anxious as he was about this strange and sudden meeting. The lack of forthcoming information made Peter feel as if he were being set up to fail—all while overdressed.

And then, as a kind of cold dread began to leak from Peter's neck down through his shoulders and back, a worse idea occurred to him: What if Charles knew more than he was saying about where Gordon had gone? After all, Peter reasoned, he was now living with the proof Charles was more than capable of deception. The notion turned Peter's dread to solid ice, freezing him whole; all he could feel was the thud of his heart in his throat, choking him.

He stood in the middle of the tiny flat, too hot and stiff in his new clothes, as the sun dropped behind the buildings outside the windows and shadows began to creep across the worn carpet. It couldn't be true, of course. Charles had not received any mail, any phone calls during their short stay in Derbyshire. He could not have been informed.

But Peter's certainty on that point did not thaw the ice that encased him. The arrow of mistrust was lodged, and to extract it would cause him to bleed out. Either way, the wound was surely mortal.

The door opened again, and Charles appeared on the threshold, the warm, weak light of the landing only partially managing to illuminate his face. "Why are you standing in the dark?"

The fingers of light showed one half of Charles's uncertain

smile, the tightness around his left eye giving away his concern as Peter struggled to formulate an answer. When he couldn't, when it became clear there was no answer, Charles added, "Car's waiting."

Peter stepped past him onto the landing, waited only a fraction of a second before walking down while Charles locked the door behind them. He found the cab, sleek and black and clearly well cared for while they'd been away. Was it Charles's? Or did it belong to the Agency? Peter did not like not knowing where one ended and the other began.

Charles came up behind him on the pavement, keys rattling in his hands. "It's unlocked. Are you all right?" And now Charles wasn't even trying to smile or hide his worry.

"I'm fine," said Peter as he opened the car door, and he was amazed at the strength in his voice, how easily the words came. It sounded almost true.

———————————————

TWO

———————————————

IT WAS the tiny and dim kind of restaurant that people called "exclusive." Peter endured the maître's sweeping examination and evidently passed inspection as the host then stiffly asked for Peter's name. When Peter gave it, the change in the maître's attitude was immediate if disturbing; first there was surprise and a reappraisal of Peter's person, then a greasy obsequiousness as Peter was led toward the back.

"Is it a private room?" Peter asked as they wove between glossy dark wood and snowy white linen, pink roses poking up from frosted glass. The maître threw a polite yet somehow strained smile over his shoulder as if Peter had told an off-color joke. And still they waded deeper into the restaurant's interior.

At first glance it had seemed small, but Peter came to realize it was also deep and got ever darker the farther they moved from the front windows. Until finally, at the back right corner, they stopped. And the man sitting there stood to greet them.

But Peter wasn't looking at him, not at first. He was frowning at the two-top. "Where is everyone?"

"We are everyone."

Peter forced himself to move slowly, though his inclination was to jerk, to jump with surprise. Instead, he lifted his head and turned it slightly to his left. The maître had gone, swift and silent as a ghost, leaving Peter faced with a ghost all his own.

"James?"

He needn't have asked, though. There was no question, even after more than twenty years. The fair hair had gone to a dirty, straw-mixed-with-grey color, and the lines around the mouth and eyes were deeply carved, but the eyes themselves were the same, sparkling and green. And the brilliant smile was as heart-breaking as ever.

"You have no idea how surprised I was when that…" James waved a dismissive hand, "brought your name up in the meeting."

"Gamby?" And now he was just filling the void and scrambling to keep hold of the traces as his thoughts ran wild.

"Is that the one? Big fellow. Sit."

James always had been bossy. He'd swept into their school and taken over fifth form. And he'd been the exact right ratio of charming and threatening that no one had questioned his authority.

Peter sat. His eyes drifted toward the rose at the center of the table, and he noticed the way death was setting in at the curled edges of the petals. If he complained, would they bring a new one? If he said he didn't like pink, would they bring him another color?

"Botany?" James asked as he slipped into his own chair, and Peter silently despised the note of amusement in his voice, felt it as nails scratching down his back. Still, he managed a bland, blank look. "You're staring at that flower, and I can't tell if you love it or hate it," James remarked.

Peter dragged his eyes from the centerpiece, though it took more effort than he expected. "I thought there would be more people. I was under the impression this dinner was some kind of business meeting."

"You're not happy to see me."

"I don't know what I am," Peter admitted before he could check himself. "Confused mostly." He looked down at the spotless tablecloth and realized he had no menu in which to take refuge.

"I asked them to prepare something special," said James. "Hope you don't mind."

"As long as it's not school food in honor of the old days."

"There you are," James said with seemingly genuine pleasure, his dazzling smile cracking his face like a lingering lightning bolt. "It always was a trick to pull you out of your shell."

"And with a smile like that you were always destined for politics."

"Genetic."

"The smile or the politics?"

But James's grin only widened as he turned its full wattage on the waiter who had crept up on their table. "Would messieurs care for anything to drink while they wait for their dinners?" The accent was thick and, Peter perceived, counterfeit.

"A fifty-three Cabernet Sauvignon, I think," answered James with a glance at Peter. "You strike me as the type to like Cab."

Peter shrugged, striving for nonchalance even as his heart skipped. How much did James know? Had Gamby filled him in? Or Trevor? The picture would be very different, depending. "I don't even know what we're having for dinner, so how can I hope to pair it?"

"It's fish." James turned and straightened himself in his chair as the waiter scuttled off. "In a red pepper sauce. You don't mind a little spice, do you?"

"You know I don't," said Peter, feeling suddenly and unaccountably sullen.

And James understood, just as he always had. "I'm sorry," he said, and all the audacity dropped away, replaced with an earnestness as he leaned forward and tilted his head in a bid to catch Peter's averted gaze. Peter conceded only in watching askance and was powerfully reminded of the facets James had shown in their school days—the leadership in the classroom and on the field versus the softness when they had been alone. James would have made a good agent. But his family had had definite plans for him.

"I shouldn't have sprung it on you," James continued. "I just wanted a chance to catch up before..." He fluttered his left hand and Peter caught sight of the ring but was careful not to react.

Peter shifted and resettled in his chair. "Yes, well, I came in from Derbyshire this morning, so..."

Their waiter reappeared with the wine and two glasses, which he set before them with a flourish before displaying the bottle's label to each of them, gesturing like a woman on a showroom floor. Peter glanced at James and caught his eye then looked away quickly for fear of bursting into laughter as the corner of James's mouth quirked in amusement.

"I'm sure it's fine," James told the waiter, his voice remarkably even given his obvious mirth. "Just pour it."

And with that, Peter felt a warm ripple tension run out of him, down his back and away as he returned James's tacit toast by lifting his glass and drinking.

"Derbyshire," James said. "I didn't think you ever went back."

"Are you so well informed of my movements?" Peter asked.

"You've never been easy to find. Imagine my surprise when I heard your name. I didn't dare hope it was the same man."

"And yet you arranged for a private dinner."

James smiled. "I did some homework first. Even politicians know how to snoop." He paused, twisting the stem of his wine glass where it rested on the table, a thoughtful frown clouding his features as the deep red liquid twirled. "I would have been easy for you to find." The green eyes shifted upward. "If you'd ever thought to look."

"When you stopped answering my letters..."

"I answered every letter!" protested James.

"Three," Peter countered. "I sent three that never received a reply. I took it as a sign you..." Peter's throat closed over the words as the bitter memory of rejection rose burning like bile. At some point he must have given up hoping for anything in the post. He'd crawled back into his studies and the life he'd led before James had broken his world open.

1947

The new boy had all the makings of a self-assured bully; Peter had heard it whispered that James's father was someone important in the government, which only made Peter wonder why James's family would send him so far away to school. Still, as James sharked around in ever nearer circles, Peter remained serene in the way of a person used to being ignored. School antics—the fights, the hijinks—raged around Peter, and he sat in the eye, usually with a book open in his hands.

Besides, Phillip would never let anyone touch his little brother.

And yet the day came when James wandered over to where Peter sat reading on a bench and demanded to know what Peter was doing.

"What does it look like?" Peter asked without bothering to look up from the page.

James glanced uncertainly over his shoulder, but he had no audience that day.

"'S not even in English," James observed.

"No," Peter agreed. It was *Le Comte de Monte-Cristo*, and Peter had read it a number of times before; it was one of his favorites. Which was why he was more ruffled than he might otherwise have been when James swiped it from his hands.

"Give it back!"

"Come on, then," James said, stepping out of Peter's reach.

Peter looked around at where other boys were chatting, playing cards, a few bent over their schoolwork. Here and there a cluster of bodies denoted a club meeting that had decided to take advantage of the fine weather. Finally, turning back to James with exasperation, Peter asked, "What do you want?"

The unexpected question froze James.

"You wouldn't bother me otherwise," Peter persisted. "And you've clearly waited until you don't have your usual following."

James feigned sudden interest in the tattered paperback. "Why not just read it in English?"

"Because sometimes the nuances of language get lost in translation."

In response, James shot Peter a look that, for all his linguistic skills, Peter was himself at a loss to translate. Then, checking to make sure no one had looked their way, James quickly grabbed Peter's hand and began to tow him out of the quad and around the buildings, putting distance and (Peter noted) many trees between them and the larger society of their school. When James at last seemed satisfied they were sufficiently masked and released Peter's hand, Peter had a moment balanced between perplexed curiosity and wariness. The former wanted to stay and find out what was going on, the latter demanded Peter run back the way they'd come.

Peter didn't move.

James noticed the book still in his hand and dropped it to the grass. Peter eyed it, the idea bouncing in the back of his mind that he'd have to find his place again, but he did not attempt to retrieve it; to do so would require coming closer to James than made Peter comfortable. Peter reminded himself that Phillip would not allow anyone to bully him, then wondered whether James knew he had a (much larger) older brother?

Still, Peter couldn't bring himself to run. And when James advanced on him, Peter found himself rooted to the spot, though he balled his hands and made ready to swing if it came to that. But when James's hands came up, they went to the sides of Peter's face, holding him in place for the kiss.

While Peter's mind worked to make sense of what was happening, his body responded quite naturally. And once James felt sure Peter wasn't going to bolt, the hands moved down to Peter's shoulders then wound themselves around Peter in a way that startled him into moving backward. James moved with him, their feet tangled, and they fell.

This is a trick, Peter thought as James rolled off him. *He's told everyone to hide and watch and any minute now they'll come through the trees laughing.* He lay still in the grass and waited, listening. But the only sound was James moving beside him, barely audible over the pounding of Peter's own heart in his ears.

When nothing happened, Peter waited still longer, assuming James would collect himself and go and this would be something about which neither of them would ever speak. James would go back to ignoring Peter, and Peter would go back to his books.

But James did not leave, and finally Peter looked over at him. James was idly pulling grass and staring at Peter thoughtfully. "Had you ever done that before?"

Peter shook his head. He'd thought about it—not about James, but there were others—but had kept it to himself. Phillip knew, and Peter supposed others had guessed, but he'd always believed so long as he never did anything about it...

"It's why I'm here," said James.

Peter's brow quirked. "To kiss people?"

James threw a fistful of grass at him. "Idiot."

Peter sat up and began to brush his uniform clean.

"There's some..." James slid closer, started to swipe at Peter's shoulder, and Peter's world slipped into a kind of slow motion. He turned to see what James was aiming for, and as his head tilted James moved in, more carefully this time. Peter would have liked to return James's embrace, but he was forced to keep at least one palm flat to the ground in order to support their exploration of one another's mouths. He didn't realize he'd put his other hand in James's hair until James pulled back and said, "Don't muss it."

So that's it, Peter thought, and his eyes fell on the paperback lying a meter or so away. He supposed he should go fetch it, give James a chance to skulk away, but James only continued to sit there and stare at him. Well, maybe he wasn't comfortable standing up yet, either.

After a minute James gave a huff of exasperation. "At least I know you won't tell anyone."

Peter looked a question at him and James rolled his eyes. "Do you ever talk?"

Peter frowned. "About what?"

James shook his head in the way Phillip sometimes did to intimate Peter was hopeless. "You're going to tutor me," James declared.

"In what?"

James shrugged, gestured at the book in the grass. "French or something."

"Do you need help in French?" Peter asked.

"Oh my God, you really—" James took a deep breath. "I have a private room."

Peter nodded; many of the wealthier boys had the luxury of not having to share their quarters.

"And you will come *tutor* me there."

Peter looked hard at James then, to be sure he understood. "All right," he answered slowly, apprehension and anticipation warring in his chest and speeding his pulse, making his lungs labor for air. "When?"

"Tonight. During prep."

"They'll come around to check on us."

"And we will be very studious," James assured him. He stood and offered Peter his hand to help him up. "You've still got grass..." Peter remained still as James rid him of the last of the clinging blades. "I'll go first," James told him as his hands swept over Peter's back. "Give it a minute then you can follow."

Peter didn't answer. The brushing stopped and Peter went to collect his book. By the time he turned around, James had gone.

1967

The server returned, this time with their dinners. It was delicious, but then James had always had a decadent palate. They ate in silence for a while before James said again, "I'm sorry. I suppose someone intercepted the letters, confiscated them. I promise I did answer every one I received." He hesitated; Peter heard the catch in James's breath from across the table, the tell-tale sound of someone unlocking his tongue to say something, and stopped eating though he kept his eyes on his plate. He was afraid of what he might see in James's face if he were to look up.

"I thought, after Phillip, maybe you..."

The words stung as much as a slap would have. They weren't

meant to hurt, of course, and the way James rushed them out of his mouth was the verbal equivalent of having a plaster ripped off in one pull. But Phillip's name always felt like a slap, even when said kindly.

"You had... changed, something had changed..." James went on. "I was sure you'd gone home, and I didn't know whether it was safe to write you there. I did want to say I was sorry. For what happened."

"You're sorry for a lot, aren't you?"

"Yes. I am."

The sincerity pained Peter, so he allowed the remark to pass as a boat on a river then mentally turned away from the riverbank, taking the conversation with him. "And aside from nostalgia, why are we here?"

James's expression was surprisingly crestfallen at the shift, but he rallied in short order, flashed a smile, and took on a businesslike air. "Gamby suggested you for Gordon Lessenby's job."

"I thought Gordon Lessenby had Gordon Lessenby's job," said Peter.

James gave a negligible shrug. "He's getting up there, as you know. And things are moving, changing faster than a man his age can hope to keep up with. And then there is the little issue of his having disappeared on us."

"I wouldn't call that a little issue. What's being done to find him?"

"Not really my department," James said. "Though if it turns out he's gone off to spill some secrets..."

"He would *never*."

James's green eyes went wide and round at the violence of Peter's reaction, and the hands came up, palms out, in a gesture of placation. "We don't know. I mean, I'm sure you're right, but..."

"*I* know. *I* know Gordon. *You* don't." Something inside Peter's chest felt aflame, and he had to grip the edge of the table to keep his hands steady, so hard were they shaking. Truth was Peter had no idea whether James knew Gordon, but no one knew Gordon the way Peter did. And even as he thought it, something terrible whispered in the back of Peter's mind that, though he trusted Gordon implicitly, Gordon had seen fit to test Peter's loyalty. And look what that hath wrought.

"Trevor mentioned you were close," said James.

"I'm sure he made it sound like no good thing."

"Well, he seemed to think it foreshadowed a lack of progress. That, were you to be put in charge, you would do things the way Gordon had always done them." James smiled again. "Have you grown intractable in your old age?"

"Haven't I always been?" asked Peter.

James's eyebrows shot up. "I found you quite adaptable. Maybe that's why Gordon considered you such a good understudy."

"It's Trevor who's intractable," Peter said. "He's dug in and now he's holding on for dear life."

"No, I'm not a fan myself," James admitted. "Dessert?"

The waiter had materialized bearing the small menus that would list their options. Peter shook his head; all at once he was tired in the way that played with light and made things fuzzy around their edges. "I'll just finish my wine, I think."

James shooed the server away, then said, "You haven't said whether you want the job."

"Is it up to you?"

"I know which strings to pull."

"Including mine," said Peter.

"Those are buttons. Pushing. That's different." The relaxed amiability of James's tone did not make the words any less true.

"And what would you program me to do, I wonder?" Peter asked.

"We have reasons for wanting the Agency under our umbrella," said James. "Not that renewing an old friendship wouldn't be enough," he added. "For me, anyway. But look at it this way: Whoever takes Gordon's chair will be in charge of the efforts to find him. Should he be so inclined."

"You must want him found," Peter said. "If you're worried he might be off tattling to the Reds."

"All the more reason to change everything. Then his information is worthless anyway."

"That's Trevor talking," Peter surmised.

"He's not wrong," said James. "I don't see him as a good fit for the throne, though. Too..." James held out a hand palm down and wobbled it. "And I don't think people will follow him."

"They won't follow me, either," Peter told him. "I'm sure Trevor filled you in on all that."

James's answering sigh assured Peter Trevor had. "Who then?"

"Gamby is the next logical choice."

But James shook his head. "Too much of a bully."

"Might be what the Agency needs, some bossing around."

"You know how it works," said James. "People get tired of being yelled at and begin avoiding the throne room altogether. Next thing, the man in charge doesn't know what's going on right under his own nose because no one is brave enough to tell him anything. With you they at least believe they'll get a fair hearing. They know you lean on justice because it's what your reputation rests on, having benefitted from it yourself." James eyed Peter speculatively. "And you never were much of a screamer."

Despite himself, Peter flinched.

James drained the last of his wine glass. "I realize you probably want time to consider, but we're going to have to do something soon. For what it's worth, I think you'd do a fabulous job. And I think you and I could make the connection between the Ministry and the Agency far smoother than it has been so far." A pause. "We still like each other, don't we?"

Peter sighed, one of those terrible, heavy, exasperated sighs that made him worry, however fleetingly, that something in him was too much like his father. Gordon would never have sighed at him like that. But Peter was tired—it was difficult to comprehend that he'd started the day in Derbyshire, been to the office and the tailor since then, or how he'd ended up here at the end of it all. Here, across from James, who that morning had been a childhood memory and had now somehow circled back into his living, breathing reality.

He'd known, of course, that James worked in the Ministry. Peter was aware enough of politics, kept abreast of current events, read papers... And if whenever the name jumped out from the print it felt like a tiny hook in his heart, well, that was the nature of first loves, wasn't it?

"You disagree," James said, drawing Peter's exhausted mind back from its wine-spun thoughts. Peter saw James's mouth made long for being pulled down into a frown and all at once James appeared sixteen again; it was the same expression he would get whenever a letter would come from his father or brothers, disappointment mixed with that trapped feeling of being unable to sway things. Peter's throat knotted at the idea that expression, those feelings now applied to him.

"I don't disagree," Peter said, and because it came out oddly hoarse, he gave a small cough. "And if you trust me to do the job, I will. At least as long as it takes to find Gordon."

"And if you never find him?"

Peter stood; everything had taken on a muffled feeling, and he felt moving was the only way to begin to clear his head. Visibly startled, James followed suit, and Peter was forced to admire the grace with which the man moved. The wedding band flashed a taunt in the dim light.

"I'll find him," Peter said.

"Well, let's hope not too quickly." James plucked the pink rose from its vase and stepped over to Peter, neatly threading it into the buttonhole on Peter's dinner jacket. "I'd hate to lose you having just found you again."

Peter blinked at the nearness of him, knowing he should move back but aware that he might just as easily fall over. And something in him didn't want to put any more air between them. That thing—and it was a truly awful thing—dared him to close the space further. But he didn't. He didn't move at all.

"It will be yours within the week," James murmured, the words soft as a lover's promise. "I look forward to working with you."

Peter drew in a slow, deep breath filled with the fragrance of rose and took one step back, though he had to expend more effort than he liked to keep from swaying. "And I look forward to meeting your wife," he said. "But for now my car is waiting." And though it felt like a physical struggle to do so, he turned and walked away.

———————————————————

THREE

———————————————————

CHARLES *WAS* WAITING, as it turned out, though Peter hadn't asked or expected him to. The cab inched forward as Peter exited the restaurant, and Peter initially ignored it, relegating it to the background of London. But as he walked along the pavement—and where was he going, really? he had no idea—and the cab rolled slowly along beside him, Peter was of course forced to acknowledge it. Bad things came to agents who went too deep inside their own heads.

Peter stopped walking. The cab stopped moving. And the window came down. And even then Peter was unduly surprised to see Charles's bright eyes peering out at him.

"Where are you going?" Charles asked.

"Have you been here all evening?" Peter retorted. He opened the rear door and slid into the back seat rather than walk around to the front passenger side. It was a cab, after all.

"I went around to Papa's for some dinner," Charles said. Giuseppe Fendi ran a small establishment for which he was not licensed, but the food was so good the law refused to close him down. "Papa," as everyone called him, maintained he simply had so many friends he was forced to run a commercial kitchen to feed them all. And there was some truth to his words, for he did not ask for money; one merely paid what one felt was fair. There was no set menu, either. One ate whatever Papa felt like cooking.

"I hope he had meatballs," said Peter. Meatballs were Charles's favorite.

"He did!" Charles answered with unfiltered enthusiasm. "How was your meeting?"

It was a smooth enough transition and, Peter supposed, a natural question, yet something small and bright flared in Peter's chest when Charles asked it. Peter did not feel ready to share the experience of having seen James again, and though part of him felt traitorous for it, Peter merely shrugged. "Boring."

"Nice rose," Charles remarked as they slid into the evening traffic.

Peter glanced down at the pink bloom in his buttonhole. "They want to give me Gordon's job."

Charles's blue eyes flashed at Peter from the rearview mirror, wide with surprise, and Peter found himself irritated. "Is it really such a shock?"

Charles didn't answer right away, though Peter wasn't sure whether that was because of the need to concentrate on not hitting pedestrians.

"What did you tell them?" Charles asked once they'd carved their way around and through several flocks of doe-eyed theatre goers.

"We should go to a show," Peter half sighed.

"What?"

"I said I'd do it, but only so long as it takes to find Gordon."

Charles swung the cab onto Bayswater Road. "I didn't think you liked pink," was all he said.

———

For a long moment after the cab came to a stop at the kerb outside the flat, Peter sat. He told himself he was too tired to move, but he wasn't really; he simply was not ready to go up the stairs and into his life. Cars were marvelous, transitional creatures, ferrying people to and from, there and back. Now that Peter had been There he wasn't sure he was ready to return.

Things, Peter felt, could not be the same now.

His world had shifted, not by a lot, but by enough to make a difference. As in a minor earthquake, when a doorway goes just ever so slightly askew. Looking at it, one might not notice, but the door never fits quite right again.

And then the door beside him opened, startling him and letting in the cool night air, and Peter looked balefully up at Charles. Peter knew he had no real right to be so irritated by the interruption, but just in that moment Charles's very existence was a nuisance, a tiresome and unrelenting chafing. Peter ducked his head on the pretense of bending out of the car so that Charles could avoid prolonged exposure to his displeasure. "Sorry," he muttered as he swung his long legs out onto the pavement. "I didn't mean for you to act as chauffeur."

"I offered," Charles reminded him.

Somehow this only made things worse in Peter's mind; Charles's presence was all at once suffocating. "You should have let me walk." And when Charles's eyes lit with concern and confusion, "I think I need to walk." And he started off toward the corner without waiting for Charles to respond.

———

There were clouds building; he couldn't see them, but he could feel the damp gathering in the air. The rose in his buttonhole began to nod as if sleepy. Peter did a quick turn around the block but was unable to collect his thoughts into any useful arrangement, and so he focused on the chill of approaching rain, on the desertedness of the street, on the sound of his dress shoes striking the pavement, on moving from one pool of lamplight to the next. It felt good to be alone, even without his thoughts. Maybe even good to be free of them for a few minutes.

By the time he'd looped back around to the building where their flat roosted above two seemingly unoccupied dwellings (Peter knew better than to believe it), his off mood had blown over just as the clouds had blown in and he was ready to see Charles—really see him—and even tell him about the dinner. He climbed the flights to their converted attic and found Charles actively wiping down surfaces that had grown dusty while they'd been away. "Did you—?" Peter began and Charles nodded his head in toward the small, round dining table. Piled on top of it was a collection of wires and listening devices.

"Can't see why they continue to bother," said Charles. "Waste of time."

"Gamby does it for the fun of it." Peter strolled over to where Charles stood beside the child-sized sink. He took the rose from his buttonhole and tucked it behind Charles's left ear, taking care not to scratch Charles with the thorns. "There. Pink suits you better than me."

Charles blinked up at him. "Was a short walk," he ventured.

"Just needed some air after being in that restaurant." Peter began fighting his silver and onyx cufflinks, the only thing on his person that he'd possessed before that morning. As he went to where their bed stood behind the screen that divided it from the lounge and kitchen, Charles trailed after him, dishrag in hand. He looked utterly absurd with the rose perched against his short ashen hair, and that pleased Peter for some reason; a warmth spread from Peter's stomach through his chest and out to his fingertips. It was as if his heart had been stopped for the past few hours and had only just begun to circulate his blood again.

Peter kicked off his shoes and shrugged off his dinner jacket, very aware of the way Charles watched him. Without prompting, Charles stepped over and began to undo the buttons on Peter's shirt. Peter could feel the gusts of Charles's breath against the hollow of his throat at even intervals.

As Charles tugged Peter's shirt free of his trousers so as to get at the last two buttons, he asked, "Was it as good a restaurant as they say?"

"I'm not sure. James had them prepare something special; I don't know what the regular menu is like."

"James…" Charles mused as if trying to place the name.

"Tarlington. From the Ministry." Peter slipped his arms free of the shirtsleeves and was instantly cold. He started to toss the shirt onto the bed, but Charles took it, turned around and grabbed an empty hanger that was hooked over the top of the screen.

Inside his socks, Peter's toes began to drum. Now that he'd begun talking, he didn't want to stop. But he needed Charles to ask something, give him an access point. Otherwise, Peter wasn't sure where to begin.

Charles hung the shirt back on the screen. "Who else was there?"

Peter let out his breath slowly and stilled his feet. "No one."

"Not Gamby? Trevor?"

Peter shook his head.

"No one else from the Ministry?"

Another, smaller shake.

Charles reached up and took the rose from over his ear, examined it thoughtfully as if it held secrets. He ran a thumb over one velvety petal. "Just the two of you then. How romantic." Despite his gentleness, the petal threatened to break under his caress and hung like a loose tooth when Charles released it.

"Not really." Peter stepped closer to Charles, put his arms around him, but when he made to draw Charles closer, Charles threw his weight into his heels and resisted. Head bowed over the rose, Charles said, "James Tarlington. He's in the papers sometimes, I think."

"And married," said Peter, urging Charles closer, and this time Charles gave a couple centimeters. He looked up at Peter from under his thick eyelashes; Peter saw the blue crescents of iris like moons.

"You know him."

It was a statement, not a question, and Peter drew in a deep breath that smelled faintly of dying rose. "We were at school together." He watched this information bounce through Charles's brain. Though Charles's expression did not change, Charles went still as he processed, and Peter used the moment to pull him closer still, stopping only when he felt the rose between them.

"It's called a bride, you know," Charles said, his voice low and mournful as if this were bad news. "This kind of rose."

"I don't care what it's called," Peter told him. He plucked the flower from Charles's hand and tossed it to the floor, the loose petal falling free and spiraling downward in a solitary Sema. Peter then brought Charles to him, closing the little remaining distance between their bodies, but Charles had gone rigid again and kept his head turned, his face averted. In exasperation, Peter released him.

"Were you friends?" Charles asked. His question appeared to be directed at the carpet. Or perhaps he was asking the broken rose.

Peter ripped his socks from his feet and tossed them into the corner he'd selected for dirty laundry. "I'm going to shower." Maybe, he thought as he stalked into the tiny bathroom, he wasn't ready to tell Charles everything. Just as likely Charles wasn't ready to hear it.

____

FOUR

____

GAMBY WAS WAITING for him first thing; Peter suspected he'd told the gatekeeper to call ahead once Peter had arrived so that by the time he'd made his way to his office Gamby was there to meet him, a hulking figure in a navy suit and vivid red tie.

"How was dinner?"

"Why are you standing outside my office?" Peter asked, fishing his pocket for his key.

"Don't think this is yours any more," said Gamby.

Peter glanced over at Simeon's abandoned desk.

"I've moved him around the corner to Sandra's old desk," Gamby told him.

"Move him back," said Peter. "I can do the job just as well from here." He opened the door and stepped into the must of an office that had been closed up too long.

"Probably," Gamby agreed amiably. "But they won't see you as king until you're in the throne room. It's a better view, anyway."

Peter watched the dust motes float in the shaft of light from his window, took in the drooping plants on the sill and sighed. "Keep this one vacant. I'll want it back once we find Gordon."

Gamby lumbered behind him as he went back past the lifts and over to the corner where Gordon's office was located. Seeing

Simeon in Sandra's space made Peter wonder where she'd gone. But before he could ask, Gamby offered, "She left when he did. Said she'd only been waiting on him."

Peter nodded. It was the way of things. Simeon looked up then and, seeing Peter and Gamby, scrambled to stand. "I have your key." He opened the middle drawer of his desk and produced a silver key, which he held out delicately for Peter to take.

In return, Peter handed over his old office key. "Keep it locked." And when Simeon only stared at the key in his palm, "In fact, go lock it now."

As Simeon started to dash off, Peter called after him, "And do something with those plants."

Beside him, Gamby chuckled softly. "Well now, key to the kingdom, eh?" he asked, nodding at Peter's hand.

"Do we have a meeting, Gamby?"

"You're going to need a right hand."

"You can't have my old office."

"Yes, you're saving it."

Peter's gaze raked Gamby's hefty build. "The exercise won't hurt you in any case." He stepped forward to the dark wood of Gordon's door, now his. *Just for now,* Peter told himself.

Gamby had the decency, or at least the sense, to hang back.

Simeon reappeared carrying one wilted plant in each hand. "I don't think they're dead yet anyway."

And from behind him Peter heard Gamby answer, "Some things don't come back, lad, no matter how badly you hope."

———

Gordon's office—Peter could not help but think of it as Gordon's —was almost as stuffy as Peter's had been. "When did he leave?" Peter asked, and Gamby stepped up behind where Peter stood on the threshold.

"Couple days after you went up to Derbyshire."

Peter surveyed the room, so well known to him. But now it

took on the role of an undiscovered country, a place no one had tread in a long while, a place of hidden treasure and secrets. The desk was clear aside from the blotter and phone and a light layer of dust. "Cleaning crew?"

"Been kept out," Gamby acknowledged.

Peter nodded his satisfaction and finally braved a step inside, the equivalent (or so it felt) of planting a flag and staking claim.

The office occupied the southwest corner and benefitted from windows in two walls instead of just one like most of the others in the Castle. The sun had not yet made it to that side of the building but even so the room was bright enough not to require any overhead lighting. In fact, upon reflection Peter could not recall ever seeing the light on; even in winter or when Gordon had worked late, it had been by the light of a desk lamp.

"Do we know if he took anything?" Peter asked. "From here or from home?"

Gamby shrugged. "Not as if we knew, particularly, what he had to begin with. But maybe *you* would know. How was the meeting?"

Peter turned to look at Gamby, trying to gauge the question's intent. "Tarlington had said he wanted to meet me."

"Yes." Gamby glanced uncertainly behind him at where Simeon sat at his desk, pulling dead leaves from the plants. Then Gamby gave Peter a nudge in the back, urging him farther into the office, and stepped in, closing the door.

"I thought it would be a nice surprise," said Gamby. "He made it sound like you'd been close."

"That's one way of putting it," Peter muttered. He walked to the desk, laid light fingertips on it as he rounded it the way a person might keep a hand on the back of a horse to keep it from kicking. But when he came to the imposing chair, Peter stopped. He merely stood beside it.

"He gave you the job," said Gamby.

"Is it his to give?" Peter wondered, then said, "Yes, he gave it to me. Said he'd bring the Ministry committee around within the week." He glanced around the office. "Means I probably shouldn't be in here yet."

"A technicality," Gamby said.

"One Trevor will exploit," said Peter.

"He's never here."

"He will be," Peter predicted.

"Sounds to me like you're looking for excuses," said Gamby. "If you don't want the job—"

"I just want to find Gordon."

"And then what?" asked Gamby.

Peter felt as if he'd been slapped by a cold, wet hand. "What?"

Gamby lumbered forward a few steps and dropped into the chair that sat in front of the desk, and for a fleeting instant Peter thought, *That's* my *chair*. But of course it wasn't. It never had been, really; its dark red leather had belonged to any and every guest in the office. Though Peter supposed—he liked to believe—he had spent more time in it than anyone.

"Even if you find Gordon, then what?" Gamby pressed. "If he doesn't want to come back? If he's a traitor? If he's dead?"

Peter shook his head, denying all those possibilities. "And if he's hurt? Being held? Are we sure he wasn't taken?"

"We're not sure of anything," said Gamby.

The phone on the desk beeped, startling Peter badly enough that he jerked away from the desk as if it *had* kicked him. He caught a glimpse of Gamby's smirk and, scowling, jabbed at the intercom button. "Yes?"

"Mr. Tillholm is here," said Simeon, not bothering to hide his dislike.

Peter lifted an eyebrow as he looked askance to where Gamby sat. "This is why you're in charge," said Gamby with a smile. "And now he's your problem."

"Send him..."

The door was open before Peter could even finish.

"Peter. You're back."

Gamby had grown suddenly focused on his fingernails. "Observation skills like that, Trevor, I can't imagine why they didn't give you the top job."

"They need me in other places," Trevor answered smoothly.

He glanced over at the sagging sofa that lined the wall, dismissed it, rocked toe to heel, slipped his left hand into his trouser pocket and jangled at something, keys or loose change.

"Keep telling yourself that," Gamby muttered.

"Gentlemen," said Peter, then to Trevor, "Sorry there's only the one chair at the moment. Can't think where the other one's gone."

"Maybe Gordon took it with him," suggested Gamby as he worried a hangnail.

Trevor lifted an eyebrow in Gamby's direction, for all Gamby didn't see. "And there's why you didn't get the job."

"They need me in other places," Gamby told him.

"Oh, for God's sake, both of you," Peter said. "Are either of you here for a reason?"

"Only to congratulate you," said Trevor, and Gamby's head came up fast enough to do him a neck injury. "I know it's not official yet," Trevor continued, "but I understand it's only a matter of protocol. It's all but done."

"Fast work," Gamby said, eying Peter. "How close were you exactly?"

"I tutored him in French," said Peter.

Gamby made a strangled sound that developed into a coughing fit as Trevor said, "Well, he's fluent in it now. James Tarlington, that is. One has to be, in his position." He turned to Gamby. "Do you need some water?"

But Gamby had lumbered to his feet. "We'll talk later," he told Peter, his massive face an alarming red-purple.

Peter and Trevor watched him go, and as the door closed behind Gamby, Trevor wondered aloud, "Is he well?"

"I'm sure he's fine," Peter said. "And thank you for your graciousness, Trevor, but—"

But Trevor had crab-walked to the chair Gamby had vacated and was settling in to the warmed leather. "You'll be after Gordon, I expect."

Peter hated that he froze, hated that terrible shock that went through him like a pinched nerve. He answered slowly, carefully, as if to be sure his tongue still worked. "It's on my agenda, yes."

Trevor nodded. "He'll have gone after her, you know. I'd heard someone was onto her and..." He hooked an ankle over his knee. "Well, but this was just as you'd been shot. That damn Miranda. One of hers all along. They told you, didn't they? You went straight out of hospital to wherever it was, so I don't know what you know."

Ah, and there was the rub. Peter felt his shoulders relax and suddenly his weight shifted to his palms as he held himself up against the desk's surface. "I've hardly had time to gather my thoughts," he told Trevor. "Perhaps you should make a list of what *you* know and I can compare it to my own notes."

Trevor's eyes were beady, like a bird's. Sharp, too; Trevor was a magpie in search of some bright bit of information with which to feather his nest. The idea of knowledge flowing out instead of in would ruffle his feathers, Peter was sure. And when Trevor abruptly unfolded himself and stood, Peter felt the rush of vindication up his spine. Only to have the fountain run dry as Trevor said, "Certainly. I'll have it to you in a day or so. Just," and he cocked his head, more birdlike than ever, "to be sure I don't forget anything."

Peter blinked his astonishment, though he was careful to keep his face set. "I'd say to take all the time you need, but we don't have it, I'm afraid. But yes, better to be thorough. Who checked the house?"

Trevor's head tilted a little farther, a visual question mark.

"Gordon's house," said Peter. "Who went?"

Trevor looked to the door as if distracted and his tone became disinterested, the way one's does when rushing to end a conversation and escape someone's company. "Gamby sent someone. Or maybe he went himself even."

Peter narrowed his eyes at Trevor's back as the little man moved for the door. "I'll be sure to ask him for a report as well then."

"Yes," Trevor agreed absently, "it will be good to have everyone on the same page again." He stopped, his hand white as it clutched the doorknob, and looked over his shoulder at Peter. "Meeting?"

"Tomorrow afternoon. In here."

"Better find another chair," said Trevor, and then he was gone.

____

FIVE

____

PETER HAD OFTEN WONDERED what homework Gordon might
have done, whether learning of the stiff relationship between
Peter and his parents had somehow moved Gordon to step into
that breach and take Peter under his wing. Certainly a man at
Gordon's level had not been required to call for Peter's services;
anyone from the Agency might have been sent, and often
someone else was. But Gordon turned up just as regularly, even
as Peter finished at uni, summoning Peter back to the unnamed
estate now and again for this or that bit of translation, or sometimes just to pick Peter's brain over a cypher. And if on one dark
and cold autumn evening Peter had let bits of his life—his
brother; his parents; the acrimonious split during which Byron
had threatened to kill Peter, or himself, or both—spill out
against the glow of a fire and the glint of brandy in cut crystal
glasses, Gordon had listened with his hands folded over his
middle and never passed any verbal judgement.

So it was that by the time Peter had graduated, he went
straight from uni to the Bastion. It might just as well have been
the military, and though Peter did not consider himself soft or
pampered, the going had been rough at first. It was his adaptable
nature that saw Peter through. He kept his head down, and he
focused on his work, did his part in field exercises. And in all

those weeks, there was no sign of Gordon. But when it was all over, Gordon was there again and saying, "I hear you have the makings of a director."

But Peter had shook his head and said, "I'm really just meaning to do translations." And he'd thought he was telling the truth. And Gordon, being the wise man he was, let Peter roost in a scribe's office at the Monastery for almost a year before asking him whether he might like to go down to Paris and help them with something. And next it was Madrid. A little hiccough in Athens that, if Peter were willing, his Greek being so fluent...

———

Peter blinked himself out of his reverie as Simeon opened the office door. "You want them on the window sill?"

"What?" But then Peter saw Simeon was holding the plants, now free of dead leaves. "They'll just die again in here," said Peter.

"Not if you take care of them properly." Simeon passed the desk where Peter sat and situated the plants by the window behind.

"Housekeeping should water them and... whatever else they need," Peter insisted.

"Housekeeping isn't allowed in here," said Simeon. He leaned back against the window. "Sandra told me she used to tidy Mr. Lessenby's office, dusting and all. Which, by the way, I won't do. Why do you even have them if you're just going to let them die off?"

But Peter was stuck on another idea. "Sandra," he repeated. "Where did she go?"

"Pensioned after Mr. Lessenby cleared off."

"But they asked her where he went."

"I'm sure they did," Simeon agreed.

"She didn't know."

"I guess not."

Peter sighed with vexation and caught sight of the foliage out the corner of his eye. "Put those someplace housekeeping *will* water them. And get me Sandra's address."

———

It was a small place, a good bit south of the river. Flower boxes attempted to make it cheerful, but the water-stained brick and peeling shutters overpowered them. And the grass in the tiny garden was somehow both too long and very dead, while along the edges of the cracked pavement weeds stood strong and sturdy sentinel.

Peter glanced up at the wooden overhang and noted the sagging, brittle and black rot from poor drainage. There was a corresponding dip in the porch where the wood had warped, causing Peter to speculate how long before it gave way. Sidestepping the potential pitfall, he took a deep breath and knocked; there was no bell. A long quiet, and Peter began to wonder whether to knock again or simply leave off. The longer he stood there, the more conspicuous and foolish he felt. But then the door (it was an astoundingly ugly shade of mud brown) opened and there was Sandra, as done up in hair and makeup as ever.

"Peter!" she gasped, and he tensed and froze instinctively, the way a boy does when his mother begins to scold him. "They never said whether you would come back! Oh, come in!"

She waved him into the entry, where the floors were warped and uneven, then led him on into the lounge. "Sit!" she commanded. "You want some tea?" And before he could answer, "Of course you do. Give me a minute."

As Sandra bustled back into the kitchen, Peter tried to make himself comfortable on a Victorian sofa that was surely more for show—perhaps a family heirloom—than was meant to be sat upon. But the only other chair in the room was a very worn rocker that Peter guessed was Sandra's own. It was situated at an angle to the window, and Peter supposed Sandra's love for gossip extended to watching her neighbors.

Sandra came back with a tray and set it on the low table in front of the sofa, pulled her rocker closer and sat down, leaning forward to pour. "Of course, *I* always said you would be back," she said as she slid the cup and saucer in his direction. "And Gordon didn't doubt it, either. He said all you needed was some time."

Peter didn't touch the tea; it was well known throughout the office Sandra's tea was always weak. "Where is he, Sandra?"

"How am I to know?" she asked. "You think they didn't ask me already? Start with them, not me! Start with yourself for that matter. You know Gordon as well as I do, if not better."

"He didn't say or do anything unusual in the days leading up to his going? Didn't at all mention..." Peter shook his head, and Sandra shook hers sympathetically, and for just one moment Peter was fascinated by the way her platinum curls refused to budge.

"You know Gordon," she said again. "Always muttering to himself in any case. I'd learned to tune it out. If he said anything about going, I never heard it."

Peter tested the tea, if only to buy time to consider. Should he press her now or only come back if he got nowhere on his own? Better not to upset her, to keep her on his side. Could he flatter it out of her? In no way did Peter doubt Sandra knew something, whether she was aware of knowing it or not. Sandra, whose ears were like radio antennae, did not "tune out." She might, however, selectively remember.

He went at it another way. "Is it true housekeeping never cleaned his office?"

This time Sandra nodded. "He didn't trust it, you see. Never wanted anyone in."

"So, it wasn't policy, just Gordon's choice," Peter realized.

"He was careful like that. Never left anything out, always locked his drawers. Would leave his waste bin outside the door to be emptied so they wouldn't have to go in. Every now and then I would go dust things off. Only when he was in, of course, because he was the only one with a key. More tea?"

"No, thank you. Sandra…" She batted her heavily mascaraed lashes at him. "How are you getting on?"

Her frosty pink smile trembled at one corner. "Oh, I'm fine, dear. Keeping myself plenty busy." And she leaned over and topped off Peter's cup anyway.

"Family?" Peter asked, apprehending with a pang that he'd never thought to ask before, that for him Sandra had only ever been a fount of office knowledge to be pumped when needed. And what was he doing now? He swallowed against the black lump that threatened to swell in his throat. A glance at the mantelpiece showed no photographs, only knick-knacks.

"Not any more than you have," said Sandra, and Peter gave a tiny start of surprise. "Oh, I mean my parents are long since gone, of course. And I never married."

Peter worked to keep his expression passive. "A pet at least?" And he cringed at the hopefulness in his tone, as if Sandra *not* alone absolved him of something. As if it meant he would not some day end up equally forgotten and spending his days watching people walk by his window.

"Adele is allergic." And when Peter gave another little jump, her smile broadened. "She still works. But I have books and the telly in the meantime."

"Oh," said Peter. "Well, that's…" Another sweep of his eyes produced no evidence of either books or a television. But maybe she didn't spend as much time in the lounge as Peter had assumed.

"Peter." Sandra leaned forward in her rocker, hands splayed on her wide knees. "He kept secrets, you know. Not just his own but others' as well. It was his job. And he was good at it."

———

"Good day back?" Charles asked when Peter stepped over the threshold. Though they only had two hobs and a toaster, the smells that had drifted down the stairwell announced that Charles had still managed to pull together something like a home-cooked dinner. More than that, Peter discovered upon entry; Charles had bought some flowers for the center of the little dining table.

"Needed some color," said Charles when he caught Peter staring at the multi-hued arrangement of daisies. "And it seems you've taken to flowers."

Peter felt as stung as he was sure he was meant to but dove low under the bait. "Smells delicious. What is it?"

"I had to make do," Charles replied by way of an apologetic preface. He frowned at the pots on the stove. "But it's something *like* bangers and mash."

"No beans," Peter surmised.

"But there *is* onion," Charles said. "It will be ready in a few."

Peter shed his suit coat, momentarily considered leaving it on the sofa, then, catching sight of Charles, went to do the correct thing by hanging it up on the screen. The lack of closet in the flat was increasingly problematic. When it had been only him, Peter had thought nothing of it, but with Charles around he always had to think not only once but twice and sometimes more. So as he re-emerged from behind the screen, he asked, "Anything good from the estate agents?"

"There are one or two worth seeing, I think," Charles said as he brought plates to the table. He turned back toward the kitchen but Peter waved him to his chair.

"I'll get drinks," Peter told him.

Charles sat but craned to see Peter over his shoulder. "I marked the ones. In the paper."

The kettle was already steaming though it hadn't started to whistle yet. Peter didn't wait. He took it off the hob and poured hot water into two mugs then went in search of tea bags.

"Upper right, just next to the refrigerator," Charles instructed.

Peter could taste Charles's impatience like copper in his mouth. No, not impatience, exactly, but there was a patronizing air in the way Charles always sought to help and do. And though Charles was sincere in all his actions, something about this made Peter grind his teeth. As if by being so helpful, Charles had rendered Peter helpless, at least in his own home.

But this wasn't home.

Peter found the tea, dropped a bag in each rapidly cooling mug, and transported the drinks to the table, where he was obliged to nudge the vase of daisies aside a bit in order to make room. It wasn't how Charles would have done it, he knew; Charles preferred to brew the tea in the pot and then pour. But something in Peter felt rebellious and exultant in doing it another way.

"I saw Sandra," said Peter, "went to see her, that is." And when Charles appeared politely puzzled, Peter added, "Gordon's girl. Assistant."

"Ah. Her Simeon."

"However you like to frame it," Peter said with a small, quick shake of his head to rid himself of the strange frisson Charles's words had given him. Charles's dislike of Simeon was unnatural and unfounded.

"But they must have already—"

"Yes, of course they did." Peter frowned down at his plate and wished for toast. "But that's beside the point. Sandra hinted..." Peter took a deep breath. "Charles, maybe we shouldn't continue sharing a flat."

He kept staring at his plate and holding his breath, unwilling —un*able*—to look at Charles, though he could still picture the exact mixture of hurt and shock sure to be hanging on Charles's face. Charles's fork clanked against the porcelain of his plate. Peter waited for Charles to say something, but there was only silence until Charles pushed his chair back and stood.

Peter looked up at him then, his heart skipping in a way that made him lightheaded. "It's not that I don't want to! But without Gordon... He was protecting us, Charles. Now I have to —to do it for us."

"This is for your image then," said Charles as he removed his mostly uneaten supper and retreated to the kitchen.

"I don't care what they think," Peter insisted. "But I *have* to care what they think now that Gordon is gone." He pressed two fingers to the spot above his nose and between his eyebrows and attempted to push away an abrupt headache.

"Everyone knows!" said Charles.

"Yes, but I can't give them anything to act on! I'm in a precarious position, Charles. And it's only until we find Gordon."

Water began to run in the sink as Charles rinsed his plate. And then, so low Peter almost didn't hear it, "He's not coming back, you know."

Peter, having started up from his chair, froze in the process of abandoning his own dinner and sat back down with a weight incongruous to his thin frame. "To work? No, I know." And Peter *did* know, but to hear it said aloud and with such finality had felt like a lead pipe to the gut. "I only want to be sure he's all right. Once I've done that, they can have the Agency, do what they like with it."

The water shut off and Charles plucked the dishtowel from the counter to dry his hands. "You'll never leave. Those months... You were miserable without it."

"I'd be more miserable without you," said Peter, but even as the words left his mouth, he began to wonder if it were really true. And when Charles turned around, Peter could see his own doubt mirrored in Charles's expression.

"Give me an assignment," Charles said.

Peter's brow quirked. "What?"

"You're in charge now. Give me an assignment, someone to vet."

The stabbing pain between Peter's eyes sharpened. "I don't..."

"Something to do, someplace to be while you sort things out. I'll wait however long you need, but Peter, I cannot sit here and do nothing. Any more than you could in Salzburg."

"And yet that's exactly what I did in Salzburg," said Peter. "Did the shopping while you..." His throat closed over the words and his body gave a great rattling shake as adrenaline and anger combined over the memory of the deception.

"Peter—"

"I'll find you somewhere, someone to bother," Peter said in a bitter rush. "I'll have to look into the files, find someone who doesn't know you, at least not on sight. You can go in under another name. I suppose you've done that? Is Charles your real name, by the way? I could check the files, but it would save me some trouble if you tell me now."

A long silence, and Peter concentrated on trying to ease his ragged breathing; it felt as if he might shake apart where he sat. Finally, Charles said, "It is. My real name. Not Toulson, but the Charles is real enough."

Peter nodded numbly. "It couldn't be... Not here at the Castle. Too many people might recognize you." Though, in fact, Peter could count on two hands the few who knew Charles for who he was and could identify him; Gordon had been careful indeed.

"You're sending me away."

"You said you wanted an assignment. If so, this is the only way." He stared at Charles, daring him to change his mind and ask to stay. But Charles only reached back to rub at his neck.

"And you'll stay here?" Charles asked.

Peter glanced around the tiny flat. "No," he decided. What he chose not to voice was his desire to start fresh, in a place void of any memories. He felt the weight of Gordon's office on his shoulders and would rather not bear additional tonnage in his personal space.

An idea struck Peter. "You should go up to the Bastion," he told Charles. "If Mr. Martin is anything to go by, they may be in need of some guidance."

Charles's face turned pink. "I vet knights, Peter. I don't babysit."

"It's almost the same thing, isn't it?" Peter asked with forced indifference. "Anyway, I haven't got anyone for you to vet at the moment. But as soon as someone begins misbehaving, I'll be sure to send him your way."

"Do you trust Trevor?"

"You can't have Trevor; he knows who you are."

"I can play that to our advantage. Particularly if it becomes common knowledge that we've parted ways."

A bolt went through Peter, so sharp and sudden he fleetingly believed lightning had struck the building. But a quick glance at the windows proved the evening was still clear. "Have we?" he wondered aloud.

Without answering, Charles pushed away from the kitchen counter and came to take Peter's plate, then carried it back to the sink and began to scrape it clean.

IT HAD to be done sideways, starting with Peter quietly telling Simeon to have Housing find him a new flat. When Simeon asked whether Peter's "friend" had any particular requirements, Peter made it clear the flat would have a solo occupant. And although Simeon was not given to gossip—more an observer, which Peter counted in his favor—the ladies in Housing were. By the end of the week, Peter had been removed to the southwest corner of Green Park, and everyone knew he lived there alone.

"And what about *him*?" Gamby asked one morning as he entered Peter's office without knocking while Simeon sputtered behind him.

Peter was tempted to feign ignorance of understanding the question then decided to ignore it entirely. "Do we have a meeting?"

From the doorway, Simeon gave his head a vigorous shake.

"You're wanted over at Whitehall," said Gamby.

Peter looked again to Simeon who appeared as thunderstruck as Peter felt. Sliding his gaze back toward Gamby, Peter asked, "What for?"

"They want to meet you. Tarlington is the only one who even knows what you look like."

Peter sighed. "I don't suppose I could just send 'round a photograph. Fine." He stood up and went for his suit coat, which he'd gotten in the habit of tossing onto the arm of the sofa. "Is it now?"

"It will be by the time we get there," said Gamby.

"Any chance they'll start letting Mr. Martin know when these things come up? My calendar is his job, after all."

Gamby only chuckled and led the way out.

———

The room was almost unbearably stuffy, the closed glass of the windows holding in all the light and heat of the summer day without offering any air to go with them. Peter and Gamby had been shown in, Trevor not long after, and they sat in silence at the bottom of the conference table, waiting for their tardy hosts. On Peter's right, Trevor fidgeted and shifted incessantly; to his left, Peter sensed Gamby trying to catch his eye, rather like a bad influence at school. And like a good boy, Peter kept his hands folded on the wood in front of him, eyes trained on it, so that he could not be accused of misbehavior.

Finally, the door opened and in came four men, James heading the line. Peter didn't even have to look up to be sure; out of the corner of his eye, he caught the neat press of the trousers and the sure stride and knew it to be James. He stood, and Trevor rushed to do the same. Gamby was slower about it, though whether it was from reluctance or just the effort of moving his massive frame, Peter couldn't guess.

Peter was prepared for reticence, but James greeted him warmly and rattled off the names of his fellows, names Peter understood he would have no need of because James, it was clear, meant to be the liaison. "We are *very* interested in making this process as smooth as possible," James said as they sat.

"What process is that?" Peter asked.

James looked with surprise not at Peter but at Trevor. "Haven't you been keeping him informed, Tillholm?"

Trevor sat forward in his chair. "Of course, but—"

"You know we're bringing the Agency in under our umbrella," said a white-haired, walrus-like man wearing the ghastly combination of a red paisley bowtie and striped blue shirt.

"I'm not surprised to hear it," Peter admitted.

"It should function more or less the same as it ever has," James put in. "Just some additional oversight given, well, you know."

Peter did know, but he only stared blankly across the table at the Ministry men while next to him Gamby exuded a strange mixture of irritation and satisfaction.

"Any news on Gordon?" James asked.

"I've only been in a week," said Peter. "But when we find something, you'll be first to hear."

James smiled, seemingly satisfied, and said, "Then there's just the matter of moving everyone."

"Moving?" asked Peter.

"Better to have everyone in one building," said one of the other men. He wore round glasses, and had thinning, straw-colored hair and an unhealthy ruddy tint to his skin that caused Peter to believe there might be a heart condition lurking beneath the man's checkered shirt.

"I don't see how we'd manage it," Peter told him.

Trevor leaned farther forward so that he was all but laid out on the wood of the table. "But the Castle is half empty!"

"And this building is more than half full," said Peter. "I've only just got into my nice new office; I'm not inclined to give it up just because a few people are adverse to some exercise. And that's not even taking into account the hazards of transporting secure files."

James's smile had frozen onto his face. "Let's discuss it over lunch," he said, standing. Everyone else did the same, though as his men seemed predisposed to linger, each of them whispering fiercely, James was eventually forced to shoo them off.

"Digging in your heels already," James remarked as he rounded the table to join Peter. Trevor and Gamby continued to hover, so Peter turned to Trevor and said, "You still owe me that report, don't you?" which was plenty enough to send Trevor scurrying off, though he did it with a resentful glare. To Gamby,

Peter said, "Would you be sure to tell Mr. Martin I'm out for lunch when you get back?" Gamby raised an eyebrow and walked away whistling.

"You aren't entirely against moving. As a rule," James said to Peter. He began walking and Peter fell into natural step alongside, just as he'd done at school, though back then James had been the taller one. Now Peter had an inch or two on him. "I heard you just recently did change flats."

"The one I was in had no closet," said Peter. "It was never meant for the long term."

"Ah, but I also hear you didn't pack everything."

Peter drew in a long, slow, steadying air and tried to decide how candid to be. "Maybe that wasn't meant for the long term, either."

"So there aren't any plans to... retrieve forgotten items?" James asked.

"Not forgotten." Peter's tone was low and mournful. "Lost, perhaps."

"Well, and I was lost to you once, too, but here we are," said James. "Let's take the stairs, shall we?"

Peter followed James down and out a door on the Embankment side of the building. It was the lunch hour and summer besides, and the gardens and pavements were choked with locals and tourists vying for space. "Where are we going?" Peter asked as James marched smartly onward, clearing a path with no visible effort.

"I keep a place just down here," James told him. "Sort of an office away from the office, someplace to go when it's been a long night and I don't want to wake Janette or Gabrielle."

"Your wife and daughter," Peter surmised.

"My wife and her daughter," James corrected.

"She's not yours?"

"Truthfully? I don't know. I've raised her as mine, at any rate, and she's a delightful girl. Just turned seven. This is it." James gestured at a tall, thin wedge of brick some four stories tall.

"The top floor?" Peter asked.

A vivid flash of white teeth as James pushed open the door. "All of it. I told Stephen to expect two for lunch."

"Of course you did," Peter murmured as he followed James inside and up two flights to a red and gold parlour with nothing but a round, black lacquer table and two chairs situated in front of the floor-to-ceiling window. The table was set for lunch with deceptively plain white china that, upon closer inspection, was finer than anything an upscale restaurant might use. Crystal goblets of ice water stood sweating and ready. The silverware, too, was heavy enough to prove its worth.

"I eat here almost every day," said James. "Much nicer than the canteen or holing up in the office. Those were Mum's," he added when he saw how Peter reacted to the fork he'd adjusted if only to have something to do with his hands. "The china is relatively new, though; a wedding gift that Janette didn't like, so I found use for it here."

Peter was spared the need for a response by the entrance of a man he assumed to be Stephen, who was carrying a tray featuring two chilled salad bowls. He set one on each of their plates, set a creamer of dressing in the center of the table, and was gone as swiftly and silently as he'd come.

James gestured for Peter to take the dressing first. "We could do this more often. There's a spacious office two down from mine."

"Did you offer that to Gordon, too?"

"I certainly encouraged him to move the camp. So many of them are already here. Trevor…"

"Not a winning point," said Peter.

"He needs to be contained, Peter. Which would be that much easier if you were on site."

"Oh, but you want oversight. *You* contain him. Better yet, get rid of him."

"Believe me, I'm watching for the opportunity," said James.

"Explains his nerves," Peter said. "He's worse even than usual."

"Well, if he has a nervous breakdown, that will save us some trouble."

Stephen reappeared and the salads were replaced with a creamy pasta tossed with vegetables and what Peter supposed were bits of chicken. He thought fleetingly and wistfully of Papa's.

"Wine?" James asked. Peter shook his head, and James waved Stephen away. "Tell me you'll at least think about it."

Peter had lost the thread of their conversation. "About what? Trevor?"

"Moving everyone over. The library can stay where it is," James was quick to put in, forestalling Peter's next objection. "We'll keep a few people there to make sure it's all right and tight."

Peter's gaze drifted out the window to where the tourists remained but the number of businesspeople was rapidly dwindling as they returned to work. "You realize I don't plan to keep the job."

"I'd very much like it if you did," said James. "I could use a little help with my French."

Peter made a point of not looking at James, though he very much wanted to, if only to gauge whatever expression James might be wearing at that moment. Peter's eyes flicked to the faint reflection in the window glass, but the glare made it impossible to discern anything more than the general line of James's profile.

"Is that why I'm here?" Peter asked. "I suppose you keep a bed upstairs."

"I do, actually," James said. "Would you like to see it?"

Peter pushed back in his chair and stood. "I should get back to work. The sooner we find Gordon, the sooner things can be settled to everyone's satisfaction."

James sat back in his chair and peered up at Peter under heavy eyelids. "It wouldn't satisfy me at all to have you leave the Agency. To have you disappear again."

An image flashed through Peter's mind: Byron, his fists clinched and eyes blazing as Peter picked up his packed overnighter for yet another weekend at the estate. How restful those weekends had been compared to dealing with Byron's intense need and fury, his hot and cold moods.

And James, what had he been? Easy going on the surface, but there was a deep well in him, dark and icy. James was used to getting what he wanted; how might he react when he didn't?

"Even if I leave the Agency, it doesn't mean I'll disappear," Peter told him.

The green-grey eyes ran Peter up and down, and finally James stood. "Just think," he said, "if you're not planning to stay any length of time, it shouldn't much matter to you if the staff changes buildings. Come on, then. Best not to leave Trevor unsupervised too long."

———

"Are we moving?" Simeon asked as Peter rounded the corner from the lifts.

"What? No. At least, not right away." It wasn't worth Peter asking Simeon how he'd known that had been the chief topic of conversation. Simeon wasn't a gossiper, but he did have big ears.

"Mr. Gamby asked that you call him when you get back," Simeon said as Peter unlocked his office door. Peter didn't answer, only went in, shut the door and shed his suit jacket, tossing it onto the sofa and dropping himself next to it. He felt in want of a shower, sticky in a way that had little to do with the warmth of the day.

There was a knock at the door. Peter ran his hands over his face and through his hair, unwittingly mussing it in a boyish way, so that when Gamby ambled in, he chuckled.

"What?" Peter asked.

"How was lunch?"

"They want us to move."

"But you told them no."

"I told them I'd think about it. If we could just find Gordon..."

Gamby snorted like an angry bull. "And what if we never find him, eh? You going to keep being half-arsed and pretending you have no stake in what's going on? Going to let them bury us under the weight of their administration?"

"Oh, for God's sake, Gamby. Did you come here just to lecture me?"

"I came to congratulate you on holding your ground. But maybe it's too soon." He sat down on the sofa next to Peter, his heft forcing Peter to move over just to keep from falling into the dent Gamby made in the leather. "Gordon wanted you for this job. He fashioned you for it. How disappointed would he be if you didn't actually *do* it?"

Peter sat back, once more risking falling into Gamby's crater. While Gamby stared at him, he stared at the ceiling. He'd known, of course, that Gordon wouldn't be around forever... Hadn't he? In truth, Peter had never thought about any future without Gordon. What he'd known logically—that Gordon would retire and he, Peter, would be expected to take up the throne—he had not prepared for emotionally.

But denial would get him and the Agency nowhere. It was a stage of grief and one Peter could not afford to luxuriate in. He *would* find Gordon, but he could not ignore every other task in favor of that one.

Gamby seemed to sense the shift in Peter. He pulled a couple sheets of paper from the inside pocket of his suit coat. They were curled from having been lightly folded to fit. "You need to sign these."

"What are they?"

Gamby didn't answer, merely handed them over. Peter took them, read the name and address on the first and the office assignment on the second, then rose and went to his desk, took his pen, and signed each paper where he stood. As he handed them back, Gamby asked, "That's it?"

"Get out," said Peter.

SEVEN

THE NEW FLAT had pale pearl grey walls and white moldings. All the lounge furniture looked like it had come from an art gallery; Peter was almost afraid to make any use of it. He spent more time in the bedroom, which had a reading nook by the window and was less intimidating. His habit had become to take his meals at the tiny table next to the primrose-colored armchair, avoiding the lounge and dining room entirely.

He had settled in with the *Times* when there came a tapping noise from another room. Peter first thought to ignore it, but the tapping got louder. Following the sound led Peter to the entry, and opening the door revealed Simeon standing there with a carton of take away.

"Mr. Gamby said I should check on you."

Peter frowned at the greasy carton.

"He also said you may not have had much for lunch, so..."

"People keep feeding me," Peter observed, stepping back to admit Simeon.

"You did have lunch then? Oh, this is nice." Simeon stopped in the middle of the lounge, and Peter, fearful the carton might not last much longer under the weight of whatever was bowing out its bottom, took the take away from Simeon's lax grip and ferried it into the kitchen.

"Of course I had lunch, and Gamby knows—" But it suddenly occurred to Peter what Gamby might have assumed about that lunch. "Have *you* eaten, Mr. Martin?"

Simeon tore his eyes from the finery and looked around to where Peter stood. "No, sir."

"Go sit at the table."

Simeon did as he was told and Peter split the dinner—some kind of beef and noodle dish—over two plates and brought them to the table before going back for forks and cans of lemonade. They ate in silence, Simeon's plate clean before Peter was half done.

"Why would Gamby think you need to check on me?" Peter finally asked, thinking to add a preemptive, "And don't shrug," just as one of Simeon's shoulders began to move.

With obvious effort, Simeon wrested his shoulder back down. "I don't know."

Peter caught Simeon in his gaze and Simeon shifted uncomfortably. "You do know."

"He only said you'd received some bad news," Simeon blurted. "And that, between that and not having eaten, you were in a terrible mood."

"And then he sent you into the lion's den."

Simeon started to shrug again but stopped himself. Peter was pleased to see the boy was at least a quick learner and somewhat self-aware.

"Well, I don't know what he expected you to do besides feed me," said Peter, standing and removing the plates.

"Oh, he..." Simeon rose, too, and began patting at his trouser pockets. "He gave me a note for you."

Peter gave a small sigh. "You might have said something sooner, Mr. Martin."

"Sorry." Simeon held out the envelope and Peter came to take it. Sealed. Peter glanced at Simeon and for the first time that evening, the boy looked a bit nervous.

"You know something about this?" Peter asked.

Simeon shook his head.

Peter slipped a finger under the flap and tugged until he

could get enough of a rip to open it. Inside was a piece of notepaper, imperfectly folded and ripped on one corner—a hasty job. Peter pulled it free and opened it.

Not Gamby's writing.

Peter swallowed against the lump that formed in his throat; he'd seen enough grocery lists in that neat hand. Even in a rush, Charles's block letters looked cleaner than most other people's best handwriting.

"Carlton," Simeon said aloud. Then, "What does it mean?"

It was the only word on the page. Peter frowned over at where Simeon stood craning to see over his arm. "I'm sure it wasn't intended for you, Mr. Martin." Which was better than admitting he had no idea what Charles could have meant by it. Nor could Peter imagine a scenario in which Charles would have gone through Gamby in order to reach him. At least, not unless there were no other options.

"I'm sure you have better things to do in any case. Your girl-friend, what was her name? Katy?"

Simeon turned pink. "Yes, sir."

"You'd rather be spending your personal time with her, I'm sure." And when Simeon hesitated, looking trapped, Peter insisted, "Go on, Mr. Martin. I will see you in the morning."

Peter waited some minutes after the sound of Simeon's foot-steps faded before going for his suit coat and slipping on his shoes.

———

The Agency was never deserted, but that evening showed it to be the nearest thing to abandoned Peter had ever witnessed. The gatekeeper was an older fellow; he checked Peter's badge in silence, and in the utter lack of sound, the lift's bell seemed far too loud. Peter would have walked up, if possible, but the lift was the only way to the second floor aside from the necessary fire exits at the back of the building. It was otherwise completely isolated, its only entrance kept under careful watch.

This was the records room.

The door was heavy, wooden, with a long, narrow window reinforced by mesh. Peering through, Peter could see the bow of the desk set off to the right, large enough to suggest the prow of a ship ready to set sail into the ceiling-high shelves that stood before it. And at the helm was Beth, her wheat-colored hair neatly secured at the nape of her neck and looking brilliant against her simple black dress. She turned as Peter pushed open the door.

"Mr. Stoller!"

Peter tried to smile and hoped it looked natural enough; maybe Beth would chalk it up to strain more than nerves. And why should he be nervous? He was not out to do anything wrong. But he was terrified, perhaps of the answers that awaited him. Ignorance was bliss, but his work did not allow for either.

"Can I help you find something?" Beth asked, and Peter took in the dip of her sculpted brows and the tiny frown that folded the corners of her mouth and read concern there.

"I'll find it myself, thank you, Beth."

Beth's eyes tracked toward the multitude of shelves, and it was clear she was not convinced. But Peter had done enough finding and fetching for Gordon—and even before that, as a scribe—and his memory was sharp enough to not require Beth's services. Thank God. He had no desire to spread the search any wider; bad enough Simeon knew as much as he did.

Beyond the desk stood what amounted to a card catalogue, though the system of organization was far different, established by and known only to the Agency. Dates, names, code words, and cross-referenced files... A certain amount of memorization was involved as key information had been reduced to numbers that were merely random and had no establishing system at all. It was central to the curriculum at the Bastion and the bane of many young knaves.

Beth cleared her throat, and Peter paused on his way to the cabinet. She smiled shyly. "Sorry, but..." One vivid pink nail tapped the register.

"Of course," said Peter. He took up the pen and signed in, glancing up at the clock behind Beth for the time.

"Pretty late," she said. "I guess your assistant has already left."

Peter wondered if she were digging for information or merely bored, being stuck in an empty room filled with papers for hours on end. He opted for another half smile and went on with his task.

The files were arranged first by current, closed, and those that fell in between—the cases that had never come to any satisfactory conclusion and were (though no one wanted to say it) dead ends. Peter did not know what "Carlton" might be. A person? With a tiny catch of breath, it flashed across Peter's mind that Charles might have been giving him his genuine surname.

But why now?

A quick search turned up a six Carltons, including one with the middle name Charles. Peter went to retrieve the files.

More than an hour later, Peter was no closer to understanding Charles's concise message. It was clear enough Maxwell Charles Carlton was *not* Charles; the man had died in 1958. But whether Maxwell or any of the other Carltons were important in some other way remained to be determined. Of the stack, two were current agents, three were deceased agents, and one had been a questionable citizen about whom no formal decision had been made, and that man had died in 1949.

Peter shifted the stack of folders to one side of the research table he had commandeered and ran his hands over his face in an effort to get the blood moving so he could think more clearly. But then the sound of a step on the worn, industrial carpeting startled him; Peter dropped his hands to the table—the resulting clap seeming outrageously loud in the hush of the room—and the stack of files slid, two of them falling to the floor.

Peter glanced to his right as he leaned to pick up the runaways. Beth stepped closer and all but leaned over him as she set a cup and saucer on the table, her flowery perfume threatening to make Peter dizzy. "I thought you might like some tea."

"Thank you," he murmured.

"Do any of these need to be put back?"

Something cold crawled through Peter, and he was perhaps more brusque than necessary when he answered, "No. I'll put them back myself when I'm done."

Beth twitched like a rabbit and, just as a paralyzed rabbit might, seemed unsure of which way to hop. Needled by sympathy, Peter said, "I thought drinks weren't allowed in here."

Beth pressed her lips together, and Peter read in her face her quandary of whether to be serious or coy. Finally, she said, "I know you'll be careful."

"I promise not to tell anyone," Peter told her.

"Just let me know if you need a refill. Or anything else."

Peter darted a look at her and realized she'd reapplied her makeup. "I certainly will," he said, and she swished away.

Peter sipped at the tea, grateful it was still hot. He eyed the folders thoughtfully and, once the tea was gone, returned to the catalogue to resume his search. After people would be places then, should that not yield anything useful, he would dig into operations names and other minutiae. And if that didn't help? He would have to begin looking outside the Agency for the answer. But God only knew how many people, places, and things would bear the name Carlton.

A momentary sense of fruitlessness fell over Peter like a wet and heavy blanket, and he found himself standing in front of the catalogue cabinet, unable to move. Aware of Beth's surreptitious glances from the desk behind him, however, Peter forced himself into action.

There were, of course, a number of towns named Carlton. In Selby, there had been some Agency action a few years before. Could that be what Charles wanted Peter to research?

Asking himself more questions wouldn't get him any answers. Peter set that file aside as a possibility and moved on to the next. Opening the folder, he was confronted with a photo of a beloved memory: an old estate house sitting in a park of savage grass. It was called—and Peter had never known its name, had never heard anyone speak it—Carlton Rise.

Heart thumping and breath caught in his throat, Peter began

flipping through the contents. The estate had been closed eleven years prior and was now held merely as a land asset for the Agency. A road map was clipped to the back of the file, with a road added in red ink to indicate the exact location. The line ended in a circle made blotchy where the ink had spread.

Peter sat back and considered. Bags were not permitted in the records room, nor was there a photocopier. Records were not allowed to leave the room unless signed for by at least two people of certain rank, thus ensuring no one took information in secret; there was always at least one other person (besides the librarian) who knew what was circulating. Even being the reigning king would not win Peter a pass.

He could call Gamby, of course. But he dreaded Gamby's prying questions, or worse, his smugness.

He thought of the tiny camera in his desk upstairs. It was small enough to fit into his jacket pocket. But even if he covered the flash, the sound of the mechanism would be too loud in the quiet.

Finally, he thought of Beth—the makeup, the perfume, the exaggerated swing of her hips when she'd walked away—and a sick sort of swirling began in Peter's stomach. He'd done it before, though not since Charles. But it was clear from Beth's behavior that Gordon really had kept a lid on things, at least at home in the Castle. The damsels still considered Peter a fair catch.

He re-shelved all but the Carlton Rise file, which he slipped into completely the wrong spot on a shelf, if only to make it quickly accessible. Then he carried the teacup and saucer up to the desk. "Beth..."

He almost froze when he saw the dark-haired woman turn from her spot behind the desk. "Good evening, Mr. Stoller. Beth's shift ended about twenty minutes ago." She looked at the teacup and raised her brows.

As he got closer, Peter saw the woman's hair was threaded with silver, her eyes lined by deep wrinkles. And he had no idea who she was. "I was only hoping for more tea," he said.

She pressed her lips into an uncompromising line. "Someone's been naughty." And when Peter failed to hide his shock, she added, "You're not supposed to have drinks in here."

Peter tried to look sheepish. "No, I suppose not. I should just go down to the canteen instead."

"I would have to leave the desk to bring you tea," the woman went on, and Peter became afraid she might begin to enumerate all the reasons she could not and would not fulfill his request. "If Beth brought you that, well... She shouldn't have. Not without calling for someone to watch the desk while she was away."

"You're right, of course."

"Did she?"

"Did she what?"

"Call for someone to cover her break?"

"I don't... Beth is the only person I've seen here tonight. Except you."

The woman squinted at him slightly, as if trying to see into him somehow. Then she reached out and took the cup and saucer from him. "I suppose the place is in good enough hands if you're here," she said and rounded the desk and left.

Peter was so stunned that for a moment he only stood there. Then, once the lift had chimed its departure, he swiftly returned for the Carlton Rise folder. He stopped on the way out to sign out of the register and debated leaving some kind of apologetic note, perhaps stating he'd been called away. But by whom? No need to make it any more complicated, and he needed to get out before she came back; if they were to cross at the lift, there would be trouble of the worst possible kind. So, tucking the file under his arm, he went and rang for the lift.

Except he pushed down.

Then realized he couldn't go down.

The gatekeeper was not going to let him walk out with a file. He would have to take it up to his office instead. Take the photos, then return the folder to the records room.

But, God, how was he going to do that? He hadn't thought this through completely, he realized, and was on the brink of going back into the library when the lift rang. And it was going up.

Peter decided to take it as a sign. He stepped aboard the empty car and rode up to the sanctuary of his—unknowingly, he'd grown accustomed to thinking of it as his—office.

____

EIGHT

____

HE DIDN'T HAVE his key.

Knowing it wouldn't be allowed in the records room, Peter hadn't brought his briefcase, and not anticipating any need to visit his office, the key was still nestled in the zippered pocket of that briefcase.

Now Peter stood outside his office door, pilfered file still under his arm. He tested the knob, just to be sure, or maybe just to try his luck, but the door remained firmly set against him.

Peter glanced over his shoulder, and his eyes fell on Simeon's desk. He stepped over to it and tested a drawer. Unlocked and filled with unused paper for the typewriter. Peter slipped the file into it and closed the drawer with a trundling thud, then opened the central pencil drawer. There were pencils, yes, and pens, but no paperclips. A second drawer produced a small note pad, two candy bars, a pack of chewing gum, and one half-full bag of crisps. But still no paperclips. A final drawer held nothing but a bottle of correction fluid with so much crust built up around the neck Peter doubted it could be opened.

Not relishing the idea of prowling the floor and searching people's desks for paperclips, Peter had more or less concluded he would have to simply take the whole thing up on the morrow (ideally arriving before Simeon so as to fetch back the file), when Gerald Kerr rounded the corner; he stopped when he saw Peter.

"Mr. Stoller..." The way his voice trailed told Peter that Gerry wanted to ask but was afraid or unsure of what to say.

"Forgot my key," Peter told him ruefully. "Can you imagine? Came all the way down here and..." He gestured, open palms up in a show of hopelessness.

Gerry's eyes strayed to the locked office door.

"It's all right," Peter told him. "It was just something that popped into my head; it will keep until tomorrow. I know no one else has a key."

Gerry lowered his brows. "Of course we have a key."

And now Peter was confused. "I thought housekeeping—"

"No, they don't have a key. Not any more," Gerry agreed. "Mr. Lessenby didn't want... But the stewards keep one. For emergencies."

"Would this constitute an emergency?" Peter asked, then realized that it was for him to tell Gerry whether it was one. "No, probably not."

"It's no trouble," Gerry insisted. "I can be right back with it."

He was lumbering away before Peter could answer. Peter waited awkwardly with his hand on the back of Simeon's chair, trying to decide whether to sit down, and then Gerry was back with the key flashing in bright contrast to the meaty flesh of his hand. Gerry held it out in offering, and Peter plucked it up. "Thank you." He went and unlocked the door, stepped inside.

Peter waited until he was sure of Gerry's departure before going back out to retrieve the file from Simeon's desk. Then he returned to his office and closed and locked the door behind him. He took the file to his desk and made to open one of his drawers, thinking to get his camera, but the drawer would not budge.

He'd locked his desk before leaving that afternoon.

Peter groaned and sat down. But he couldn't wallow for long; his training wouldn't allow for that. He asked himself—demanded, really—what he would do if this were a field situation. And he answered himself with two choices: either commit the information to memory, or try to get it out of the building. If not by camera, then on paper.

Peter opened the file for another look. How much of the information there did he really need? Only the map, he decided. He only needed to be able to get there. He pulled the corresponding pages free and folded them into as small and tight a rectangle as he could, then slipped that into his suit coat pocket.

As for the rest of the file... Peter went to the cabinet against the wall, drew open the bottommost drawer (not locked, something in him noted; he'd finally won a round), and dropped the file below those that hung inside, so that Carlton Rise lay below the swinging folders as if lost and forgotten.

———

He had to knock four times in ever increasing increments of loudness before Simeon opened the door. The young man's hair was disheveled and he had not taken the time to put on a shirt, which enlightened Peter to the fact that when Simeon blushed, his chest turned red as well as his face and neck.

"Mr.—Mr. Stoller!" Simeon stammered. "I, uh..." He glanced over his shoulder and Peter wondered whether the lovely Katy were somewhere within.

"I only need your car, Mr. Martin."

"My... Hang on. Come in." Simeon stepped back to allow Peter to enter the flat, smaller even than the one Peter had so recently shared with Charles, and not in as nice a part of the city, either. It was not, Peter surmised, a place to bring a lady after a certain hour unless one were prepared to fight off potential thugs, and evidently Simeon thought as much as well, since there was no one else in the bed. There would not have been *room* for anyone else in the bed, shoved into a corner as it was, and only just large enough to fit Simeon. There was a telly on a bureau placed so that one might sit on the bed and watch, another tiny table beside the bed with a can of soda on it, and something that barely passed as a kitchen, with a door leading to the bathroom. The whole of the place would have fit in Peter's current lounge with room left over.

As Peter took it in, Simeon swiped a t-shirt from its careless placement on the deep blue carpet and slipped it over his head. "Why do you need my car? You could just call the service. Unless..." Simeon's dark eyes darted speculatively at Peter's narrow profile. "Carlton?"

"The keys, Mr. Martin. Oh, and..." Peter reached into his pocket to remove the stewards' key to his office, though as he drew it out, a corner of folded paper appeared. "Return this to Gerald Kerr, would you?"

Simeon accepted the key, trading it for a small ring of several similar keys. "You'll need a navigator." And before Peter could deny it, "Driving in the dark and all. You won't be able to see whatever map or directions you have there."

"Nor would you."

"There's a pen light in the glove box. But it would be easier to have someone else use it."

Peter asked himself why he'd elected to go to Simeon rather than Gamby and concluded it was *not* because he thought Simeon would be less likely to demand answers. Had Peter honestly believed he would be able to go alone? Had he wanted to? If so, why not hire a car instead? No, the truth was if he were going to have a long drive in the middle of the night with someone—and he was, for whatever uninspected reason he'd clearly chosen to have company—he'd rather it be Simeon.

Well, and Gamby would have insisted on driving.

"Comb your hair and put on some real trousers," said Peter with a nod at Simeon's pyjama bottoms, and when the young man flushed again, Peter added, "I'll wait in the car."

———

It would take some two hours to get there, by Peter's estimate, less if he chose to drive faster than the posted limits. But getting there any sooner would make little difference; it would be very late (or early) either way.

They drove in silence until London was behind them. Then Simeon asked, "So who is Carlton?"

"Not a who," said Peter. "A where." He pulled the map from

his pocket and handed it to Simeon, who wrestled with the tight folds then peered at the paper in the darkness.

"What's there?" Simeon asked.

"I thought you had a pen light."

Simeon opened the compartment and fumbled around before producing the promised light. But he didn't bother to use it, only sat staring into the darkness beyond the windscreen. After a moment, in a voice so low Peter almost couldn't make out the words, Simeon asked, "Is Mr. Lessenby there?"

"If we're lucky, yes."

Simeon's head whipped around, and in the gloom his dark eyes glittered. "Why if we're lucky? What difference does it make if we find him?"

"Mr. Martin!" Repressive. The same voice, Peter reflected, his father had used when confronted with something he did not want to acknowledge.

"It's not as if he's going to come back to work," Simeon pressed. "So if you find him, what then? Are you going to quit, too?"

"No." And beside him Simeon let out a long breath like a balloon exhaling its contents, all tension released. Peter realized it had been the right thing to say, even if he was not entirely convinced it was true.

They rolled on in quiet for a good while, and once or twice Peter was induced to glance over at Simeon just to see if the boy had fallen asleep. But every time Peter turned his head, Simeon responded by turning to look back at him, until finally Peter quietly asked Simeon to check the map. From there on conversation was made up of a series of murmurs designed only to press at but never shatter the lull that seemed to have settled over them as they sped through the dark countryside.

The landscape became familiar yet not familiar, like flashes from a half-remembered dream. Then all at once the gates were there, looming as they always had, and if they were a bit rustier than before, Peter could not tell. Still, as he brought Simeon's car to a halt before them, Peter realized it had been a bad idea to leave London so late—or so early. Why hadn't he waited at least a few hours? Then they might have arrived at a somewhat reasonable hour. As it stood, it was coming up on three in the morning, and Peter found himself staring mournfully out the window at the call box, reluctant to use it.

"What are we doing?" Simeon asked, and Peter could only answer truthfully, "I don't know." He should have gone to Charles first, however awkward that might have been, and found out how Charles had discovered this place. All at once Peter felt the collar around his neck, the tugging of the leash—he'd been led, had allowed himself to be led by the promise of something wonderful at the end of the road.

Well, this was the end of the road. His progress was barred.

The sound of the door unlatching startled Peter from his thoughts. Simeon was climbing from the car.

"Simeon!"

The young man ducked and tipped his head to see Peter, and said, "You never call me Simeon."

"Get in the car."

"I'm going to check the gate." And before Peter could protest further, Simeon walked over to the tall iron bars and tested them, first pushing, then pulling. Nothing happened. Peter watched through the windscreen as Simeon went to examine the gate hinges then turned his attention to the call box.

Peter got out of the car then, angling to intercept anything Simeon might do. But Simeon was already poking experimentally at the buttons. "I don't think it's connected."

Peter glanced up at the camera mounted above the box, but there was nothing to indicate it was working. "I'm sorry, Mr. Martin. It seems we've come a long way for nothing."

"So we just go back?"

Peter tried to decide what he would do if Simeon were not with him, but it hardly mattered. With the young man watching, Peter felt compelled to act as a good role model. Upon revised thought, however, Peter considered that giving up was not a terribly fruitful example; in the field, agents were often forced to come up with plans on the spot.

He eyed the gate. It was sturdy but not particularly tall, made to stop cars rather than people, while the higher walls of smooth grey stone were what would keep people from climbing over. "No," Peter decided, "so long as you don't mind my standing on your car."

Simeon glanced at the automobile and Peter went to pull the car closer to the gates, all but nudging up against them. Once standing on the bonnet, Peter was nearly as tall as the bars.

"What about me?" Simeon asked.

"Can you climb?"

With a grimace for his paint job, Simeon joined Peter on the car.

"Go on, then, Mr. Martin."

The boy was not as tall as Peter, but he had youthful energy on his side. He launched himself at the iron. "Like climbing the rope," Peter told him. Of course there wasn't room to get his legs wrapped around any one bar, but somehow Simeon managed to shimmy up and seat himself on the gentle curve of the top of the gate, pausing to catch his breath.

"I can probably..." Simeon lowered himself down the other side of the gate, his feet dangling as close to the ground as he could possibly get them before letting go and dropping.

"Very good, Mr. Martin," Peter told Simeon when he reappeared, disheveled and dirty, long blades of dying grass clinging to him.

Peter reached out and took hold of the iron bars of the gate, hauled himself up to the top, and was just swinging himself over when the sharp squeal of the mechanism and unexpected movement startled him into releasing his hold. He tumbled, landing hard on his back on the dusty track that served as the drive.

"Mr. Stoller!" Simeon's face appeared above Peter's. "The gate is opening!"

"So I gathered." Peter sat up, gave his head a moment to clear before getting all the way to his feet. He considered the car but hesitated to bring it up to the house, lest they end up trapped inside the gates with no transportation on the outside.

"Mr. Stoller..."

Peter turned and saw the bobbing of a torch, growing closer

as its bearer made his way up the path from the house. It was not a perfectly straight route, and from time to time the light would turn as whomever carried it must. But then it came straight again, and for the last few meters the round, yellow-white of the torch came at them like the lamp of an oncoming train.

Beside him, Simeon shifted his feet as if anticipating trouble. Without thinking about it, Peter slanted himself between Simeon and whoever was coming. And then came the familiar chuckle, quiet but carried clearly through the still darkness, and behind the brilliance of the torch, Gordon Lessenby appeared.

"I'm sorry, Peter. I should have opened them sooner. I just wondered what you might do." And he gestured at the camera Peter had thought wasn't working.

Peter squinted over the torch to better see Gordon. "You're looking well," he decided, and indeed Gordon did appear fit, his shoulders less stooped, his eyes less heavy. But rather than grati-fied, Peter found himself oddly disappointed. This was not a man who needed him.

"Come up," said Gordon, and then to Simeon, "It's your car, isn't it? Give us a minute to get out of your way, then bring it through."

———

"How did you find me?" Gordon asked as he and Peter walked back toward Carlton Rise. And before Peter could admit it had been someone else's idea, Gordon went on, "I knew you would, of course. Eventually."

"Why did you leave?"

"Some day, Peter, you'll discover it *is* possible to get tired of fighting. Of scaling the gates that are locked against you."

"What's locked against you?" Peter demanded. "You were in charge, you—"

But Gordon was shaking his head. "And you can't do my fighting for me, either. No matter how badly you want to.

"I planned it, you know," said Gordon as the house came into view, a black hulk blotting out the starry sky. "Closed the house, locked it up, made sure it was forgotten. Trust you to remember it." The affectionate, lop-sided smile that Gordon bestowed made Peter's throat tighten. He wanted desperately to be able to say yes, he'd worked it out, but he hadn't.

"I didn't—"

Behind them came the coughing of a car engine brought to life. Though Gordon glanced over his shoulder, he did not quicken his pace.

"Someone else knows you planned it," Peter said, the sound of the car prompting him to haste. "At the very least, knows where you are."

The pop and hiss of a slow-moving vehicle crept up on them. But Gordon had stopped walking now. "No, Peter, I don't think—"

As if the lion that had been stalking them had decided to make its move, the car engine roared with a sudden application of speed. Peter saw Gordon frown and turn again to look over his shoulder. But before Peter could follow his gaze, Gordon was suddenly gone, replaced by the blackness of the sky. And then Peter, too, was gone, airborne, the only concrete thought he could cling to in the swirl of confusion being: *The car*.

―――――――――――

NINE

―――――――――――

HE DID NOT KNOW where he was, but it hurt to be there. And *he* hurt as well; his back, his head, there was not a place on his body that was comfortable.

Before attempting to move, Peter first took mental stock. Here was grass, and the jabbing behind his knee was almost certainly a stone. The grey above him was sky, showing signs of dawn. He was outside on the ground, then, but was at a momentary loss as to why.

And then: *Car.*

And: *Gordon.*

Peter struggled to sit up, ignoring the warning screams of his muscles and bones. How long had he lain there? Was Gordon hurt? Where was Simeon?

It became almost immediately clear to Peter his left ankle would not bear any weight, nor was his left hand inclined to do more than hang limply at its wrist. The rest of his body moved only reluctantly, but he did finally manage to get as far as his knees; his foot did not allow him to fully stand.

He was only a couple meters off the path that led up to the house; the car had struck them forcefully but had not had time to garner much speed. There was no sign of the vehicle now and, at first glimpse, no sign of Gordon or Simeon either. Until

Peter's eyes fell on a dark point that contrasted with the untended, half-dead grass on the other side of the path, an odd arrow of dark brown as if pointing to heaven.

The toe, Peter slowly came to understand, of Gordon's shoe.

There came a low moaning sound, and a minute or so passed before Peter became aware he was the source of it. He dragged his useless foot along to the dirt drive and over, seemingly unable to stop the keening whine issuing from his throat. If anything, it was getting louder the more he saw. The shoe, followed by the foot that was mostly free of that shoe, as if Gordon had just begun to slip off his loafers; the Argyle sock; the clay-colored trouser leg; the belt that was the same brown as the shoe, its buckle winking in reflection of the rapidly bluing sky; the cream-colored jumper; and finally, the head, face turned away from Peter at a horrifyingly unnatural angle. And now the long, low moan took on substance in Peter's throat, became a bulbous entity threatening to choke him, so that the sob was abruptly cut short.

Peter swayed on the edge of the path, not wanting to get any closer, but knowing he had to confirm what he already knew. If he could put it off a few more minutes, then for that short while it might not be true. But perversely, the longer he waited, the more real and true it became; there was no escape, and finally Peter was motivated to put an end to it by closing that last bit of distance and folding himself beside Gordon's body.

Left hand useless, Peter shifted so that he could more easily use his right to press at Gordon's ruined neck in vain search of a pulse. The skin was still lukewarm, still elastic, but there was no telltale thrum, no hint of a heart. Peter blinked a few times, waiting for tears, but though his eyes felt hot, none came.

Simeon. Peter struggled to his knees once more, and now his body was beginning to tingle with a kind of numbness—shock. He looked up the path toward the house; from where he knelt, he could see clearly to where the drive formed a circle to allow cars to turn around, but there was no car there now. So Peter turned to look back toward the gate, but from the turns in the path and the few trees, it was not visible.

He started the slow and painful journey back toward the gate and, once there, found what he'd expected to find. The boy was breathing at least, but the bruise on Simeon's forehead was bulging and almost as dark as his hair. Which meant there was a chance Simeon had seen who it was.

They'd left Simeon's car, too, though its front bumper was now hanging on one side and there were sizeable dents in the bonnet.

Peter wasn't sure how long he sat there, but once he'd satisfied himself that Simeon was alive, the exhaustion hit him and he hadn't the energy to move again. He thought about what he should do: crawk up to the house, call in, try to get Simeon inside, get the gate closed at the very least. But all Peter could do was sit there on the warming gravel as the sun made its way up for a better look at them.

And then Simeon started to move. Peter looked down at him, watched as the young man stirred and winced and tried to open his eyes only to close them again against the glare of the morning. "Mr. Stoller..."

"Yes, Mr. Martin?"

"Something happened."

"Yes, Mr. Martin."

There was silence for a moment until Simeon tried to sit up. Then turned over and vomited. "I feel seasick."

"Concussion. You've got a lovely egg on your head there. Do you remember anything?"

Simeon started to shake his head but gagged again at the motion. "Only coming to get the car, and then..."

"And then?"

"Something hit me."

"Some*one*," Peter corrected. "Though they probably did use something. Can you stand?"

"I can barely sit," Simeon complained, but he got to his feet anyway, then found himself looking down at Peter. "What about you?"

"I've broken an ankle and a wrist. Go up to the house and call Gamby."

"Where's Mr. Lessenby?" asked Simeon.

Something acrid flooded Peter's mouth, and his throat tightened. "You'll pass him on the way," he managed. "Just go."

For a second it seemed Simeon might argue, but finally the boy turned and shuffled his way up the path, pausing now and again to get his bearings. It was only once Simeon was out of sight that Peter allowed himself to cry.

———

Some amount of time passed; Peter looked at his watch only to find the glass netted with fractures and the hands stopped at 3:49. Beginning to worry that Simeon had not made it to the house, Peter struggled up again, this time determined to get all the way to his feet. He rested against the car a moment, then followed the boy up the path, gritting his teeth against the pain in his ankle. If Jules could survive weeks while injured in the field, Peter knew he needed to be able to do at least this much. He passed the place where Gordon lay, this time noticing the marks in the dirt that showed where they'd stood when they'd been hit; Gordon had been a step or two nearer the car, which was why he'd been struck first and borne the brunt of the impact.

Peter forced himself to continue on up to the house. The door hung open, and Simeon was seated on the needlepoint chair in the entry, next to the telephone table. He looked up as Peter closed the door, dark eyes filled with anguish. "I'm sorry..."

"It's all right. You phoned Gamby?" A tiny nod. "We need to close the gate."

Simeon rose, none too steadily. "I'll do it. You should sit. I'll..." Simeon's gaze traveled down the hall, its once polished wood now scuffed for lack of Imogen's care. Peter tried to imagine Gordon knocking around the massive space, alone...

"The kitchen is straight back and around the first corner," Peter recalled. "You'll find the gate switch in a small room behind the pantry."

Simeon nodded again and Peter collapsed into the chair. When Simeon returned, he brought tea with him. "Can you make it into the front room?"

Peter assured him he could and did, settling into a much more comfortable, if worn and vilely mustard yellow, armchair. The chair Gordon had always sat in, but Simeon had taken the brown one Peter thought of as his own, even after a decade of not having been to Carlton Rise. Simeon silently poured out tea, added sugar just as Peter preferred it, and nudged the cup and saucer across the small table that spanned the space between the chairs to within Peter's reach.

They sipped tea and gazed out the window. After a moment, Simeon asked, "Should we... Bring him in?"

"Wait until they can take some pictures for the file."

"Oh, God," said Simeon, his cheeks losing color. It was the last thing either of them said until the buzzing of the call box alerted them to Gamby's arrival.

———

"Leave your car at the gate," Peter instructed, and a minute later Gamby arrived on foot. Not bothering to knock, Peter and Simeon heard the front door open, followed by Gamby's bellow of, "Peter! Where the...?" And then, "Oh," as Gamby reached the front parlour.

"I came in advance of the housekeepers," Gamby said without preamble, "but they're right behind, won't be long. What in blazes happened?"

"He's outside," Peter said dully.

"I saw. Looked like Martin here hit him with the car."

Simeon gave a little yelp, and Peter replied evenly, "It wasn't Mr. Martin. Though they did use his car."

"Who then?" asked Gamby. "You were followed?"

"No. This person was on foot. May have parked farther along the road so as not to be seen, but didn't follow us in a car, not all the way up. Whoever did this already knew Gordon was here and was waiting for an opportunity. The open gate gave him one."

"Or her," added Simeon quietly, almost to himself, so that he was startled to look up and find both Peter and Gamby staring at him. "Well," said Simeon, "it's not as if we've had much luck with women lately. Mrs. Lessenby and Miranda…"

"Who knew he was here?" Gamby asked. "How did you find him?"

"The note you had Mr. Martin deliver, the one that came from Charles," said Peter.

"And where did he get the information?"

"The gate is still open after you," was all Peter said. "Someone should close it."

———

Housekeeping came and two of them set to work on Peter's wrist and ankle while another kept admonishing Simeon to sit still while she tended to his head. Through the closed windows, Gamby's shouts were muffled but no less forceful as the team took photographs, made notes, towed Simeon's car, and finally removed Gordon.

Wanting to remain lucid, Peter had declined painkillers in advance of the questioning he knew was coming. Simeon was led from the room, looking confused and stricken, to be interviewed elsewhere. Meanwhile, Peter stayed put, elevating his foot on an ottoman as prescribed, and finally an unprepossessing man in grey tweed and wire rims arrived to take his statement. Peter gave it as dispassionately as he could manage, only needing to pause when describing finding Gordon.

"And what prompted you to come out here in the middle of the night?" the tweedy man asked.

"I only wanted to see it again," said Peter.

"It couldn't wait until morning?"

"I thought I would come, have a look, and be back in London by morning."

"Nostalgia. That was all?"

"That was all," Peter assured. "The past is all we have to build on."

————

After tasking the housekeepers with cleaning then closing up the estate, Gamby herded Simeon into the back of his car and Peter into the passenger seat for the long ride back to the city. "Boy has enough sense, I hope, not to say anything about the note?" Gamby asked Peter.

Simeon's voice floated sullenly from the back. "I'm right here. And I only said that Mr. Stoller had turned up wanting to borrow my car. I never mentioned the note."

Gamby threw an impressed look at Peter. "He's learning."

"He's not a dog, Gamby," said Peter. "Nor is he a fool."

"Nor do I have a car any more," Simeon muttered, but Peter and Gamby ignored him.

"Charles has been out here before?" asked Gamby.

Peter shook his head. "No idea. It's been closed for years. Gordon said... He said he'd planned it. Had closed the house so that everyone would forget it."

Gamby grunted. "Damn strange retirement plan."

"What was he going to do with Mrs. Lessenby then?" Simeon asked.

Peter craned around to look at him. "What?"

"If Mr. Lessenby was planning to retire out here... Was he going to bring Mrs. Lessenby too?"

Peter sat back hard against his seat. He tried to picture Elinor enjoying the rural life, but his imagination refused to cooperate; Elinor had enjoyed socializing and shopping and would have hated being in the middle of nowhere. And Gordon would certainly have known that.

"We need to talk to Charles," Gamby said, "see what tipped him off." He glanced over at Peter. "I'll do it, if you want."

Peter felt sick at the idea of putting Gamby and Charles in the same room ever again. "No. I'll do it. Mr. Martin, when we get back, you'll have Mr...." Peter struggled with the new name, "Ennion brought round to my office."

Simeon mumbled something that Peter took as aquiescence, and Peter spent the remainder of the drive wishing he'd asked for the painkillers after all.

TEN

IT WAS, Peter discovered, supremely difficult to do anything with one's arm in a sling and one's ankle in a brace. Gamby had dropped him at his flat so he could change and clean up a bit before returning to the office. Easy enough if he'd had use of both arms and legs, and thank God the building had a lift, but things like changing clothes and washing up proved to be a constant wrangle.

Always thinking ahead, Gamby had also sent an Agency car around to bring Peter to the Castle when he was ready. He found Simeon already at his desk, fresh bandage covering his bulging bruise. "I'll call him now," Simeon said and was already on the phone by the time Peter had unlocked his office.

Peter was still trying to find a comfortable way to sit when the knock came, followed by the door opening a crack and a familiar crown of greying hair and a blue eye slipping through.

"How did you know?" Peter asked.

Charles stepped the rest of the way into the office and closed the door behind. "I heard... I'm so very sorry, Peter. I know he was like a fa—"

"How did you know where he was?"

Charles inched toward Peter's desk, and for the first time Peter realized Charles had brought something with him—a book, which he now held out to Peter like an offering of raw meat to a ravenous tiger. But instead of reaching for it, devouring the information, Peter actually drew back slightly, eyes trained on the book.

Decamerone. An old copy in the original Florentine and likely worth a great deal. "He sent it to you," Peter said, a dripping sort of numbness starting at his head and working its way down. "One of your messages."

Charles laid the book on the desk. "Peter..."

"Why?" Peter asked. He lifted his eyes from the book and met Charles's brilliant gaze. "Why you and not me?"

"Peter," Charles sighed again. He glanced around the office. "You don't keep any hidden...?" He made a gesture that suggested a drinking glass.

Peter was beginning to have the dooming feeling one got when a doctor was about to impart bad news. "I could have Simeon bring tea."

Charles blinked. "When did you start calling him Simeon?"

"When you left," said Peter, feeling needled. He thought the pain in Charles's face would salve him somehow but discovered it only left him feeling hollower. Quite a feat considering he hadn't thought it possible to feel any more empty than he already had.

"I'm not sure tea will be strong enough," said Charles. "But it certainly couldn't hurt."

Peter reached for the intercom button on his phone and asked Simeon to bring in the tray. There was a pause long enough to make Peter wonder whether Simeon had wandered away from his desk, but at last a faint, "Yes, sir," floated back to them.

Charles settled himself in the chair and said, "He can't be an assistant forever."

"He's hardly your concern," Peter retorted, and they sat in silence until Simeon arrived with tea, which he set on Peter's desk for lack of any other surface. Peter watched Simeon's face as the boy absorbed everything: the quiet, the strained expressions, the book on the desk. Simeon's dark eyes flashed at Peter, and Peter saw he'd put the pieces together. Good lad.

"Thank you, Mr. Martin, that will be all for now."

Simeon beat a hasty retreat.

"I'll play mother," Charles said, drawing his chair closer to the desk. And with a nod at Peter's sling, "Broken, is it?"

"Shouldn't need surgery," Peter said, and Charles nodded and handed him a cup.

"At least it's the left."

Peter sipped at his tea; Simeon was getting better at making it. Finally, he asked, "What was Gordon's message to you?"

"The moment I received it, Peter, I sent it to you."

"Through Gamby," Peter pointed out.

"I thought it would be better that way."

Peter tried to comprehend the vast change between them, one that would make Charles feel more inclined to approach Gamby than Peter himself. An arrow of regret shot up from Peter's stomach and into his throat, and he set down his tea, unable to drink any more.

"And was that it? 'Carlton'?"

Charles set his cup down as well, and Peter was momentarily distracted by the dainty vessel with its blue roses and gilded rim, so out of place in such a masculine setting. A reminder, he supposed, of the gentility they hoped to adopt or at least affect when in reality they worked under harsh conditions and were harsh men.

Yet Charles, with his thick fingers, was gentle as he set the cup down, and equally gentle as he said, "The full message was, 'Bring Elinor to Carlton.'"

"Elinor," Peter echoed, and for a minute he did not know who Elinor was because Gordon could *not* have meant his wife. Not the woman who would have used both Peter and Gordon to a bad end. Not the woman who had mentored Miranda and possibly even been the one to order Miranda to shoot Peter. "What could he want with Elinor?" Except maybe to punish her, of course. But if that, he could have, should have, *would* have had her brought back to C&I.

Peter looked at Charles, who was leaning forward, watching

and waiting for Peter to follow the thread to its ultimate frayed end.

"He must have been planning a counter…"

"Peter…"

"She would have come more willingly to a quiet place, thinking he wanted to talk," Peter went on, building it as it should have been. "Would she have gone with you?"

"I don't know."

"Where is she now?"

"I don't know," Charles said again. "Possibly still in Salzburg, waiting for me to come fetch her to Gordon."

"We should bring her in," said Peter, without enthusiasm.

"It would be the right thing to do," Charles agreed.

Peter began toying idly with the curved handle of his teacup, running a finger over the smooth and glossy china. "Who else knew he was there?"

Charles shook his head. "No one, so far as I know."

"And why did you tell me?" He wanted to hear, of course, that Gordon had asked for him, had wanted him and needed him.

"It meant so much to you," said Charles. "And…" Charles attempted a sheepish smile that came off more as an apologetic grimace. "I had no idea what Carlton was but thought you might know."

Peter sat back in his chair and considered. Gordon would not have known that he and Charles had parted, would have perhaps counted on their working together to do as he requested. *Trust you to remember it.*

But how could Gordon have possibly believed Peter would willingly play a hand in bringing Elinor to him?

"He loved you," Charles said. "It's why he never wanted you to come back. And why, when you did, he tried to make you as secure as possible."

"By distancing himself," said Peter. "He should have hated her."

"Why? Because you do? Oh, Peter, you blame her for breaking up what you thought of as your happy family. And maybe she did. But you know as much as anyone there is no accounting for where love lies."

"Then why didn't he just go to her?" Peter asked bitterly. He thought of Simeon's comment in the car and repeated it. "What was he planning to do with Elinor out at Carlton Rise?"

"Maybe that's best left unknown." Charles stood and returned the chair to its usual position, his careful self making sure to fit the legs back into the carpet dents. Then he stepped over to the desk, returned the stray cups to the tea tray, and picked the tray up.

"If no one else knew..." Peter began.

At the door, Charles turned, the tray balanced so that he could open the door.

"The car," said Peter.

"Maybe that's best left unknown," Charles said again before slipping away.

ELEVEN

"LUNCH?" James asked as they exited the meeting. He tipped his head in the direction of Peter's arm sling. "Though I see I may have to feed you by hand."

Peter was exhausted from the long roll of questions regarding Gordon's death and not the least bit hungry. "I'm afraid this situation requires all my time and effort at the moment."

"All the more reason to take a break," said James. "And as good an excuse as any for us to be closeted together for any length of time."

"You're enjoying this."

James flashed his too-white grin. "I enjoy *you*, Peter. Is that such a crime?"

Logically, Peter understood it was not, but it somehow felt like it should be. Still, he fell into step beside James, and something in him savored their almost equal footing. In their school days, they had not enjoyed an open friendship; Peter had been widely known merely as James's tutor—and who would question James having selected the best French student—and privately as James's secret. How novel to be walking beside James now, where anyone might see.

And did their observers assume it was only business? Peter saw heads turn their way as they passed. Then, as they came to the staircase, Trevor's slick, dark head rounded up from the landing, Charles's contrasting flyaway fair-to-grey coming in his wake. Glancing up, Charles saw Peter and James and paused.

"And then if we—" Trevor took in Charles's expression and looked up to see what had grabbed his attention. "Was there a meeting?" Trevor asked.

"Not one you needed to be involved in," said James. Peter thought as far as Trevor was concerned there was no such thing as a meeting that didn't call for his input, but far from voicing this, Peter merely gave each man a polite nod and made to move past. So he was startled when James stopped beside them on the stairs.

"This is your new staffer?" James put out his hand, clearly under the impression he required no introduction himself.

Trevor shot Peter a snakelike look. "An inheritance. It seems I get Peter's castoffs."

Charles dropped James's hand, fidgeted, and finally found something interesting to look at out the window, though it was almost entirely obscured by a tree that needed cutting.

James looked from Charles to Peter. "Ah. Well, I'm sure we could find another place for... Charles, is it? Maybe he'd rather go back into the field."

"We're blocking the stairs," Peter said levelly, trying not to reveal the strange, crawling panic that had been lit in his chest.

James ignored him. "Should we have a meeting?" he asked Trevor. "We could discuss your placement while we're at it." And with a glance back at Peter, "I'm sure you have some changes you'd like to make to Gordon's hierarchy."

"One thing at a time," said Peter, his desperation rising steadily, making him feel like a man treading furiously to keep his head above water. "Let's put Gordon to rest first."

"Bury Gordon," James said. "We need a clean slate. Quickly."

"Then perhaps we should get on with our lunch," suggested Peter. "And Trevor and I can discuss his staffing concerns later." He gave Trevor a look that did nothing to disguise his contempt.

"You're keeping the job, then," said Trevor. "I always had the notion you regarded it as temporary. Now that Gordon has been found... And lost... Though not necessarily in that order, as I understand it."

Peter knew he was being baited, and he hadn't the energy for it. He saw Charles's eyes slide in his direction, though Charles never turned his face from the window.

James saved Peter having to reply by stating, "Peter and I have a very solid working relationship; it would be difficult for me to accept anyone else in the role. And would set us back quite a bit on our progress," he added, though it rang in Peter's mind as an afterthought, and he could tell from the way Trevor's gaze bounced between them that Trevor had the same feeling.

"It's not that you're not wanted, Charles," James went on, and Charles turned a startled face to him. "It *is*, perhaps, that your talents are being wasted in your current position. Think about what you might like to do and let Peter and I know."

Peter became aware now of people coming to the stairs behind them, seeing them clustered there, and finding various detours. *Just business.*

Charles looked a question at Peter, but Peter kept his face carefully blank. "I haven't really gone over the personnel situation," Peter said. "There will certainly be some rearranging."

"We can talk about it over lunch. Gentlemen," James said, and without further ado he continued his way down the stairs, giving Peter no choice but to follow.

"You gave him to Trevor," James said once they were outside. Slowly, Peter began to take in air again, his apprehension dissipating with each breath and the increasing distance from the building. "He must have really offended you."

Peter sidestepped the issue by asking, "What did you mean by 'bury Gordon'?"

"Only that you shouldn't expend too much time or energy on it. This is the start of a new era, Peter. And you and I are going to be at the head of the charge."

"And all that questioning—"

"Just for the record. Gordon wasn't a public official; we don't have to answer to anyone but each other. When is the funeral?"

"Tuesday. And Elinor?"

"What about her?"

"We should send someone after her. Try to find Miranda." They had arrived at James's townhouse, and as James threw open the door, Peter asked, "Does she know?"

James looked back at him, clearly confused by the question, and Peter noticed how less handsome he was when he knitted his brow and frowned, how much older the pronounced lines made him appear.

"Your wife," said Peter.

"You'd like her," James said. "And she would approve of you, I think. Would you like to meet her? We could—"

"No." Peter stepped back from the doorway, which suddenly seemed like a yawning mouth waiting to swallow him. He stepped back from James and all the "progress" James represented. "It's the wrong direction."

The lines on James's face grew deeper still. "What?"

"I'm sorry, James. I just recalled I have lunch plans elsewhere." And he turned and walked away, out of the shade of the trees and into the light and warmth of the London summer.

About the Author

M holds a Master of Arts in Writing, Literature and Publishing and a Bachelor of Science in Radio-Television-Film. She has a love of Shakespeare, having both performed and taught his work, and also interned on Hollywood film sets. She then worked in publishing before deciding to write full time. M lives in Livermore, California with her family and cats.